THE FALL

SHARI LOW

ROSS KING

Boldwood

First published in Great Britain in 2023 by Boldwood Books Ltd.

Cover Design by Alice Moore Design

Cover Photography: Shutterstock

A CIP catalogue record for this book is available from the British Library.

Paperback ISBN 978-1-80426-790-5

Large Print ISBN 978-1-80426-789-9

Hardback ISBN 978-1-80426-791-2

Ebook ISBN 978-1-80426-787-5

Kindle ISBN 978-1-80426-788-2

Audio CD ISBN 978-1-80426-796-7

MP3 CD ISBN 978-1-80426-795-0

Digital audio download ISBN 978-1-80426-793-6

Boldwood Books Ltd
23 Bowerdean Street
London SW6 3TN
www.boldwoodbooks.com

ABOUT THE AUTHORS...

When a budding radio DJ and actor met a young nightclub manager in Glasgow in the late 1980s, little did they know that over thirty years and thousands of miles later they would still be friends.

Los Angeles-based Ross King MBE is a four-time News Emmy award-winning TV and radio host, actor, producer, writer, voice-over artist and performer. King has starred in London's West End, appeared in over ten movies and hosted TV shows in the UK, Europe, USA and Australia. He has also presented countless radio shows and pens a Sunday newspaper column. In 2018, he received an MBE from the Queen for services to Broadcasting, the Arts and Charity.

Best-selling author Shari Low released her first book in 2001. Since then, she has published over thirty novels, selling over two million books worldwide, including the recent hits *One Last Day of Summer* and *One Day With You*. Shari splits her time between Glasgow and Los Angeles, and wherever she is, she's probably writing the next chapter of a book.

Visit Ross's website at www.rossking.com
Instagram & Twitter – @therossking
Visit Shari's website at www.sharilow.com
Instagram – @sharilowbooks
Twitter – @sharilow

From Ross – For David Johnston King and Isabel King, my heroes, my pals and my 'Pops and Wee Bella'. Forever in my heart.
With thanks and all the love in the world to the best sister, Elaine, and the family, Jim, Hollie and Euan.
And to all my dear pals – you know who you are.

From Shari – For my love, John, and our family, who are everything, always.
And for the incredible women in my life for the strength, the support and the laughs that get us through everything.

INTRODUCTION

Welcome to *The Fall*!

This is the third book in the Hollywood series featuring movie star, Zander Leith, TV producer, Davie Johnston and writing legend, Mirren McLean.

If you haven't read *The Rise* and *The Catch*, the first two books in the series, don't worry, because here's everything you need to know to catch up...

Mirren McLean, Davie Johnston and Zander Leith – three Hollywood superstars who grew up together in a tough housing estate in Glasgow.

Back then, Mirren's mother, Marilyn, was the mistress of Zander's father, a violent gangster called Jono Leith.

Neglected, living in poverty, the three youngsters were inseparable, the family that they chose for themselves.

Until the unthinkable happened.

Jono Leith raped seventeen-year-old Mirren and her mother killed him. Not because Marilyn was protecting her daughter, but because she was consumed with jealousy that Jono had touched another woman.

Desperate to escape the horror of what had just happened, the three youngsters covered it up, burying Jono's body under the shed in Davie's garden.

Marilyn disappeared into the wind, and the world thought Jono had gone to ground to avoid rival gangsters. He wasn't missed.

That could have been the end of it. Case closed.

However, as a way to process the trauma, Mirren wrote the story of what happened and, against all odds, it found its way to a Hollywood producer, Wes Lomax.

He turned Mirren's words into a movie, *The Brutal Circle*, a cult hit that unexpectedly became a box-office smash, winning Mirren, Davie and Zander an Oscar for Best Original Screenplay.

The whole world believed it was fiction and the success brought brand new Hollywood lives for the three Scots. Zander became an A-list star, thanks to his leading role as spy, Seb Dunhill, in a hugely successful movie series, Davie went on to make millions as producer of some of the biggest shows on television and Mirren secured her position as a powerful player in the industry by writing, directing and producing one of the most iconic film franchises of all time.

But fame and fortune came at a price.

The shame and pain of finding success by capitalising on the worst moment in their lives drove the three of them apart. They didn't speak for twenty years, until a young journalist from Scotland, Sarah McKenzie, began digging into their past.

Eventually, Sarah discovered the truth about what happened to Jono Leith, but by then it was too late. She'd fallen in love with Davie Johnston and killed the story to protect him.

Along the way, the ghosts of the past brought the hope of resolution.

Sarah's investigation forced Mirren, Davie and Zander to reconnect, two decades after they'd walked away from each other. It wasn't always easy. The pain was still there. Davie's discovery that Jono Leith was his father too was tough to digest. Mirren's mother was dead to her, but her presence aways lingered. And Zander's demons from his childhood still pushed him towards a bottle.

But in *The Catch*, all of those issues were set to one side when the three famous names were targeted in a series of violent, disturbing incidents. Davie's house was attacked, shots were fired at his gates, an arsonist set fire to his home, and he was ambushed by a stalker.

Zander was busy fighting fires of a different kind. His apartment was ransacked, he was falsely accused of a sex crime he didn't commit, and his integrity, friendships and career teetered on the edge of destruction when he gave a positive drug test, despite being clean since the death of Mirren's eighteen-year-old daughter, Chloe, a fellow addict that he'd tried desperately to save.

Mirren had her own demons to combat. Still grieving over Chloe, her world was rocked when Marilyn came back into her life in the most brutal way. At first, the three friends suspected that Marilyn was at the root of all their troubles, but a violent explosion at the Academy Awards in 2014 claimed Marilyn's life, and the truth was revealed – Davie and Zander had been targeted by people they'd crossed in the past, enemies who would no longer trouble them after their acts were exposed and justice was served. And not necessarily in a courtroom.

The Catch ended with peace. With resolution. With the three of them battle-scarred but still standing.

Mirren found love with studio head Mike Feechan.

Zander married Hollie, the assistant who'd stuck by him through years of off-screen struggle.

Davie and Sarah were committed to a future together.

And all three of them saw their careers soar.

However, in Hollywood, happy endings don't last for ever.

Sometimes they're just the calm before the storm...

THE HOLLYWOOD CAST

Mirren's World

Mirren McLean: Born and raised in Glasgow, now a major Hollywood player, best-selling author, Oscar-winning screenwriter, director and producer of the iconic Clansman movies, epic tales of a heroic warrior and his clan in 16th century Scotland.

Mike Feechan: Mirren's husband of four years. CEO of Pictor, the TV and Movie studio that makes Mirren McLean's Clansman series. Father of Jade, 16.

Chloe Gore: Mirren's daughter, wild child, addict, troubled soul. Died in 2013 from an overdose, aged 18.

Logan Gore: Mirren's son, gained worldwide success as former lead guitarist and singer in South City, the boy band that was on the walls of teenagers across the globe from 2012 to 2016. Now a solo artist, married to...

Lauren Finney Gore: singer, songwriter, global sensation, first came to fame as winner of Davie's talent show, *American Stars*.

Marilyn McLean: Mirren's mother, who killed her lover, Jono Leith, in cold blood. Now deceased.

Lou Cole: Mirren's best friend of over twenty-five years, journalist, gossip queen, and editor of the *Hollywood Post*.

Lex Callaghan: movie star, plays the lead role in *The Clansman* but shuns the limelight when he's off-screen.

Cara Callaghan: Lex's wife, a Native American beauty who runs an equine therapy centre at their fifteen-hundred-acre ranch in Santa Barbara.

Jack Gore: Mirren's ex-husband of almost two decades, movie producer turned mid-life crisis cliché.

Jason Grimes: a counsellor at one of the branches of Chloe's Care – the drop-in centres Mirren funds for young addicts.

Davie's World

Davie Johnston: multi-millionaire presenter/host and producer of some of the biggest reality hits on American television.

Jenny Rico: Davie's ex-wife, lead actress on hit TV cop show *Streets Of Power*.

Darcy Jay: Jenny Rico's partner both on and off screen.

Bella and Bray: Davie and Jenny's fourteen-year old, red-haired twins, child stars of sitcom *Family Three*, Bella is now the next Hannah Montana, while Bray shuns the limelight.

Ena Johnston: Davie's mother and keeper of his secrets, still lives in his childhood home in Glasgow.

Cal Wolfe: Davie's ruthless, sharp-suited former agent. A moral vacuum in a world where all that matters is power and profit.

Drego and Alina: Davie's loyal gardener/driver and his tempestuous housekeeper.

Mellie Santos: the mildly terrifying, caustic producer on Davie's talk show, *Davie Johnston: As It Is*.

Lainey Anders: country music legend, friend, and former judge on Davie's old show, *American Stars*.

Zander's World

Zander Leith: icon, actor, action hero and star of the Dunhill movie franchise. Former loner, addict and no stranger to uninvited violence, rehab and jail cells – now happily married and has found peace for the first time in his life.

Hollie Leith: Zander's former personal assistant, right-hand woman, and unfailingly loyal, smart-mouthed friend – now his wife of five years.

Jono Leith: Zander's father, Glasgow gangster and one of the most evil bastards to ever walk the earth. Killed in 1989 by his mistress, Mirren's mother, Marilyn.

Wes Lomax: Legendary studio head, with a sexual appetite that's as ferocious as his temper.

Sarah's World

Sarah McKenzie: Scottish journalist, who came to LA to investigate rumours about Davie, Zander and Mirren's past lives, but fell in love with Davie Johnston. Now Davie's fiancée, she is the author of two best-selling books on the dark side of Hollywood and is currently writing a third. She also has a new role as investigative journalist for the crime documentary show, *Out Of The Shadows*.

The *Out Of The Shadows* Team

Chip Chasner: executive producer.

Meilin Chong: investigative journalist and co-anchor.

Shandra Walker: super-smart young researcher.

Hank Travis: Head of Legal for the production company that makes the show.

PROLOGUE

'Fame' – David Bowie

Myla Rivera reporting for the Fame Channel:

'Welcome to the 91st Academy Awards, live from the Dolby
Theatre, in the heart of Hollywood. And what a spectacle this
promises to be! We'll be sharing every moment right here on the
Fame Channel. Behind me, the stars are just beginning to arrive for
Hollywood's biggest night, and we'll be chatting with them soon
and checking out all the fashion on the red carpet. Of course, we'll
have some hot gossip for you too, plus we'll be sharing our predictions as to who will be heading home with the most wanted man in
Hollywood... Oscar!

'We'll also be keeping you updated on the biggest story of the
day so far, the tragic situation unfolding in Malibu right now, where
an unseasonal wildfire has reportedly claimed the home of Zander
Leith, a much-loved friend of many of the industry names who will
be arriving this evening. Let's take a look at the moment Zander

won his Academy Award, back in 1993, for the original screenplay written by Leith, Davie Johnston and Mirren McLean.'

Cut to a VT package – The Academy Awards 1993. Actress Lana Delasso announces the winners in the category of Best Original Screenplay. Zander Leith, Mirren McLean and Davie Johnston, all barely in their twenties, take to the stage and pick up the gold statue for their movie The Brutal Circle.

Cut back to Myla Rivera...

'At the moment, we've no information on Zander Leith's location, but before today's events, he was expected to attend tonight's ceremony to present the award for Best Director – a category in which one of the nominees is his old friend, and no stranger to controversy this year, Mirren McLean.

'So, be one of the billion people worldwide tuning in tonight for all the latest news, fashion, and of course, the awards. Stay right here on the Fame Channel, and we'll be right back after these messages...'

Broadcast ends. Myla Rivera looks off camera, taps her earpiece, speaks to the producer in the gallery.

'Billion people, my ass. Why are we still peddling that bullshit? Lucky if it's even half of that. Okay, I need to know exactly what's happening with Leith. Let's run the package about his wife in the next segment, but you guys keep the cameras on the limos. Make sure you get Mirren McLean's face on a close-up when she arrives, and I want Davie Johnston's first words. Do your work, people. This is going to be a shitshow and we want the whole fucking world to be watching it here.'

1

'Standing In The Shadows of Love' – Four Tops

The limo slid to a halt in the line that stretched back from the entrance to the Dolby Theatre. Inside the cars was the action that the audience at home didn't see. The chaos. The waiting to arrive. The last slug of straight vodka. The last line of coke. The last adjustment to a dress to ensure the greatest exposure of both the body and the star. The last-minute phone calls to publicists, screaming about the lack of coverage on the story that had been planted to ensure the flashlights on the C-lister would elevate them, just for tonight, to the spotlight of an A-lister. Even the entrance to the theatre was a façade. The shops that lined the walkway to the theatre were covered for one evening only with luxurious drapes. It would be so easy to pull back the curtain on Hollywood in every sense of the word. But, of course, no one ever did.

Six cars back from the beginning of the red carpet, in a smooth black Bentley limo, Mirren McLean was one of the last to arrive for the night's proceedings. On the cream leather seat, she sat bolt upright, to accommodate the boned corset of her bespoke gown – a work of body-hugging, crystal-beaded artistry that had been designed for her by fashion students at the Glasgow School of Art. For the first time, no major designer had offered to dress her. Over the last year, she'd discovered who her friends were, and she'd found that there were fewer than she could ever have imagined. Now, she wasn't sure if it was the constraints of the dress, the prospect of tonight's public appearance, the man sitting next to her or the call she was taking on her phone that was forcing her lungs to work way too hard to get breath into her body.

'Lou, I can't go in there if I don't know he's okay,' she told the one person who had never let her down. Not ever. Lou Cole. Editor of the *Hollywood Post*. The sister she'd chosen for herself when she'd met her back in 1989, a few months after she'd arrived in Hollywood. Lou Cole was Sasha Fierce with a pen, a magnificent woman of colour, a media queen who controlled the Hollywood press, who knew where the bodies were buried, and, more importantly, knew who'd buried them. There was barely a hotel manager, a club promoter, or a service-industry employee in this city who wasn't on her list of informants. For a price, of course.

'Don't worry, babe, I'm on it. I'll find him.'

'Okay, call me back. Love you.' Mirren ended the call, dropped her phone into her Judith Leiber crystal clutch and snapped it shut. She could already see the flashes of the cameras up ahead, and the very thought of going out there made her stomach churn.

The single wave of titian hair that flowed over her right shoulder, held in place by a diamond clasp and made rock solid by a two-thousand-dollar-an-hour hair guru that afternoon, barely budged as she turned to her companion. 'I don't know if I can do this, Mike.'

Mike Feechan, Head of Pictor, a movie studio that carried as much weight as the bigger boys at Lomax, Warner Bros, Universal and Paramount. The third love of her life and her second husband. The one she truly thought would last until the end of time. Not anymore. Not now that he could barely look at her when he spoke. 'If I can walk out there with you after everything that's happened, you can damn well play your part.'

'Even if it's pointless? Come on, Mike. They only nominated me because Clansman had the biggest box office this year and they needed a woman on the ballot sheet. There's no way they're letting me win. Not now. The Academy would never withstand the backlash.'

His jaw pulsed as she watched him bite back the obvious reply. *He'd* withstood it. He'd taken the charge. The body blow. He'd let the whole world tear her apart and destroy everyone she touched, and he was still here. At least today. For this. Because this wasn't just personal, it was work. The Clansman movies – Mirren's series of box-office-breaking films about a heroic warrior in sixteenth-century Scotland – had earned Pictor billions of dollars. His presence here today wasn't love – it was protecting his investment.

'Suck it up, Mirren. This is one deal you don't get to quit.'

The bitterness in his voice made her flinch, and the worst thing was that she didn't blame him one bit. He hated her because she'd humiliated him. Taken a wrecking ball to their marriage, their careers, their future, and most painful of all, her reputation. All that was left in the rubble was disdain, disgust and a sign saying 'cancelled until further notice'.

Mirren McLean had well and truly screwed up her life.

Millions of movie fans watching this spectacle on their televisions around the globe would give anything to be here. Mirren would give anything to be anywhere else. That wasn't strictly true. The only place she wanted to be right now was with her friend, Zander Leith.

* * *

Two cars behind Mirren, Davie Johnston was sweating through the fine layer of foundation his make-up artist had applied an hour before, as he read the headlines on the TinselTownTrials.com article that had just dropped on to his phone.

'How The Mighty Have Fallen.'

It was the zinger of a line underneath that made him want to kill someone.

'After blowing his nine lives, have last rites been delivered to Davie Johnston?'

The grind on his teeth was so violent, it risked his fifty-thousand-dollar veneers.

The very parasites that had sucked on him when he was at the top now gloated when he was at the bottom. It would be tempting to respond. If his PR agency hadn't dumped him the month before, perhaps he would have. Now they were all just rats deserting a sinking ship. And he was the *Titanic*.

Against the orders that were screaming from the tiny cell of dignity that remained in his body, he began skimming the rest of the piece, absorbing the lines that jumped out.

'Believed his own hype.'

'Dinosaur who didn't read the room.'

'Broke the unspoken rule.'

'Used his own cash.'

He didn't need to read every word to fill in the blanks. Hell, there wasn't a television-viewing person in the USA who didn't know the details of his demise. A few years ago, he'd had three of the top-rated shows on TV. He'd produced and starred in a talent show called *American Stars*, that imploded when the ex-boyfriend of one of the winners killed one person, seriously injured several more and tried to murder Davie in twisted revenge attacks because he believed the show had taken away the love of his life. Davie survived; *American Stars* didn't.

He'd also produced the reality show *Beauty and The Beats*, featuring a washed-up, drug-addled, eighties rock star and his twenty-five-year-old cokehead model girlfriend. That one had taken its final soundcheck when the rock star had the temerity to drop dead on the first episode of Davie's former talk show, *Here's Davie Johnston*.

That was his other hit, and after the huge publicity of actually killing a guest on episode one, it had found a ratings-busting niche as the midnight safe space where the stars who didn't want the Ellen afternoon audience or to sing for their supper on Fallon or Kimmel came to just lay it all out. No holds barred. They could say what they wanted, curse when they liked and there was only one rule – no woke PR shit was allowed. He'd brought in politicians. YouTube stars. Disgraced public figures. Actors who could handle the challenges and deliver honesty instead of soundbites. Famous names who wanted to be real. Every time a star claimed to be 'blessed' or that working with another huge ego was an 'honour', the audience were encouraged to show their displeasure with boos and cries of 'bullshit'. At first it was a novelty. A massive hit. Meteoric. But it wasn't long before one too many offensive comments riled the woke agenda and the most virtue-signalling town in the USA rebelled against it. Against him.

But still, he kept going, convinced that he was right. That the backlash wouldn't last. That the new generation of snowflakes would toughen up and stop being so fucking offended by everything.

And that's when he'd danced with the two unspoken rules in Hollywood. Number one, never use your own money. Number two, never, EVER, use your own money.

Davie Johnston gambled with his cash. He'd been accused of

having BDE – big dick energy – and he'd showed it. Defiant. Furious. Determined that being cancelled by the chinless cretins wouldn't dent him, he'd ploughed every penny he had, and some more that he didn't, into launching a new talk show, *Davie Johnston, As It Is*. He couldn't even take credit for the idea to self-finance. Back in 2004, Mel Gibson had rescued his career by using his own cash to make *The Passion Of The Christ*. But then, he'd had Jesus on his side.

Oprah had gone one step further, launching her own fricking network, 'OWN', although back then she'd had big bucks partners in Discovery Communications.

That was his planned trajectory. Make a brilliant show, then watch as the big players – Warner Bros, NBC, Sony, ABC, Paramount, CBS – came flocking to buy in.

In Davie's case, no one gave a flock.

Oh, but he did get fucked in the process. He couldn't even think about that now. Denial, that's what he was going for. Especially when it came to his empty bank account and the huge new loan on his forty-five-million-dollar Bel Air mansion.

He'd also discovered that there was something much worse than failing, than losing everything, than blowing up his life – and that was becoming irrelevant. A new generation was reshaping Hollywood and there was no place in it for a middle-aged, anti-woke maverick who'd thought his star would never fade. And that big dick energy? Decidedly flaccid.

A few years ago, he'd presented the Oscars. Not last year, when they'd had the lowest ratings in recent history. Nope, that didn't happen on his watch. His show had brought in the highest viewing figures of recent years. Changed times. Tonight, there would be no host, after Kevin Hart lost the gig, and Davie had to call in favours just to get on the guest list. Man, that stung. And he didn't even have his family to fall back on. Revelling in his misfortune was his ex-wife's favourite sport. His kids acted like they couldn't stand him, and they were way too famous to give a toss about their embarrassing old man. And Sarah, the love of his life, had walked away from him. Cancel that, she'd run. Actually, she'd fucking sprinted. One mistake, that he still didn't even understand, and she'd bailed on him.

'Bastards!' Unable to read any more of the crap, he threw his phone against the glass privacy window between him and the driver, who hadn't been keen to take this job in case he didn't get paid. Rumours of Davie's financial difficulties were already swirling around town and he wasn't sure how much longer he was going to be able to keep a grip on any of this. He needed a miracle, and contrary to the shit romcoms that drew in millions for the streaming services every Christmas, the reality was that they were in short supply.

The pain that struck his cheek was as sharp as it was unexpected. Thanks to a rubber, shatterproof case on his phone, the damn thing had come right back like a boomerang and slapped him on the side of the face. With rueful resignation, he decided that was that a metaphor for his whole life these days. Shot himself in the foot. Slapped himself in the face. *Stay tuned for tomorrow, folks, when a meteor lands in my bed and kills me while I sleep.*

Oh, and the irony? Despite playing frisbee with the phone, the damn thing still worked, as he realised when it began to ring, blaring out the theme tune to *Braveheart*. Cheesy, sure, but it was the ringtone he'd allocated to Mirren years ago and he had never changed it. He checked the screen. FaceTime audio call from Mirren McLean.

'Hey,' he answered, on the fourth ring.

'Where are you?' Her voice, even after all these years, made something inside him soften. She had been his first love, and he'd been hers. Sixteen years old, and a world away in a rough housing scheme on the outskirts of Glasgow. Urban depravation, they'd called it. He disagreed. There had been no depravation when Mirren had been pressed up against him in a single bed, in a bedroom that was a quarter of the size of his walk-in closet now.

'In the limo line. Probably ten minutes out. Right at the end. Guess they're hoping the cameras will have moved inside by the time I get there.'

'Yeah, me too. Have you heard anything from Zander? I've been trying to get him all day, but he's not replying. The footage is horrific, Davie. CNN showed aerial images and his whole house is decimated. Burnt to the ground.'

'I know, I saw it.' There was a sudden self-realisation that, yep, that was the kind of selfish prick he'd become. Enraged about a stupid article when his half-brother and lifelong friend was missing, his home incinerated in a wildfire that was raging through Malibu.

Zander had moved there a few years ago, after he married his assistant, Hollie. It had been his wedding gift to her and they'd adored it. Made it their home, their sanctuary. Zander had found peace there. Davie had envied him that, until the unthinkable had happened. Not the fire. That didn't even come close to the tragedy that had blighted Zander last year. No. What happened six months ago was brutal, horrific...

Mirren's voice cut into his thoughts. 'I don't feel right coming tonight, but I'm hoping we can't get a hold of him because he's already here, ready to present as planned. I'm praying he's hiding out somewhere backstage, being Zander.'

Davie knew exactly what she meant. To the outside world, Zander Leith was the biggest action hero in the movie-verse. He'd played Dunhill – a tough, super-suave spy who had fought terrorists, organised-crime and mendacious third-world dictators in ten movies now and neither his popularity nor his box office showed any signs of diminishing. Of course, his image had fed the hype. For almost twenty years, he'd been the incorrigible Hollywood bad boy – hard drinking, drugs, jails and rehab were way too familiar to him. But the rest of the world also saw the good-looking, self-deprecating Zander, the one who didn't go looking for trouble but who found it any way. The one who punched out a vapid, attention-seeking reality star – twice – for insulting women he loved. The one who couldn't be sexier, even when he was in handcuffs. To them, he was just doing what Dunhill would do and, perversely, his popularity had grown with every flying fist and scandal.

Only the few people on the inside of Zander's world knew different. They knew he was fighting a lifetime of demons formed by a childhood of violence and poverty, and a malevolent bastard of a father, Jono Leith, whom teenage Zander had helped bury with his own hands after Mirren's mother killed him. The trauma had left him damaged, with a deep-rooted conviction that he was unworthy of love until two women changed him. Chloe. Mirren's eighteen-year-old daughter. A fellow addict, who'd brought out a paternal side that Zander never knew he had. He'd fought with everything to save her, but still failed, and that moment had changed him. He'd never touched alcohol or drugs again. That left space for Hollie, the person who'd loved him whether he was on top of the world or in a gutter. Her job description had changed from assistant to wife, and they'd found the kind of happiness they truly deserved, until…

'Davie! Are you listening?' Mirren blasted. 'Shit, hang on, Sarah is trying to FaceTime me. I'll switch this call to video and add her in…'

Davie's hand began to tremble as anxiety kicked in, just as it had every time he'd seen Sarah since she left him.

Davie's ex-fiancée's face filled half of the screen. He knew she was ten miles away, in Malibu, far from the glitz and glamour of the

91st Academy Awards, trying to find out if Zander was there, or if he'd made it out before the fire took hold. Davie could see that the smoke was thick around her, could almost taste the ash and carnage that was choking her, so that her words came out as hoarse barks of desperation. 'Mirren! Mirren! Zander is... is...'

The line died and for the second time tonight, rage and fear exploded inside him, taking his heart rate to triple figures. He wanted to scream, to kick out the limo windows, to smash his phone to pieces. This time, he didn't even try, because if Sarah called back, he needed to be there for her. Like he hadn't been when it mattered. When he'd let her walk away from him.

'What the fuck was that?' He was screaming at Mirren now, who was still on his screen, now trying to calm him.

'Davie, I don't know, but we will get her back. I'll call Lou right now and we'll keep trying, we'll find her. We'll... Shit, Davie, I'm here. I'm at the circus.' Mirren shielded her eyes from the flashlights of dozens of cameras and had to speak louder to be heard over the wall of noise as the limo door opened. 'Find me on the inside, Davie. I'll wait for you.'

* * *

Mirren's split-second decision had been made. If she stayed in the car and drove off now, it would pull attention her way, cause a scene, and her no-show would be perceived as an admission of guilt over the scandal that had been swirling around her for months. Although, none of that mattered. What truly mattered was that the last thing Mirren wanted to do was put herself at the centre of what was going on with Zander. This was his pain. His heartbreak. And the most important thing right now was finding out if he was safe, if he was already inside, if he'd made a private entrance to avoid the cameras and was right now sitting in a dressing room, mourning his losses and needing a friend. She was the friend. And she had to get to him.

'Ready for the performance of a lifetime?' Mike asked, dread in every word, and she saw the pain in him too. She deserved his anger and all she could do was take it.

Smile on, she came out of that limo waving like a pro. The first person she saw was Mishka Alves, her head of PR, who'd be in front of her on the red carpet, preparing the way through the gauntlet of press. 'Don't allow questions about Zander or anything personal. I'm only talking about the movie and the Oscars.' she hissed, through a megawatt smile that had been compared to the iconic grin of Julia Roberts by a thousand lazy journalists. She had the same waves of red hair too, but that was where the similarities stopped. Mirren McLean had a pale West of Scotland complexion, her mother's blue eyes and an angular bone structure that was more Blanchett than Roberts.

Right now, she worked the smile, and she worked the wave, with the arm that wasn't threaded around the elbow of her dashing, relaxed, partner. Yeah, Mike was putting on the performance of a lifetime too.

Just as she'd asked, Mishka steered her through the crowd on the red carpet. The A-listers, acting like they loved this, even though they despised every second of it. The plus-ones, either basking or seething in the shadows. The interviewers, desperate to land another soundbite that would be viral within the hour. Ryan Seacrest, Giuliana Rancic, Ross King, Sam Rubin, Jessica Holmes, Myla Rivera and a few others, all schmoozing the stars.

Mirren passed right on by, but she could hear the shouts of the journalists on the balcony above.

'Mirren, do you think you're going to win tonight?'

'Are you taking legal action?'

'Mirren, do you have any comment on the allegations against you?'

'What do you say to victims of sexual abuse in the workplace?'

'Have you spoken to Zander?'

She ignored them all, just kept smiling, moving forward, waving, dying inside, every second feeling like an hour as she travelled in slow motion up the red carpet of fame and achievement that she loathed with every fibre of her being.

As soon as she got to the end of the carpet, she was greeted by one of the dozen clipboard militias. 'Miss McLean, we're running late for the live start, so we have to get you straight to your seat.'

She scanned back the way she came, hoping to see Davie, but he wasn't there. Anxiety crushing her chest, she slipped her phone back out of her purse and called Zander again. Still no answer.

'Is Zander Leith here?' she asked the twenty-something blonde behind the clipboard.

'I'm sorry, Miss McLean, I've no idea. Right this way please.'

There was no point objecting. This event was run with military precision and defectors were shot on sight – usually by an errant photographer who would then fuel the rumour that a star was 'difficult', or 'in crisis', or 'out of control'. She didn't need more scurrilous accusations, so she went along with it. Mike dropped his arm, avoiding contact as they were led to their seats, past three decades of friendships. If she hadn't been panicking inside, she might have noticed their reactions, spotted the minority who still smiled at her in solidarity, and the majority of fair-weathers who averted their gaze, desperate not to be caught being kind to the woman who now came with the stink of cancellation.

Mirren McLean had become a pariah.

And as she reached her seat, at the very end of a row and out of scope of the cameras that would pan the room as awards were announced, she caught sight of Davie, being seated in the same row, but at the opposite side of the Dolby Theatre. Another one in the pariah wings. They should have sat them together and given the cameras one less area to avoid.

Before she could catch his eye or signal to him, the house lights went down, the stage lights went up. Mirren had seen the rehearsal and read the script, so she knew what to expect. The red curtain was about to rise with an explosion of light and sound. Queen would open the show in a riot of smoke and attitude, to the sound-track of Brian May's searing guitar, Adam Lambert's pitch-perfect vocals. No doubt the stars would immediately jump to their feet, clapping and dancing, aware that acting like they were having a great time would bring the camera focus to them for an extra second or two. A video montage of some of the year's big movies was scheduled to follow the opening number – among them, *Bohemian Rhapsody*, *Deadpool 2*, *Black Panther*, *Vice*, *A Star Is Born*, *Roma*, *Green Book*, *The Favourite* – before Tina Fey, Maya Rudolph and Amy Poehler would take to the stage to announce the first award.

But not yet. First, there would be some off-camera activity in preparation for the live broadcast. One of the producers came on to the stage, checked some technical stuff with the gallery, then ran through a few announcements, sharing the news that there would be a last-minute change to the schedule.

A hush descended as the audience realised that this wasn't part of the plan. This broadcast ran like clockwork, was drilled, timed and rehearsed weeks in advance. They rarely veered off script, although it often overran, usually due to winners deciding to thank everyone they'd ever known. Or sobbing unconsolably – otherwise known as doing a Gwynnie, after the overly emotional speech by Miss Paltrow when she picked up the little gold guy for Best Actress in 1999 for *Shakespeare In Love*. If there was an unexpected alteration to the script at this stage, then it was something big, something unexpected, something way too cataclysmic to ignore.

Mirren felt her whole body begin to tremble as Paula Leno, head of publicity for Lomax Films, the studio that had launched Mirren's career and that had made all of Zander's movies, took to the stage. 'Ladies and gentlemen, the live broadcast will start in a few moments, but the Academy felt it only right that you should know that in the last few minutes we've learned of the death of a friend, of a legend, of a man that many of you know and love...'

That's when Mirren knew what Sarah had been trying to tell them.

'Zander is... is...'

Her best friend, the man who had shared her life since she was twelve years old... Zander Leith was dead.

EIGHT MONTHS EARLIER

JUNE 2018

2

MIRREN MCLEAN

'God Is A Woman' – Ariana Grande

'Ladies and Gentlemen, my name Is Lou Cole, and I can't thank you all enough for coming tonight to the opening of Chloe's Care Downtown – the fifth Chloe's Care Centre to open its doors in the last four years. As you all know, these centres were established in honour of Chloe Gore, a remarkable young woman whom we lost to addiction at just eighteen years old. Now, I'd like to welcome to the stage a woman who is many things. Best-selling author. Director. Producer. Creator of one of the most successful movie franchises in Hollywood history. The founder of Chloe's Care, the huge chequebook...' That got a few laughs, before she went on, 'And the reason that so many people are helped by these incredible facilities. Please welcome my best friend and Chloe's mom, Mirren McLean.'

Even though many in the audience were holding phones in one hand, recording the event, the applause in the room was raucous.

As Mirren passed Lou on the stage, she leaned in to hug her. 'I'll bloody kill you for all that acclaim bollocks,' she whispered, out of earshot of the rest of the room.

'Give it your best shot, girl,' Lou laughed, kissing her on the cheeks, then taking her place at the side of the stage, next to Mirren's son, Logan Gore, and his wife, Lauren. Thankfully, they were pretty much standing in front of her ex-husband and Chloe's father, Jack Gore, who, despite contributing nothing to these centres, always turned up to share the glory.

On the other side of the stage stood the director of the centre and the counsellors that would be working here. Lynette Washington, the head of the centre, was alongside Lebron Ray, a therapist who had worked with Zander and Chloe back in the day, and four other experienced addiction specialists that had been recruited to the team. Mirren didn't glance their way, unwilling to make eye contact with someone who was... a mistake. A moment of weakness. She knew Jason Grimes would be clapping, could hear him cheering, and her face flushed. Not today. Not tonight. Not ever again.

Mirren nodded gratefully, even though the applause went on a little longer than she was comfortable with. There was a reason she chose to write, to direct, to do anything that kept her behind the camera and out of the spotlight. She didn't do interviews, didn't participate in 'behind the scenes' documentaries about her success, and point blank refused to do anything that made her centre of attention, preferring to just keep her head down and get on with the work. Despite that reticence, she'd still made her fair share of headlines over the years.

Almost a decade ago, her face had been on every tabloid when Jack had been caught screwing Mercedes Dance, the twenty-something star of a movie he was producing at that time. Despite Mirren's fervent wish that his dick would fall off and he'd seek a life of obscurity, she wasn't that lucky. The asshole had now been

through half the reality stars and Z-listers in town, losing his career
and credibility in the process. He'd been through his mid-life crisis,
his fast-car stage, his bomber-jacket years, his rocker vibe, his
metrosexual interlude and his hair transplant. He was still in his
twenty-three-year-old girlfriend stage, but now it came with a yoga
mat, a man-bun and conversations about chakras and being
lactose-intolerant. All of which tended to make her Jack Gore
intolerant.

Her son brought fame to their door too. He'd been a singer in
South City, the most famous boy band of this century, who were
now officially 'on a break'. Nowadays, boy bands never officially
broke up, because they knew it was far more profitable to keep the
fans onside for their solo projects. It was a strategy that clearly
worked, because Logan was killing it in his solo career. It hadn't
hurt when he'd married Lauren Finney, who was beaten in global
record sales last year by Ed Sheeran, Drake, Taylor Swift and...
actually, that was it. The fourth best-selling artist of 2017. It was a
source of much friendly rivalry that Logan only charted at number
six on worldwide record sales, but when it came to live performances, Logan still won top prize for tickets sold. No one else could
touch his popularity, as he continued to sell out stadiums in cities
across the globe. It would be easy and lazy to class him as a nepo-
baby – the term used for children of stars who then use their
parents fame or fortune to create their own success – but that had
never happened because it was well documented that back when
he was sixteen, Logan had ambushed his parents by auditioning for
the band. He was in before they even knew he could sing. At the
start, Mirren hadn't been up for it at all, but his father had
persuaded her to let him do it. For once Jack had been right.

Of course, her ex-husband couldn't help but milk their attention, turning up at every gig, every award show, every photo oppor-

tunity, but Mirren stayed out of it. Logan's success was his own and she didn't want or need to take the credit for it.

Her only unavoidable exception to the 'no publicity' rule had been her work with Chloe's Care, the chain of centres she'd set up to support young addicts and street kids, in memory of her daughter, Chloe. When her daughter had died an addict at eighteen, Mirren knew her heart would never be whole again, but these centres put a patch on the cracks. Five of them now, all in different areas of LA, all open 24/7, saving the lives that wanted to be saved and taking care of the ones that were too far gone to turn back.

'Thank you,' she said, into the microphone, as the hundred or so people in the room gave her their full attention. 'I'm not one for speeches, but I'd like to say this...'

Her focus was distracted momentarily by a new arrival who'd come through the door at the back of the room and was now standing against the back wall, watching her.

Well over six feet, he moved with the easy confidence of a guy who was used to commanding a room and now his gaze was on her, eyes narrowed, taking in every word that she said. It was only then she realised she'd been waiting for him, hoping he'd come.

She stuttered, flustered, then inhaled, steadied herself, found her voice again.

'I adored my daughter Chloe. I loved her with everything I had, but it wasn't enough to save her. Along the way, I learned a lot, met many experts and addicts, and families who cared for them, and all of that expertise and love has gone into building the facilities that we have here now. I so wish that I'd had somewhere like Chloe's Care back then. We can't save everyone blighted by the disease of addiction, but we will try. I couldn't save Chloe, but hopefully we can help many more young people in her name. Thank you to my family, to our donors, to our incredible staff here and at all the

Chloe's Care Centres across the city. We couldn't do this without you.'

Another round of applause. Cheers of congratulation. Hugs from her family and friends. As always, Mirren struggled with the emotion of it all. What should be a happy moment was numbed by the reminder that this was only here because Chloe was dead. And nothing she could do would change that.

Her family and best friend understood that.

'Do you want to go grab a drink and something to eat?' Lou asked, with a squeeze of her hand, her long manicured nails a kaleidoscope of colour. Lou had barely aged since they'd met when a young reporter interviewed a writer who'd landed in Hollywood from Scotland and won her first Oscar in her early twenties. Wes Lomax had discovered Mirren's script on a golf holiday to St. Andrews and, in one of these million-to-one scenarios, had made the damn thing into a movie, *The Brutal Circle*, starring Davie and Zander. It had been the biggest shock to them all when it became an instant classic that had won them a gold statue.

Back in the late eighties, Lou had called it, had told her she was about to hit the big time, then she'd suggested they go for cocktails and, thirty years later, they were still doing it.

'We are gonna head to Giorgio Baldi. Come on, I'll treat you to your favourite Dover sole,' she added. 'You can help me convince the young ones that we're in our prime,' she joked, gesturing to Logan and Lauren, who were busy schmoozing the donors, interacting with the guests, half of which were only invited so they'd open the apps on their phones and Venmo some four-figure donations to the QR code on the autograph cards the two singers were doling out. Most of them would take the bait, then drive home in hundred-thousand-dollar cars that cost more in gas every year than the cash they'd just dropped to make themselves look good. Mirren didn't care. She'd take all she could get. Half of the profits from her company and 100 per cent of the royalties from her Clansman novels already financed the centres, so she'd welcome any extra funds she could rustle up.

'No, I'm good. I'm just going to slip out the back. But thank you, honey. I'll call you tomorrow. Logan, you got this?' she asked her son, who'd wandered over to her, leaving his dad, who was very clearly hitting on her PR manager, Mishka. Mirren wasn't worried. Mishka liked them somewhere between Thor and Momoa on the body scale. Mirren was pretty sure Jack drew in his abs with bronzer.

Facially, there was no mistaking that Logan had his father's DNA. Chloe had come from Mirren's Scottish side of the gene pool, with her red waves and pale complexion, but Logan had the blonde hair and chiselled jaw of the Gore side, a fact that wasn't missed by the millions of teenagers who had his gorgeous face as their screensaver.

'I've got it, ma,' her son assured her, using her favourite Scottish word for mom. Since Chloe had passed, for every tear she'd shed for her daughter, she'd given up a prayer of gratitude for her son.

'Thanks. I'm just going to go and—'

Logan's wife, Lauren, one of Mirren's favourite people on this earth, had come up behind her and wrapped her arms around her. 'We know. I'll call you in the morning. Love you, Mamma.'

'Love you back,' Mirren whispered, before quietly making for the exit. She never stayed longer than she had to at these events, too scared that she'd crack and every pearl of devastation and grief inside her would roll right across the floor for all to see.

Her gaze went to the back wall, to where the late arrival had stood, but, of course, he was gone. She'd known he would be. He wouldn't stick around for the small talk either. It wasn't his way.

The mild chill of the LA evening made Mirren shiver as she slipped out of the fire exit at the back of the building and into her car. Mercedes. A basic model though. She didn't need the attention, the ego boost or the dent in her bank balance for the kind of swanky rides that were usually seen in this city's streets. She'd sold her top-of-the- range, pimped-out, swanky Range Rover to buy furniture for the third Chloe's Care Centre. Which was an eminently more sensible decision than when she'd rolled her ex-husband's Lamborghini over a cliff the first time she'd caught him cheating.

She sat on the speed limit as she headed west, onto I-10, the freeway that would take her all the way to Santa Monica, where she'd veer right on to the Pacific Coast Highway, the legendary stretch of road that snaked up the west coast from San Diego to Washington. Abbreviated to PCH, it would pave her way, mountains on one side, sea breeze on the other, all the way to her Malibu Colony home.

Only, tonight she didn't take that route.

Instead, without even making a conscious decision, she cut a right just after Will Rogers Beach, and headed up to Pacific Palisades, to a home that was in darkness when she pulled into the long, concealed driveway. It didn't matter. She knew why she was there and where she had to go.

The security lights came on at the side gate, as she punched in the numbers that granted access to the back of the building. Treading silently, her shoes discarded back at the car, she made her way around to the pool, barely acknowledging the stunning view of the lights of Santa Monica below. In daylight, she would be able to see all the way to the ocean.

'I wondered if you'd come.' His voice, from one of the loungers at the side of the infinity edge pool.

'Me too,' she told him, dropping her jacket, opening her shirt, then the buttons of her jeans as she went towards him. By the time she reached him, all he had to do was pull off her jeans and she was naked. She straddled him, kissing him, recognising his smell, his taste, pulling off his shirt, then his belt, then the waistband and zip of his pants, until he was free.

Silent, except for the sound of their breaths and their moans, they made love in the open air, and then he carried her into bed, where they made love again. It wasn't just sex. This was more than that. It was twisted, complicated, gut-wrenching love, the kind that hurt more than it soothed the soul.

It was dawn when she sat up, pulled the sheet around her, ready to go.

'Thank you for coming to the centre last night.'

'I wouldn't be anywhere else,' he told her, his fingers tracing a line down her spine. The room was cold now, the glass doors out to the pool deck still open wide.

'We can't keep doing this,' he said.

Mirren stood up, taking the sheet with her. 'I know.'

'So change it. Let me come home to my wife.'

Even in the dawn light, she could see the determined set of her husband's jaw. Mike Feechan was a man who was used to getting what he wanted and the problem was that he wanted too much of her. More than she could give. Their marriage had been great for the first couple of years, until he'd grown impatient with the time she gave to everything else but their lives together. In the industry, she was one of the rarefied few, the untouchables, that pulled in a massive slice of the global box office. She was a triple threat. Writer. Producer. Director. And none of that came without total focus. Then there was her obsession with Chloe's Care. Her son. All of them came before Mike, before her own happiness. Over the last year, she'd pushed everything to the limit in preparation for opening this centre, immersed herself in the shoot for the new Clansman, drowned in grief and she'd shut Mike out. She knew that. He'd begged her to give him something, but somehow self-imposed solitary confinement was the path of lesser pain.

Eventually, he'd had enough, moved out, and this was what married life looked like now. Separate houses. One foot in, one foot out. He'd thought leaving, taking a break would make her re-evaluate her life. In the meantime, it had just turned him into an estranged husband with benefits. And her into a lonely workaholic who sought him out for sex, but who didn't think she'd ever match up to his expectations as a wife. Now maybe she thought she could.

He was right. They belonged together. It was time. Now that the new centre was open, she could let the professionals take over, step back for a while. The space from him had shown her how much she'd missed him, ached for him. Time to stop living in the pain of the past and move forward. It was time to prioritise her life, her future, her marriage and concentrate on making this work.

'You really want to come back?' she asked him, leaning back, kissing his neck.

'I do. But only if you're in. If we're going to give it everything.'

'I'm in,' she told him, truthfully. She meant it. Mike Feechan was the love of her life and she'd let him go. Time to change that, before it was too late.

'I'll move my stuff back tomorrow,' he whispered, climbing on top of her, sealing the deal by reminding her just how good it felt to be loved by him.

An hour later, the sun was bright when she climbed back into her car and headed down the canyon towards home, feeling something that took a moment to identify. Joy. She was happy. Mike was coming back and this time they were going to make it.

The feeling lasted until she slowed to leave the PCH, turning left on to Webb Way, when her phone pinged to signal an incoming text. At first, she assumed it would be Mike. It wasn't.

Hey, baby. You looked amazing last night. I wanted to speak to you, but I know you're not ready yet. Just don't say it's over, because it isn't. I need to see you. Today? Tonight? You say where and when. Jx

Nope, not Mike. Someone else. Her mistake.

The one that refused to stay in the past.

The one that could destroy any chance of reclaiming her love, her marriage, her future.

Mirren McLean picked up the phone and pressed delete.

3

ZANDER LEITH

'Truly Madly Deeply' – Savage Garden

On a scale of one to ten, dangling a hundred feet in the air with his bollocks trapped inside a safety harness was a solid zero on Zander Leith's scale of enjoyment. He only started breathing again when the director yelled 'cut' and the stunt team hauled him back up.

Rick, the stunt double he'd worked with on the Dunhill movies for the last two decades, got ready to take his place and be dropped back down the side of the skyscraper in downtown LA.

'You okay, man?' Rick asked as they passed each other on the roof.

'Yeah, but fuck Tom Cruise. Life was so much easier before he shamed us all into doing more of our own stunts.'

'I hear you, bud,' Rick agreed, laughing.

In a dim light, he could be Zander's brother: the same wavy fair hair, same wide shoulders, same physique, thanks to daily martial arts and gym workouts. Even when he'd been in the worst grip of addiction, Zander never missed the gym, knowing that his career and his earnings depended on his ability to embody a kick-ass, military-trained, fearless international secret agent. Dunhill, the character he'd played for two decades, didn't do double cheeseburgers and a six-pack of beer every night for dinner.

Zander patted his mate on the back, grinning. 'You be careful down there. I'm not feeling the need to die today.'

'I'll do my best, bro. Got plans tonight and dying would definitely screw them up.'

With that, Rick stepped backwards, only his harness, skill and a dozen safety protocols preventing him from plunging to ground.

Zander shook his head as he watched him drop. If there was a more crazy-ass way to make a living, he didn't know what it was. Over twenty years as Dunhill, he'd been shot seven times, blown up four times, been exposed to radiation, been infected with a killer contagion, fallen from an aircraft at least twice, suffered several forms of torture, drowned, dangled from countless helicopters, participated in car chases through several of the world's biggest cities, and once, oh yes, had stowed away on a space shuttle to prevent a nuclear weapon being unleashed on earth.

It used to be that the stunt guys did all the work and the stars were just brought in for face shots, but, well, Tom Cruise... Zander didn't mind the work, but he fancied Rick's chances of surviving the jump from a burning building way more than his. And shit, the falls hurt so much more now than when he first took this gig.

Dunhill had been going strong for almost twenty years, but unlike Bond, the studio, Lomax Films, had stuck with Zander, deciding the public didn't want a new, younger Dunhill every few years. He mostly owed that to Wes Lomax, the founder of the organisation, who'd recently retired after a heart attack had felled him during a threesome with two A-list actresses who looked like sisters. Their new movie with Lomax Films was announced the next day, while his heart attack had been kept under wraps until it was clear Lomax was going to make a full recovery.

Once upon a time, the movie mogul had been a father figure to the young Zander Leith, but no longer. A few years back, Lomax had believed a false drug test when Zander was clean, and Zander had never forgiven the lack of trust. Personally, they were done. But, professionally, Leith and Lomax made each other a shit ton of money, and until that stopped, Zander Leith would play Seb Dunhill in Lomax movies for as long as the public wanted him and his bollocks could still squeeze into a harness.

He headed back to the temporary production centre that had been set up in a vacant office floor, one level down. A considerable chunk of the movie was being filmed on location in this building so the huge open-plan area was buzzing with staff from every section of the team: make-up, wardrobe, stunts, lighting, sound and a dozen others. The only private areas were the converted side offices being used as dressing rooms, and Zander headed straight for his.

When he opened the door, he was greeted with, 'Hey there, aren't you Zander Leith? I heard you're a tremendous shag and I'd be prepared to test that theory.'

Zander felt his shoulders relax and drop at least an inch, as they always did when his wife was nearby. Just knowing that Hollie was there made everything better in this world.

'Yeah, whoever told you that is a liar,' he replied, closing the door, then leaning against it, arms folded. 'Just wanna manage the expectations.'

Over at her desk in the corner of the room, she sat back in her chair and sighed. 'Really wish you'd done that before we got married. But divorce lawyers are way too expensive, so s'pose I'll just hang on to you for a while longer.'

He could look at her all day, especially when she smiled at him like that. There was not an inch of this woman that Zander didn't adore and the best thing he'd done in his life was marry her four years before. Their path hadn't been easy. She'd been his assistant and best friend for ten years before he'd realised that what they had was so much more than that. It was the forever stuff.

Not that it mattered, but most of the world seemed to agree. There had been overwhelming support from fans and commentators, with the exception of a few tabloids, who couldn't seem to get past the fact that Hollie didn't fit the movie-star-wife stereotype. She wasn't a size four, she wasn't in her twenties and she had no desire whatsoever to hit the red carpet, hanging on to his arm, grinning for *People* and *US Today*. Nope, she was a thirty-five-year-old, gorgeous, curvaceous US size 14, with wild brunette hair and a business brain so sharp she could be successful in any role she put her mind to. Thankfully, right now, her choice of positions was his wife and manager.

'Okay, since you're not offering any perks of the job right now, let's run through the next couple of days.'

Zander kicked off his boots, pulled off his shirt and took up residence on the battered brown leather sofa that sat against the wall next to her desk, grabbing a packet of wipes to remove the make-up that had been applied for that morning's shoot. It seemed like every year he got older added another layer of concealer. George Clooney still claimed he never wore make-up in his movies, but Zander wasn't buying it.

'Okay, so you've got an interview tomorrow morning with *Entertainment Tonight*, to talk about Dunhill 10, then a live link to the GQ awards, to accept an award for something – film star who farts the most is my bet – and then day after is Davie and Sarah's wedding, up at the Callaghan ranch in Santa Barbara. You're off the shooting schedule next week because they're doing the location stuff in Morocco, so after the wedding, we're going to stay at the ranch for a few days with Cara and Lex, then we're back here

Friday, because they need you for a couple of shots on Saturday morning.'

'Are we driving?' Zander asked, hoping it was the case. It was his favourite time, just the two of them, on the road together. They'd leave the Aston Martin at home and take his old beat-up pickup truck, and as long as they dodged any paps when they were leaving the house, no one knew where they were or where they were going. They'd taken an extended honeymoon in that truck, just the two of them, working their way right up to Montana, staying in out-of-the-way beach shacks and mountain cabins that Hollie had booked in her own name. Zander had grown a beard, left his hair to get long, pulled on a baseball cap and shades, and if anyone they met had recognised him, they didn't mention it. It had been four weeks of anonymous freedom and the best days of their lives.

'We sure are, honey,' she said in her best hillbilly accent. 'Oh, and we also need to talk about...'

He didn't hear the rest, because her phone began to ring and she answered it straight away.

'Hollie Callan.' She'd kept her maiden name when they'd married, saying it had done her fine for thirty-odd years and she had no reason to change it... unless she got arrested or needed same-day restaurant reservations somewhere trendy. Thankfully, the first of those occasions hadn't been tested.

'Hi, Joanna, good to hear from you.'

Zander guessed she was speaking to the only Joanna they knew – the VIP manager at the Louden Hotel in Toronto. Zander had just spent six solid months filming Dunhill up there, and that would continue for the next couple of years, so they kept their own two-bedroom penthouse suite there all year round so that they could make it personal and comfortable.

Zander could only hear Hollie's side of the conversation, and at first it sounded light-hearted. 'What? No, not this week. Clearly, since I'm talking to you right now.'

It soon went left. 'What?' You're kidding. Holy shit. No. Has to be a mistake.'

He sat forward on the sofa. 'What's going on?'

'Hold on, I'm going to put you on speaker so you can say that again and Zander can hear you.'

'Hi Zander.' Joanna's voice filled the room. This was a woman who'd worked in many of the top hotels in the world, so fame and stardom had long since ceased to faze her. It was just one of the reasons Zander and Hollie loved to work with her. Although, it had taken her a while to get used to their insistence that she drop the formalities and call them by their first names. That didn't happen often in the VIP world.

'Hey, Joanna. Whatever is going on doesn't sound like something I want to hear.'

'It isn't. Look, I'm really sorry about this, and I take full responsibility for it, but we've had a breach of protocol up here. I was off for a couple of days so I'm only catching it now, but basically, someone checked into your suite, saying she was Hollie and she'd lost her key.'

'And your staff gave it out? Hell, Joanna, that's some breach...' Hollie interjected, shaking her head and raising her arms to him in a 'what the fuck?' gesture.

'I know, I know. But please bear with me, because this is a bizarre one. The woman stayed there for two nights this week, and the only reason I was alerted to it was because housekeeping flagged it up to me when I came back in today.'

'Wait, so you're saying that someone stayed two nights in our suite?' Zander clarified, immediately running through the personal stuff that was left there. Not much, this time. Filming in Toronto had wrapped a couple of weeks ago, and now there was a two-month break for LA location shoots, so they'd brought most of their stuff home.

'Yes. I'm so sorry to share that with you. I understand if you're pissed.'

'Look, it's not the end of the world,' Zander began, hearing the regret in Joanna's voice and instinctively trying to make her feel better, while ignoring Hollie's thunderous expression. He was definitely way more chilled than his wife when it came to shit like this. What did it matter? 'So someone got a couple of free nights. Just have the place swept for devices and cleaned before we get back up there and we'll be cool.'

Hollie motioned pointing a gun at him and pulling the trigger.

'I appreciate the understanding there. Hollie, you've gone quiet...'

'I'm not quite so understanding as Gandhi over there,' Hollie bit back.

'Look, I understand and I feel the same. But there's a couple more things you need to know. Housekeeping alerted me because there were two framed photos of you guys in the suite and both of them have been smashed to pieces.'

'Shit, Joanna, that's messed up,' Hollie blurted.

Zander was paying attention now. His wife rarely got concerned or upset, especially since he'd got sober and she no longer had to pull him out of gutters or check him into rehab.

'It really is. And I'm not trying to deflect blame here, because we screwed up by letting her in the room. But the thing is, it was an understandable mistake because, like I said, this is a bizarre one.'

Hollie shot that right down. 'How the hell could it be understandable?'

'Are you guys near a computer? Can I email you some footage from our security system?'

'Sure.' For the first time in years, Zander was beginning to feel a rising sense of dread, the one that used to make him reach for a bottle of Jack Daniel's.

Hollie refreshed her screen a few times, until the email dropped, then waited a few more seconds until the attached file downloaded and opened.

It wasn't TV quality, but it was colour, and it was pretty clear. The date in the top right-hand corner was three days ago and Zander immediately recognised the scene. The Louden reception area. The back of the head of a receptionist. She lifts her head as someone approaches, speaks to her and...

Hollie's gasp was somewhere between incredulity and horror. 'What the...?

Zander was on the same train to WhatTheActualFuck. Because there, on the screen, was Hollie.

Only it wasn't. It couldn't have been.

Because, three days ago, she had been right here with him.

4

DAVIE JOHNSTON

'Spaceman' – Sam Ryder

Davie Johnston unpacked four suitcases from the trunk of his Bentley and counted to ten. *Do not lose your shit. Do not lose your shit.*

'Seriously? Never figured you for a ranch in the country kind of dude. I mean, we got married at the Four Seasons and even then, you were pissed because the ballroom could only fit two hundred.'

Why? Why had he chosen to pick up his ex-wife, Jenny Rico, her partner, Darcy Jay and his teenage twins, Bella and Bray from the private airfield a couple of miles away? He had a driver for that. Drego was probably sitting buffing his fricking nails in the garage here, while Davie was subjecting himself to the ex-partner version of waterboarding.

Do not lose your shit.

He lined the cases up next to each other on the driveway. Actually, driveway was a bit of a reach. It was a dirt track road that they'd travelled two miles along to get to the ranch, and now they were here and he was unloading more luggage than a travelling ice hockey team from the vehicle.

'Yeah, well, times change. I change. My bride changes. And that's happened for a reason,' he said, aiming for the higher ground, then being shot by a sniper when she came back with the killer retort of, 'Preaching to the lesbian choir, Davie Boy.'

She accessorised that with a smug grin and he counted to ten again. After all these years, she could still press his buttons more than his bank manager. And he really, really hated his bank manager.

Five years after they split, it was still a source of endless amusement to Jenny and Darcy that what had started as an occasional threesome for a bit of fun had ended with Jenny and her gorgeous co-star on the cop show, *Streets of Power*, Darcy Jay, shutting him out of the picture. And the bedroom. Eventually, the two women had gone public with their relationship, it had been written into the show's storyline, and the ratings had doubled, with the watching world loving a high definition view of the dynamics between numbers three and six on *People* magazine's Most Beautiful Woman list that year.

Davie dropped the last Louis Vuitton suitcase on the gravel, earning a yelp of outrage from Jenny.

'Look, didn't we call a ceasefire?' he demanded. 'I was under the impression that we were the poster folks for congenial co-parenting these days, yet I'm sensing a smidgen of animosity has returned to paradise.'

She threw her Gucci Diana tote over her shoulder and came back oozing contempt. 'We did. But that was before you refused to build the kids a guest house on your property.'

'We already have a guest house on the property.'

'But it doesn't meet with Bella's specifications. It's smaller than her closet.' There was at least a hint of evil amusement in her voice and Davie had the distinct feeling she was playing with him. Winding him up was her very favourite game and he fell for it every time.

'And that's why they should be living in the main fricking house! They're fourteen!'

'They're not normal fourteen-year-olds. How many kids that age do you know that have seven figures in the bank?'

'Then they can build their own house,' he spat back, unsure what was pissing him off most: the entitlement of his kids, the fact that their mother encouraged it, or the reminder that these days, with the massive residuals from their show, his kids were on track to be wealthier than he'd ever been. They were probably more popular too. They'd been stars of the hit TV soap *Family Three* since they were four years old, until it finally wrapped last year. Bella had catapulted her fame into endorsements, a fashion line and a new role in a Disney series that was turning her into the next Hannah bloody Montana. Bray, meanwhile, had turned his back on the whole scene and spent all day, every day at Zuma beach surfing the waves, ignoring the rest of the world. Davie was worried about him, but it didn't help that Jenny liked to undermine his relationship with the kids by pointing out Davie's flaws, his failures and his flagging career at every opportunity.

However, the career element of that was going to change soon. True, he'd slightly overextended himself. Okay, fucking massively overextended. But when his new show launched next week, the big players in the industry would recognise the genius of it and he'd recoup every cent of his investment and more.

Right on cue, Bella and Bray disembarked from the vehicle and stood, staring at him.

'What?' he asked, genuinely puzzled. They hadn't heard the hissed conversation, because, God forbid, that would have required removing their earphones.

'Isn't there a concierge? Or a doorman to take our stuff to the room?' That came from Bella, who had overcome any notion she'd ever had of being a daddy's girl and was now a full-on tweenage terrorist.

'There is. It's a female. Called Bella. And she carries her own cases because that's what her arms are for.'

Davie thought her head was going to explode.

Why? Why had he invited them to his wedding? He'd been trying to do the right thing and the result was serial persecution. And they were only just out of the car. The only blessing was that his mother, Ena, was already in the house and she'd keep them in line over the weekend. She'd arrived yesterday from Scotland, and despite her deep conviction that his lifestyle was built on frivolous nonsense, she was the only person that, for some staggeringly unfathomable reason, his kids listened to.

Davie helped them with the cases as far as the door, where Cara Callaghan, the owner of the ranch, came to meet them. This had been their first choice of wedding venue because Cara was a friend, and the wife of Lex Callaghan, who played the Clansman in Mirren's movies. Cara ran this place as an equine therapy centre for addicts, but this weekend there were no other guests, just the wedding party. Davie had a feeling she'd be glad to get back to dealing with the damaged in society after a weekend with his brood.

He was about to go inside when he spotted Sarah over at the fence that surrounded the nearest paddock to the house. She was the first and only choice for company on any day of the week, so he left his unwilling collective of dysfunction to get settled and strolled off to join her.

She turned when she heard his boots on the gravel. 'Yay, you're back. Did you pick everyone up?'

'I did. But tell me why we didn't elope?' he asked, as he leaned over the fence beside her.

She didn't hesitate. 'Because you're too much of a people pleaser and you love to be the centre of attention?'

'Sad but true. Are we too late to change our minds?'

A lock of her chestnut hair had escaped from her ponytail, so she tucked it behind her ear. She rarely wore make-up and today was no exception, so her freckles were on full display. Davie loved every one of them.

'Davie, you're about to spend the weekend on a ranch with your ex-wife, who thinks you're a knob, and your kids, who barely tolerate you. It'll never be too late to change your mind. Say the word, and I'll meet you in Vegas. But then you'd miss the confetti and the party and that would kill you because you're inherently shallow.'

They both laughed, mostly because, again, it was true.

He slung his arm around her shoulder, not caring that the afternoon sun was beating on his head. Usually, that would cause a dash inside to lather up on factor 100 and pull a cap on. Wrinkles were the enemy for anyone on TV in this world of 4D definition. But no, he stayed put. That was how much he loved this lady.

In fact, one of his first memories was of her sitting by his pool in the morning sun, eyes closed, face lifted towards the sky. It was only hours after they'd met in a private club in LA, before he knew she was a journalist, over from Scotland to try to dig up the true story of Davie, Zander and Mirren's lives in Glasgow. She'd learned it all. How Zander's father had been an abusive monster. How his lover, Mirren's mother, had killed him. How the three of them – Mirren, Zander and Davie – had covered it up and buried the body – and how they hadn't spoken to each other for twenty years because they couldn't bear to face their memories.

That had all changed. Sarah had killed the story, but her investigations had brought them all back together again and he was grateful. Even more grateful that after almost five years of asking, she was finally going to marry him. Until now, she'd said she wanted to make it on her own terms before she'd consider going public with him. Wasn't that a role reversal. The only person on the planet who didn't want the world to know that a Hollywood star was in love with them. He'd honoured her wishes though, and it had been worth it.

Her first book, a deep dive into the Hollywood underworld, had made the bestseller lists and had led to a second book deal. Her exposé of scandals in the music industry had been even more successful than her debut, topping the bestseller lists for three weeks and staying in the charts for another twelve. For the last year, she had been working on book number three: a commentary on the #MeToo movement and the women who had found the strength to come forward with their own stories as a result of the change in the social justice landscape. He could tell it was having an effect on her. Over the last few months, she'd been a bit distant. Quiet. He figured it was an occupational hazard. Or perhaps she was just feeling over-loaded. Her background as a journalist, and a few insightful, hard-hitting television interviews discussing the subject matter in her books, had earned her the job offer of her dreams – as an investigative journalist on *Out Of The Shadows* – a weekly TV show that exposed injustices, abuses and conspiracies across the country.

On the day she got the offer, she'd finally said yes to his marriage proposal, on the condition that it was a small, intimate ceremony and, afterwards, she would still keep her own name and wouldn't be forced to do all that mindless public appearance shit that made her itch. Now Davie was locking that in before she saw sense and changed her mind.

'Maybe we can just steal that and flee?' he suggested, nodding to the helicopter that had just appeared over the trees a couple of hundred yards in front of them.

They both watched as the imposing black chopper came towards them, getting lower with every spin of its blades.

'Who is that? Zander? Mirren?' Sarah asked, as he squinted in the same direction.

'No, Zander's driving and I think Mirren is too. She's coming up with Mike.'

'They're back together? Oooh, I like that.'

He kissed her forehead. 'I knew there was a romantic heart in there somewhere.'

'Just pragmatic. They belong together.'

'Like us?' He pushed, enjoying the flirtation. It seemed like the last few weeks had been a chaotic bedlam of meetings, recordings, financial discussions and a whole lot of convincing everyone from sponsors to producers that his show was going to work, that he was going to get the ratings, that the country was ready for straight talking and programming that didn't clutch its pearls when it came to the occasional profanity. This was real-life TV. Not the sanitised crap that the big networks were pushing now.

It took a few moments for him to realise that Sarah hadn't answered, and a couple more to understand why. She was staring at the helicopter, her eyes narrowed. He followed her gaze. Now that it had turned, he could see that it said Lomax Films on the side.

Davie felt a split second of triumph. He'd come. Wes Lomax. His original mentor, the man who was responsible for Davie's career at the start, and the newest, and only investor in his latest enterprise. They hadn't worked together after *The Brutal Circle*, because Davie had quickly realised that his talents lay in hosting and then producing, but nevertheless Davie owed Wes the life he'd had here. The fortune. The fame. Hell, even the fuck-ups wouldn't have been possible if he hadn't met Wes. And he hadn't forgotten it. That's why he was one of the first people Davie had spoken to about investing in his new venture.

They'd had a couple of meetings over the last year, one before Wes retired on health grounds, then a lunch at the Polo Lounge in the Beverly Hills Hotel last week. Wes didn't look like a guy who was three months after a heart attack. Didn't act like it either. Wes's investment made even more sense now, Davie had argued in the second meeting, because the old man needed a side project to keep him occupied since he'd stepped down from the studio he'd founded. Wes Lomax wasn't a man who would spend the rest of his days on a golf cart at the Bel Air Country Club. He needed to be busy. In the mix. At the centre of whatever was making waves. He needed skin in the game. And all the other clichés the execs in this business threw out in every conversation.

While Davie was schmoozing and hustling his thousand-dollar Prada boots off in last week's meeting, he'd casually dropped into the conversation that he was getting married.

Wes had roared. 'Don't be a fool, son. Haven't you learned a lesson after giving away half of everything you worked for to Jenny? You know that old saying? Be quicker just meeting a woman you don't like and giving her a house.'

Davie had shrugged. He'd long since made peace with the settlement he'd given Jenny. It wasn't the 50 per cent he'd have had to cough up if they'd stayed together past the ten-year California threshold, but it was a sizeable chunk of change. A high price for freedom, but, hey, they'd had a good run and she'd always taken the biggest share of responsibility for the kids. 'She deserved it,' Davie had objected. 'Don't get me wrong – she's still the biggest pain in my ass, but that doesn't detract from the fact that she deserved the cash.'

'Nothing worse than a man that doesn't learn his lesson,' Wes had muttered, condescension batting every word towards him. 'So who's the lucky lady then?'

The question didn't surprise Davie. Sarah's insistence that he kept their relationship under wraps had led to endless gossip that he was celibate, gay or – in one particularly outlandish website – had an old lady fetish. He was now careful to avoid streets with senior care facilities.

'Sarah McKenzie. She's a Scottish journalist, but she lives here now and—'

The older man had tossed his napkin on the table. 'Fuck. Really? Dark hair? Skinny chick? I think I know her.'

That had surprised Davie. Sarah had never mentioned running into Wes.

'Really? From where?'

'I bumped into her at the Beverly Hills Hotel. We were chatting about all that #MeToo stuff. Fucking Weinstein has got the whole town paranoid and making up shit that didn't happen. Nice girl, though. I enjoyed speaking to her. Look, tell you what, Davie. I'll come in for twenty million dollars. Call it a wedding present for you and that lovely lady.'

It had taken Davie a moment to process that. Twenty million dollars, just under half of the budget for the first six month run of the show. You fucking dancer. Somewhere in the jubilation and celebration of that, the invitation was out of Davie's mouth before he'd even thought it through.

'Come, then. Next weekend. Lex Callaghan's ranch. Wedding is at 6 o'clock on Friday. We'd love to have you.'

Yeah, it was a great idea. It would give him more time to solidify Wes's investment, maybe even milk him for some more, and at the same time, Zander – Wes's superstar action dude – would be there to reinforce the connection. Mirren and Wes had a long history too, and Wes's studio had made a couple of her Clansman movies, until she'd taken them back to her old home at Pictor. The whole gang was going to be back together.

At least, that was the thought he'd had until he'd left Wes's table, phoned his business manager to tell him the news and promptly forgotten that Wes might come along today. Shit. He should really have told Sarah, but in his defence, he'd thought it pretty unlikely that a man whom he'd barely communicated with for twenty years would actually pitch up at his wedding.

Only he had. The gust from the blades of his chariot were blowing dust up into their eyes, and Sarah didn't look thrilled.

'Davie, is that Wes Lomax?'

Well, she knew now, but he was sure she'd be fine with it once she realised that he was Davie's new investor.

'Yeah, I forgot to say, he's agreed to back my show. Twenty million. When we were discussing it, I mentioned to him that we were getting married and I might have thrown out a casual invitation. Didn't think for a minute that he'd come.'

The chopper had landed now, and the blades were beginning to slow, but even at their top speed they wouldn't have been as fast as Sarah's head as it whipped around to face him. He could see that he was wrong. She wasn't going to be fine. In fact, she looked about as far as she could be from fine.

'You. Forgot. To. Say.' She spat out the words like bullets.

'Yeah, why? Is... Is... is it a problem?'

He couldn't even begin to understand the expression on her face. Horror. Fear. But most of all, fury. What the hell was going on?

'It's a problem, Davie. A huge fucking problem.' She was speaking through gritted teeth now, but there was something more. Clenched fists. A straight, stiff posture. If she swung a punch at him right now, he was ready to duck.

'Davie, I love you, but I need him gone. Right now. If you don't get rid of him, there won't be a wedding.'

With that, the love of his life walked away and he was left with absolutely no clue what the fuck had just happened.

5

SARAH MCKENZIE

'It Must Have Been Love' – Roxette

Sarah could feel her heart race and her temper boil as she stormed through the huge open-plan living area of the ranch, so focused on getting to a private, safe space that she didn't even register Jenny and Darcy over at the stunning rustic mahogany dining table, chatting to Cara Callaghan.

When she'd begun dating Davie, she'd had a rocky start with his ex-wife, mainly because Jenny thought so little of Davie, and that made her fairly sure anyone who wanted to be with him must be deeply flawed. But that had been then. Over the first couple of years, they'd warily danced around each other, and now, to Davie's undisguised irritation, the two women had become friends. Actually, the three women – Sarah loved Darcy too. Jenny and Darcy had even been gracious enough to contribute to an episode of her show, *Out Of The Shadows*, where the team had been investigating the homophobia that still existed in some corners of the entertainment industry.

'Well, here she comes,' Jenny whistled. 'The one woman crazy enough to want to marry my ex-husband.'

It wasn't a dig, more just the back-and-forth jousting that had become both women's favourite part of their friendship. Usually, Sarah would throw a dig right back – 'You okay there, Jen? Feeling insecure because he traded up to a younger model?' Then Jenny would laugh, and they'd head to the nearest bar for a couple of rounds of mimosas. Not today. Nope. Today, Sarah barely registered the comment, too consumed by the uncharacteristic rage that was exploding in her head.

Wes Lomax.

Wes. Fucking. Lomax.

She got to her room and, without realising it, slammed the door behind her, every one of her senses drowned out by the fury that had taken a grip of her soul. She pulled her suitcase onto the bed, opened it and started stripping her clothes from the hangers in the wardrobe and tossing them in.

Wes. Fucking. Lomax.

Cara had left a tray on the credenza with bottles of red wine, vodka, gin and some mixers, but Sarah had been pretty sure it would remain untouched. Davie was a beer guy, and she only ever drank beer or the occasional cocktail. Not today. She poured a shot of vodka and threw it back, then shuddered as the liquid slipped past her disgusted tastebuds and down into her gut.

Breathe.

Just breathe…

But Wes fucking Lomax.

The truth was, she wasn't furious at Davie for inviting him. He didn't know the history because she'd chosen not to tell him, so that had been an innocent action on his behalf. The problem – the knife-twisting, rage-inducing problem – was that the bastard had chosen to come. The arrogance of him. The sheer fucking audacity. It was a power play on his side and Sarah wasn't going to shut up and let it go. She'd come too close to that already.

Davie burst in the door, with 'Sarah, what the fuck was that?', then caught sight of her face, her posture, of the turmoil that was oozing from every pore, and immediately de-escalated. 'Babe, what is it? What's going on? It's only Wes. I had a meeting with him last week, forgot to tell you, and he mentioned he'd met you, so I invited him along. I don't get the problem.'

The reality was he truly didn't. He wouldn't think twice about inviting someone to their small, intimate wedding without running it past her. Awareness and empathy had never been on the list of things she loved about Davie Johnston. He was shallow. Self-involved. Overconfident. Occasionally delusional. A hustler who had crawled to the top on not much more than charm, self-belief, ruthless ambition and the kind of raw determination that only very few possessed. But she saw so much more than that. She saw a guy who was shaped by poverty and violence in his childhood, who had a good heart under all that bravado crap and who made her laugh like no-one else ever had. More than that, there was a chemistry that she couldn't explain. She felt a connection to him that made her happier when he was around, that made her smile when she saw him, made her accept his flaws, just as he accepted hers but loved her anyway.

Five years ago, after meeting Davie on a brief trip, she'd travelled 5,000 miles and given up her life in Scotland to be with him, although she'd taken it slow, refused to move in with him, avoided the limelight, kept their relationship completely private and would only now marry him because she'd forged her own career. Now, she had the job, she had the man, she had the life she'd always wanted...

Until Wes Lomax had pitched up and wrecked it.

Davie was standing right in front of her now, waiting for her answer.

'I don't want him here,' she stated simply.

'But why? You're gonna have to give me more than that.'

Christ, she was going to need another vodka for this.

'Because...' Every ounce of air left her body as she exhaled, and she wasn't sure how much longer her shaking legs would hold her, so she sat down in the armchair beside the bed, aware that she was going to have to have the conversation she'd been dreading for months. 'Like he said, I met him once. But it wasn't accidental. I tracked him down as part of the research for my #MeToo book. Davie, he's another Weinstein. And he's every other sleazeball big shot in this town who uses power and fear to silence women, no matter what he's done to them. Come on, you know that's not a surprise. You've heard the rumours.'

Davie poured a vodka of his own, sat on the bed opposite her. 'Look, I know what he's like. Everyone does. Hell, he's built his reputation on being a serial shagger.'

Sarah wasn't having that. 'No, don't dismiss it like that. It's more than just being someone who is there for the party. Since I started working on the #MeToo cases, I've heard horror stories about the things he's done to women. The assaults. The rapes. The threats. The manipulation and intimidation.' That was true. The problem was all the stories were second-hand. *Were.* Past tense. She had a first-person one now, but she wasn't ready to share that. 'The man is a monster. And now that I'm telling you this, I need you to believe me. I need you to tell him to leave.'

A voice inside her head begged, *Do it. Please do it now. Then this conversation can end here for now and we'll save the rest for another day.*

'Look, I'll tell him to leave if that's what you want.'

Yes. Do it now. End this. Go.

Sarah watched as his eye twitched, his reaction to stress since he was a child, and she knew he wasn't going to leave it there.

'But, Sarah, come on. It's Wes. I owe that guy everything. How do you know the stories are even true? How do you know this isn't just some money-making con? That these claims aren't just desperados looking for five minutes of fame or a payout?'

The fact that he was still pushing back was making her fury rise again and she fought to keep it under control.

'I know they're true. I can't tell you why,' her words were coming through gritted teeth. 'I just need you to trust me, Davie. As a journalist, as your partner, as someone who knows what she's doing. I need you to do as I ask. Get rid of him. And then I need you to cut off all contact with him.'

He came straight back at her. 'No. I get that he's an asshole and he's made mistakes, but they're fuck all to do with me and I'm not getting involved. And to be honest, if you cared about me, you'd drop this. He's just agreed to invest shitloads of cash in my company. I've known this guy for more than half my life. He brought us here, he made us, and back then he was like a father to Zander, to Mirren, to me. I'm not going to turn my back on him.'

'And right and wrong don't matter?' she spat, challenging him.

'Loyalty matters more. God knows, none of us are perfect.'

'Davie, did he agree to give you the money before or after you told him we were getting married?'

He reeled back, confused. 'What? I've no idea. Why does that even matter?'

'It matters.'

Before she could decide whether to elaborate, there was a knock at the door, followed by Cara's voice. 'Sarah, is everything okay? Can I help?'

There was nothing she wanted to do more right now than open the door and let Cara put her arms around her. She wanted to hand over her care, her stress, this whole situation, to someone whom she knew would do the right thing. She just wished that person was the man sitting in front of her, the one she was about to commit the rest of her life to.

'I'm okay, Cara, but thanks,' she lied. She was definitely not okay.

'Okay, but holler if you need me, honey.'

There was the sound of steps on the Spanish floor tiles as Cara retreated.

Sarah found a way to lower her voice, so her words came out calm but direct. 'What about loyalty to me?'

'Babe, they're just rumours. Like I said, they're probably not even true.'

Was he really doing this? Was he really still arguing with her, dismissing her thoughts and her concerns? But even as she thought that, she knew that she had a skewed perspective, because he didn't have all the information. She did. And every single fact and story absolutely sickened her.

'And like *I* said, I believe them so you need to trust me. And I want you to get rid of him, and to cancel his investment in your company, and to cut him out of your life.'

His eyes were wide and his voice oozed exasperation as he replied,

'Sarah, if I cut ties with everyone I've heard a sleazy rumour about, I'd be doing podcasts for one out of a basement in Ohio.'

The journalist in her knew he wasn't wrong, but still, it took everything she had to keep her cool.

'That's the problem. It's so widespread that you're immune to it. I'm not. Be careful who you put on a pedestal, Davie. People like Wes need their comeuppance and their victims need justice. I'm going to prove that everything I've heard about him is fact.'

'And if it is, I'll back you 100 per cent,' he said.

'You'll speak out against him, if I need you to?'

A pause and she saw his reluctance. In the years before the media storm leading up to his arrest, she hadn't seen male stars in the industry publicly raising concerns about Weinstein or supporting the allegations made against him. Rumour was, Brad Pitt once confronted him, but that was never quoted as fact, so she couldn't say for certain it was true.

'And you'll tell him you don't want his investment?'

She now knew exactly what a rabbit in the headlights looked like. And even though it broke her heart, she had to run right over it.

'Too late,' she said softly, calling out his hesitation. 'I need to do this, Davie, and I'm not going to do it while worrying about your feelings or the consequences for you. This is so much more important than that, so I need you to back off, give me space...'

'What the hell are you talking about? Sarah, we're getting married tomorrow! What are you saying? You're cancelling? Is this a postponement? A break-up?'

'I don't know. I just know that I can't marry you this weekend. Not now. Not when he's infected it.' Him, of all people. Lomax. That rotten, disgusting bastard had spoiled this, and that made her want to rage, to defy him, to tell Davie the truth about everything and find a way to salvage this, but the damage was done. There was no bringing the wedding back from here.

'Babe, I love you. Don't do this,' he pleaded, desperately. 'Let's have the wedding, let's talk about all this shit tomorrow, or the next day, or next fricking month. I don't care. All I care about is marrying you.'

She shrugged. 'I can't. Not now. Not now that he's here. I thought I could work on this story about him over the next few months and then tell you about it when I had more. I hadn't realised he was back in your life. I hadn't realised you were taking his money. That's a deal-breaker for me, Davie.'

'Okay, I won't! I'll refuse it!'

'And then you'll resent me for making you turn him down? No. You make your own decisions. I just hope they're the right ones. Let's talk about us when this is over, Davie.' With that, she zipped up the suitcase, pulled it off the bed and made to leave. 'And if you want to help me, then stay out of my way and let me concentrate on what I'm doing, because I don't need the distraction.'

He stood there as she walked past him, and again, she held in her rage, her tears, her desperation to melt into his arms and tell him everything.

The truth was that she had to follow this story because she did have one victim who was willing to speak out, but only when she was certain that she'd win.

The woman had met Wes Lomax in a bar a few months ago, planning to suss him out and see for herself how he treated women.

She'd heard rumours.

She'd wanted facts.

She'd thought she was safe because she went in with her guard up.

She wasn't.

He'd tried to drug her.

He'd attacked her.

And now she was determined to bring him down.

The victim's name was Sarah McKenzie.

6

ZANDER

'I Need You' – Tim McGraw (feat. Faith Hill)

Traffic had been heavy, and there had been a couple of truck fires that blocked the highway, so the journey back down to Malibu from Santa Barbara had taken almost three hours instead of the usual hour and a half, but Zander didn't much care. He had his wife in the passenger seat, some Blake Shelton on the sound system and he was cruising in his pick-up – this was about as close to heaven as it got for him. Many times, he'd wished he had discovered much sooner that this was what it took to make him happy. Maybe then he wouldn't have spent twenty years soaked in Jack Daniel's, snorting coke from the dashboards of cars and waking up next to whatever woman had picked him up from the floor or the rehab centre the night before. He'd once met a beautiful woman for drinks, while she was on the way to LAX to catch a flight to the UK, and then later that night he'd hired a private jet to join her there, where they had a wild weekend of passion and excess. So much for impulse control. Dick move. Especially when it transpired that she was married, and her husband was the type of guy who doled out cement boots and river trips to anyone who crossed him.

'You know, I'm still gutted for Sarah and Davie. I really think those two are meant to be together and I'm so confused. Tell me you've found out what happened?'

He glanced at Hollie, face blank.

She threw her hands up. 'Of course you haven't. God forbid you and Davie would talk about anything concerning emotions. You know, I once knew a guy who played golf with his best buddy every week and had no idea his wife had divorced him. I will never understand it. It's like they teach you repression of feelings and ignoring emotional situations in Man School.'

Zander shrugged, mostly because it was true. Avoiding hard situations by hanging out with his buddy Jack Daniel's had been his playbook for life. But on Davie and Sarah, he shared Hollie's confusion. By the time they'd reached the ranch last Friday, the wedding had been cancelled and Sarah, Davie and the rest of the wedding guests were already gone. Zander and Hollie had planned to stay the rest of the week up there with their friends, Lex and Cara, so they'd stuck to that, and Zander had tried to reach Davie all week, with no success. Davie wasn't returning calls, or answering texts.

If Zander had to apportion responsibility for the wedding cancellation, his first bet would be his half-brother, the other son of Jono Leith. Yeah, that lack of impulse control and propensity for shit decisions was in the genes.

As if reading his mind, Hollie pressed a few buttons on her cell phone and he could hear the rings at the other end, then her sigh as it clicked on to voice mail. Hollie waited for the pre-recorded message to end before she spoke.

'Sarah, it's me again. Just calling to check in. Honey, I'm sensing by the million ignored calls that you don't wanna talk, but when you do, call me back. If I worry about you anymore, I'm gonna need Botox for my frown lines and you don't want to be responsible for messing up this pretty face. Love you.'

She sighed as she hung up. 'Too pushy?' she asked him, then immediately, 'Why am I asking you? You're a relationship desert.' Not strictly true, but she enjoyed the exaggeration. He had a couple of friends, a lot of acquaintances and one wife he adored. That was all he needed. Hollie was still sharing her thoughts. 'The million was a slight exaggeration, but I've called every day this week, and every time she just texts me back and tells me she's ok, just needs some space to work some stuff out. I mean, she could be in a hostage situation and the kidnapper could be writing the texts.'

'Glad you're not getting dramatic about this though.' Zander deadpanned.

Hollie wasn't listening, and he figured she'd be replaying the phone message in her head. He wasn't surprised that she'd tried to keep it light because she wouldn't want to pile any more pressure on whatever was happening there. The two women had been friends for a long time, and they had the kind of easy relationship that was based on love, trust and the firm conviction that all this Hollywood stuff was pretentious bullshit. With that kind of perspective, Zander was pretty sure that Davie's life was a whole lot better with Sarah in it.

Just as his was so much better now that Hollie had taken leave of her senses and married him.

How his life had changed in the last five years. Sobriety. A wife. Mirren and Davie back in his life. A home that he finally felt connected to. He still remembered the day of his own wedding, when he'd woken up and felt something that he'd never experienced before, something that it took a while to put a label on. When he finally did, he realised that it was the opposite of lonely. He felt like he had people. He had connections. He belonged somewhere. And that was the kind of high he'd never managed to buy from a dealer or a liquor store.

'What are you thinking?' Hollie asked, then followed that immediately up with, 'Go on – shock the crap out of me. Tell me you were pondering global warming. Or international politics. Or the history of atomic research.'

He responded to her sarcasm with a wry grin and a side eye of disdain – which she clearly thought was hilarious.

'Okay, okay,' she conceded. 'I know my audience. Sport or sex?'

'Sex.' Which was almost true. She'd think he was kidding if he said love.

'Okay, you've twisted my arm. Want to pull into a lay-by or wait till we get home?'

He was still laughing when the song went from Shelton's 'Mine Would Be You' to Tim McGraw's 'I Need You'. This song said everything. He reached over for his wife's hand. This was all he needed, right here.

They'd both been wound tight on the way up to Davie's wedding after they'd discovered the whole intruder fiasco at the hotel in Canada. They'd notified the police, and John Wood, head of security for Lomax Films, had a team on it too. So far, all they'd established was that someone had used a wig, and make-up, and possibly even prosthetics, to look like Hollie in order to get into the suite. They were pretty sure it was probably some Instagram prank, or a journalist trying to drum up a reaction and a story. Either way, Zander and Hollie had decided to let the professionals handle it. No point in stressing when there was nothing they could do. A few days at the ranch had helped them relax and Zander just wanted to keep that vibe going when he got home.

They pulled up into the driveway of their house on Broad Beach, a few miles along the Pacific Coast Highway from where Mirren lived in Malibu Colony. They'd moved here when they'd married, from the only other home Zander had ever owned – a top-floor apartment on the boardwalk at Venice Beach, overlooking the ocean, but right above the crazy hustle of the streets below. Moving had been one of Hollie's non-negotiables, given that the marijuana use was so extensive in that area, she swore she got high when she stood at the open window. She probably had a point. As a recovering addict, it wasn't the healthiest place for him to be. And besides, he'd lived there for twenty years as a bachelor and she said she was scared to touch anything if she wasn't wearing rubber gloves, so a fresh start was a no-brainer.

Zander's only stipulation was that it had to be a beach house and this one had everything he needed: an unobstructed view of the ocean at the front, and the stunning vista of the mountains behind it. He could grab his surfboard and be on the waves in two minutes. But the most important thing was the privacy. They were near-neighbours to celebrities like Goldie Hawn, Pierce Brosnan and Robert De Niro, but this wasn't the kind of place where you hung out in next door's backyard with a beer. It wasn't the kind of place that tourists could easily access with their cameras either. They felt safe here and after a couple of scary experiences a few years back, when his Venice Beach house was broken into and ransacked, that mattered.

The security system recognised the transmitter in his car and automatically opened the gates for them. They'd gone with a fairly minimal security approach – full-height gates at the front, with cameras and controlled entry, and then lights and perimeter cameras around the property – because he didn't want to feel that he was living in a fishbowl. They'd also made the decision to have no live-in staff: no housekeeper, no driver or gardener, just a cleaning company and landscapers that both came in once a week.

'Hey, the lights aren't working,' Hollie remarked. Then, with what he sensed was a nervous laugh, she added, 'This feels like the opening scene of every *CSI* episode I've ever watched.'

'Probably shorted again. There was a pretty bad storm last week,' he shrugged. Outages in LA were not unusual after bad weather and getting a generator was on his list of things to do. But even as he said that, there was a tiny wave of that anxiety again, lying low in his gut. He didn't like this. Not one bit.

'Or maybe the cleaners switched them off accidentally?'

Zander scanned the front yard and entrance. Other than the security lights being off, everything looked completely normal. The downlights on the outside of the house were still lit. The front door looked fine. Everything was completely normal. But still… the stuff with the hotel in Canada made him second-guess himself.

'Holls, you stay here and let me just go check everything is okay inside.'

Predictably, Hollie disapproved of that message.

'Are you kidding me? What am I, the poor defenceless woman who has to be protected by big, brave action-hero guy? Zander Leith, I've pulled you out of more crack dens and strip joint toilets than I've had tacos on a Tuesday, so don't fricking start with all your big-man shit now.'

That went just about how he'd thought it would, but he'd given it a try.

'Anyway,' Hollie was still speaking, 'the security camera at the front gate is monitored, so if anyone unexpected came in, we'd have been alerted. Stop worrying and take me in there and make good on that whole sex suggestion you had earlier.' Although he did spot that she was pulling pepper spray out of her purse, just in case.

Okay, so go on in there, or put a call into the Lomax Films security team and wait until they sent someone over?

What Hollie had said about the monitoring made sense. If he was on his own, he wouldn't even think twice about this. Guess that

was the thing when you finally had someone you cared about...
Made you antsy about taking any kind of risk at all. Nah, it was fine.
But he still reached down below the back of his seat and pulled out
a baseball bat.

'You have got to be kidding me.' Hollie didn't even try to hide
her incredulity. Or her irrepressible need to tease. 'Aren't you a bit
too old for Little League?'

Zander shook his head, grinning. This woman. This funny,
gorgeous, smart-ass woman. She was everything.

Still, he took the bat as they jumped out of the pick-up,
unlocked the front door, went through it and...

Before he even switched the inside light on, he knew that something was up. It was the sixth sense that he used to get when he
heard his father coming home when he was a kid and knew that
either he or his mum was in for a beating. It was the dread he used
to feel when he knew he'd fucked up. It was the fear that used to
make him tremble every time he opened a bottle of whiskey.

'Holy. Fuck.' That was Hollie, and her pepper spray was held
out in front of her now.

One of the things they'd loved about this home was the open
layout, the fact that you opened the door and could see every
corner of the ground-floor living space, the lounge area over to the
dining table, then the double kitchen islands, right through to the
pool at the back. They could see all that. And more.

They saw the blankets on the cream chenille sofa, as if someone
had been lying there watching TV. They saw the used glasses on the
lacquered jet coffee table and, yes, this was definitely a half-empty
situation. They saw the chairs that had been moved at the dining
table, as if someone had been sitting there. The dirty bowls and
plates littered across the kitchen island. The trash stacked at the
kitchen unit, empty cartons of milk and pizza boxes.

'It looks like someone's been living here,' Zander said, pointing out the obvious, but still saying it out loud in the hope that he was seeing things, that this wasn't real.

Hollie gasped, and Zander immediately followed her gaze.

Their wedding photo, the one that sat on the console table by the door, was smashed. But beside it was another one... Zander, in his wedding suit. Next to him, a bride. A woman with Hollie's hair. With her figure. With her face. With her dress.

'That's not me,' she whispered.

He saw it too. From a distance, it was Hollie. But the way she stood, the way she smiled, the way she held his arm, that wasn't his wife. It was a top-class Photoshop, that would fool almost anyone.

'Who is she, Zander? Who the hell is doing this to us?'

7

MIRREN

'I Should Have Known Better' – Jim Diamond

'Have you heard from Davie or Sarah?' Mike asked, as he emerged from the bathroom. Watching him in the reflection of the dressing-table mirror as she dried her hair, Mirren was distracted from the question by the fact that he was walking across the room wearing just a towel, his upper body still wet from the shower.

'No, I've left a ton of messages for them both, but they haven't called back. I guess they're still working it out.'

It had been two weeks since the call from Davie, telling her that the wedding was off and that he'd phone back to explain it all later, but the second call had never come. She'd seen footage of him on TMZ at the Lakers game a couple of nights ago, so she knew he was still alive.

That was Davie all over. His world could be falling apart, but he'd put that grin on his face and he'd be out there, acting like there was nothing wrong. She also knew that there was no point pressing him for answers, because he'd tell her what he wanted her to know in his own time.

As for Sarah, she'd texted to say she'd be in touch when she was ready, so Mirren was giving her the space she asked for. It was understandable. She adored Davie's fiancée, but at the end of the day, she understood that Sarah wouldn't want to discuss what was going on with someone who was Davie's lifelong friend and former love.

'You good for the Clansman scheduling meeting this afternoon?' Mike asked, as he came up behind her and placed his lips on her shoulder.

She'd forgotten how good this felt. To wake up next to him. To do the morning chat stuff. To feel like someone had her back again, was on her side.

'That depends. Are you going to give me everything I want and tell me how wonderful I am?' Her knowing smile showed she already knew the answer to that question.

'Almost definitely not,' he replied, working his way along to her neck. Kissing her skin with the lightest, sexiest of touches.

'Can you be bribed?' she teased, dropping the towel that was wrapped around her so that she was naked from the waist up. Heading towards fifty now, her body wasn't what it used to be. Her stretch marks showed. Her breasts were on a new downward trajectory. And she didn't give a damn, because she didn't waste a moment of her life worrying about stupid shit like that. Mirren knew who she was. And right now, she was Mike Feechan's wife and about to show him exactly what that meant.

They didn't even make it to the bed.

She stepped over the towel, pulled his off too, and in a tussle of grabs and moans, they made love right there, on the dressing table, Chanel No5 bottles, hairdryer and brushes swept away while she told him every single thing she was about to do to him.

And she did, until they both came and then sank onto the thick, cream carpet, limbs still intertwined, bodies still hot, hearts still racing.

'Was that your shot at bribing me?' he asked, his husky laugh making her want to do that all over again.

What had she been thinking, letting this guy go, even for a moment? Even as she thought it, though, she knew the answer. Every time she was working to set up another centre in her daughter's name, the project consumed her, the stress altered her, and the grief overwhelmed her until she came close to losing her mind. Mike had only wanted the best for her when he'd said she had to pause, had to step back and take her foot off the gas, but she hadn't wanted to hear it. Now she knew it was time to listen. And the best thing about that was that it meant he was here again, doing this to her in the mornings.

'Maybe. Did it work?' Mirren pulled back so she could get some air to help her cool down.

Mike shook his head. 'Sorry, not this time. But you could try again...'

Laughing, she pushed him off her with mock indignation and headed back to her bathroom for another shower. Screw yoga. If there was a better way to start the day than the cardio she'd just done, she hadn't found it.

By the time she was finished, he'd also showered again in his adjacent bathroom. The irony wasn't lost on her – growing up in a tiny terrace house, she'd never even contemplated a world in which she'd own a home with more than one toilet.

Downstairs, in the kitchen, they both grabbed coffees to go. On his way to the door, he kissed her again as he passed.

'See you at the office, babe,' he murmured.

'If you feel like you might like some more bribery, come find me,' she offered, unashamedly flirting.

This felt... she struggled to pinpoint the word. Joyous. That was it. After all the stress and struggle of the last few years, allowing herself to be happy filled her with joy. And that was something she hadn't felt in a long, long time.

'I might just take you up on that. Haven't flirted with a work colleague for a long time. Just don't tell my wife,' he joked, heading off down the hall to the front door.

They always travelled separately to work, even though they were both based on the Pictor Studios lot. Pictor had been making her Clansman movies since the very first one, with the exception of Clansman 5 and 6. In a bolshy move that had rocked the industry and her relationship with Pictor chief and then-boyfriend, Mike Feechan, she'd taken them to Lomax films, because Pictor had refused to agree to her contract terms. What the world didn't know was that Mirren had also done it as a bargaining ploy with Lomax to save Zander from losing Dunhill. Anyway, Mike had been royally pissed off, but it drew a line for them and taught them to separate the personal and professional. They hadn't made that mistake again. She'd been happy to return to Pictor for Clansman 7, delighted to reclaim the McLean Production offices that sat in the grounds of the Pictor compound, and thrilled to see her husband whenever they had reason to discuss budgets, schedules, marketing plans or any other aspect of the Clansman franchise.

Mirren dressed in a variation of her usual office outfit of jeans, boots, white T and smart blazer, grabbed her briefcase, then slung her Prada backpack over her shoulder.

As she left, she was running through all the things she had to get done today, so she wasn't paying much attention as she went through the motions of setting the alarm, going out the front door, taking the few steps to her car, and...

'Good morning.'

The voice made her jump, and when she realised who it belonged to, every muscle in her body sagged. Shit.

'How did you get in here?' The question was out before she'd even thought it through. One of the perks of living in Malibu Colony, an exclusive street of some of the most expensive houses in the nation, was that it had a guarded entrance. All visitors had to be authorised by a resident before the guards would let them past the gates.

He moved towards her, sexy smile on his face. 'Came through the beach.'

Ah. The one flaw. Strictly speaking, Malibu Colony beach was public land, not something that was advertised to tourists. For those in the know, there were a couple of gates which gave direct access on to the beach. This guy had been here once before. He knew which house was Mirren's. It was a fair conclusion that he'd come onto the property from the beach, then come around the side wall to the front of the house.

'Jason, you shouldn't have done that.'

'Didn't have much choice. You're not returning my calls and you're blanking my texts, so I was out running this morning and, well, I guess I'm here.'

It was only then she noticed that he was in running gear, his blue vest soaked in sweat and clinging to his ripped, hard torso. In a way, that made this slightly less freaky. She knew that Jason Grimes ran 10 miles every day, and he lived only a few miles away, just off Malibu Canyon Road. In fact, this wasn't the first time he'd passed by her home on a run. Although, she could guarantee that this encounter was going to end very differently from the last one.

'Yeah, I'm sorry about that.' She wasn't usually one to prevaricate or to walk away from difficult situations, but the truth was, she'd been putting this conversation off for weeks. 'Look, I'm sorry. I should have called you. I thought...'

'You thought I'd take the hint and just fade away?' he asked, but in a semi-amused way, with the easy, casual attitude that she'd found appealing the first time she'd spoken to him, a few months ago, on the day that he'd come to interview for a position at the Downtown branch of Chloe's Care. She'd already read up on his background when Lynette Washington, the head of the centre, had shared his CV. Mirren left the hiring to the experts, but she usually sat in on the interviews for the therapist roles. Chloe had fought addiction for years, and the whole family had been dragged into the world of rehabs and therapy, so Mirren had a good handle on the approach she wanted her personnel to have – caring, empathetic, knowledgeable, capable of setting boundaries and reinforcing them. Pity she'd forgot about that last one herself.

He'd fitted her criteria, and he'd impressed the panel too. Sure, he was young, but at twenty-five he already had extensive experience. He'd interned at The Ocean Path, the famous Malibu rehab centre, while he'd been studying for his degree at Pepperdine. He'd then been taken on full time by them and worked there until he'd come for the interview.

'So why do you want to work for us here?' Lynette had asked him.

'Because at The Ocean Path, we deal with all ages, and mostly with people who have the finances that allow them to be there. I've done that now, and I think that my skills lie in connecting with young people. I'm probably the same age as some of the people that come through your doors looking for help. And, to be honest, at The Ocean Path, their cars cost more than my student loan. I want to work with people who genuinely need my help, not just the ones that can buy the best care and not even think twice about how much it costs.'

Mirren had been won over there and then. Chloe's Care was a non-profit, and although it paid well, it couldn't match the salaries of the bigger clinics. The fact that he didn't just want to stay in a comfortable job, and stick with the highest earning capacity, impressed her. His credentials and references made it a done deal for the rest of the panel too. He'd got the position and for a while he'd had her friendship too.

And later, just once, he'd had more than that.

Mike had moved out and, at that point, she had little hope of him coming back. Jason's age seemed to become irrelevant as she'd welcomed the conversation and the chat with someone who didn't work with her on Clansman, or see her as a mom or a wife. He was an old soul. A great listener. Easy company. For a couple of months, there was harmless companionship. Coffees while they worked on getting the facility set up. Long conversations about Chloe, too. Mirren had wept as she'd told him everything, every damn detail of how she'd failed her daughter, been unable to protect her from a disease that Chloe was way too young to survive. He'd held her while she'd cried. And one morning he'd run past her house on the beach, and he'd seen her there, sitting on her deck, looking out on to the ocean where she'd scattered the ashes of her daughter. No Mike, no Chloe, and Logan was at his own home in West Hollywood with Lauren. Not that loneliness was an excuse. A reason, maybe. Perhaps that's why she'd smiled at him, why she'd spoken to him, why she'd invited him in for coffee, and why she'd kissed him. He may have come there for a reason, but she'd made the first move. Now she had to make the last.

He'd just asked her if she'd thought he'd fade away. Time for honesty.

'I guess I... thought you'd see it for what it was,' she admitted gently. 'I'm sorry, Jason. Mike and I got back together and—'

'So we were, what? A one-time thing?'

Almost. The truth was, he was friendship, and a tiny bit of selfish pleasure during a horrible period in her life.

'We were... a moment. But things have changed. I'm sorry.'

He shrugged. 'Hey, no worries. I'm happy for you. Truly. You have a good life.'

He backed away, then he turned, and began to run, but before he did, Mirren saw something she thought she recognised from her childhood. Something in the way a man used to look at her mother. She saw a glance of malice and it caused prickles of anxiety under her skin.

Jason Grimes was her mistake. Her twenty-five-year-old mistake. And if she'd learned anything in life, it was that mistakes rarely stayed hidden for long.

8

DAVIE

'Sorry' – Justin Bieber

'Davie, will you concentrate? What the hell is the matter with you? You've got the attention span of my last boyfriend, the thirty-second wonder,' Mellie Santos, ball-breaking producer extraordinaire, blasted in his ear.

Davie thought for a second about replying with complete honesty. What was the matter with him? The list was too long to get out before the start of the show, but he'd go with the fact that two weeks ago he was getting married, then – as they said in Glasgow – he got chucked, and now Sarah had just called him and politely asked him to stop sending flowers, texts, emails and calling her.

Okay, so 400 roses to her office might have been a tad excessive, but he was desperate. He loved her. He wanted her back. He'd told her he'd rejected Wes's investment, hoping that would sort everything out, but it clearly hadn't had the desired effect.

'Davie, please. Stop with the gifts,' she'd snapped on the phone earlier. 'I need you to back off. Give me time. You're not helping me or yourself and this relentless pushing me is having the opposite effect. I'm asking you to give me space.'

'How much space? Are we talking a week? A month? Six months?'

She'd sounded weary and pissed off.

Did he regret how he'd handled their conversation up at the ranch? Of course. But he hadn't realised it would lead to her leaving and pretty much cutting him dead.

'As long as it takes,' she'd replied with a sigh.

'And what about us?'

'I can't answer that. Look, Davie, please. All I can think about, all I want to do right now, is concentrate on work and do this story. If you can't respect that, and me, then there's no hope for us.'

'And if I do?'

'Then... we'll see. But for now, just leave me be. Please.'

We'll see? That sounded to him like a lose/lose scenario. Bug her and it was over. 'Leave her be' and it was probably over too.

When she'd hung up, he'd punched a wall, thudding the knuckles that were only just healing after their meeting with Wes's jaw. Fuck!

Mellie was still waiting for a reply, and he wasn't going to tell her any of that, so he went with, 'I'm good. Don't worry about me.' He was mic'd up so she'd hear him up in the gallery. Mellie had been with him for over a decade and it was a love/hate relationship built on her having a rancid mouth and him putting up with it because, as far as he was concerned, she was the best. Also, he found her abuse amusing. It was like the non-sexual, TV version of BDSM.

'I couldn't give a fuck about you. It's my car payments I'm worried about. Okay, so are we ready to go? We're doing this, sunshine, so get your A-game on.'

Davie didn't need to ask what she meant. This was it. Final rehearsal for the first night of his new show, *Davie Johnston As It Is*. It was going out at midnight, his old time slot, but this time there was a difference. It was on the Fame Channel, one of the smaller networks, and he'd leveraged every penny he had to finance it himself. The Fame Channel was the kind of smaller network that was prepared to take risks for ratings and stick with the variety of shock content Davie did best. Besides, Davie knew all about risks. And if he forgot, his bank manager would remind him, because this could quite easily wipe him out.

What choice had he had? His old network had cancelled him, and he'd been left with no career, no options, nothing except the belief that he knew what he was doing and he was the best at it. Actually, there had been one other option – oblivion. His divorce and a couple of previous dips in his career had hurt him financially, but until he blew it all on this show, he'd had enough to live out a quiet life until he dropped dead, probably of boredom.

Nope. That wasn't happening. Davie Johnston wasn't built for obscurity. Front and centre, that's where he belonged, and just because the woke assholes at his previous network had decided that the days of shock TV were over didn't mean they were right.

That's why he'd decided to write his own cheque, to bet everything he had on himself. He'd committed to a six-month run; the contracts were signed. It was going to cost him around... he could barely form the thought... forty-five million dollars. Fuck. That made him sweat, but it was the only way. It had to have huge production values, great guests, no expense spared, because the only way to do this was to do it right. Go big or go home. Speculate to accumulate. All or nothing. Bang or bust. Yes, it was all of those clichés, but he'd built a career on trusting his gut, and it wasn't over yet. The big guys would be begging him to come back after he made this new show the biggest hit on late night TV.

The premise of the deal with the Fame network was simple – it was all on him. However, there was a financial clause in the contract that he was counting on. He'd put up the initial costs for the show – a cool twenty-five million – but he would keep the advertising revenue from the commercial sponsors, which would fund the twenty million or so that would be required for running costs over the season, and hopefully repay his investment as time went on. His name had been enough to attract some decent advertisers, so as long as he didn't piss them off, he should be good.

Of course, it would have been a whole lot less terrifying if he still had Wes's twenty million dollar investment, but after the fiasco on the wedding weekend, most of which was still a complete mind fuck to him, that money was gone. And so was Wes. And Davie still wasn't quite sure what the hell had happened.

That day, after Sarah had gone, he'd gone back over to the helicopter. Wes had been standing there, leaning against it, a smirk on his face, watching Sarah's car roar down the drive.

'She had a change of mind? Lucky escape, I'd say.'

Davie felt the rage before it reached his gob, so he'd managed to keep his tone low but filled with warning. 'Don't do it, Wes. Don't speak about her like that.'

'You've got to learn that about women, son. They're just out for what they can get.'

Davie had never been known for his restraint. Or his ability to make sensible decisions in the heat of the moment. He'd swung his right hook before he could stop himself, ignoring the fact that a swing for a guy who was 5ft 9 in shoes with lifts wouldn't connect well with a bloke who, despite his advancing years and the fact he was recovering from a heart attack, was still 6ft 3 of sinew and muscle.

As he'd made contact with Wes's chin, he'd heard his knuckles crack, then Wes's foot came up in front of him and booted Davie in the balls so hard he went down like he'd fainted. He'd just hit the grass when the second kick connected with his ribs. 'You just backed the wrong horse, son.' Davie was still lying on the grass when the older man climbed back in the helicopter and he'd stayed there until it had taken off, reluctant to add decapitation to his list of ailments.

Meanwhile, Wes had flown off, taking his bottomless bucket of cash with him.

Fuck him. Davie didn't need him. He'd make this work. He already had all the elements for success – big stars, great house band, and he'd managed to persuade some of his old team to come with him, including Mellie Santos, who, right now, was doing what she did best – riling him up by giving him abuse from the gallery.

'We need this to be the most sen-fucking-sational opening show since you killed Jizzo Stacks on live TV,' Mellie was saying, bending the truth slightly.

Davie wouldn't actually be averse to another sudden death. Last time, the frenzy that ensued had given Davie the kind of publicity that you couldn't buy, and it had carried through that whole season of his show. Now it was time to do it again, to make this the show that no one would miss, because they'd know it would be the water-cooler conversation the next day.

That's why he'd booked Princess for tonight, an absolute brat of a female pop star, who'd once been a judge on his talent show, *American Stars*. She hadn't come easy or cheap. She had nothing to promote right now, so he'd had to stump up a hundred grand fee, wired to her Cayman Islands bank account, to get her on, but she'd be worth it. She was due in any minute, so they could have a run-through before the show went live in six hours.

'Oh shit. Oh shit. Oh shit.'

Davie could hear Mellie in his ear but wasn't sure whether it was a great 'Oh shit', or whether it was a 'thirty seconds to live because a tornado was about to hit the building, oh shit'.

'Guys, guys!' he shouted to the band, who were belting out the intro song a few feet to his left. They hadn't come cheap either, but these guys were some of the best in the business, and led by a legendary sax player called Randy Volts – a name so ridiculous, it could only be real and have come from parents with a sense of humour. Although, Davie wasn't laughing when he'd had to cough up another four hundred grand to keep the band on retainer for six months.

He gestured to them to stop playing and in a cacophony of missed beats and sounds, they all finally ground to a halt.

'You okay up there, Mellie?' he said into the mike. 'Or was there an orgasmic dirty-talk situation going on there?' If they had an HR department, there would be written warnings flying about his conversations with Mellie – but they'd been friends and worked together for so long that mutual trash talk had become their platonic love language.

'Davie, we have a problem. A big, fat, fucking problem.'

He could feel his blood pressure rising with every word.

'Tell me it's a burst pipe. Or a positive test for herpes. Something that isn't gonna ruin my day.'

'Sorry, bud, you're gonna be wishing it was herpes. It's Princess. She's just cancelled. Laryngitis. Can't speak.'

The tornado hit, but it was inside his skull.

Princess was his star for tonight. The promotions and adverts had been running all week on the channel and on every social media platform. He'd even done a fucking dance to her biggest hit and paid bots to send it viral across Twitter.

Every word in his head had four letters and began with a C.

Mellie was already past the freak-out and aiming for a solution.

'Davie, we need someone else to fill in tonight. Who's huge, can be here in two hours and will do this for you?'

He gazed straight into the camera in front of him, so that, up in the gallery, she'd have full view of the expression on his face and interpret it correctly.

Don't. Be. Insane. No-one was going to be available at such short notice.

But... what were the options? Cancel a live show? No. Not happening. He'd rather shoot himself in his still-bruised balls with a rusty bullet.

Okay, solutions. He pulled his phone out of his pocket and made the call he never wanted to make. Cal Wolfe. His former agent of almost thirty years. A ruthless maniac that Davie had fired after his previous network had cancelled his last show. He firmly believed Cal should have stopped that happening. Cal firmly believed Davie was a deluded asshole whose career was on the skids. Still, Davie made the call. Cal had at least a dozen high-profile clients who could travel to the outskirts of Van Nuys for some live exposure tonight.

'Cal Wolfe's office, Araminta speaking.' A cool, cut-glass London accent. Davie would bet a thousand dollars she'd come here to act or model, and Cal had come across her at some event, thought she was gorgeous and offered her a job, even though she refused to type because it wrecked her manicure.

'Davie Johnston for Cal Wolfe.' He knew he sounded agitated, but he didn't care.

'Hold on, please.'

Thirty seconds passed before Araminta returned.

'Mr Johnson?'

Davie bristled. She didn't even pronounce his name right.

'Yes.'

'I'm terribly sorry, but Mr Wolfe is unavailable and has asked me to pass on a specific request.'

Davie's heart soared. Did Cal want to see him? Take a meeting?

'Sure. What does he want me to do?'

'Erm, he requested that you fuck off and die.'

Davie disconnected the call, swearing under his breath, furious that he'd even considered Cal might help him.

Okay, who else? Start at the top. Zander.

Davie placed the call, but it went straight to voicemail.

He tried Hollie too, same result. Shit.

Right, still at the top. Logan Gore or Lauren Finney. Husband and wife. Mega stars. Both of them bigger than Princess. That would teach the cow that she was dispensable.

He called Logan first, straight to voicemail.

Did nobody answer their bloody phones anymore?

Lauren next. 'Hi...' Another voicemail? Shit. Then, 'Davie! I'm so happy to hear from you. How are you doing?'

First, thank God she'd answered. Second, there was a sympathy in her voice that told him Mirren had filled her daughter-in-law in on him getting jilted on his wedding day. Great. Pity party for one.

'Yeah, good, sweetheart. I miss you.' He felt that catch in his throat, because, he realised, it was true. He'd discovered her, made her a star, and she was still the small-town angel she'd been when she was nineteen. True, her ex-boyfriend had tried to actually murder him because he blamed Davie for taking her away from her old life and him. But, that aside, Lauren was one of the few that Davie genuinely loved and felt protective towards.

'I miss you too.' He could hear that was genuine too.

Logan Gore was a lucky guy. If Davie was twenty years younger, six inches taller, had the body of a Chippendale and Justin Bieber's voice, he was pretty sure he still wouldn't have a shot of winning Lauren away from Logan, who was all of those things.

He snapped out of it. He didn't have time for the niceties right now.

'Lauren, honey, I'm calling for a favour. Are you in town?'

'No, we're in Cabo. Come join us!'

Bollocks. The rusty bullet was getting more likely by the second.

'Ah, great offer, but I'm working, honey. No matter. Give Logan a hug from me and let's grab dinner when you get back.'

He hung up before she could even ask him what the favour was.

'Mellie, I can't find—'

'I know, I was listening.' He'd forgotten he was mic'd up.

'Look, Davie, there's the obvious one...'

He knew who she meant before she even said it. No. He couldn't. His ego absolutely wouldn't allow it.

'No.'

'Davie this is no fucking time for your macho bullshit. Make the call.'

'I can't.'

'Don't make me come down there and beat you...'

Even in the depths of his misery, that almost made him laugh – but in a nervous way, because there was every chance she meant it.

Although, right now, a punch in the face would be a welcome diversion from the reality that she was right. He had no choice.

He made the call. It was immediately answered with, 'Tell me you managed to get Sarah back, because she's the only decent thing about you.'

'Nope, but thanks for the reminder. Another piece of my soul just died.'

'Mine too. She's my hall pass.'

'There's an image that will give me nightmares until the end of time.' Did everyone have an ex-wife that mentally tortured them or was he just lucky? 'Listen, Jenny, I need a favour.'

'No.'

'I haven't asked it yet.'

'I don't care. It's a no.'

'It needs to be a yes, because here's what's happening...' He went on to lay out the full story. First night. New show. Princess had cancelled. Disaster. His own money was in this.

'You. Have. Got. To. Be. Kidding. Me.'

'Not kidding.'

'Davie, why the hell would you use your own cash?' she screeched, then, 'Actually you don't need to answer that. No one else would touch you?'

He hated that she got that bang on. 'Wes Lomax offered twenty million, but we had... creative differences.' He went with the well-worn cliché because this wasn't the time or place to get into what had happened. And he didn't want to drag up Sarah's input into the parting of ways with Wes. Too messy. Jenny and Darcy hadn't seen the altercation at the helicopter. He'd just gone back in, tried not to show that his ribs and his nethers felt like they'd been hit by a baseball bat, and informed them that he and Sarah had had a fight and she'd cancelled the wedding. Jenny didn't need much more depth than that. She was already so convinced he was an idiot, that it was no more than she expected.

'That's not a bad thing that you're not getting into bed with him,' Jenny murmured, surprising him. 'I can't stand him. Misogynistic, sociopathic asshole who belongs with all the other depraved dinosaurs in the bone yard. Watch your back though. He's not one to cross.'

'Thanks for the tip. Makes my heart swell that you still care,' he said, resorting to his default position of humour in really shit circumstances.

'I don't,' she clarified. 'Actually, I'm sure I've still got a life insurance policy on you, so if you piss off the wrong people it could be a win for me.'

'Excellent. I promise I'll try to aim for an early death, if you just come and do the show tonight. I'm begging. On my knees. Come on, Jenny.' He hated himself for the desperation in his voice, but this was how far he'd sunk.

Jenny took a beat before replying. 'So what you're saying is that if this show fails, you'll have nothing?'

'That's about it.' He wondered if she was going to gloat, to be smug about it, but she took a different approach.

'And I won't get my alimony or child support?'

'Nope.' Humiliating. Embarrassing. Mortifying.

'You're such an asshole.'

'Yep.'

'I'll be there in an hour.'

9

SARAH

'Fire Away' – Chris Stapleton

Sarah glanced around the room and reminded herself, as she'd done every week for the last few months, that this was a dream come true. The weekly planning meeting for *Out Of The Shadows*, the news-magazine show that was up there with *60 Minutes* and *Dateline*, and she had a seat at the table. The kind of job she had only dreamt about when she was studying journalism at Napier College in Scotland, and then freezing her bits off rustling up crime stories on the streets of Glasgow for the *Daily Scot* – Scotland's biggest selling newspaper.

Back then, she'd thought that would be the extent of her career. Maybe promotion to Chief Crime Reporter. Maybe even write a book about an interesting case. But this? An anchor on an American show watched by millions? Once again, dream come true. And it wouldn't have happened if she hadn't taken a two-week holiday five years ago and come to LA on her own time to chase down a lead that Davie, Zander and Mirren were connected to a notorious Glasgow gangster who had mysteriously disappeared at the end of the eighties. It was the story of a lifetime, but she'd never regretted giving it up when she'd fallen in love with Davie and decided to stay in LA.

Look where that had got her. Anchor on *Out Of The Shadows*. Yes, her relationship had been shredded, but that wasn't Davie's fault.

That was all down to Wes Lomax.

She could still hear Davie asking how she knew the rumours about Wes were true. What was she going to say? The truth? Was she really going to talk about that on her wedding day? The one Wes Lomax had stolen from her?

I know because it happened to me. Wes Lomax attacked me.

And how would she have had to spell it out? Would he need the details? That she'd been working on her #MeToo book when his name cropped up time and time again? That she'd wanted to suss out the situation for herself, so she'd done a bit of digging, found out that he had drinks and dinner most nights at the Beverly Hills Hotel. That she'd gone to the bar, made conversation with him, told him her name was Sarah and she was there on holiday from Scotland.

'I've been there. Golfed and fucked my way around the country,' he'd boasted. She'd pretended to be impressed, even when he'd gone on, 'That's where I found one of my biggest movies. *The Brutal Circle*. Ever meet Zander Leith?' he'd gloated.

Sarah had tried to stay on top of her nerves. Not the time to bottle out. Lomax had no idea of her connections to Zander, Davie and Mirren, and she wasn't about to share them. Stick to the gullible tourist act. 'No, but that must have been amazing,' she'd purred. 'What is he like?'

'Ungrateful,' he'd spat. 'They always are. I make these nobodies into fucking megastars and then they act like I don't exist.'

Wow. Clearly some bitterness there. Sarah hadn't delved further though. The last thing she needed was a melancholy Wes calling it a night when she still had questions to answer – the biggest one being whether he really was as much of a predatory sleaze as everyone said.

She'd soon get her answer.

The contemptuous bastard had been way too busy talking about himself to notice that she'd had barely one glass from the bottle of champagne he'd ordered in the bar, so she was completely sober when she'd taken him up on his offer to let her see his bungalow there. All the greats had stayed there, he'd told her. Sinatra. Monroe. Taylor. Burton.

At his invitation, she'd sat on the sofa, and he'd joined her, given her another glass of champagne, this time from his own collection. She'd taken a couple of sips, then stopped. It could have been her imagination, but she'd thought it tasted off. She'd read the Cosby transcripts. That wasn't something she was going to fall for now.

She'd been there about half an hour, discussing movies and listening to him bang on about how impressive he was, his many achievements, the people he'd made, when he'd moved from the seat across from her, sat beside her on the sofa and tried to kiss her. She remembered saying no. She remembered his sneer. She remembered being pushed down, him being on top of her, one of his hands around her neck, the other ripping her T-shirt, then pulling at her bra, as he smiled at her, told her how much she wanted it. She remembered screaming, struggling, kicking, then her hand came up and slammed her crystal glass against his head. It was so thick it didn't break, but it was enough to shock him for a second, long enough for her to kick him off her.

'You nasty fucker,' she'd spat, as she got to the door. She'd turned round, desperate to see the kind of fear on his face that he doled out to everyone else.

'I told you my name was Sarah. Let me tell you more. It's Sarah McKenzie. I'm a journalist. I live here in LA and I know what you fucking are. Remember that.'

The fear never came. Instead, he'd shrugged, an arrogant leer on his face. 'So what? Nothing happened here. I invited you, you came – two consenting adults.'

Even as she ran, she knew that was the line he would spin and she had no proof that it hadn't gone down that way. She hadn't wanted to risk recording him. Hadn't thought for a moment it would get this far. It was a mistake, and she should have known better. But, right then, all that mattered was getting out of there.

Holding her top together, she'd slowed when she went through the lobby, so as not to attract attention.

It didn't work.

There was a woman there who had made eye contact, then hastily looked away. There was a moment. A hint of recognition. Sarah didn't have time to question it.

The next time she remembered breathing was when the valet returned her car, and she'd climbed in and locked the doors. She'd waited there for a moment for the shaking to subside enough that she could drive, then headed for home. Her home. The tiny Marina Del Rey studio that she'd lived in since she'd arrived in LA. This wasn't a night for staying over in Davie's Bel Air behemoth mansion. This was a time to be alone. To think. To cry. To rage.

Her first reaction had been to call the cops, but every bad court show cliché came into her mind. Her word against his. Who was going to call Wes Lomax a liar? Who would believe her?

Just as those arguments came in for the defence, so did another one for the prosecution. She was her own first witness, but she already knew that there were others.

Now, she needed proof. She needed someone to corroborate her story. She needed to find someone else that this had happened to and she needed them to tell their truth.

That had been her mission back then, but it just hadn't happened yet.

And that's why, rightly or wrongly, she hadn't told Davie. She needed time to process it. To come to terms with it. But, more than anything, she hadn't wanted to tell him, because that would make it real. Put it out there. And once it was out, there was no way to take it back, to make life normal again, no way to bury it and block out that it had ever happened. She'd managed to convince herself that she could compartmentalise it, keep it from Davie until she was ready to deal with it. Now she knew she'd been lying to herself.

It was time to tell the story, but she was going to do it her way. That's why she'd walked away from her wedding at the ranch. Wes's appearance had brought it all back, and his arrogance had forced her hand, baited her, pissed her off so much, she knew she couldn't wait. His audacity was astounding. As was his manipulation. Davie had told her Wes had offered the cash after he'd told the asshole who he was marrying. She could only assume that Wes had put two and two together and come up with twenty million dollars. Sure, it was for Davie's show, but why? Was it second-hand hush money? Did Wes think that by giving her soon-to-be husband a big fat chunk of change, that she'd shut up and forget what he'd done? Wrong conclusion. Wrong woman.

'Morning, you fine people, how are we doing today?'

Chip Chasner, the executive producer of *Out Of The Shadows*, took his seat at the head of the table. In his fifties, he was a notoriously hard-headed, quick-tempered, old-school journalist who had risen through the ranks of the television world after a career in newspapers. Sarah admired him for many reasons: he hated injustice, he hated bullies and when it came to his moral courage, he remined her of Ed McCallum, her old editor and mentor at the *Daily Scot*. Rough, gruff, chain-smoking and always armed with a bottle of Scotch in the drawer of his desk, Ed had taken a chance on her when she was a twenty-one-year-old rookie and he was the reason she had this career.

Chip started the meeting by recapping on the ratings for the previous show to the thirty or so assembled producers, journalists, researchers and lawyers. Over six million viewers. Just thinking about that many people watching gave Sarah both a thrill and a feeling of utter terror. Suddenly, she wasn't sure which one was going to win.

Chip discussed a few other points of interest – current legal challenges, staffing changes, new network protocols – then, as always, went round the room, getting updates on the stories the team were already working on, firing in opinions, hustling up ideas and berating any dropped balls or slow progress. He hadn't made the show what it was by taking a laid-back approach to the graft.

Sarah felt her pulse quicken as she prepared for what was coming next.

'Right, gang, my favourite part of every week,' he said, sitting back in his chair, hands behind his head.

Sarah could totally see why Chip and his husband had been together for three decades. There was something about that mix of intelligence, ferociousness and a pretty obvious gym habit that made this man highly attractive. But, right now, there was no space for thoughts like that in her head, because her mind was engaged in a war of self-doubt. Now that it was the moment of truth, could she do this? Could she really put this out there? Could she live with herself if she didn't?

Her arm gave her the answer, slowly raising, as if working autonomously of her body.

'Okay, Braveheart, shoot. What you got?' Chip had reminded

her many times that his mother was half-Scottish and it was his favourite holiday destination, so she knew the nickname came from a place of endearment. Yet, it didn't stop her hands from shaking.

Could she do this?

Every single person in this room was subject to a watertight non-disclosure agreement, so if she were ever going to say this aloud, this was the safest place to do it.

'I... I...'

Get a grip, Sarah. She inhaled. Screw it, she was tough enough to handle this. That's why she was in this room.

'As you all know, my current writing project is a book about the #MeToo movement. As part of my research, three months ago, I decided to engineer a meeting with a Hollywood icon whose name kept cropping up in conversations. I met him in a bar, then he invited me to see the bungalow he keeps at a hotel. When he gave me a drink, it seemed... off, so I ditched it without him realising. After some more small talk, he suddenly grabbed me, lay on top of me, put his hand around my neck and tried to remove my clothes. I fought him off and I left. I didn't go to the police. I should have, but I didn't. So now...'

There was not a sound in the room. Not a single sound. Just intent gazes and some visibly shocked expression. Sarah kept her stare fixed on Chip. He was her safe space. Right now, no one else existed.

He interjected, filling her pause, his troubled expression clearly coming from somewhere between horror and concern. Sarah noticed the knuckles of his clenched fists were white. 'Sarah, let me stop you. I'm so sorry that happened to you. I also have a duty of care. Do you want to take this conversation somewhere private? My office?'

Sarah shook her head. 'Thank you, but no, because I'm sharing this for a reason.' She cleared her throat. 'I'm telling you this because I want to do this story. I know I'm not the only one, so I want to find the others, I want to bring this out and I want to show the world what he is.'

She deliberately kept it unemotional, factual, professional.

Chip was sitting forward now. 'Shit, Sarah. I'm so goddamn sorry,' he said again.

Her thanks were conveyed with a nod, but her voice was gone for a moment, busy fighting back the tsunami of grief and rage that was rising in her chest.

'Are you comfortable telling us who it is?'

This was it. Do or die.

Do.

'Wes Lomax.'

There was a silent reaction, played out only in expressions, exhalations, tight jaws.

Chip never took his gaze from hers. 'Okay. You need to know a few things. First, I believe you. I know that goes without saying, but I want you to hear that from me. Second, you need to be aware that if you want to do this, we've got you. All the way. But I need to be sure you understand... It's Lomax. He's a fucking titan. As soon as he gets wind of this, he's going to come after you, and he's going to bombard you with threats and litigation until you don't know what way you're facing. He'll try to destroy you. And he'll play dirty. That's what this is. You need to decide if you can handle that. Not now. Take your time. But know we'll be with you either way.'

'I don't need time. I wouldn't have brought this to you if I wasn't ready to do it.'

It wasn't strictly true. Until ten minutes ago, she wasn't sure if she could bring herself to say it. Now she had. No going back. That's why she couldn't have Davie in her life right now. First of all, she didn't trust him to stay out of it. She had no doubt Davie would kill him. Or at least he'd try. And where would that get them? No, this was her battle and she wanted to fight it.

But more than that, if she was going to expose Lomax, she couldn't be worrying about what that would mean for her boyfriend. And if Lomax found out she was working on a story on him and decided to retaliate, she didn't want Davie anywhere near his wrath.

Chip glanced around the room. 'Thoughts?'

None. For a solid ten seconds.

Then, Meilin Chong, journalist and one of her co-anchors, nodded slowly. 'We've all heard the rumours about him,' she said, then locked eyes with Sarah. 'I care for you. I don't want anything to put you in a situation that could damage you. But if you say go, we go with you.'

The dominoes of retribution linked together as they fell.

'We go.' Dallas Manners, producer.

'We go.' Latoya Dawson, journalist.

'We go.' Shandra Walker, researcher.

Round the room, a dozen others, all saying the same thing.

'We go.'

Sarah had to sit rock still to keep her strength, to remain unbended by the power and force of the people around her.

Chip searched out the show's chief lawyer. 'Hank?'

Hank Travis, their notoriously restrictive counsel, took a moment. 'I can't think of a fight I want to have less.' For a moment, Sarah's hope stuttered until he went on, 'But I'm all in. Just keep me in the loop with every detail and I'll run defence.' He had a habit of using football analogies that Sarah didn't understand, but she caught the gist of that one.

'We go,' Chip echoed, his pride in the team and in Sarah now written in every line and crevice of his face. 'But, Sarah, you call the shots at every stage. How do you want to play this?'

10

MIRREN

'Celebration' – Kool & The Gang

'Mirren, am I good to shoot off? I've got acting class in an hour and I really want to get there early.'

Mirren glanced up from her computer to see Devlin, her assistant, standing in the doorway. He'd been the gatekeeper to her office for eight years now, since he was barely in his twenties, and to her, he was family.

Most of her staff were the same. Her lawyer, Perry, had been with her for almost thirty years. Lex Callaghan, leading man in her Clansman movies, had been here for two decades. Most of her production staff had also been with her since the first Clansman. She surrounded herself with the tightest of teams, treated everyone well, and in return she got their loyalty and hard graft.

Devlin was a six-foot New Yorker, who'd had a couple of roles within her company. He'd started as her assistant straight out of college, then he'd set his mind on a move into the production side of the operation. He'd enjoyed that, but being on set had given him a notion to act, so he'd come back to his office-based role so that he could have a more regular schedule to accommodate the acting classes he'd been taking for the last two years. Mirren was more than happy to go with the flow of his aspirations. He was a young guy, trying to figure out the rest of his life – of course, he was going to want to try different things and she was happy to stick with him until he got there.

She took her glasses off as she gave him her attention. 'Sure, but I wanted to have a quick word. The dialect coach tells me you're doing great with the Scottish accent.'

'It's not easy, but I'm getting there. I've gone from Mrs Doubtfire, to Sean Connery, to Zander Leith, so I think I'm going in the right direction.' He said every word in a pitch-perfect Glaswegian growl that impressed her as much as it made her laugh. She'd already been to a couple of his showcases, so she knew that, as far as acting went, he was working on his craft and he was putting in accomplished performances.

'Oh my, you're giving me PTSD – that sounded exactly like Zander when he first landed here.'

Devlin was leaning against the doorway. 'I studied his first Oscars speech. He had that whole "brooding male" thing down.'

Mirren shook her head. The thought of that night used to make her sad, because it was the start of a twenty-year estrangement between them, but now that the three of them – her, Zander and Davie – were back in each other's lives, there was nothing but fondness for the memories. 'Wasn't an act. He was just raging with the world back then. Took him about twenty-five years to lighten up. Anyway, what I wanted to talk to you about... We're casting Brodie, the Clansman's son tomorrow. The one he never knew existed.'

Devlin, like most of her team, had read all the Clansman novels, so he'd know exactly who she was referring to. She'd written twelve books in total now, but the movies were a couple behind.

'I'd like you to audition. I've set it up with casting, if you feel ready to—'

'Yes!' he gasped, but in his lower register it came out more like a bark, and right back in his Hell's Kitchen, New York accent. 'Honestly? Tell me you're not shitting me?'

'Nope, today isn't "shitting my staff" day, so you're good,' Mirren chuckled, loving the absolute glee on his face. What he didn't realise was that he was the only one she was considering for the part and she had every faith he'd kill it.

'OMG, can I kiss you?' he exclaimed, his excitement palpable.

'Definitely not. HR would have my arse. But you can take the audition script to your acting class tonight and rehearse. I've emailed it to you.'

'I fricking love you, boss,' he said, dropping his usual professionalism. Mirren didn't mind. This could be a life-changing moment for him and he deserved it.

'Yeah, well I fricking love Brodie, so go do him justice.'

He practically danced out of her office, and his excitement was infectious.

A few moments later, she sensed another presence at the door, and wondered if Devlin had come back with questions. But no. Her husband was the one leaning against the doorframe, in black trousers, black shirt and the Hermès belt she'd bought him for his last birthday. Even from a few feet away, she could detect the faintest whiff of Creed Aventus, his favourite aftershave.

'Man, my wife looks pretty hot when she's working,' he teased. 'If we weren't running late, I'd be wanting to do things to you on top of that desk.'

'If we weren't running late, I'd let you,' she replied tartly, quickly shutting down her computer, slipping her bare feet into the heels that were by the side of her chair and then grabbing her purse as she stood.

'Let's go, Mr Feechan – come show me a good time. With our clothes on.' It was ridiculous how much pleasure she got from flirting with him again. The separation had been the best thing for both of them. It had showed them what they had, who they truly loved, and how much they wanted to treasure it.

She left her Mercedes in her spot right outside her office, a one-storey building on the back corner of the Pictor lot, and jumped into Mike's Range Rover. He didn't do the whole sports car thing. Said he wanted a car he could use to pick up his daughter, Jade, on a Sunday morning, and then throw a couple of bikes or surfboards in the back.

Traffic was pretty light, so half an hour later, they were pulling up outside her favourite hotel, the Casa Del Mar, right on the spec-tacular sands of Santa Monica Beach. The place held so many memories for her. When she was still married to Jack, they'd kept a suite here that they used for special occasions, for romantic week-ends, for every kind of celebration. Of course, that had backfired spectacularly when she'd discovered fifty-year-old Jack was using it to screw his twenty-three-year-old actress girlfriend, Mercedes Dance, behind Mirren's back. She and Lou had discovered them in the bath, and she was pretty sure he beat the world record for a deflating erection. She'd had the room fumigated after that encounter. Now, she still rented the same suite whenever she wanted to have any kind of social gathering.

'Happy anniversary!' The cheer went up as soon as she opened the door and Mirren's heart swelled. Her life was feeling pretty good right now. This was her favourite thing to do here – bring all the people she loved together in complete privacy, espe-cially to celebrate her and Mike being back together. She was only sorry Jade couldn't make it, because she was on vacation with her mom in Europe. Everyone else she loved was here in this room though.

If she'd tried to dine with Zander Leith and his gorgeous wife, Hollie, Logan Gore, Lauren Finney, Sarah McKenzie and Lou Cole in a public place, there would be a paparazzi feast and a storm of fans there in minutes. Zander's devotees were a bit older and more restrained now, but Logan and Lauren attracted the under-twenty-fives, who could communicate with each other and muster an army for invasion within minutes. They would be swarmed, besieged, and photographs of them chewing their dinner would be on Instagram and Twitter within the hour. It was a no-brainer. The privacy of her own suite won every time.

The room had been set up beautifully for dinner. Mirren always used the same party planner, Charley King, and she knew her so well that Mirren just had to tell her the occasion and she knew that Charley and her team at Bluebell Events would deliver. As always, she wasn't wrong. The table was breath-taking, laid out like a mediaeval Scottish banquet, with spectacular centrepieces crafted from lillies, roses and thistles, dozens of candles on huge silver stems, and crockery and cutlery that had come from Mirren's own collection of Scottish antique tablewear, procured over the years from auction houses and estate sales. Mother Nature very kindly added the final touch to the room. The setting sun was streaming in the balcony doors, with the glistening ocean on the horizon. Everything she loved outside, everyone she loved inside. That joy thing assaulted her once again.

Alfie, her favourite barman at the hotel, had set up a satellite bar with her signature drinks, and the champagne was flowing as she greeted everyone one by one, getting high on the hugs, the love, and the sound of their voices.

When they sat down for dinner, she took the seat next to Hollie, and for the first time noticed that there were dark circles under her friend's eyes, and a tension across her brow that was an unfamiliar sight on her beautiful face. Mirren adored this woman and never let Zander forget, for a single second, how lucky he was that Hollie had fallen in love with him. She was everything her Zander needed, and the kind of girlfriend Mirren had really appreciated when she'd been going through her separation from Mike.

Mirren, Lou, Hollie and Sarah had established a regular Thursday night soiree here in the suite at least once a month, for drinks, for dinner, for laughs, and for long conversations about everything and anything. They'd usually sorted the whole world out by midnight, only for it all to go to shit again on a Friday, but they didn't care. The hangovers were always worth it.

Mirren nudged Hollie's shoulder. 'You okay, honey? You look a little tired.'

Hollie's reaction was too quick, too bright, and 100 per cent faked for Mirren's benefit. 'Of course! Now stop worrying about me. It's your anniversary, and you've reclaimed that gorgeous man of yours, so let's celebrate!'

Mirren knew there was no point pursuing it right now. Like her, Hollie hated to be centre of attention, hated to cause drama or make anything all about herself, so if there was anything wrong, or something was bothering her, there was no way she'd say anything here or now. Mirren made a mental note to get her alone for a moment later, or she'd call her first thing in the morning to find out what was up. Unless...

Mirren couldn't stop the smile that was spreading across her face. Could Hollie be pregnant? She sent up a prayer of hope, but that was dashed a few seconds later when Hollie accepted a glass of wine. She put a pin in that one for further investigation, squeezed Hollie's hand under the table and turned to her other side, where Sarah was already chatting to Logan.

Only seven years apart in age, the two of them had been firm friends for years, since Sarah had joined Logan on tour with his band, South City, as research for her first book on the dark side of Hollywood.

When there was a break in the conversation, Mirren leaned towards her. 'I'm so glad you came.'

Tonight had been in the diary for a couple of months, since right before Sarah and Davie's almost-wedding, because that's how much notice she had to give to get all these crazy busy people in the same place. When Mirren had texted Sarah to remind her, she hadn't even asked if Davie would be here, because they both knew that with a live midnight chat show, he'd be at work right now, getting ready to go on air.

Sarah's hair was tied back, she was wearing a killer suit, and she looked every inch the hotshot TV anchor that she was fast becoming. Mirren's love for her had an extra layer of sentimentality because she still spoke with her soft, Scottish accent. 'Me too. Although, I might leave at any moment. It's my thing these days when I'm at special occasions.'

Mirren got the memo immediately. *So we're still handling the cancelled wedding with dark humour and self-deprecation.*

A couple of weeks after the trip to the ranch, after several calls, she'd finally got through to Sarah on the phone, and they'd spoken a few more times via calls or texts since then, but she wasn't ready to talk about what had happened and said she'd explain everything next time they met in person. That had been two months ago, and Sarah had been a no-show at the last two girls' nights here at the suite. At least she'd turned up tonight, but just as with Hollie, Mirren knew this wasn't going to be the time for Sarah to share any of the deeper stuff that was going on in her life.

'Have you spoken to Davie?' Mirren asked casually, gently fishing, but not saying anything that would make Sarah uncomfortable.

'A bit. Not really. We're still taking some space. Listen, can I come talk to you, sometime this week? I've got some stuff I want to run past you.'

Mirren took a sip of her champagne, an infrequent indulgence, but hey, it was her anniversary. 'Of course. Name the day and time and I'll make it work.' One thing she'd learned lately was that the people she loved had to take precedence over everything. First Mike, now Sarah. She'd be there whenever the other woman needed her.

However, she was surprised when Sarah immediately came back with, 'How about if I come over tomorrow night? To the house?'

Mirren sat back to let the waitress put down the first course of Scotch broth. An unusual choice for this part of the world, but she liked to put together her own personal menu for her dinner parties and it invariably consisted of her favourite meals from her childhood. Scotch broth. Fish and chips or steak pie. And an apple crumble with custard for pudding. Definitely not Keto, but she didn't give a damn.

'Yeah, sure. I'll put the kettle on and the wine in the fridge,' Mirren assured her, before Logan took Sarah's attention away again.

At the other side of the table, Lou began telling a story about the time she and Mirren had got trapped in a lift at a famous New York hotel, and Mirren had called Zander for tips, because he was the only person she could think of that had rescued people from an elevator shaft.

Zander filled in the rest of the story. He'd actually been in New York at the same time and had come over to the hotel, getting there just as the engineers got it working again and freed them. When the doors had finally opened, in front of a lobby full of guests and anxious staff, Mirren had nodded in his direction as he came up behind the crowd.

'Thank you. He'd have saved us a while ago, but he was busy.'

The reaction as at least twenty people turned to see the super-spy, action hero they knew as Seb Dunhill, walking towards them was one of the funniest moments of her life.

As with most occasions when they were all together, that story led to another, then another, then another, until the food was eaten, the glasses had been refilled many times and the setting sun outside had faded into complete darkness.

Yet Mirren still wasn't ready to go home, and the laughter and chat of her guests told her they felt the same. Just as at the start of the night, she had a moment of love, of gratitude, for her family. Logan was her only living blood relative, but all of these people with her tonight – and the absent Davie – were family.

She was basking in the happiness of it when she spotted Lou glancing at a notification on her Apple watch. The flame-haired Scot and the African American goddess considered themselves sisters, and Mirren immediately read the expression that crossed her best friend's beautiful face. Trouble.

Acting as if nothing was amiss, Lou got up and excused herself and took her purse with her to the bedroom next door, on the pretext of going to the washroom. Mirren immediately followed her and wasn't surprised in the least to see Lou sitting on the bed, staring intently at her phone. As the editor of the *Hollywood Post*, there wasn't a fart in this town that Lou didn't hear about first.

Mirren opened with, 'Hey...'

Her voice made Lou jump. 'Yow! Girl, have you been practising some kind of ninja silent assassin shit?'

'Indeed. Mirren The Perimenopausal Ninja. I think it's got a ring to it.'

One of her favourite sounds in the world was Lou's loud, raucous laugh, the one that always sounded like she'd just been told a filthy joke.

As Mirren sat down beside her, Lou immediately moved her

phone out of Mirren's eyeline. Okay. This wasn't good. This was just like every time Lou had heard that Chloe had been arrested or found OD'd in some sleazy club toilets. It was like every time she got word that Mirren's ex-husband Jack was shagging someone young enough to be his daughter. It was the same pause, as Lou digested the information, assimilated it, and worked out how to tell Mirren in the way that would hurt her or enrage her the least.

'What's going on? And don't give me the "it's your anniversary so we'll save it for later" line – I've had that twice tonight already.' Her tone was still light, still hopeful that she'd picked this up wrong and that Lou was only reading some salacious rumour about some A-lister with a vice. Just like every other day that ended in a Y.

The anxiety on Lou's face told her otherwise.

'Okay, I'm just going to lay it out. Someone is trying to sell a story on you.'

Confusion knitted Mirren's brow. This certainly wasn't the first time – Jack, Chloe and Logan had all brought shitloads of publicity to this family, and all for very different reasons.

She rolled her eyes and tried to banish the tiny seed of panic in her gut by laughing it off. 'What have I done now? And who did I do it to?'

'Mirren, it's not good. Do you know some young guy called Jason Grimes?'

That was the moment, the very instant, that Mirren knew the party was over.

11

ZANDER

'Someone You Loved' – Lewis Capaldi

Zander was thinking this was the first time he'd seen Hollie laugh with her usual free and infectious abandon for weeks. This was what she'd needed. A night with great friends, great food, great wine, in a private setting where she wasn't constantly looking over her shoulder.

His wife was a tough cookie, who'd handled some serious shit in her time and dragged him out of some dark, troubled places, but this latest stuff had, quite understandably, rattled her more than anything that had happened before.

The intruder in the hotel in Canada had been worrying, but they'd both put that down to a one-off stunt by someone with a twisted mind or a strange sense of humour. They'd half expected footage to turn up on Instagram, with some Hollie-lookalike bragging how she'd managed to blag her way in and run riot with the room service and mini-bar.

That hadn't happened though. Actually, the reality was a little more troubling. The hotel's investigation had turned up evidence that the same person had been seen outside the building on multiple days, at both the back and front, scoping the place out and, incredibly, on one of the pieces of footage, Zander and Hollie had left the hotel and climbed into their car only a few yards from where the woman stood watching them.

That one made them both shudder and escalated Zander from mildly irritated to fucking furious. Who was this? And what the hell was going on? Sure, stalkers were nothing new to him, or to anyone else with his level of fame. The problem was that, nowadays, fans were only a Google search or a social media post away from finding out where their idol was, who they were with, and if they had semi-decent detective skills, they could learn where anyone lived, what they drove and where they vacationed. A couple of years back, he'd been a hundred yards out to sea, surfing with some of his buddies, when they'd realised a drone was above them, following their every move. If Zander had a gun, he'd have shot it out of the sky.

In fact, with what they now knew about the break-in at their house, a gun was starting to sound like something they might want to consider, because if the hotel stuff was disturbing, the home invasion was utterly chilling. The police had dusted the whole place for prints and used the security footage from the perimeter cameras to establish what had happened and it was, as Hollie put it, 'a terrifying head fuck'. It was also disturbingly easy and simple. The woman, clearly the same one from the security footage in Canada, had driven in right behind the gardening team who came to the property once a week. She must have known exactly when they would be there. She looked so like Hollie that the gardening boss thought it was her and didn't think twice when she went to the door and punched a number into the biometric lock to enter the house. It was one of those security ones that could be opened by a key or a code, and the code was normally only used by the cleaners if no one was home. Zander and Hollie had no idea how she'd got it. Once inside, she'd stayed there for three days – a fact that chilled Zander to the bone. Three. Days. And in that time she'd eaten their food, she'd drunk their booze, she'd slept in their bed and, as before, all the photos of him and Hollie had been smashed.

As soon as the police had let them back into the house, changes were made. The next morning, John Wood, the Lomax Films head of security, had arranged for the top security company in the city to be there, and a state-of-the-art, comprehensive system had been installed. Now, Zander and Hollie could just tap their phones and see every room in the house, and outside too. And it was all connected directly to the local police station. The other upgrades had included high-spec security lights, new locks on every door and window, and a replacement system at the gate that gave razor-sharp images and sent alerts every time they were opened. The police were still looking for the culprit, but in the meantime, the new layer of self-protection made him feel better.

'I'm starting to feel like the President,' Hollie had said as she'd watched the security guys work. They were both standing against the garage wall, scanning the mass force that was swarming around the property, taking steps to ensure their safety.

Zander had thrown his arm around her shoulders and kissed the top of her head. 'You're not getting a bulletproof car for Christmas. Just sayin'...'

That had made her smile. 'I'll score that off my list then. How about a West Wing or my own jet?'

He'd thought the assurance that they were protected would have made her feel more secure and at ease, but, strangely, it was the opposite. It was almost as if it was a reminder. Every time she had to tackle a new lock or a security light came on, it freaked her out.

He would wake up during the night, and she'd be lying next to him watching TV on her iPad with her earphones in, or reading a book on her Kindle. He didn't think she'd had a decent night's sleep in weeks. He'd even offered to move them to another house, or a hotel, to give her peace of mind, but she'd refused. 'Hell, no. I'll get addicted to room service and gain twenty pounds and then I'll have to take up Pilates. Not a frigging chance.'

That, right there, was why he loved his wife.

And that's why it was so great to see her relax and have a great time with their friends tonight.

It was almost midnight when she nuzzled in his ear. 'Right, Zander Leith, take me away and do filthy things to me, but only for five minutes, because you've got an early call in the morning.'

Right at that moment, Mirren and Lou came back to the table. Mirren looked exhausted, so he figured it was a good time to wrap up the party.

Sarah obviously had the same thought, because he saw her pull her jacket on and grab her purse.

'Are you heading home? We can drop you,' Zander offered, slipping his hand around his wife's shoulders. A couple of glasses of wine too many had been consumed, so it took concentration to keep up with Hollie's gentle sways from side to side. It was on nights like this that he'd love a drink. Actually, that wasn't true. Over five years sober, and still every night he wanted a drink. Some more than others.

'No, that's okay – you're going in the opposite direction, so I'll just grab an Uber.' She wasn't wrong. Marina Del Rey was a few miles along the coast in the opposite direction, not that he minded that in the least, but Sarah was insistent. 'Plus, I can't stand to look at you two all loved up and happy,' she joked. 'Urgh, it shouldn't be allowed. I much prefer people who are wallowing in pits of misery.'

'Nope, not tonight,' Hollie chirped, snaking her hand around

Zander's waist. 'I've had enough misery lately, so I'm choosing happiness. I'm over letting other people piss me off. Oh my God, I sound like a self-help book. Let's go, before I start coming up with inspirational quotes.'

They left in a flurry of hugs and goodbyes, then Sarah walked with them to the elevator.

As soon as they got inside, Hollie took Sarah's hand. 'So how are you doing, my friend? If I wasn't completely sure of your undying love for me, I'd think you've been avoiding me for the last couple of months.'

'Just... you know, working on a big story that has me feeling all kinds of ways. But are you free tomorrow night? I'm going over to Mirren's house to talk to her about it, and I'd really appreciate it if you were there too.'

Zander knew Hollie's reaction would be instant. She showed up for people every time, especially someone she loved as much as Sarah.

'Yesssssss! Two nights in a row with my favourite ladies. I'll be there. What time?'

Sarah filled her in on the details, and as the elevator lifts opened on the ground floor, she switched her focus to Zander. 'I hate to ask, but have you seen Davie? I know that sounds like I'm fifteen and we're in the school canteen...'

'I did his show last week,' Zander told her. 'There was some kind of problem and his guest didn't show.'

'Again?' Sarah exclaimed. 'That's happened a few times since he launched.'

'Yeah, he said that too.'

Zander left it there because he wasn't one to get into anyone else's business. It was Davie's place to tell Sarah what was going on with the show, not his. Zander had been surprised to get a call from him around 5 p.m. that day. Davie had explained that the booked guest had pulled out and begged him to step in. Luckily, Zander was free and he was happy to help. That wasn't strictly true. He hated talk shows and was long past the early days of his career when he'd had to plug his movies relentlessly, so he only did a select one or two around the release date now. But for Davie, he'd pocketed his dislike of the format, and showed up.

Sarah's Uber was waiting at the door for her, so she climbed in and waved to them as the Prius drove off.

Zander's car had been parked by the valet, and he was about to retrieve it when Hollie tugged at his hand. 'C'mon, let's go for a walk on the beach. It's been way too long, Mr Leith. And no one's around, so I'll get to feel you up.'

Zander grinned, taking his jacket off and slipping it around Hollie's shoulders. This was the kind of stuff they used to do all the time, when they first fell in love and he'd lived just a mile along the shore at Venice Beach. They'd wait until late at night, when the tourists were gone, and they'd just walk and talk, and sometimes just sit and stare at the waves. The ocean was peace for him, and back then, the crash of the waves stopped the recurring voice in his head, telling him to drink, to party, to cause chaos.

'Are you sure? You don't want to go home...?'

'Nope, not even a tiny bit. I think we need to talk about that place, Zander. It's like it's tainted now. I want to stay out here and breathe. Come with me, please?'

She was up on her toes now, landing pecks on the side of his face, and he knew he was beat. He couldn't refuse her anything. Nor did he want to.

The valet was the epitome of discretion, but Zander could see he was amused at what was playing out here. 'I'll be back in a wee while for the car.' His Scottish vernacular still popped out sometimes.

'No problem, Mr Leith, I'll have it ready.'

He took Hollie's hand as they cut down the side of the building onto the boardwalk, where she slipped off her strappy sandals and dangled them from her wrist as she walked barefoot beside him. There were very few people around, just the occasional late-night jogger, one or two couples with the same notion for a romantic midnight stroll, and a couple of homeless people camped out on the beach or lying on the ground. One of them glanced up as they passed him, and Zander dropped a few twenties on his blanket. No judgement. That could so easily have been him. By the time he was fifteen years old, he was addicted to alcohol, he was a product of a violent home and he hated the world. All he cared about was drinking until he was numb.

'Thanks, man,' the homeless guy mumbled.

'No problem, pal,' Zander replied. 'You stay warm.'

If he hadn't had Davie and Mirren and a few lucky breaks back then, he could easily have gone down the path that would end on a cold pavement. Instead, they were discovered by Wes, brought to LA, he'd made it in the movies and then Hollie had come to work for him and saved his arse and his career, time after time.

'What are you thinking?' she asked him, as she did at least once a day. He'd never been one for small talk, and she regularly complained that she had to prise his thoughts out of him.

He shook his head. 'Can't tell you. You'll be so overcome with adoration for me that you'll faint right here.'

'I'll take my chances, Romeo,' she shot back, the combination of her laughter and the breeze of fresh air making her look happier than she had in a while.

He went full romantic, sexy Zander Leith, the heart-throb who had made over a billion dollars at the box office. 'I was just thinking you saved my life.'

'Was it that time I did the Heimlich when you choked on a rib?'

'Damn, you know how to take the romance right out of a man.

That was it. My one slushy moment of the year and you blew it. You're not getting another one.'

Her head was back and her throaty laugh was the loudest thing on the street. She swung around in front of him, put her arms around his neck and began kissing him, both of them swaying as they grinned, as they kissed, as they...

He was so busy loving her, that he didn't even register the female coming towards them, but then he felt the pressure of Hollie's body as it was suddenly pushed against him again and again. That's when he realised the woman had stopped right behind Hollie, and over her shoulder he saw the stranger's twisted face, heard her haunting, demented screams of, 'He's my husband, not yours! Get away from him. He's my husband! He's my husband!'

What the fuck was going on? Who was this? What the fuck was she doing to his wife?

After a split second, before it was physically possible for him to react, he felt Hollie sliding downwards. Instinctively, he caught her and pulled her up again, but now... what had happened? Her back was wet and her head was falling to the side, and she was mumbling his name over and over.

There was a commotion going on to his right, but it barely registered as her eyes closed and... noooooooooooooo.

'Hollie! Hollie!' Her legs had given out, so he slid to the ground with her, holding her tight, keeping her on top of him, so that she wasn't on the cold concrete. Her head was on his lap, her face towards his. 'Hollie! Oh, baby, no...' He raised his head. 'Get help! Get help!' he screamed. Again. Again. Again.

That's when he saw the two other bodies to his side, the woman who'd attacked them, the homeless guy he'd spoken to a minute ago on top of her, holding her down. There were people running towards him. Screams. Noises.

'Get help!!!!!' he howled again in a voice he couldn't even begin to recognise.

Then he looked back down, and his vision narrowed in and all he could see was Hollie's face, just inches from his, her eyes closed, but she was whispering, saying something...

'Love. You.'

Two words. That's all he heard in this new world, where only he and Hollie existed, just the two of them, alone, separate from what was going on around them.

He pushed her hair back off her face, but his hand left a streak of red across her cheek and that's when he made the connection that the dampness on her back, the stickiness on his hands, the smear on her face... it was blood. Hollie's blood.

His love. His life. Everything he had.

'Hollie, stay. Please stay,' he begged her, sobbing. 'I love you, babe. Please don't go.'

She didn't make a sound. She didn't move a muscle.

And that's when Zander Leith raised his head and he roared.

12

DAVIE

'Yesterday' – The Beatles

Davie placed the mug down on the step of the wooden deck, next to where Zander was sitting. 'Hey, pal, here's a coffee. I'm just going to leave it here. I can stay, or you can tell me to fuck off.' Maybe it was grief. Or shock. Or the desperation to turn back time to when Hollie was still with them, but over the last week, whenever he spoke to Mirren or Zander, Davie's accent slipped back to the Glasgow brogue of his youth, leaving behind the American twang he'd adopted over almost thirty years here.

Zander didn't say anything, so Davie sat down on the step too, about a foot away from his oldest pal. That's how Davie always thought of him, even though, technically, they were half-brothers. They'd only discovered that a few years ago, though, so it hadn't quite sunk into the brain yet.

It was a warm day, but there was a strong breeze coming off the Pacific Ocean towards the back of Mirren's house where they sat.

Zander had been staying at Mirren's place for seven days now, since the brutal assault on Hollie, since she was pronounced dead where she lay, on top of her husband. Her assailant had been arrested and taken into custody, after being heroically subdued by an army veteran who'd been living on the streets since his return from Afghanistan.

Davie took a sip of the other coffee he'd brought out with him. This was the kind of occasion he'd usually need a stiff drink for, but he wasn't going to be the asshole who risked Zander's sobriety, especially not at the worst time in his life, when all his demons were already fighting for supremacy in his head.

These two men, with Mirren, had faced death together before. After their father had raped Mirren, they'd dug his grave with their bare hands and buried him. They'd held Mirren when Chloe died. And they'd come together when Mirren's mother was brutally killed too. Although, on that occasion, there was more relief than grief.

But this... Davie didn't even know how to begin to handle it. Security cameras on one of the apartment blocks at the beach had caught everything and the footage had been released by the vultures at StarSpy – the online celebrity website that had taken over from Twitter, TMZ and Radar Online as the most popular place to get celebrity gossip.

He'd watched the video once and that had been enough. It had showed a woman who resembled Hollie so closely she could have been her twin, approach them on the boardwalk. Zander and Hollie were kissing, so they hadn't even seen it coming, until the woman had pulled back her arm and plunged a ten-inch blade into Hollie's back, once, twice, three times in total. Zander had caught Hollie as she'd fallen and gone down with her. Meanwhile, a homeless man who'd been lying a few yards away, ran towards them and tackled the killer to the ground, knocking her out with one punch as she struggled and then keeping her there until the cops came. Davie knew the rest. First responders had swarmed the area, inevitably followed by a couple of members of the press, who had either been tipped off by police, or perhaps alerted because they monitered the emergency frequencies. One of the journalists had called Lou Cole, who was still with Mirren at a hotel just a couple of hundred yards along the beach. Both women had raced there, distraught. Mirren had eventually prised Zander's arms from his wife and had held him as he slipped into a deep fog of numb detachment, a cognitive shutdown to protect himself from the agony.

That's how he'd pretty much been ever since. Mirren had brought him back to her home, and since then he'd eaten little, slept less and the rest of the time, he'd sat on the step of the back deck, staring at the ocean. He hadn't shed a single tear.

When the cops had first come to interview him, he'd told them what happened, although when the footage was released, like everyone else, they'd learned everything they needed to know. Mirren, Davie, Sarah and Zander had then listened as they were given the details of the person they'd arrested. A woman. Debbie Butler. Thirty-eight years old. No known family. Two previous arrests for stalking, three for assault, and several for shoplifting and for passing dud cheques.

She'd had countless cosmetic procedures done to look like Hollie, had copied her hair, her style and her habits. When she'd been asked her name by the police, she'd told them it was Hollie Leith, that Zander was her husband, that she was just protecting him. After her arrest, arraignment and initial evaluation of her mental and physical state, she'd been taken to a prison medical facility, where she was still being held, while prosecutors got to work on the case.

Mirren had quietly ensured that the hero who had tackled her,

Chuck Jones, had been given a place to stay and she'd already put in place the support he'd need to help him get through this, and everything else he'd dealt with since leaving the military.

'It's all my fault.' Zander's words were barely louder than the whispers of the ocean in front of them.

Davie shook his head. 'Don't, Zander. Don't take this on.'

Even as he was saying it, Davie knew his response didn't matter because nothing would change how Zander felt. He'd been that way since they were six years old. A loner. A brooder. Someone who lived in his own head. Hollie had been the best thing that had ever happened to him, had given him the kind of security he needed to let his guard down and be happy. Now she was gone and Davie was fucking enraged by the cruelty of that.

Zander was still staring straight ahead, his voice still low. 'It's true, though. If she hadn't married me, she'd still be alive. I should have let her have a normal life instead of bringing her into this fucking circus.'

Davie didn't know how to reply to that, so he shut his mouth. He was well aware of his limitations in any situation that required an appropriate emotional response. Zander was pretty much the same. They were both products of their environment, growing up on the same street, in a world where emotion or tears were seen as weakness to be preyed upon, usually by the one man who should have protected them both.

That's probably why Mirren had always been the buffer between them, the link that made them work, and without her, they were just two grown men who could have a beer, watch a game, but who definitely were not equipped to deal with any kind of emotional need in the other. But that didn't mean Davie wasn't going to sit here and hope that his presence was enough.

There was a noise behind him, and Mirren came out with another coffee.

'How're you doing there, gents?' she asked, forcing a sad smile as she sat down next to Zander.

Out of his eyeline, she gave Davie the smallest, saddest of smiles, and the slightest of gestures of her head. He knew what it meant. Over the last seven days, they'd developed a shorthand, telepathic connection, not unlike the one they'd had when they were teenagers who had no one else but each other.

Now she was silently saying, 'I've got this, you're good to go.'

Davie nodded and stood up, resting his hand on Zander's shoulder. 'I'm just going to work, pal, but I'll be back later. If you need anything, just let me know.'

Zander said nothing, Davie wasn't even sure if he'd heard him, but Mirren's hand gently touched his as he walked past her.

This was their routine now. For the first two days, they'd all stayed here with him round the clock, but as of Monday, they'd settled into a pattern. Mirren had taken time off so she could be here all the time, and if there was an urgent work issue, she'd go upstairs to her home office to take care of it. Davie worked in the mornings, then came here for a few hours in the afternoon, before heading back to the studio around 6 p.m. Davie's mom, Ena, hadn't yet returned to Scotland, having decided to stick around in case her son needed her after getting jilted. Of course, she'd known Zander and Mirren since they were kids too - she'd been the one safe adult for all three of them, had protected them, kept their secrets and loved them. Now, she got Drego to drive her over for a couple of hours most days with her home-cooked food.

At night, Mike was here too, and Davie knew Sarah came by after work, while he was doing his show, and stayed until late. Their paths rarely crossed and much as he missed every second she wasn't with him, he was glad of that because this wasn't the time or place for them to talk. Besides, he had so many other things on his mind right now. *Davie Johnston, As It Is*, was heading towards the edge of a cliff and he needed to find out how close it was to drop-ping to its death, and what he could do to save it.

An hour later, Davie slid the Bugatti into his parking space outside the studio and jumped out, looking every inch the Holly-wood legend that he'd once been. No one needed to know that he'd only kept the Bugatti because he was famed for having the limited-edition supercar and knew he had to maintain appearances, but he'd sold the Bentley, the Mercedes G-Class, the Audi R8 and a couple of classic vintage cars that were his pride and joy. He'd almost cried when his convertible E-type had gone. He'd dreamt of that car since he was a kid, when he'd seen a picture of footballer, George Best, driving one. It broke his heart even more that selling it still wasn't enough to stop the haemorrhaging of his bank balance.

He went into the studio building and straight into the board-room for the meeting that should have started half an hour before.

'Good of you to join us,' Mellie barbed, which Davie knew she'd never have said if she was aware that he'd just come from being with Zander. The whole city, hell, the whole country and beyond, was in utter shock over the callous murder of Hollie Leith, and the release of the footage had given most people who'd watched it a personal emotional investment. The raw horror. The savage grief. The devastating sadness. There wasn't a media outlet that hadn't covered it or an influencer who hadn't commented on it.

Davie had done a special monologue the following night and for once the tears in his eyes were real, and they weren't for himself. He didn't want to be accused of exploiting Hollie's death, or playing on his connection to Zander, so he'd simply talked about how she was his friend, how she was an incredible human being, and what a devastating tragedy this truly was. Even his ex-wife, Jenny, had shown up at the studio after the show that night to have a couple of beers with him in his office. And she hadn't even charged him for them.

Davie took the chair at the head of the boardroom table and answered Mellie's jab with, 'People don't make a habit of going early to their own execution.'

That's what this was. Or at least, maybe it was life without parole. Either way, it was a fate he wasn't ready to face, but he'd run out of excuses to delay it.

Cyril Hemson, his business manager, the only member of his former team that was still on the payroll, glared at him. Davie was obviously keeping him late for his next eighteen holes on the golf course. At seventy-four, the old git could have bought the fucking golf course with the money Davie had paid him over the years.

'Okay, Cyril, shoot.'

It wasn't necessarily just a turn of phrase. Davie hoped he had a gun. It would put him out of his misery, rather than this slow painful public death.

Cyril went for the non-homicidal interpretation and passed documents to both Davie and Mellie, then started reading from the notes on the folder in front of him.

'I've summarised everything in the reports I've just given you. As you can see, our breakdown of costs is as follows: Hire of the studio for the six-month series – $1.2 million. Design and construction of the set—'

'I don't need the breakdown,' Davie interjected, scanning the rows of numbers in front of him for the figures he was looking for. 'Just give me the big picture. How deep in the shit am I?'

Cyril took his glasses off, the numbers clearly ingrained in his mind.

'Drowning in it. Basically you started with a six month budget of just over forty-five million dollars. You put down twenty-five million for initial set up costs and early cashflow. The deal with the network was that, in lieu of payment, you would keep the advertising revenue, and that would make up the shortfall needed to sustain the show. Unfortunately, that has run at...' Glasses back on, he checked his notes again, 'Eighty per cent less than projected. And without that revenue being achieved and diverted into the running costs, cash is only going in one direction. And that's a problem.'

Davie's gut was churning. The sponsors and advertisers had started out well, but one by one they'd dropped out, citing inconsistency in the quality of guests, disappointing ratings and a rising swell of stories appearing in the press and on social media platforms criticising the show. At one point a couple of weeks ago, he'd woken to see that he was trending on Twitter and his heart had soared, until he realised that the hashtag on every post was #daviejohnstonisover. There was even a Twitter challenge to fit the words 'Davie Johnston is a douche' into the lyrics of any famous song. So many Coldplay songs had been wrecked in the process, the band was probably considering suing.

Davie didn't get it. He just didn't fucking get it. Not to be paranoid – actually, fuck it, he was being hugely paranoid – but it was as if the whole world was conspiring against him.

It had started that first week when Princess had dropped out and he'd had to call in Jenny. He'd put that one down to bad luck. But the next week, it was A-list actor, Charles Power. Then the Governor of the State a few nights later. The following week, Mercedes Dance had bailed. And then Carmella Cass, the dippy cow who owed her whole career to him, had cancelled with only a few hours to go. He'd had to mine every friend he had, and a few people who hated him but owed him favours, to fill the slots. His ex-wife that first night. Logan and Lauren had helped him out on two other occasions. His daughter, Bella, had done it in return for a Mercedes, and she wasn't even old enough to drive. The week before Hollie died, Zander had stood in. And much as it had made his scrotum suck right back into his body, he'd even had to beg

Darcy Jay, his ex-wife's partner and co-star to fill an empty chair for one show. The chaos had two knock-on effects, aside from the drop in advertising revenue. First, he didn't deliver on the promos that he'd run for the stars who'd dropped out, so it just made his whole show look shambolic. Okay, so he'd recouped their fee, but that wasn't the point – what mattered was that they were booked in the slot and then bailed. And secondly, he was now having to pay celebrities way over the odds to appear. It was a perfect storm of humiliation and financial devastation.

He was on death row and his only hope was a Hail Mary, a last-minute reprieve.

'Cyril, give me the bottom line,' he demanded, then had a fleeting thought that folding into the brace position might be a good move right about now.

Cyril's specs were back off. 'We're not even halfway into the run and you've already blown through almost thirty million dollars. Given current running costs, and the lack of forecasted advertising revenue, if you don't get a massive injection of cash within the next month, you're going to have to shut down production. And that won't even solve your problems, because the network has a heavy penalty clause in the contract, so they'll sue the crap out of you.'

Davie felt the hum of the electric chair being fired up.

Mellie leant forward and, for once, didn't fire off some wise-cracking insult. Instead, she went for straight-talking truth.

'Davie, I'm so sorry... but I think what Cyril is trying to say is that you're fucked.'

In the depths of his mind, he could hear himself scream, but that's not what he put out there. Fuck that. He wasn't losing every-thing, not now. Not yet. There was still a chance. If he could just raise enough to keep the show on air for the rest of the season, and then get commissioned for another six months, then he could go back to plan A. His luck had to change. His guests had to start showing up. He had to find a way to bring his advertisers back. And he'd get the ratings. Because what was the alternative? If he called it quits now, he had nothing, except a house he'd have to sell to pay off debts. No job. No future. Ten years ago, he'd been the most successful guy in TV, and he wasn't going out like this.

'How much do I need to keep going?'

Cyril shook his head. 'Davie, I don't recommend—'

'How. Much. Do. I. Need?' he asked again, through gritted teeth.

Cyril thought about that for a moment.

'Twenty million. That'll cover the debts and get you to the end of the run. But I don't...'

Davie stopped listening. Fuck that. Fuck the debts. And fuck giving up. He hadn't worked like a dog all these years to lose it all now. There had to be a way to save this.

Twenty million. That's what he needed. All that mattered right now was where was he going to get it?

Mirren had it, Zander too, but asking either of them was out of the question right now. His ex-wife couldn't liquidate that kind of cash, and she'd rather toss her entire fortune from the top of a building than give anything to him.

Without another word, Davie got up from his seat and headed to his office. Okay, he'd tried to rustle up investment before and the only offer he'd had was from Wes. But he must have missed someone. There had to be another angle.

It had to be the house. It was worth forty-five million dollars. He couldn't sell it, because the market was in the toilet, and even if he could find a buyer, it would take a couple of months minimum to close. He could mortgage it, but he'd have to jump through hoops, and again, he didn't have the time.

'Well, that sure looks like a face that needs a friend.'

Even in the depths of hell, Davie would smile when he heard Lainey Anders' voice. One of the best moves he'd ever made was putting the country music legend on the judging panel of his old show, *American Stars*. The exposure had put her right up there with Dolly and Reba in fame, fortune and the affections of the nation, and if Davie was twenty years older, he'd have learned to ride, bought a Stetson and gone off into the sunset with her. As it was, they'd settled for friendship and platonic adoration. He'd decided he needed some of that when he'd booked her to do the show tonight.

'There is no one I'd rather see right now than you, Lainey Anders.'

Chuckling, she did a twirl for effect, and the fringes on her white leather mini-dress blew out like the brushes on a car wash.

'I can sit on your knee, if that would cheer you up?' she joked, sliding into the chair at the front of his desk.

'Baby, I think that would just be giving me a taste of something I don't deserve,' he joked, with so much charm she almost blushed.

She leaned forward, elbows on his desk. 'So, tell me why you're looking like a steer just kicked you in the nuts.'

He had to get back to trying to solve his finance issues, but hell, he could take a five-minute reprieve just to feel normal for the first time in months. 'Ah, just a bad run of luck, sweetheart.' He'd always been unable to stop himself slipping into Southern lingo when he spoke to her.

'Anything I can do to help?'

He shook his head. 'Not unless you've got a spare twenty million lying around.'

'Well, I might just manage that,' she chirped. 'What are we buying? A small island? I'll go half with you on that.'

'If only,' he said. Okay, a choice. Should he carry on with the flippant nonsense or get real for once? She made the decision for him.

'Hey, what's really going on?' she asked, showing genuine concern as she sensed his mood.

'It's fucked, Lainey. It's all fucked. If I don't find twenty million, I'm done. The show's done.'

She went quiet for a moment. This was the point he'd find out if she was a Hollywood friend or a real friend. If it was the former, her sparkly stilettos would be clicking right out of his office any second now. The heels didn't move. She stayed exactly where she was.

'Well, honey, you invested in me when you gave me that seat on the panel of *American Stars*. So I guess it's my time to invest in you.'

Davie was rarely lost for words, but right now was one of those times. He cleared his throat.

'I can't work out if you're serious or not. I'm talking about a twenty-million-dollar investment in my show.' This couldn't be happening. Lainey? Sure, she had the money, but would she really help him out here?

'Oh honey, I'm serious as a heart attack,' she drawled, chuckling. 'Davie, I'm a businesswoman. I've seen what you can do. And hell, I know it's been rocky, but I have faith and I have investors, too. Ones that trust me to back the right horses.'

If he was a praying man, he'd have slumped to his knees and thanked God. This was it. His Hail Mary. His pot of gold. His fucking jackpot.

Over the next hour or so, they framed up a deal. Twenty million. He'd have to put his house up as security, but that was no different than taking out a mortgage and so much quicker than having to deal with the banks.

'When can you have this done?' he asked her, still stunned that this angel had almost literally fallen in his lap.

'Baby, I can have my lawyers send the paperwork to you tomorrow and have the cash in your account the day after. God only knows how much time we have left in this world and I'm not one to waste it.'

Her relentless cheeriness and positivity made him melt. This was the first piece of good luck he'd had in years. Wasn't it about bloody time? He deserved this. This was just the start. He could feel it. Things were turning round for him and it was only up from there.

He was still grinning when Lainey clicked her heels out of his office and over to make-up.

Mellie was the next one through the door, and she stopped, stared at him quizzically.

'Have you just snorted coke? Because if you have, you'd better share it out. It's not my thing, but then neither is unemployment and I'm about to try that.'

'No coke,' Davie replied, still grinning.

'Then what? Davie, I swear if there's someone under that desk giving you a blow job right now, I'll break your face.'

'No blow job. Although, if you're offering...'

'Fuck off.'

'That's what I thought. No blow job. But I do have a twenty-million-dollar investment that will be with us before the week is out.' He punched the air, swirled around in his chair and hollered something approximating a yee-hah.

'Shut the fuck up! You're kidding,' she exclaimed.

'Nope. Lainey Anders just saved our asses.'

That left Mellie even more stunned. It took a few seconds before a smile crept across her face. 'Man, I don't know how you did it, but I love you for it.'

'So you'll reconsider the blow job?' Davie teased. They both knew he wasn't serious and he braced himself for the usual rejection.

'Urgh, I could never love you that much.'

Yup, there it was, swift, definite, and it made him laugh. He was back in business. Execution cancelled. He'd been given a partial reprieve and enough time to make this show work so that a big network would come in and snap it up.

Lainey Anders had just handed him a shovel. Now all he had to do was use it to tunnel his way to freedom.

13

SARAH

'Lean On Me' – Bill Withers

Sarah was sitting in her favourite café in Venice Beach, wondering if she'd been stood up. The woman she was meeting was half an hour late and she was about to give up hope.

She checked her phone for the tenth time. No messages. Sighing, she slumped back against the wood panelling behind her, grateful the Gucci shades Davie had bought her in New York last year were covering up the fact that she'd closed her eyes.

That was a mistake. Every time she did it, she saw Hollie, that night at Mirren and Mike's anniversary party, and heard her agreeing to meet her again at Mirren's home the following night. 'Yesssssss! Two nights in a row with my favourite ladies. I'll be there. What time?'

Barely an hour later, Hollie was dead.

Sarah felt her ribcage constrict and her throat tighten. The three weeks since then had been the longest of her life, and she'd give anything to go back there and change that night. If only she'd agreed to Zander's offer of a lift home, then Hollie wouldn't even have been on the damn boardwalk. When she'd voiced that thought to the cops, the detective in charge of the case had told them that Debbie Butler had been stalking Hollie and Zander for months, and that if she hadn't struck that night, it would have been another night in the future. That should have alleviated Sarah's guilt just a little, but it didn't. Maybe on another night, she could have been stopped.

Wringing her hands, bare now that she'd removed her engagement ring, Sarah had to remind herself to breathe, but her mind was still back there. If she'd known that would be the last time she'd see her friend, she'd have held her tighter, she'd have stared at her face for longer, held her hand and never let her go... Instead, in just a few hours, she would be going to her funeral service.

Zander had decided to go with a short, early-evening service, with the very minimum of ceremony, saying Hollie would hate a fuss or a spectacle. Knowing her friend as Sarah did, she felt he was right.

'Are you Sarah?' The voice was quiet, uncertain, and immediately snapped Sarah back to the present.

She opened her eyes to see a woman that had one of those faces that onlookers might think was vaguely familiar. The feline green eyes. The defined cheekbones. The natural full lips. But they wouldn't be able to place her because the woman that they knew didn't have black shadows under her eyes, her face wasn't gaunt, there weren't lines of stress and anxiety across her forehead, and a demeanour that screamed uncertainty.

'Lisa? Hi. Yes!' A wave of gratitude overtook her. She'd come. Lisa had actually showed up.

When Chip had given Sarah the green light to work on the story she'd been absolutely insistent on one thing – she didn't want Wes

Lomax to see her coming. That's why she'd asked for only two people to work on the investigation with her, fellow journalist and co-anchor, Meilin Chong, and bright, dedicated young researcher, Shandra Walker, and emphasised the ring of complete confidentiality that they had to create around their team. Everyone in this town knew someone, who knew someone, who knew someone, and she wasn't risking anything leaking on this before she was ready. That's why she'd only spoken to people she trusted.

The conversation she'd planned to have with Mirren the day after her party hadn't happened for obvious reasons, and since then, there hadn't been a time that felt right. Mirren had enough on her plate protecting and caring for Zander right now. However, Sarah had forged ahead with her enquiries, contacting every woman who'd mentioned Wes during the interviews for her book on the MeToo movement, as they'd all already signed non-disclosure agreements, prohibiting them from sharing details of their conversations. It wasn't fool-proof, but these ladies were rooting for her. And she was rooting for them.

The first time she'd talked to them, she'd focused on their experiences, but this time she specifically discussed Lomax, asked them if they'd heard any of the rumours first-hand, from any of his victims. On the fourth phone call, she'd found what she was looking for. One of her contacts, Jodie, had a friend, an actress who'd had decent parts in a couple of movies made by Lomax Films until she'd crossed Wes. Jodie said she'd ask permission to pass on her details to Sarah. An hour or so later, she'd called back with the name and number. As soon as Sarah had googled her, she'd recognised the face of the woman and from what she read, gathered that she'd been in the spotlight for a moment, before, inexplicably, dropping out of the public eye. Lisa Arexo. A British actress. Thirty-five years old. Had played opposite Zander Leith as Seb Dunhill's love interest in two of the spy flicks, until she was killed off in a gruesome torture scene in the opening seconds of the next movie.

Sarah had even seen the movies that the actress had starred in, back when she was still a journalist in Glasgow, and had been researching Zander.

The star on the screen had been a brighter, lighter, younger and more confident version of the person who had just joined her at the table.

Sarah stood up, ready to hug Lisa if she made a motion to do that. She didn't. Her eyes flicked around the room, as she pulled out the chair opposite Sarah and sat down. 'Thank you so much for meeting me,' Sarah said warmly, desperate to unfurl the tension that was in every part of Lisa's demeanour: the hunched shoulders, the firm set of her mouth, the gaze that couldn't quite meet Sarah's eye.

'That's ok. But I can't... stay long.' Sarah had expected that. In her experience, people often opened awkward conversations by setting up an excuse to bail if the discomfort got too much.

Sarah tried to put her at ease. 'No worries at all, that's fine. Just let me know when you need to go. I'm really grateful to you for talking to me, though. How about I get us some coffee? Or something else?'

'Tea, please.'

Of course, Lisa was a Brit. Tea was the standard drink of crisis.

'Something to eat too?'

Lisa shook her head.

Sarah went to the counter, ordered two hot teas, then carried the cardboard cups back to the table. Relieved that Lisa was still there, she checked that no one was in earshot before she spoke.

'Would you like to stay here? Or we could go for a walk? Whatever you're more comfortable with.'

Lisa immediately nodded. 'A walk. Can we do that?'

Sarah was already out of her chair. She'd got the teas in 'to-go' cups just in case this happened. 'Of course, let's go,' she said, with what she hoped was warmth and reassurance.

They went out onto the street, and Sarah let Lisa take the lead, turning right towards the ocean and walking with similar strides.

In a few moments, they were at the grassy area next to the beach, and as they veered around the skateboard park, Sarah opened the conversation with, 'Thank you for coming. I can't tell you how much I appreciate it.'

Lisa had stopped at a tree that was casting a shadow and slid down onto the grass. 'Is here okay?' she asked, nervously.

Sarah kicked off her shoes. 'It sure is. It's lovely to hear a British accent. Where are you from?'

Now that the breeze was blowing Lisa's hair back, Sarah could see the incredible beauty of her bone structure and her long graceful neck.

Lisa smiled at the mention of her background. 'Manchester. But I've been here for ten years now, so it's home. I married an American guy when I was twenty-five. I did it for love, but it didn't work out. The green card was the consolation prize.'

Sarah understood. It had cost her over ten grand in immigration lawyers to get her green card, and before that she'd had to leave the country every ninety days so that she didn't outstay her tourist visa.

Sarah could see Lisa beginning to relax, so she decided to gently ease her way into the reason for being there.

'Lisa, I don't want to rush you, or to take this too slowly or do anything you don't want to do. I know that Jodie told you I'm looking into Wes Lomax's history with women...' she said, mentioning her original source, the one who had, after checking it was okay, given her Lisa's contact details. 'And I think you have a story to share. If you feel able to do that with me, I'd be so grateful.'

There was a pause as Lisa stared at some kids playing further along on the grass.

'I'll tell you, so that you know, but I hope that's enough, because I don't think I could share this with the world, and I already decided not to go to the police.'

'That's okay. We'll do this on your terms, however you want it to be.'

Sarah had seen all the movies where the journalist persuaded someone to go public with a story of their personal trauma. Hell, she'd done it a few times when she was still working on the paper back in Scotland, but this was different. There were too many factors in play. This was Lisa's life, her career, everything, and Sarah had already decided that she wasn't going to violate the trust of any of Wes's victims. If Lisa didn't want to take a public stand, she'd just wish her well and keep searching for someone who was ready to speak out.

Lisa sat back against the tree, gaze downwards. Exhaled.

'I was in two of the Dunhill movies for Lomax Films. Played Dunhill's girlfriend.'

Sarah nodded, immediately putting a pin in the first question that had come into her mind. She'd worked with Zander. Had he noticed anything? Now wasn't the time to interrupt. She could come back to it.

'I had been given a contract for two movies, with an option for four more, because the plan was that my character would marry Dunhill and become a permanent addition. I was ecstatic. Actually, that didn't even begin to cover it.' Lisa gently tugged on the grass beside her as she spoke. 'It was everything. The dream I'd had since I was a kid, doing school plays and putting on shows in my living room for anyone who would pay attention. I'd made it.'

Lisa raised her eyes, and Sarah met her gaze, gave her a sad smile of understanding and encouragement.

'We filmed my second movie in Toronto, and I was staying in the same hotel as most of the rest of the cast. When the movie wrapped, Wes Lomax flew in for the last day. There was a bar and pool on the roof of the hotel, and Wes threw a huge party there that night. The cast, the crew, we were all there.'

She paused, cleared her throat.

'After the speeches, and the toasts and a couple of hours of drinking and dancing, Wes called me over and, wow, I thought that was everything. Wes Lomax knew my name. He wanted to speak to me. It honestly felt like one of the best moments of my life.'

Another pause.

Sarah wondered if she'd lost her, if it was too painful to continue, but no...

'He said that he'd invited the leads and the top production guys to his suite – he was staying in the penthouse – because he wanted to thank us all personally. He asked me to join them. I didn't think anything of it and now... I can hear how fucking naïve that sounds and I hate myself for it. I'm not a stupid woman. I don't get taken in by shit like that. But... I guess I did.' Lisa spat the last words out, words full of contempt and self-reproach that Sarah knew she didn't deserve. How many women beat themselves up for the vile behaviour of others?

Sarah didn't hesitate to contradict her, speaking softly, truthfully.

'You're not stupid, Lisa. The guy was your boss. I think anyone else would have done the same thing.'

Lisa gave her a look that said she didn't quite believe that but was grateful for the thought.

'So down I went with him. One floor. As soon as I got there, I realised it was just us and I got the worst feeling. And I could have left, but I didn't, because... I couldn't quite get my head around the thought that I was in danger.'

'You couldn't have known...'

'But that's the thing, I did,' Lisa objected, pain in every word. 'I knew then, but something in my head kept telling me I was wrong. That this wasn't a set-up. That I was mistaken. That this wasn't going to happen, but it did. And it didn't even take ten minutes. He just pushed me against a wall, and when I screamed, he put his hand over my mouth and told me he knew I'd like it rough.'

A tear slid down one cheek and Lisa angrily rubbed it away, as if it had no right to be there. 'Then he ripped my dress, and my underwear, put his hand inside me, then... worse...' She closed her eyes for a second, unable to say the words, before snapping back to the present. 'I don't really know what happened next.'

'Do you think he drugged you?'

Lisa shook her head. 'No, I was aware. I knew. I knew he was inside me, and I knew he walked away when he was done. Went for a shower, like it was all perfectly normal, and I did nothing. Nothing! I just left. Why?'

Sarah reached for her hand.

'Why didn't I go in there after him? Why didn't I use my rage to hurt him? I don't know. I don't know why.'

'Because it's not that simple,' Sarah offered gently, knowing that was true. She'd asked herself the same things.

'The next morning, I went back to his room, and this time his secretary was there. Monica. She answered the door and I demanded to see him. He was in the other room. I could hear his voice. Monica said he wasn't available, I told her I'd wait. I was agitated. Angry. I had no idea what I was going to say or do, but I just knew I wanted him to see the bruise on my face, to let him know that he'd marked me. It seemed... important. None of it makes sense now. Anyway, she just kept repeating that he wasn't there and eventually she threatened to call security. I gave up. Walked away. No girl code in that bitch.'

'I'm so sorry.' The words weren't even close to being enough, but Sarah had to say them and Lisa's sad smile acknowledged them.

'The next day, my agent called to say that my contract had been cancelled. They were killing off my character. The next movie opened with a twenty second flashback of me being caught by bad guys, tortured and left to die, then Dunhill mourning my loss. How fucking ironic and sick was that?'

Even as she tried to contain her inner fury, Sarah realised she remembered that scene. It had been so well written, using flashbacks and what she guessed must have been body doubles and CGI, that no one had given Lisa's departure a second thought.

'The thing is, he didn't just take away that job. He took away my whole career. My confidence. My belief in myself. In everything I thought I was and thought I wanted for the future. I don't know how to be me again. I don't even know who that person is anymore. Since then, I haven't booked a single job. Not one. Lomax bad-mouthed me throughout the industry, told people I was a nightmare to work with, that I had a drug addiction, a drink problem, you name it, he said it,' her hopelessness was rising now, making her words sharper, angrier. 'My agent dropped me, I can't get another one, and no one answers the phone to me. It's like I no longer exist. He's somehow cancelled me. Now, I'm nothing.'

'Lisa, I promise you that's not true. You're a survivor. I'm sorry – I know that's a cliché, but it's true. And I say that as someone who tells themselves the same thing every single morning.'

A realisation made Lisa lock on Sarah's gaze. 'You too?'

Sarah nodded. She didn't need to say the words. 'I promise you right now, I'm going to get him. I don't know how long it will take, but I will.'

That thought was still revolving like a mantra in Sarah's mind when she walked into Hollie's funeral service that evening. She was with Zander, with Davie, with Mirren, but she hoped that Wes

Lomax, sitting in the second row, knew that she didn't need any of them for protection. She was enough. Her fury was a bigger force than he could ever be.

Somehow, some way, no matter how long it took, she was going to end him.

The corners of his mouth turned up when he saw her as if daring her to go ahead. Given her current surroundings, it was a heinous thought... but she'd never wanted to kill someone more.

14

ONE MONTH LATER – MIRREN

'Why' – Annie Lennox

Mirren stared at the ocean, wondering if the people who glanced her way as they walked along the beach thought she had the perfect life. Successful career, beautiful home, millions in the bank, a wonderful son and daughter-in-law, great friends, and a husband she truly adored.

Of course, it wasn't perfect. She'd swap all the success in the world to have Chloe back. To have Hollie here with her too. But as far as work and marriage went, she could see that she was close to a dream life.

This was the pinnacle. The reward for the years of struggle and devastation that began when she was just a child, when she used to sit outside shivering against the wall of her house so that she didn't have to listen to her mother, Marilyn, and Jono Leith having loud, uninhibited sex upstairs. Her mother hadn't given a toss about her. The only person who'd mattered to her was Jono, her obsession, the swaggering gangster who promised he'd take her away from the sewer of her life, despite having a wife and kid just two houses down. He was still all that mattered when she'd discovered that Jono's sexual desires extended to seventeen-year-old Mirren and Marilyn eventually plunged a knife through his chest. Even then, all she cared about was the loss of her lover, not the daughter who had been brutalised.

Mirren had absolutely no doubt that those two bastards had rotted in hell, and she hoped that was true because she couldn't stand the thought that their spirits were out there and that they might be about to witness her blowing up the illusion of her perfect life.

And she had no one to blame but herself.

Dealing with Jason Grimes had been the least of her worries over the last few weeks. Hollie's death had been devastating, and her focus had immediately become taking care of Zander. He'd lived here with her and Mike until the day after the funeral, when he'd decided it was time to go home. Since then, she'd dropped in on him every day. If he was sleeping, she didn't wake him. If he was silent, she didn't force him to talk. If he was hurting, she held him. She did all the things for him that he'd done for her after Chloe had died, when he'd slept on her couch and held her up until she could stand by herself again.

He had been her priority. He had been the friend that she thought about all day. But, eventually, there came a moment when he could stand up and her issues could no longer be ignored. And the biggest issue of all was Jason Grimes.

Lou hadn't been wrong about him shopping around a story.

A week or so after they'd lost Hollie, while Zander was sleeping, Mirren had called the branch of Chloe's Care where he worked. She'd contemplated going in person, but she didn't want to leave Zander, and she didn't want to be swarmed by the pack of paps and reporters that were staking out the street outside the Colony gates, hoping for a shot of a grieving Leith. Parasites was too generous a term for how she felt about them.

On the second ring, LeBron, the assistant manager at the centre had answered. He'd become a friend of the family after he'd cared for Chloe and Zander at another clinic, Life Reborn, many years ago. He'd reacted immediately to her voice.

'Mirren, I don't even know what to say about Zander's lady. I met her a few times, and she was something else. Something really special. Please pass on my love and tell him I'm praying for him.'

Mirren wasn't a religious person, but she appreciated the sentiment and she'd take any prayers that were going for her friend.

'I will do, Lebron, thank you.' After some more chat about the centre, she'd finally got around to the reason for the call. 'While I'm on, I was hoping to have a quick chat with Jason Grimes. Is he around?'

A pause.

A longer pause.

The nausea Mirren had been suffering since the night of her anniversary party had taken hold again.

'Erm, he's not here.'

Oh. So he wasn't on shift right now. No big surprise. The counsellors worked a three-shift pattern so that there was someone there 24/7.

'No worries. Can you check when he's next on the rota?'

Another pause. 'That's the thing, Mirren. He left. Last week. Just said it wasn't working for him and up and quit. I thought you'd been notified.'

She probably had, but she was so far behind on her emails, she must have missed it. Damn. 'Ah okay. Thanks, Lebron. You take care of yourself.'

When she'd disconnected the call, her chin had dropped to her chest. Shit. This wasn't good.

Against her better judgement, she'd tried calling his number, knowing that Lou would be furious at her for establishing any kind of paper trail involving her initiating contact. Mirren had decided that could be explained away as just an employer calling her ex-employee. It didn't matter, because he didn't pick up. No point in leaving a message. He'd see that she'd called and he'd either call back or ignore it. He'd ignored it.

Mirren had reported all this back to Lou, who had predictably chided her for trying to contact him, then given her verdict on the situation.

'Damn, sister, this dude is a piece of work. Didn't think you could find a bigger douche than Jack Gore. If it wasn't for Mike and your excellent taste in friends, I'd be seriously questioning your judgement. What were you thinking with this one, girl?'

It wasn't the first time Lou had asked the question. When Mirren had told her about Jason, she'd initially been supportive, understanding that a bit of physical intimacy could be a necessary distraction from the loneliness of where she'd been in her life back then. But as it became clearer that Mirren had left herself vulnerable to a man who saw her as some kind of meal ticket, Lou had understandably become more frustrated.

'I think the point was that I wasn't thinking,' Mirren had conceded.

'I hear you,' Lou had said, and Mirren could picture her nodding. Both of them had made mistakes in their lives, and they never judged each other.

'Look, I've got you. Leave it with me and let me see if I can make this go away.'

That had reassured Mirren a little. If she had to bet her salvation on anyone, it would be Lou Cole.

Jason probably thought Christmas had come early when he got an offer to meet with the editor of the *Hollywood Post*, the biggest payer for authentic, proven stories.

Lou had met with him in the lobby of a hotel in West Hollywood, and she'd recorded the meeting on a lapel camera. Mirren had seen the footage Lou had recorded, and later she'd watched as Lou had got straight to the point. How much was it going to take for exclusive rights?

Jason had raised his eyebrows as if he appreciated the direct approach. He'd come dressed to do business, in his smart black pants, and white Prada shirt, distinguishable by the unmistakable logo on the breast pocket. That was a thousand-dollar shirt – and Mirren knew that because she'd bought a similar one for Logan for Christmas the year before. The commonality wasn't lost on her. Her twenty-four-year-old son, and now, here was her twenty-five-year-old one-night stand. Again, the same question – what the hell had she been thinking?

It hadn't taken him long to give Lou her answer.

A hundred grand.

Mirren's hopes had soared at that point. It was a lot of money, but cash wasn't something she was short on, and it would be worth it to avoid any kind of attention or scandal coming her way.

'I think I can make that happen,' Lou had agreed.

At that point, Jason had looked way too pleased with himself, until Lou went on, 'But there are conditions. Exclusive rights.'

'Done,' he'd said, with all the cockiness of a man who had just been offered a shitload of money for little effort.

'And an NDA. Without limit of time.'

For the first time, he'd appeared rattled, but he tried not to show it.

'That doesn't work for me. That means I can't talk about what happened? And if you decide not to run the story, then no-one will ever hear about it?'

'Correct.'

So it's a catch and kill,' he'd spat, quoting the well known term for a story that gets purchased by the press and then squashed to protect someone. 'Fuck that.'

That was the moment Mirren knew what was happening here.

'It's not the money,' Mirren had sighed, when Lou had stopped the playback on the recording at that point.

Lou was on the same page. 'Nope, it's the publicity. He wants to be the stud who slept with the Hollywood powerhouse twice his age. He wants to milk it for attention, for fame, and if he can leverage it into some kind of influencer/reality TV deal, then that's what he's going for. So much for the humanitarian that just wanted to help people.'

Mirren had felt it churlish to point out that she was only forty-seven and not quite twice his age. The principle was the same and so was the conclusion. She'd been played. This had probably been the game plan from the start and she'd been too sad, too wrapped up in her grief, too stupid to see it.

Now, it was crystal clear and so were the consequences.

One of which, had just come into the kitchen to pour himself a coffee.

She'd thought about telling him so many times, but every time, she'd decided against it. What was the point? They'd been separated when it had happened. Mike had left. And, no, they hadn't explicitly discussed what that meant in regard to seeing other people, but the implication was clear. This wasn't some *Friends* scene, and they weren't Ross and Rachel on a break. This was real life and at that time she was pretty sure they were over. She'd never asked Mike if he'd seen anyone else because she didn't want to know. It was none of her business. And if Jason Grimes hadn't turned out to be a publicity-seeking douche, he'd have been a closed chapter, one she felt no obligation to share with Mike. Now the asshole was about to create carnage, not only in her life, but more importantly, in Mike's life too, and the very thought of hurting him made Mirren's heart sore.

Mirren was standing at the island in the middle of the room, holding her mug with both hands as he passed her, kissing her on the top of the head as he went. 'Morning, gorgeous.'

Just like most Saturdays, he was in jeans and a white T-shirt, his feet bare and his face unshaven. It was Mirren's favourite look.

'What? Why are you staring?' he asked as he poured a mug of Columbian roast from the machine on the wet bar.

She hadn't even realised that she was. 'Because I know I got lucky,' she answered truthfully, making him grin. Before he could take that further by suggesting they get romantic or naked, Mirren pivoted the conversation to the one she'd been dreading.

'Mike, I need to talk to you. Can we sit?'

He knew her well enough to immediately pick up on the tone.

'What's happened? Are you okay? The kids? Zander?'

Of course, his first thought would be everyone else's well-being. That was who she'd married. She'd just forgotten it for a minute.

'Yes, everyone's fine.'

They both slid into the booths on either side of the round kitchen table in the corner of the room. This had been the scene of so many important conversations in her life. There had been many good times. Chloe and Logan had both blown out their birthday cake candles a dozen times right here. And there had been a few occasions that had broken her heart. She was pretty sure she'd been right here when she'd discovered that Jack, her husband of twenty years, had been having an affair. That was a circle of life that she didn't want to contemplate right now.

She felt a flush of red begin on her chest and work its way upwards. 'I don't know where to start with this, Mike.'

His expression of expectancy immediately turned to concern as he leant towards her and took her hand. 'Hey, what's going on? You sure you're okay?'

'Yes, I just... Mike, I slept with someone.' So much for any gentle build-up or warning. She'd blurted it right out and now he was just staring at her, but his hand had slipped right off hers.

'You're going to have to give me that one again.' His voice, low and deadly, made the flush of red seep across her neck like a bloodstain.

'I slept with another man. Once. While we were separated.'

A frown of confusion melded with his anger.

'Mirren, we were never separated. We were giving each other space. It's two very different fucking things.'

That jarred her. Mike rarely swore, usually leaving that to the Scottish DNA of Zander and Davie, but now his words shot into the air between them, hanging there, making everything else she could say seem like a petty excuse.

He was right. Kind of. Yes, they were living apart, but she'd definitely viewed it as a potentially permanent separation, positive that she could never give him the wife he wanted. That being said, she knew the respectful thing to do would have been to clarify things, get closure on where they were before embarking on any kind of relationship with anyone else. The fact that it was a one-night stand as opposed to long term intimacy was just semantics.

'I'm so sorry, Mike.' It seemed woefully insufficient for how she was feeling right now.

Mike's eyes had darkened, his voice low and taut. 'Who is he?'

'A counsellor at one of Chloe's Centres. He's gone now. It was a one-night thing, Mike, I swear. One night. Just sex. That was it.'

'So what, you never spoke to him before that?'

'Just as friends. He was someone to listen when...' She didn't finish that. Someone to listen to her when Mike wasn't there. Someone to listen to her grief and her pain over Chloe, when everyone she knew had heard it too many times. Someone to make her forget, just for a moment.

'No, no, no... you don't get to do that. I would have listened to anything you wanted to say, Mirren, but the problem was you were never fucking here. You drowned yourself in work. I was here for you – it was you who checked out.'

He was right, but at the time, it had felt too suffocating. With him, she had to be Mirren, his wife. With Jason, just for a second, there were no expectations. Not that it was an excuse and she wasn't trying to defend herself.

'I know that. You're right. Mike, there is nothing you can say that could make me think less of myself than I already do.'

She was trying to work out where to go next when he showed her the way.

'Why tell me now? We've been back together for months. Why now? Guilt?'

If only it was just that.

Mirren shook her head, unable to look him in the eye. 'He's sold his story to StarSpy. They're going to go public with it.'

'Mirren, no...' He closed his eyes, and she was sure she could see the contours of his face age in front of her. He'd been in this business a long time and he knew exactly what that meant. This would be a media frenzy, a hot topic and the subject of endless chat on social media. There would be fricking memes, hashtags and a million comments, all trashing them both. More than that, their kids would suffer. Logan could withstand it – he was a twenty-four-year-old music superstar with his own robust social media presence and a team of publicity experts that would manage this. But Mike's daughter, Jade, was sixteen, still in high school, still finding out who she was and carving her place in life. Now she'd have to do it all while enduring the sniggers and the gossip about her father's marriage. Just like her dad, she didn't deserve this. Mirren had put them here, and now, the least she could do was be honest about just how bad it was going to get.

'You need to know something else. He's twenty-five.'

'Almost the same age as Logan,' he said, shocked.

'I'm aware,' she fired back, then took a breath. He was entitled to this anger. She reset. Steadied her voice. Went on. 'The reason he's selling his story is that he's trying to use it as a platform for a career. Maybe reality TV. Modelling. Acting. I don't know. All I do know is that he's not going to go quietly. Lou already tried to shut it down.'

'Wait, so Lou knows?' Mike threw his hands up. 'Of course, she does. Who else? Am I the last fucking chump to find out that my wife screwed someone else?'

'No one else knows, only Lou. But that's going to change. We just need to tell the kids before it gets out there.'

'No.' Mike stood up, and began pacing, thinking. All Mirren could do was wait until he could vocalise his thoughts. 'No. I'm not having Jade dragged into this. Get ahead of it, Mirren. Have Lou release the story tonight, in your words, make it as gentle as possible on yourself. It's the only way.'

Mirren's hopes were on a seesaw of positivity and despair. On the one side, she was so grateful he was considering her feelings in this; on the other, he was pushing her to release something that she couldn't bear to have out in the world.

'I'll do whatever you need me to do, but, Mike, we need to be realistic. That won't stop Jade being dragged into this.'

He stopped just a few feet away from her.

'Yes, it will. Because you're going to announce tonight that we separated a year ago. That we're still friends, so that's why we've occasionally been seen together. But that you did not, I repeat, DID

NOT, destroy our marriage by being unfaithful to me. That takes me out of the picture and protects Jade. I'll give a statement tonight corroborating that, and confirming that we're divorcing. And then the only story you'll have to worry about is that you shagged some twenty-five-year-old guy, and he might give away some of your bedroom secrets. Embarrassing, sure, but it'll be forgotten by next week.'

'And then what? Where do we go after that?'

As he stared at her, she took in the blaze in his eyes.

'I already covered that. Seems lies are your thing, Mirren, but they're definitely not mine. You betrayed me. Wrecked us. Risked my daughter's happiness. None of that is forgivable. I'm releasing a statement saying we're divorcing, because it's true.'

15

ZANDER

'My Fault' – Imagine Dragons

Zander had been staring at it for hours. Just staring. Straight ahead. It sat there, alternating between taunting him and telling him how much he needed it.

Come get me, it said. *I'll make this all better. I'm here for you.*

A few times already, it had thrown out an extra comment.

You killed her. You. You did this.

He didn't argue, because the bottle of Jack Daniel's that was sitting right in front of him on the kitchen table, calling to him, was right. He'd killed Hollie. Sure, Debbie Butler used the knife, but it was Zander's fault. If Hollie hadn't met him, she'd be working for someone else, dating a regular guy, maybe married, perhaps even picking up their kids from kindergarten. She'd have had a big, beautiful life and she'd have deserved it.

But now she was gone and even her funeral service had been a blur. Mirren had arranged it all and he'd no idea who'd even been there. Hollie's family. Their friends. A hundred other people he hadn't even glanced at. A choir had sung her favourite songs. A preacher had spoken about her. Zander hadn't listened, because that would have meant he was really there, at his dead wife's funeral, and that would have killed him too. When her coffin had slipped behind the curtain to be cremated, he'd closed his eyes, shut down completely. He only knew it had happened because now there was a small oak box full of ashes in their bedroom, with a tiny brass plate on the lid engraved with Hollie's name.

Meanwhile, the trial of the woman who had knifed her had been delayed. Someone, somewhere, was waiting for multiple forensic psychiatry reports, for opinions from her doctors, for her lawyers to prepare her case. Zander honestly, deep in his core, didn't care. Debbie Butler thought she was his wife, so she'd killed Hollie to protect him. She was obviously deranged. Unwell. And Zander couldn't find it in his heart to hate her, because he was too busy hating himself.

The bottle was still calling him. *Come get me. I'll make this all better. I'm here for you.*

His phone rang, and he thought about ignoring it, but when he saw it was a FaceTime from Mirren, he answered. If he didn't, he knew she'd drop everything and be at his door within the hour. That would only disrupt the conversation between him and his friend Jack over there.

'How are you doing, my love?' she asked, as she did on every call. She looked tired today. Pale. Weary. Probably because she was trying to have a life and look after him at the same time. Every morning, she was here at 7 a.m., with coffee for them both, and they sat on the deck out by his pool. Sometimes they chatted, mostly they sat in silence. Some days she brought food to stock up his refrigerator, and some evenings, she'd come back and have dinner with him too. He'd cancelled the cleaners and the gardeners, to avoid seeing anyone else, so Mirren also helped him clean the house and last week she'd cleared the leaves off the pool while he'd mowed the lawn. He'd told her she didn't need to do it, but she insisted. Zander Leith. The gift that just kept on giving.

'I'm okay. I made some lunch.' A lie. 'And I'm going to work out this afternoon.' Another lie. The gym in his home, usually his first stop of every day, hadn't been entered since he'd returned from staying with Mirren.

'I'm going to come over later. I'll bring pizza. I could do with the carbs.' She was trying to lighten the conversation, and he went along with it because Hollie would tell him it was the polite thing to do.

'Add in wings, and I'll let you in,' he said, hoping she bought the act. *Humour by grieving widower in a tale of murder and tragedy.*

'Done,' Mirren agreed, and the forced hope in her voice made him ache. He knew she was desperate for him to be okay. Right now, he couldn't imagine a time that he'd ever be okay again.

'Ok, see ya, Mirr.' He hung up, and went back to staring at the bottle. It was still there. Still taunting.

The last time he had a drink was hazy to him now. An act of self-sabotage that he'd chosen to block. Was it the night in his Venice Beach apartment, when he'd got trashed just hours after leaving an AA meeting? Or maybe the time he'd dragged Raymo Cash, a cretin of a human being, out of a nightclub, pummelling his face every step of the way?

And what about the coke? When was the last time he'd touched the white powder? Was it the morning he'd said goodbye to Chloe, who was in the same rehab, promised he'd stay clean, then pulled his Aston Martin over to the side of the road and broke the top off the Seb Dunhill bobble head attached to his dashboard, to get to his secret stash of the snowy stuff?

The time stamps on the memories were blurred to him now.

The only thing he knew for sure was that the night Chloe had died in hospital, overdosed at eighteen, was the night he swore he'd honour her by staying sober. And he'd kept that promise every day since then.

Now Jack over there was making him question whether there was any point. Who would know? It would take the edge off the pain. Right now, all Zander wanted to be was numb.

Come get me. I'll make this all better. I'm here for you.

He wasn't even sure how it had got there. Every day for the first month he'd been back at the house, there had been letters of condolence, sympathy cards, flowers and deliveries of care packages. The Jack Daniel's had been in one of the boxes last week, but he hadn't even checked to see who'd sent it. He'd just put it in the cupboard, and every morning, as soon as Mirren left, he'd taken it out and stared at it. It was his own personal brand of self-harm.

A noise shattered the silence and startled him at the same time. The buzzer at the gate. He checked the security screen, wondering if it was Davie and he'd forgotten the code. A few days a week, his brother would come over at lunchtime, armed with huge bowls of chicken and rice, because that was the only damn stuff he ate. They'd establish quickly that neither of them knew what to say, so they'd just sit next to each other on the sofa, put on an old *Die Hard* movie and watch it in silence. It passed the time and Zander was grateful. His only other regular visitors were Sarah, who often came with Mirren in the evenings, and Davie's mum, Ena, who had Davie's driver bring her over every couple of days with pre-prepared comfort food. He was grateful for her love, but most of the food usually made its way to the bin. Mince and tatties wasn't going to fix this.

He peered at the screen. Not Davie. The car was a vintage 1965 Shelby Cobra Roadster CSX, a legendary muscle car that Zander knew had been purchased for over a million dollars a few years ago. And, of course, Wes Lomax was at the wheel of his pride and joy.

Shit. Zander had zero desire to see his boss right now, but he knew if he ignored him, just like Mirren, Wes would just keep coming back until he got him. Wes Lomax wasn't the type of guy who ever stood for being ignored.

Zander pressed a button to let him in and watched as the gates swung open. He went to the front door to greet his unwelcome guest and Wes strode straight in, shaking his hand and doing the whole hug/back slap thing on the way past. If he saw the bottle of Jack Daniel's on the table, he didn't mention it. If there had been a line of coke, that would have been a different story.

As the leading man in Lomax Films' most profitable franchise, he'd made this man billions, but he'd also had his fair share of fuckups. For well over a decade after Wes had brought him, Davie and Mirren to Hollywood, Wes had stuck by him, giving him the part of Seb Dunhill and playing almost a fatherly role in his life. Some would say he just knew where his box office came from, but Zander, for his own sake, chose to believe that it was because the two men had a genuine bond. That had lasted until Zander had a few false positives in drug tests a few years ago. Wes had refused to believe his innocence and, faced with the insurance company shutting down filming, had fired him and decided to recast the role. Zander had only got his job back because Mirren had made a deal that allowed Wes to produce two of her Clansman movies on the condition Zander was reinstated. Zander had found out about the agreement years later, and he'd been pissed off at Wes, but, at the same time, beyond grateful for Mirren's faith in him.

From that day forward, Zander had truly understood his relationship with his boss. Zander played his role, earned obscene amounts of money from it, and in return, he didn't rock the boat with Wes. In fact, he feigned friendship, something that used to have Hollie making gagging noises in the corner of the room. She had no time for Wes Lomax. And she was the best judge of character he'd ever known.

Wes took a seat on a sofa, slung his arms over the back, and brought one ankle up to rest on the opposite knee, his standard Alpha male body position.

Zander sat on the sofa opposite. He didn't need the posturing.

'So, how have you been then, son? We've missed you.'

Zander had a vague memory of Wes being at Hollie's funeral, but he wasn't surprised that Wes didn't lead with that. Lomax wasn't the type of guy to dwell on sadness or show empathy.

'Yeah, I'm okay.' Man of few words. Even less when he was lying.

Wes took that in, and Zander wondered how long it would take before he dropped the niceties and got straight to the point. Five, four, three, two...

'Listen, Zander, I'll cut the bullshit and get straight to it.'

Bingo.

'We need you back on set. It's been two months now, bud. Trust me, no one is more sympathetic to your situation than me...'

Now Wes was lying.

'But the truth is, we've got two more weeks of filming and the shutdown is costing me hundreds of thousands of dollars every week.'

Zander resisted the urge to point out that was small change to Wes Lomax.

He did, however, challenge Wes's argument. 'Costing you money? I thought you'd retired, Wes.'

'I still own the company and it's still my bottom line, so I need you back next week.'

'No.'

'What?' Watching Wes's expression change was like seeing a dark cloud come down over a mountain.

'I'm not coming back, Wes.'

'Until when?'

'I don't know.' He wasn't being difficult, just honest. He couldn't go back. He couldn't look at the pity on people's faces. He couldn't act like he was okay for fourteen hours a day on set. He couldn't sit in his trailer, without Hollie right there with him, helping him run lines, organising his life, being his wife. He couldn't do it without her.

'Zander, I need you to—'

'I said no.'

'You selfish bastard,' Wes hissed. There it was. There was the truth of how he felt.

Zander stood up. 'Get out, old man. Before one of us does or says something that we can't take back.'

Lomax got the message, stood up, then took a step towards him. At six foot two, Zander was used to being the tallest in most rooms, but Wes was an inch closer to the sky.

Wes was in his face now. 'After everything I've done for you. For you all. Ungrateful cunts. I should have left the three of you back in Scotland. I'll expect you on set Monday morning. Fucking be there.'

In his head, Zander could see Hollie rolling her eyes, telling him for the hundredth time that Lomax was a narcissistic douchebag with overtones of downright nastiness, who relished the fight and always played dirty.

'Oh, and if you see Mirren, tell her that being a whore isn't a good look on her.'

Zander had no idea what that meant, but apparently his fist wasn't going to wait to find out. His arm flew back, then came forward at speed and cracked Wes on the jaw.

His reaction? Some kind of twisted, evil laugh.

'You're the second son of a bitch that's hit me in the last few months. Your pathetic little prick of a sidekick tried that too. He's still paying. Fucking pathetic, all three of you. But, you know what, I'm going to let it go, son, because it's a helluva time to be you. Be back at work next week, or I'll find a way to finish this movie without you and then a fucking Hemsworth brother will be wearing Dunhill's suit next time round.'

Zander didn't even answer because there was not one cell in his brain that cared.

All of this was pointless. All of it.

Wes Lomax opened the front door, but before he could take a step outside, he slid to his knees, then toppled forward until he was lying, flat out in the doorway, absolutely still.

Zander didn't go to check why.

Instead, he went over to the dining table, picked up the bottle and opened it.

16

DAVIE

'So What' – Pink

Davie pushed the bacon sandwich on white bread away. 'Ma, I can't. If I ate that, my internal organs would drop out of my body. The only meat I eat is lean chicken and I haven't had white bread since 1992.'

Ena drew herself up to her petite, yet terrifyingly intimidating, five foot one inch. 'Davie Johnston, you will eat that and be grateful. There are people lining up at food banks for a square meal, so don't you think for a second that you can turn your nose up at decent, nourishing food.'

He could have argued, but this was his mother's specialist subject. After four months in LA, she was heading back to Glasgow tomorrow, and within twenty-four hours of landing, she'd be back at work on the soup bus – the local term for the vehicle that parked on Glasgow's Sauchiehall Street every night to provide food and care for the homeless and street workers in the city centre. It was completely voluntary, but she religiously did two nights a week – more if they were short-staffed – for no payment. Ena had started volunteering when she'd retired years before, and she'd never worked harder, despite Davie offering her money, cars and every other material thing she could ever want. The only thing they never discussed was a new house, but that was because they both knew that Ena's home – the tiny two-bedroom terrace that he'd grown up in – held way too many secrets to leave. Jono Leith's resting place was only yards from her kitchen window, and Ena would take that story to the grave to protect her son. That's if she didn't kill him with white bread and bacon first.

'It's a nonsense, this diet of yours. Just like the rest of this,' she gestured around his kitchen. 'I mean, you're one person, Davie – there is no good reason for you to live in a house that's big enough to be a homeless hostel. It's shameful, it really is.'

Shameful. Any other mother would be bursting with pride over Davie's achievements. He had five bloody Emmys and a People's Choice award. Not to mention a forty-five-million-dollar home and a twenty-five-year career in the industry. But none of that meant anything to her at all. Her socialist, working-class Scottish upbringing had left her with a genetic code that frowned on excess and thought anything more than basic needs were wasteful and frivolous. Oh, and boasting or conspicuous displays of wealth could give her a conniption, such was her disdain for the pursuit of riches over humanity. All of which made it even more surprising that she'd had a child to Jono Leith, the maddest, baddest, swaggering gangster in their area of the city. She'd had sex with him once, but it was enough to make her pregnant and give her a son who shared his father's enjoyment of acting like the big shot.

'Are you sure you don't mind Drego taking you to the airport instead of me?' Davie asked her for the third time that morning, deciding that changing the subject was a better option than arguing over the size of his kitchen.

'Of course I don't. He's a lovely man, that one. Did you know his father was Ukrainian but his mother was Russian, like his wife?'

Davie didn't want to state the obvious, but no, he was not aware, because he'd never asked. Drego had been his driver, groundsman, and all-round general handyman for two decades, while Alina was Drego's 120lb, country-music-loving, quick-tempered, fiercely loyal wife, who treated Davie with a strangely potent mix of adoration and disdain. He had never quite worked out whether she loved him or dreamt about killing him in his sleep, but she didn't make him bacon sandwiches for breakfast, so she was a keeper.

'Anyway, I've spent more time with him than I have with you on this trip.' That could have come out as a passive-aggressive dig, but the sadness in her tone just ripped out Davie's heart.

She was right. Ena had come over for the wedding, and then, when it didn't happen, had insisted on staying to spend time with Bella and Bray, popping down to Mexico for a day trip at one point, so that she didn't break the terms of her ninety-day tourist visa. Davie was grateful that she'd spent time with her grandkids. Bella had even taken her to the recording studio for a couple of sessions as she laid down tracks for her new album. It wasn't lost on Davie that the same offer had never been extended to him. In fact, that went for both his kids. Ena had burnt her forehead, sitting on Zuma Beach, watching Bray surf too. Even picturing that scene made Davie smile. Ena, in her bucket sun hat and the only pair of sandals she'd ever felt the need to own ('They go with everything, son – why do I need more than one pair?'), hanging out with a bunch of surfer dudes, telling them to get their suntan lotion on and not to be doing any of the big waves in case they got hurt.

Her time had been filled with more than just her grandchildren, though.

To salvage her soul, Ena also visited Zander regularly, and did volunteer shifts at the Chloe's Care centre over on Sunset most days. At home, her prevailing focus, though, was to make sure Davie was okay. He wasn't. However, she probably wouldn't know that because he'd been so consumed by work that he'd barely seen her.

Now that they were in November, she'd decided it was time to return to Scotland because the winter was getting harsh there and she wanted to get back to help with the soup bus at its busiest time.

Davie walked her to the door, where Drego was waiting, leaning up against the pick-up truck that came with the job.

Ena wrapped her arms around her son and murmured in his ear. 'You make sure you get Sarah back, Davie. That one is a keeper, and you should never have let her go.'

Great. Just what a forty-seven-year-old man needed. A reprimand from his mother on where he was going wrong in his relationships. Especially one that overlooked the fact that Sarah had left him, and that, other than when they both showed up for Zander at the same time, there had been virtually no contact for months. It was clear to him that it was over, although he still didn't completely understand why. His only assumption was that she was so wrapped up in her work, so consumed by this whole mission to crucify Wes Lomax, that she had no headspace for anything else. In a way, he understood that. She was still establishing her career here, and when he was at that stage in life, he'd been an obsessive workaholic who'd put ambition before everything and anything else. Not much had changed.

'I'll try my best, Ma,' he told her.

'And also...' She began.

He braced himself for whatever little nugget of wisdom was about to come next.

'I love you more than life, son, but remember this is all bollocks,

Davie. And before you say it, no, that's not a swear word in my mind, so I'll use it if I please.' She gestured around her, getting back to her point. 'None of it is real and you don't need it to be happy.'

Her familiar refrain and, as always, Davie answered with, 'I know, Ma. You're right.' If only she knew he once spent a hundred grand on a custom drum set just because he knew Matthew McConaughey had one, or that his season ticket for his courtside seat at his beloved Lakers cost almost double that, she would have had him sectioned.

She was a sight to behold as she took Drego's hand and, displaying admirable agility for a woman of her diminutive size and age, managed to climb up into the cab of the pick up. 'Love you, son,' she shouted as they began to drive. 'I'll give you three rings to let you know I'm home.'

That almost felled him. The safety cry of the Scottish women of that generation. They'd call, but hang up after three rings, so that the other person knew they'd reached home in one piece, but because the call didn't connect, they wouldn't be charged for it. It didn't matter that Davie had paid her phone bill for the last twenty-five years. Or that calls were free on her service plan. It was bred into her DNA, just like her caring heart and her fondness for fish and chips on a Saturday night.

Davie watched as they disappeared down the driveway, surprised by the feeling of loss that was wrenching his gut. Maybe she was right about this lifestyle, the house, the car, all being totally excessive and irrelevant to his happiness. That sentiment lasted about five seconds, until he brushed it off and jumped into his Bugatti.

He roared down the drive and made it to the studio in twenty minutes.

Mellie was arriving at the same time and drew into the spot next to him.

'Not a bad car for a man that's got more debt than a third-world nation.'

Jesus Christ, what was it with the women in his life? There wasn't one of them that wasn't busting his balls these days. Although, the moment Mellie Santos started being sweetness and light to him, he'd know he must only have a short time to live.

'Not letting it go,' Davie told her, shaking his head. 'Soon as I show up here in a Prius, the tabloids will pronounce me over. And that's worse than being poor or dead.'

'Let's hope we don't have to find out if that's true,' Mellie murmured. 'Is it just me or does this feel like the Alamo? And we're on the wrong side?'

Davie didn't argue. They were four weeks away from the end of the initial six-month contracted run, and right now, the chiefs at the Fame Channel were waiting in the boardroom to discuss the future of the show.

Six weeks ago, he'd thought he'd solved his problems, thanks to his very favourite country superstar. Lainey had delivered as promised and the twenty million dollars had been in his bank by the end of that week. Davie had been like a twenty-one-year-old that had just got his first credit card. The only way to get out of the situation, to raise the profile, was to spend. And shit, twenty million didn't last long when you were trying to save a show and make it the hottest thing on TV. He'd booked the biggest stars, paid them handsomely and had a 100 per cent cancellation fee written into their contracts if they didn't show. He'd bought thousands of clicks and likes on social media. He'd upped the advertising, spending fortunes on TV ads on other channels, on radio commercials and billboards. That was why his face, and his laconic grin, now stared down at everyone driving along Sunset Boulevard.

Throw in the fact that he had gone back to his initial strategy of no-holds barred discussions, and there had definitely been a dramatic shift in both the perception and popularity of the show.

Some of the best moments had gone viral. Camilla Cass had finally come on and told an outrageous story about a three-way with actress Mercedes Dance and actor Charles Power. Charles's wife had left him (again – it was a regular occurrence), and both him and Mercedes were threatening to sue, but Davie knew they were bluffing. Both of their careers were in a slump and this was giving them the kind of relevance money couldn't buy.

Logan had done him the biggest favour and got the whole of South City on the show to discuss a reunion. It would never happen, but that had got the under-thirty demographic tuning in and saturating social media with memes and overdramatic celebrations.

And it was all working.

Ratings had soared. People were talking about him again and he was getting the chance to remind everyone who he was and why he was the best at what he did. Fallon, Kimmel, Colbert and that bloke with the Carpool Karaoke schtick couldn't touch him.

The network had to be feeling that too.

Loaded up on bravado, Davie went in all swagger and big dick energy. His phallus soon shrivelled when he saw who was waiting there.

Clint Hunt (yes, Davie really had to be careful with that one), chief of the Fame Channel, was bordered on both sides by lawyers. That wasn't good. If they were going to talk about a future, then there would be someone there from marketing, from advertising and from production. Shit.

Hunt got straight to it. 'We're not renewing, Davie. I'm sorry.'

Davie barely let him finish. 'Don't be so fucking stupid, Clint. We're on the up. We're coming into our moment. Another few months and we'll be the biggest show on your network.' That was true. And then Davie's value would rise, and the big networks would start a power play for him. Right now, they were waiting to see if he could sustain this. He just needed a few months longer to prove that he could. No matter what, America loved a comeback story.

'Another few months and you'll be out of funds, Davie.'

Dread and fear were making Davie's hands sweat. How the hell did Hunt know that? Sure, he was cutting it close, but he knew he could still turn this around. Advertising was beginning to rise again and bringing in the revenue he needed to balance the books, so he was going to find a way to keep that going. Just a bit longer. That's all he needed. But if he didn't get it...

He was sweating all over as a voice in his head answered that. If he didn't get more time to make this work, he'd be left with nothing except a whole shitload of debt.

'Look, Davie, I'm not here to drag this out and there's no negotiation on it. The truth is, we've been offered another show for your slot and the terms are way more favourable. It's a done deal.'

Another show? Offered by who? What. The. Fuck?

Davie's brain exploded.

He'd gone in there all guns blazing.

And they'd shot him dead.

'Sorry, Davie. No hard feelings.'

Hunt stood up, motioned to the lawyers to follow him. When they trooped out of the room, spineless fuckers that they were, Mellie sighed.

'What do you reckon, boss. Time to order the Prius?'

Before he could answer, his phone rang. Mirren. The one person he never ignored.

She bypassed the niceties.

'Davie, can you get over to Zander's house? We have a problem.'

17

SARAH

'Don't Lie To Me' – Barbra Streisand

Sarah had been waiting for half an hour outside the coffee shop that her target went to every day for lunch. She knew that because Shandra Walker, her brilliant researcher at *Out of The Shadows*, a USC graduate who'd majored in journalism and minored in communication technologies, had found out more about Monica Janson than her best friend, her mother and the IRS combined. Shandra was also on the university's athletics team, so she'd taken to running past Monica's place of work every lunchtime. That's when she'd realised that every single day at noon, Monica came to the Sweetbitter Café, bought one decaf coffee, one water, an avocado on rye sandwich, and walked around the little park right next to it for forty-five minutes before getting in her car and driving back to work on the Lomax lot.

Monica Janson had been Wes Lomax's secretary and personal assistant for forty years of her life and she'd been notoriously well rewarded for keeping his secrets. Rumour had it that on top of her generous salary, he gave her a Chanel bag and a ten-thousand-dollar allowance every Christmas for one of the best plastic surgeons in the city. Monica obviously followed the Jane Fonda path of 'little and often' and kept it looking natural. No duck pout. No wind-blasted face. No frozen forehead. That's probably why, despite being sixty-six last month (another nugget of information established by Shandra), she could pass for a woman in her mid-forties.

Sarah knew exactly what she looked like. It had been just one of many shocking discoveries in her investigation so far. She'd googled Monica's name and the recognition was instant. Monica's face was imprinted in her brain. The reception at the Beverly Hills hotel. The woman who had caught her eye. The connection. Then Monica had glanced away. Did she know? Had she seen something?

Sarah had a hunch that Monica was a smart cookie who would remember her too. That's why she had held off on this moment, waited until she was ready and prepared to show her hand, before coming here to speak to her.

Over the last few weeks and months, Sarah had been obsessed with this investigation. She'd followed up on every single lead and chased down every person mentioned in her interviews, while being respectful of their boundaries and trauma.

Lisa, the British actress who had shared her story with Sarah right at the start, had been an invaluable help. She'd put the feelers out, talked to friends, worked tirelessly on connecting with other women who shared her pain, and the results had been horrific. They'd tracked down woman after woman – there had been seventeen so far – who had been assaulted or violated at the hands of Wes Lomax. Sarah had spoken to them all, either by phone, video call or in person, leaving it up to them to decide how to communicate. She never pushed, and she never led the conversation, preferring that they tell her their story in whatever way they were comfortable. Some were angry, some broken, some sad, some devastated, their vulnerability achingly obvious as they shared their experiences. She'd also stopped being surprised that most of their stories had stunning commonalities. He'd invited them somewhere on the pretext of a confidential chat about their ambitions, their work, or their prospects, and once there, he'd dropped all pretence and gone straight in for the sexual thrill. In some cases, he'd given the woman a drink that had caused her to feel unwell; in others, he had just used his power or his physical strength to get what he wanted. He was a monster. And Sarah was consumed with slaying him.

There was just one, recurring, major problem. None of the women wanted to go on the record. She'd hoped that the strength of the #MeToo movement would somehow empower them to stand in their truth, but, understandably, the women didn't want to let Wes Lomax take their privacy, their anonymity or any chance they still had of forging a career in this industry. Even now he was retired, he still had the power to kill careers, blacken names and have projects cancelled on a whim. That's why, months after she'd begun the hunt, she'd come to the conclusion that she needed something else: the smoking gun. She needed someone with first-hand knowledge of his behaviour and his crimes to come over to their side and expose him for the psychopathic monster that he most definitely was.

That was why she was still standing outside a café, just off San Vicente Boulevard, waiting for Monica Janson to get here. Sarah's logic on this was simple. Monica was in story after story that she'd heard from Wes's victims, either introducing them, showing them to his office or suite, or even, in some chilling cases, seeing them out after they'd been with him. Surely she must have known something, must have suspected?

The problem was obvious, though. There was a very real possibility that as soon as Sarah spoke to Monica, she'd go running back to Wes with the story, and the bastard would bury her in litigation until the end of time. However, at this point she was all out of options, so all she could do was take her chances and pray that Monica had a soul and a conscience.

'Hey, has she appeared yet?' The voice beside her made her jump, and Sarah's head whipped around.

'Lisa! What are you doing here?'

'Would you believe me if I said I was just passing?'

'Definitely not.'

Sarah's heart sank. She should never have mentioned that she was coming here today. It had been a passing comment yesterday, when Lisa had called to give her the contact details for someone else who might have had experience of Wes Lomax's violence. Lisa was still wavering about taking the stand and Sarah understood that. Speaking out against Weinstein had wrecked the careers of many, sometimes before they'd even got off the ground. Lisa wasn't ready to say goodbye to any tiny chance she still had of reclaiming the professional life she'd worked so hard for. However, Sarah was coming to realise that Lisa's obsession with bringing down Lomax had become as all-consuming as her own. Every day, there was a message or a question from her, and Sarah had seen her in online forums time and time again, asking questions about Wes, making implications, writing blind pieces that other victims would recognise, always careful to stay on the right side of any kind of slander or potential litigation. Of course, she used an anonymous profile, but Sarah knew it was her. MancGirlHollywood was her pen name. It hadn't been hard to work it out.

Sarah's feelings were torn. On the one hand, she understood Lisa's pain and her need for justice, but on the other, she was getting concerned that Lisa's fixation was becoming unhealthy for her. Her third worry, that Lisa would get caught in the crossfire of the investigation, was niggling at her too.

'I just needed...' Lisa began, then paused. Changed tack. 'I don't know what I needed. I just wanted to be anywhere but at home. I don't know what else to do any more.'

Sarah reached for her hand and held it. 'Honey, I get it and I'd probably feel the same...'

Lisa sensed what was coming. 'But?'

'But I need you to leave this to me for now. I promise I'll call you tonight. I'll let you know every single time we make progress, and you can phone me day or night too, but I need to do some of this on my own.'

'I hear you.' Lisa pulled her beige chunky cardigan around her, and it struck Sarah how much weight she'd lost since they'd first met.

'Have you eaten today?'

Lisa shrugged, scanning around for sight of Monica. 'I think so. Maybe some toast.'

Prickles of anxiety made the hairs on the back of Sarah's neck stand up. That wasn't a normal answer. She made a note to check if Lisa had been visiting the therapist that *Out of The Shadows* had agreed to finance for her. Sarah felt strongly that they had a duty of care to the women who helped them, and Chip had agreed, setting aside a budget for counselling. Lisa had been the first person Sarah had referred and, as far as she knew, she was talking to the trauma expert twice a week.

'Wait here.' Sarah went into the café and came back out a few minutes later with a coffee and a salmon bagel. 'Here, hon, eat this. I'm worrying about you.'

Lisa took it gratefully. 'Thank you. And please don't worry. You don't understand. This is the first thing that's given me a reason to get out of bed. The fight had gone out of me, but I guess now that

I've got someone to talk to, someone who believes me, I feel stronger again.'

Sarah wasn't convinced, but she didn't get a chance to ask any more questions because over Lisa's shoulder, she saw Monica Janson climbing out of her car.

'Please stay here and keep out of sight. Keep your back to us so that she doesn't spot you. Let me do this alone.'

Lisa nodded, pulled out a chair at an outside table and sat down with her food, flipping up the hood of her cardigan and facing away from Monica so she wouldn't be seen.

Sarah took a similar approach, keeping her head down as she approached Monica, so she didn't get spooked and flee.

'Monica?' she began, when she reached her, although she already knew the answer to the question. Lomax's secretary was clearly someone who took very good care of herself. The work on her face was flawless, her long mane of chocolate brown hair gleamed and her body was the taut, well-postured frame of someone who never missed a daily yoga session. 'I don't know if you remember me...'

'No. I'm sorry.' Her easy smile indicated that she hadn't quite clicked that this wasn't an accidental encounter. Or that they'd met before.

'I'm a journalist. My name is Sarah McKenzie. I wondered if we could have a chat? Maybe a coffee while you're here?'

That changed Monica's demeanour and her eyes narrowed. 'Why? What's going on?'

Her eyes darted from side to side, until they rested on Lisa, over at the outdoor seating area. Of course, she hadn't been able to remain hidden, or facing the other way, too intent on watching what was happening. There was an instant reaction of recognition and Sarah cursed in her head. Shit. So much for trying to have a casual coffee and then easing into the real reason she was there.

Monica's gaze came straight back to Sarah as she made the obvious connection. 'You're with her.' She tried to pivot away from Sarah. 'I can't talk to you.'

Sarah darted around her, so she was by Monica's side as she walked quickly back in the direction of her car.

Two choices: let it go and leave the confrontation for another day, or understand that this could be her last chance, because as soon as Monica told Wes about this, he'd be straight on the phone to his lawyers.

'Monica, please. Look, I know she's made accusations, but she's not wrong. I know you must have seen things.'

That wasn't working. Monica's steps were just getting faster and Sarah could see she was about to break into a sprint. She decided to go for shock value.

'Monica, you saw me that night at the Beverly Hills Hotel. I know you remember. I was in Wes's bungalow. He attacked me too. I need you to hear that. There are many of us. You need to understand, to be on the right side of this. Please talk to me, or at least listen. I think when you hear our stories...'

She didn't get any further. Monica reached her car, wrenched the door open and jumped in, immediately locking it behind her.

'Damn it!' Sarah hissed, quickly jumping back so that she didn't lose her toes under the tyres of a Range Rover Evoque.

Exhaling, she tilted her head back, looked up at the sky, closed her eyes. Shit. She'd spectacularly blown that.

After a moment, she'd gathered herself enough to go back over to Lisa, who immediately greeted her with, 'I'm sorry. She saw me. I should have known she'd react like that. I'm probably on every security poster in the Lomax lot.'

Sarah shook her head. 'No, it wasn't your fault. She'd probably have bolted anyway.' Sarah wasn't sure that was true, but she didn't want to pile any more stress or guilt on to someone who was very obviously fragile. 'I'm going to have to come up with another approach.' She reached over and hugged Lisa, feeling the bones through the thick wool of her cardigan. 'I need to shoot back to the office. Can I give you a lift?'

'No, that's okay. I brought my car.' Lisa nodded to a beat-up old Toyota that was parked at the other side of the café. 'I bought a Porsche with the pay cheque from my first Lomax movie. Now I couldn't even afford the gas.'

It was a stark illustration of everything she had lost. Everything Wes Lomax had taken from her. A tiny piece chipped right off Sarah's heart.

'Let's have coffee tomorrow, okay? I'll text you.'

Lisa nodded and Sarah made a note to remember to do that, even though she didn't really have the time to spare. If she made it lunchtime, she could at least make sure that Lisa ate something.

They said goodbye, and Sarah dialled the office as soon as she got into the car. Meilin answered on the first ring. Before Sarah could begin to fill her in, Meilin cut her off.

'Has your phone not been blowing up for the last twenty minutes? Mirren McLean has been trying to get a hold of you.'

Sarah flicked to her notifications. Shit. A whole list of them.

'I'll call you back.'

She dialled Mirren's number, and it was answered straight away.

'Sarah!' Mirren's voice was as urgent as it got.

Crap. What had happened now? The dickhead who had been coming after her friend with his stories of their affair had been getting solid traction in the press and online. Mirren had told her, Hollie and Lou about the hook-up at their first Thursday night cocktail session after it happened. None of them had seen the harm in it. Mirren had been in a dark place back then and if that was what she'd needed to get her through it, well that was okay with them. They couldn't have predicted that he was a manipulative douchebag who would try to wreck her life.

The story had hit the press two weeks ago, when they were all in the depths of shock and grief, and of course it had gone viral. Sarah was pretty sure the asshole had hired a publicity team, because he was everywhere and he was spinning angles that were guaranteed to get his pretty face all over social media. He must have sold his story for big bucks because that kind of service didn't come cheap. He'd managed to turn a one-night stand into a meal ticket and a political cause, and Mirren was the target in the crosshairs.

'Yes! Sorry! I was trying to get an interview and I had my phone on silent. Are you okay?'

'Yes. No...' Mirren sounded flustered – another unusual event.

When Sarah had met her five years ago, her first impression had been that Mirren was the calm voice of reason, the clear-headed thinker in the middle of brooding, troubled Zander and ruthless, egocentric, extroverted Davie. Much had changed since then. Chloe had died, Zander had got clean, Davie's stock in the town had plummeted, and Mirren had remarried, but the dynamics of the trio had remained pretty much the same, with Mirren as the steady force in the centre of the maelstrom of the others' lives. If she was sounding agitated, there had to be something serious going on.

'Where are you?' Mirren asked, without stopping to explain her mixed reaction.

'I'm on San Vicente. Just heading back to the office. Why? Do you want to meet?'

'No, but can you make a detour? Can you come to Zander's place?'

Sarah pursed her lips. Bollocks. She did not have time to drive an hour up to Malibu today. She adored Zander and he was one of her closest friends. Also, she felt a responsibility to Hollie, one of the loves of her life, to take care of her husband now that she was gone. And, of course, there was nothing she'd refuse if Mirren asked. But the need to focus on the Wes Lomax case was like a burning fire in her gut and she hated to take her eye off it even for the people she loved.

That being said... Priorities. If Mirren needed her, she'd be there.

'Of course. Do you mean right now?'

'Yes. Soon as you can. There's been an incident and I could do with the help.'

'Oh God, that doesn't sound good.'

'It isn't. Wes Lomax is here...'

Sarah's attention immediately shot to 100 per cent.

'...and he's collapsed. I think he's had a stroke.'

18

MIRREN

'Sign Of The Times' – Harry Styles

After speaking to Sarah and Davie, Mirren hung up the phone and put it down on the cool cream quartz of Zander's breakfast island. What. A. Clusterfuck.

There had been something in his voice earlier, when they were speaking on the phone, that had made her feel so uneasy that she couldn't shake it off and had to come check on him. It was more than melancholy. It was... emptiness. The kind that she used to sense in Chloe, right before her daughter would get wasted or high.

She remembered the first time Zander took a drink. It was back in Glasgow, in the eighties, and they were about fourteen. Maybe fifteen. His father had taken a night off from screwing Mirren's mother and gone home to his own house, just two doors along a five-home terraced row on a slum estate that Jono ruled with fear, intimidation, violence and swagger. Zander lived in the house at one end. Davie at the other end. And Mirren's house was right in the middle. The three of them were inseparable, each other's insulation against the poverty, the neglect and the bleak brutality of their world. Somehow, when they were together, it didn't matter what else was going on.

Even then, Zander had been a guy of few words, but God, he was beautiful. Every single girl Mirren knew was enthralled by him. Not that she knew big words like that back then. And not that they actually told her either. Nope, the other girls kept their distance. Mirren had come to their school at twelve, when Jono had used his contacts to get them a house in his street because he wanted his wife and his mistress close to each other. Made life easier for him to go between them. Bastard. The girls at school already had their friendship groups and Mirren wasn't interested in trying to be included, so for five years of high school, as far as her peers were concerned, she was the weird, sullen girl in the corner with her head in a book, who didn't care what anyone said to her or about her.

But Zander Leith and Davie Johnston, the cheeky guy who had more energy than them all, were her friends. And she was theirs. The three of them against the world. No matter what.

The night Zander had started drinking, his father had come home with a couple of his sidekicks, and his mother had made a harmless comment that Jono decided to take offence to. He'd beaten her to a pulp – a regular occurrence – in front of them all. Then, without a care in the world, he'd gone to the pub and been the life and soul of the party. When he'd come out, Zander had been waiting, and when Jono had turned to face a wall to pee in the street, Zander had taken a baseball bat to the back of his head until it burst, then he went home and drank a bottle of straight whisky.

His dad never did find out who attacked him that night – his guess was that it was a rival gangster. For Zander, it was the first of many times he'd defend his mother, and the first step in alcohol addiction that had almost ended his life on too many occasions to count.

For a moment, when the niggling feeling had brought her to his Malibu home today, she'd thought that he'd gone right back to the booze and that terrified her, because if he had, it would mean he was on a personal crusade to join Hollie. And this world was a much better place when Zander Leith was in it.

Thank God, she'd been wrong. She'd got to the gates, punched in the code, watched as they opened and that's when she saw Wes Lomax in the open doorway. He saw her, raised his hand as if to wave, and then slumped down to his knees, before falling forward onto the gravel of the driveway. Mirren had raced in the drive, braked, flown out of the car and ran to him, her nervous system firing straight up to high alert. What the hell had just happened?

When she reached him and threw herself to the ground next to him, his face gave her the answer. It was pulling down to one side, and he was trying to speak, but only garbled sounds were coming out. She'd seen this before. A stroke. The other side of his face was red, as if he'd hit it on the way down.

'Zander! Zander, call 911. Zander!'

For the first time, her gaze went into the open-plan kitchen and she saw Zander, standing calmly at the island just a few feet away, emptying a bottle of Jack Daniel's into the sink.

'Zander! What the hell is wrong with you? Call 911 right now.'

That seemed to snap him out of whatever fugue he was in, and he slowly walked back over to the sofa, picked up his phone and did as Mirren ordered. Wes had passed out by that time, so Mirren put him in the recovery position, then shouted for a pillow and a blanket to make him comfortable. She then slipped off her fitness watch and put it on Wes's wrist so that she could monitor his heart rate, ready to do CPR if needed. She'd heard he'd had a heart attack a few months ago. Now this. Shit. Wes Lomax, Hollywood icon, wasn't her favourite person. Sure, he'd discovered them, but their relationship had hit the skids when she'd told him she was taking the Clansman movies back to Pictor after their brief two-film spell at Lomax.

God, he'd been furious. When she'd told him she wasn't renewing the contract, he'd picked up one of his Oscars and hurled it at the original Picasso on the other wall of his office, immediately wiping millions off his assets. 'Don't you fucking dare,' he'd roared.

Mirren knew she should probably be scared, but she wasn't. She'd known the worst that a psychopathic, evil bastard could do to her, and this didn't even come close. 'I dare, Wes,' she'd replied calmly, before walking out the door, hearing his bellowing rage behind her.

That was the last time she'd seen him, but that didn't mean she was going to step over a sick man.

When the medics arrived, they took over, and when he left in the ambulance, he was stable and breathing. Wes Lomax didn't die. Not on her watch.

Now, in the aftermath of the chaos, all she cared about was making sure Zander was ok.

'That was Sarah on the phone. She's on her way over. Davie too.'

Zander shrugged. 'They don't need to be here, Mirren. I'm good. I don't need babysitters.'

Mirren pushed back. 'Zander, you just calmly ignored a man who dropped down in front of you.'

He shrugged. 'Just like Hollie did. How come he gets to live? Hollie was worth so much more than him.'

Fear was making Mirren's skin itch now. This wasn't Zander. This was someone called Grief. Called Heartbreak.

She checked herself, remembering what she'd seen when she arrived. He needed love and support right now, not questions and challenges. He was on the sofa now, so she went over and sat next to him, put her head on his shoulder, their usual positions when they were alone and sorting out the world.

'I saw you pouring the whiskey away. I'm proud of you.' She was wearing jeans and sliders, so she kicked off the shoes and curled her legs up beneath her.

'I don't know how long I can keep doing that,' he said, and she could hear the raw honesty in his words.

'That's okay. Just as long as you tell yourself not to do it today. And then tomorrow you do the same thing. I don't want to pour on the emotional blackmail, but you got clean for Chloe. I think you need to stay that way for Hollie. She loved you, honey. Seeing you go back there would break her heart.'

His reply came out as a low rasp. 'I know.'

They sat in silence, just like that, for a while, both of them lost in their own worlds. It was Mirren who broke the silence first, when she spotted the red marks on Zander's knuckles. Her first thought was that he'd punched a wall out of anger or frustration. It wouldn't be the first time.

'I'd hate to see the other guy,' she said, gently touching the inflamed skin with her thumbs.

'You did see him.'

'Wait, what? Do you mean Wes? You punched him? Why?' She lifted her head so she could see his face. Zander wouldn't lie to her, but if he tried to fudge the truth, she'd see it on his face.

He shrugged. 'He's got a big mouth. Pissed me off. Anyway, you want to tell me what's happening with you?'

Mirren knew he was deflecting, but she wasn't letting it ride. She hadn't told him about Jason Grimes or about the absolute shitshow of a media frenzy he was whipping up. Appearances on celeb gossip shows. Influencer blogs. Relentless social media posts. The unremitting self-promotion. The asshole even had his own website and a weekly podcast now. However, it was the manipulation of the facts, the lies and his insistence on riding the back of the social justice zeitgeist that was the toughest thing to deal with. The headlines had been crushing.

Mirren Mclean Targets Young Employee For Sex.
#MeToo #MenToo
When The Predator Wears Heels – The Twisted Needs of Mirren McLean

And her personal favourite...

#MeToo – The Wolf In Clansman Clothing.
#victimequality #notallpredatorsaremen

Her legal team were sending out cease-and-desists on a daily basis, but it was like playing Whac-A-Mole – the minute one was shut down, another one appeared.

Legal action was difficult because Grimes stopped short of putting lies in print and stuck to the facts – he was twenty-two years younger than her, it was the daytime equivalent of a one-night stand, she was his employer. He then spoke of his 'feelings' – that his job was at risk if he didn't comply, that she wouldn't take no for an answer, that she could damage his future career if he didn't submit to her demands. He'd taken every true and worthy emotion of many of the women who had shared their personal stories of abuse in the #MeToo movement and manipulated them for his own gain. And there wasn't a damn thing Mirren could do about it because she'd given him the ammunition to blow her life up. He had everything he needed to portray her as the female equivalent of all the casting-couch wankers who ever thrived here – the ones with the power, who wielded that in return for sex and cheap thrills. It was every bit as tawdry as it sounded and it felt like the world was believing it.

Over at the *Hollywood Post*, Lou was mitigating as much as possible with counter articles and some opinion pieces coming to Mirren's defence, pointing out the lack of substance to his claims, but of course, they weren't getting the same traction as the scandal pieces.

There were only two consolations in the whole devasting saga. The first was that Mike had managed to escape relatively unscathed by releasing the news that they'd been separated for over a year and were in the process of divorcing. Even the thought of that made her catch her breath. Mike. Her love. And she'd lost him because of her own damn stupidity.

The only other comfort was that Zander Leith didn't know a thing about it because he didn't do social media, he hated the celeb websites and he had been living in a vacuum of grief, regret and isolation since Hollie died.

Now he was asking her what was going on and she wasn't going to volunteer the information.

'Nothing, why?' she replied to his question.

He nodded slowly, face set in firm irritation. 'Okay, so we're lying to each other now. Good to know.'

She should have known better than to try.

'Mike and I are over. I messed up.' Once that bit was out, the rest came right behind it, and Zander just held her gaze, listened until she was done. No tears fell down her face, and there was no self-pity, because the reality was that no matter what she'd been through, it didn't even come close to what had happened to Zander.

'So there it is,' she finished. 'One mistake, a devious prick and it's all my own fault. Thoughts?'

If this had happened at any other time, Zander would have been the first person she'd have come to. His life had gone through such lows that he always boiled everything down to what really mattered.

'Mike shouldn't have left you. Fucking coward.'

'I don't agree. He was protecting his daughter from the shit-storm. He was right to do that.'

'So who is protecting you?'

That raised Mirren's blood pressure a few points on the scale. 'I don't need protection. I did what I did. It was a mistake. I'll ride the storm and I don't need anyone else.'

It was true. She'd never even considered for a second that Mike should have stayed and defended her. His daughter was what mattered here, and Mirren wasn't letting her toxicity spread to his family.

Zander wasn't buying it. 'I think the first time you told me you didn't need anyone else, you were twelve. Maybe time to change that tune.'

'Maybe you should too,' she challenged, surprised at how good it felt to get angry, until a realisation clicked. Why had he suddenly asked her what was going on in her life?

'Wait a minute. Wes. He said something about me, didn't he? That's why you punched him?'

Zander's silence was her answer. Crap. Wes had a heart attack last year, and now a stroke. Had the punch caused that? Or was it just coincidental timing? And if he didn't make it...

Had her one-time thing with that conniving little shit just caused the death of a Hollywood legend?

19

ZANDER

'How Long Will I Love You' – Ellie Goulding

Zander truly didn't care if Wes Lomax lived or died.

He meant nothing to him. Once upon a time, he had mattered. Back when Zander first came to LA, Wes had made him into Seb Dunhill and then protected him in his early days of addiction. A few years ago, he'd given a speech at a ceremony to celebrate Wes Lomax's forty years in the film business. Zander still remembered every word.

'Ladies and gentlemen, thank you so much for being here tonight to honour a man who is one of the greatest producers we have ever known, one of the greatest visionaries in the history of our industry, one of the greatest inspirations to a generation of film-makers.'

He wasn't lying. Over four decades, Lomax Films had grown from one man with balls of steel and a vision for the types of movies people wanted to see, to one of the biggest production studios in town. In that time and since, Wes Lomax had been thanked by at least a dozen directors, producers and actors in Academy Awards speeches.

One actor had even lifted the gold statue and said something like, 'Thank you, God... by that, I mean Wes Lomax.'

That was the kind of reverence he commanded, and he had the receipts to prove it. Lomax Films didn't have the box office income of, say, Sony or Warner Bros, but they'd topped Lionsgate and Miramax for the last four years running.

In the early days, Wes had been like the father he'd never had, but Zander's feelings for Wes had changed years ago, when three things had happened. First, he'd got sober. Second, Wes had fired him when he'd doubted Zander's sobriety, and then brought him back only when Mirren intervened. And third, he'd married Hollie and he'd begun to see the world through her eyes too. Through eyes that hadn't been blurred by a lifetime of alcohol and drugs and fighting invisible demons that had carved their presence on his soul.

And one of the things that had become crystal clear was that the same psychotic temper and ferocious reputation that Wes had used to protect Zander in the early days came from the same School of Mad Bastards as his father.

Being with Hollie had changed everything for him. It was the first and only time he'd ever felt safe, felt in control of his life, felt... happy. Truly happy. Now she was gone and he knew, deep in every cell in his body, that he would never be happy again. It hurt just to breathe, just to exist.

'I'll be back in a minute,' he told Mirren, not because he had anywhere to go, but because he just couldn't be there, in a room with someone else, no matter how much he loved his friend.

He got up off the cream chenille sofa that Hollie had picked, walked past the dining table she'd designed, under the lights she'd had installed, and into the bedroom where she'd loved him. In every way. Now Hollie was ashes in a small oak box on her dressing table, next to the brush she'd never use again, the perfume she'd never spray, the make-up she'd never wear.

He lay on his bed, closed his eyes, and pressed play on his favourite movie in his mind, the one that was a collection of some of his most precious moments with Hollie, the ones that defined where they started, and how they got to where they should be. Married. Forever.

The collection of scenes that he'd watched on repeat in his head every day since she'd left him always opened with the same one. Back in the early days, when Hollie was his assistant and best friend, the person who fearlessly and loyally defended him to the world, but was never slow to berate, call him out and hold him accountable behind closed doors.

Opening Scene...

He was supposed to be on set early one morning, but, as usual, his excesses had derailed him and Hollie had stormed his apartment, to find him hung-over, with a random woman in his bed.

'Okay, hero, get up.' She pulled back the Pratesi sheets.

'I can't.'

'Don't make me kill you.'

Hollie turned to Dixie. 'Nice outfit. Look, honey—'

'Don't call me "honey". I'm, like, a feminist,' Dixie announced.

Zander closed his eyes. He couldn't look. No one should witness blood being spilt at this time in the morning.

'Okay, let me try that again, Hillary Clinton. Can you please do something for me?' Not bad considering every word was spat out through clenched teeth.

'Can you, right now, take your skinny, half-covered ass and remove it from my sight?'

'But...' Dixie began to object.

Hollie was one step ahead of her. She pulled ten hundred-dollar bills from her wallet.

'For your lingerie fund. Stick with purple – it's your colour.'

Fast-forward to the next scene...

A photo shoot for Adrianna Guilotti, the menswear brand he'd once endorsed, until a tempestuous affair with Adrianna had ended both business and pleasure. That day, he was in the midst of yet another of his endless attempts to get sober, although he hadn't yet said goodbye to his other vices.

Hollie appeared at his side. In her jeans and white shirt, she was a healthy contrast to the skeletal, black-clad fashionistas who had worked on the shoot.

'Man, that lot need to go eat a pie,' she murmured at the retreating crowd, before continuing, 'Okay, I'm off the clock and I finally have a date with a real, live man tonight. But if there's any possibility whatsoever that you're going to go sample anything stronger than coffee at the bar, I'll stick around.' She went misty-eyed. 'Ah, the good old days – gutters and groupies. I miss the old fuck-up you sometimes.'

Zander threw an arm around her. 'Me too. Who's the date?'

Her eyebrows shot up, always an early warning system for acute irritation. 'What are you, my dad? The morning I pulled a stripper called Stardust out of your bed, you lost the authority to judge my relationships.'

Fast-forward...

Hollie had just picked him up from the airport after a trip to New York and he was explaining to her that his affair with Adrianna was over.

'I told her I wanted her to leave her husband.'

'Oh dear Christ, you didn't,' Hollie exclaimed, taking her eyes off the road to look at his stony face. 'Oh dear Christ, you did. And she turned you down.'

Hollie's eyes were wide as he nodded ruefully. 'Yep. And now's the time you tell me what a dick I've been,' he said, resigned to the truth.

'Zander, I've been with you for ten years. You've made so many fuck-ups that on your scale of dickdom, this barely makes a spike.'

Fast-forward to the next scene...

After Chloe died, and he'd got sober, yet he'd tested positive for drugs. It turned out Adrianna's powerful husband had arranged for the results to be falsified. Wes didn't believe him, but Hollie did.

'I. Didn't. Use,' he told her, praying that she'd see his truth.

Her gaze had locked on his. 'I know. I believe you.'

'Why?'

God knows, he'd lied to her before, usually right before she found him lying upside down in a pool of his own vomit beside a dumpster in a strip club's alley.

'Because if you were using, then right now you'd be ranting and raging and you'd probably have punched at least one wall on your way out. You get crazy defensive when you're guilty. But more than that, I've watched you every day since Chloe died and I know that even when you want to get completely wasted, she stops you. I think she always will.'

Fast-forward...

To the day when he'd suddenly realised that the only person whom he wanted to be with was the one who'd been there all along. And Hollie had made it clear that she wasn't someone to be toyed with. They were standing at a fence surrounding a paddock at Lex and Cara Callaghan's ranch in the searing midday sun.

'I want to kiss you. Is that okay?' he murmured, his voice thick with emotion that had come out of nowhere.

'No!' She pushed him back. 'Don't you dare. Don't do that, Zander.'

Her voice wasn't angry. It was something else.

Something he wasn't understanding.

What just happened had taken him completely by surprise. It wasn't planned. And, hell, she wasn't happy.

'I'm not some chick for you to play with. If you're going to be an asshole, go do that to someone else.'

Fast-forward...

The night in the hospital, after an explosion at an Academy Awards after-party had almost killed them and had hurt several of their friends, including Cara Callaghan. Just him and Hollie, in an empty room.

'I learned something tonight,' he said.

For the first time ever, Hollie didn't have a smart-ass retort, so he continued, incredibly calmly, sure of what he needed to say, even if he wasn't sure how to say it.

'When I almost kissed you at the ranch, it was spontaneous. In the moment. A reflex.'

Hollie nodded sadly. 'I know.'

'And I'm sorry. Impulse control has never been my strong point.'

'I know that too. It's okay, Zander – you don't need to say it. It's gone. I knew then what it meant, and I know now too.'

'You don't.'

'What?'

He totally broke the moment by laughing. 'Hollie, I swear you don't know everything.'

'I do,' she retorted automatically.

'I love you.'

'I know that,' she said, softer now, like a friend reassuring another.

'No, Hollie...' He was getting exasperated. 'I actually love you.'

Their eyes were locked now, hers questioning, his hoping.

'Zander, I can't. I know you too well. This will pass, like everything else. Like the booze. Like the pills. Like Adrianna fricking Guilotti. Things come and go with you, Zander. It's your nature. It's who you are. I can't come and go.' Her voice cracked. 'I just can't.'

He reached over, put his hand on the side of her face, wiped away the tear that was falling there.

'Hollie, tonight with Lex, I watched him suffer because he thought he could lose Cara and I realised the one person I couldn't lose was you. It's

not a craving, or an obsession, or the need for a fix. I just love you. And not as a friend. As you.'

He leaned forward, kissed her, and breathed again when he felt her arms go around his neck. Eventually, her mouth left his as she pulled him into an embrace.

'Zander,' she whispered in his ear.

'What?'

'I love you.'

'You do?' he teased.

'I do. But if you fuck this up, I'll kill you.'

Fast-forward...

Their wedding day. On the beach in front of Mirren's home, when the most incredible woman he'd ever known had agreed to be his and he'd become the luckiest guy who ever lived when he agreed to be hers.

'Zander, Hollie...' Mirren, who was officiating the ceremony, reached for them, gently pulled them towards her so they were facing each other.

'Zander Leith, with the powers invested in me by an ordination website...'

Laughter.

'Do you take Hollie Callan to be your lawfully wedded wife, to have and to hold her, to love her, adore her and be faithful to her always?'

'Always, the lady said,' Hollie repeated for emphasis. 'That means forever.'

'I do,' Zander said, laughing.

'And, Hollie Callan, do you take Zander Leith as your lawfully wedded husband, to have and to hold, to love, to cherish, to keep on the straight and narrow and out of trouble... Always?'

'Yes. Yes, I fricking do.'

'Then I now pronounce you man and wife.'

The applause had thundered, just like the roar of pain in his head did now.

The scene in his mind faded, while inside he screamed, begging her to come back. The pain of this, oh God, the pain was unbearable. Physical. The kind that should only ever be inflicted with anaesthetic, but Zander had none, and that made this evisceration of his heart, his gut, his soul, too much to bear.

He couldn't do this life. Not without her.

So no... Zander truly didn't care if Wes Lomax lived or died.

Because without Hollie, he didn't care if he lived or died either.

20

SARAH

'Don't Let Me Down' – The Chainsmokers

'Siri, call Meilin Chong.'

Sarah had just turned onto the Pacific Coast Highway and was racing along the straight stretch of road that would take her right up to Zander's home at Broad Beach, when she made the call. Meilin answered on the second ring.

'I'm already hearing it,' Meilin blurted. 'They took him to the emergency helipad at Zuma Beach and they're flying him to Cedars Sinai.'

'Any word on how he is? I heard it's a stroke?'

There was a splutter at the other end of the line. 'Where did you hear that?'

'I'll fill you in later.' Sarah wasn't prepared to say on the phone. If it wasn't out yet that this had happened at Zander Leith's house, or that Mirren McLean was there, then she wasn't going to let that slip on a phone call. She trusted Meilin implicitly, but there was still the slim possibility that someone in the office could leak the news. There were websites that would pay life-changing cash for that kind of info. Shows like TMZ had so many people on the payroll: waiters, concierges, hospital staff and every other trade that came into contact with a star whose privacy was up for sale. And if there were images or video to back up the scoop, the cheques were huge, so all boundaries were off and people would go to any lengths to get footage. The images of Michael Jackson being wheeled into the hospital where he'd be pronounced dead. Princess Diana as she lay dying in a car in a Paris Tunnel. Britney Spears as she was put into an ambulance during an alleged mental health crisis. And it wasn't just professional paps. Every mobile phone was a camera now, and most stars would give anything to return to the days when fans wanted an autograph instead of a ten-second video for their mother, their friends or Radar Online.

'Keep me posted on anything you hear, Meilin.'

'Will do. I'll let Chip know too. That fucker had better not die before we get to tell the world exactly who he is.'

Meilin had just voiced the thought that was ricocheting around Sarah's mind. No. Not yet. Don't let the bastard die before he knows what's coming.

It took another half-hour before she drove through the gates at Zander's house, and there was a tiny sigh of relief when she saw that Davie's car wasn't in the driveway. For the last few months, they had been like two satellites orbiting the same planet. They could see each other in the distance, they occasionally crossed paths when they were spending time with Zander, but since the phone call when she'd told him to back off, there had been no direct one-on-one communication. There were a dozen reasons she had to keep it that way, but in the rare moments in the early mornings or late at night, when her mind wasn't 100 per cent focused on this case, she missed him. Just not enough to take a step back towards him. There were too many entanglements. Too many conflicting priorities. He was just another complication and she was already dealing with plenty of those.

Mirren let her in and Sarah followed her to the kitchen island, where Mirren offered her coffee, then said, 'Sorry for calling you. I just panicked because I thought I was going to have to go to hospital with Wes and I didn't want to leave Zander alone, but it was a moot point in the end. They decided to take him to the helipad, so they wouldn't let me travel with him. I've called Monica, his secretary, and she's going to take it from here.'

Just at that, Zander came out of his bedroom and hugged Sarah, then retreated to the sofa. It was difficult to say this about Zander Leith, globally acknowledged as being one of the world's most handsome guys, but he genuinely looked like crap. Unwashed hair. Grey skin. Bloodshot eyes. Lips that had pale cracks of dehydration.

It wasn't only his appearance that concerned her, though. Straight away, Sarah could sense a tension in the room that she didn't understand.

'Did I interrupt something?' she asked, taking the mug of coffee that Mirren was holding out to her.

'Nope,' Mirren replied sharply. 'I just have a bit of an issue with Rambo over there.'

Sarah pulled out a stool from the underside of the granite island, mind racing to process their overlapping worlds. Just a couple of hours ago, she was staking out a coffee shop, trying to speak to Monica. All the while, Wes Lomax was here with Zander. 'Okay, you're going to give me it from the start. Including the reason you're pissed off with Zander.'

Zander came over from the sofa and caught that last line. 'Because apparently Mirren needs no one. Doesn't share shit with her friends. That's just how she rolls.'

Ouch. Sarah had no idea what was going on between these two, but she wasn't getting in the middle of it. If there was one thing she'd learned, it was that Zander, Davie and Mirren had complicated relationships with each other, vibes that could swing between, love, hate, loyalty, irritation, fury and support, but if anyone went after one of them, the other two closed in like wolves protecting the pack.

Mirren took the seat opposite her, and Zander filled up his own mug, then joined them, while Mirren ran her through what had happened. Wes had come here to persuade Zander to go back to filming, they'd had a disagreement, Wes left, but when he got to the doorway, he'd collapsed, just as Mirren arrived.

The whole time she was relaying the info, Mirren and Zander didn't glance at each other, not even once, sending Sarah's journalistic senses from curious to high alert. Something was up. They weren't telling her everything. But then, she hadn't been straight with them either. Time to change that.

When Mirren got to the point when paramedics took Wes away, Sarah felt a prickle of anxiety under her skin, just like she had on the day that she'd shared her story with the boardroom at an *Out of The Shadows* team meeting.

The difference was, these people here were her friends, and the problem wasn't that she didn't want to tell them, it was that she knew she should have told them before now.

She put her mug down on the table. Took a breath. 'Quite a day,' she said, mind still racing as to the consequences of what had happened here. 'Did the paramedics give any indication of his prognosis.'

'No, but I'm not sure anything is going to take Wes down. The bastard will live for ever.'

'I hope not.' Sarah spat the words out with such unexpected vehemence, Mirren and Zander both stared at her, startled.

'Sarah?' Mirren, perceptive as ever, tuned in to her anger.

Sarah exhaled. Took a moment. 'Okay, I need to tell you both something, but I need you to swear you won't tell Davie. Please. You'll understand why.'

It was one of her biggest fears – that Davie would find out, do something stupid and land himself in more trouble than he could talk himself out of. She couldn't have that on her conscience. They both nodded their agreement to her confidentiality request, with Mirren adding an, 'Okay,' in case it was needed. Short of getting it in writing, that was going to have to do. She inhaled, exhaled, spoke.

'Do you remember, at your anniversary party, I asked if I could come talk to you the next day? We never had the conversation because...'

That sentence didn't need to be finished, because both Mirren and Zander's faces shadowed. They both knew exactly what night that was and why everything else had been put to one side.

'Hollie was meeting you too,' Zander said, and Sarah realised he must remember the conversation. She wondered if every single moment of that night was now imprinted in his brain and hoped beyond words that, eventually, the worst of it would fade a little and allow the laughs and the love to take over.

'Yes,' she agreed softly, before going on, 'It was because I wanted to talk to you about Wes. I'm working on a story about the women that he's hurt over the years.'

That got Mirren's attention. 'What do you mean "hurt"?'

'I've spoken to more than twenty women who have been assaulted by him over the years. Credible stories. He should be sharing a cell with Weinstein so they can wallow in each other's filth. Zander, one of the women was in a Dunhill movie. Lisa Arexo.'

Now it was Zander who was leaning forward. 'Lisa?' Sarah watched him flip back through the memories. 'Lisa was great. The initial story arc was that Seb Dunhill was to marry her. The writers told me she pulled out of the next movie because of some kind of family emergency. That wasn't true?' As he asked, Sarah could see he was landing somewhere between confusion and shock.

'Wes Lomax raped her, then dropped her from the franchise.'

'The evil fucker. Hollie was right. She always hated him.'

'She was,' Sarah agreed.

'Shit, I should have questioned why she left.'

Sarah shook her head. 'You'd never have found out the truth. I can only tell you this now because she's just agreed to speak out. It's taken her a long time to make the decision, because we all know how much courage it takes to go up against someone like Lomax. Even then, it's still her word against his and that won't fly. Mirren, can I ask, did he ever...?'

They all knew what she meant, and Mirren was quick to answer. 'No, but when I met him, Davie and I were a couple...' Sarah still found it difficult to imagine Davie and Mirren together, but they'd been childhood sweethearts until the pressures of fame had caused them to split not long after they'd arrived in Hollywood. 'And then I had no close contact with Wes for years afterwards. By the time we were in the same circles again, I was married to Jack and I'd had a few massive movies, so I guess he didn't have any kind of power over me. Look, I've heard plenty of stuff about him over the years – his voracious appetites and stories about his high-freak factor. I didn't question whether it was all consensual. I guess I should have. Shit. What can I do? Tell me how I can help you.'

Part of Sarah's training to become a journalist on the crime desk of a tough Scottish newspaper was learning to isolate her emotions. She didn't do rapturous excitement. It was one of the reasons she'd adored Davie – his enthusiasm and lust for life were exhilarating and forced her out of her controlled, orderly box. At the same time, she could switch off fear and worry and she rarely let tears get the better of her. That's why the pools of water on her bottom lids took her by surprise and she had to furiously blink them back.

'You just did. Help me, I mean.'

Mirren's puzzlement was obvious. 'How?'

'You didn't ask me if I was sure the women were telling the truth.'

Mirren pulled the sleeves of her sweater down and hooked her thumbs through the holes in the cuffs. 'Because I know you wouldn't be telling me this if you had any doubt. Sarah, you're the best journalist I've ever encountered – with the exception of Lou, who would never forgive me if I said otherwise. You unearthed our secrets going back twenty years, and you were the first person to even suspect that there was more to the story. I'd never doubt you. If you're saying that's what happened, I believe you. And it's already making me think I should have left the bastard to die this morning. I'm sorry.'

Sarah felt a real hesitation. This was the moment that she should share what had happened to her, yet every one of her senses was screaming at her to stop. Shut it down. Say nothing. Mirren had already bought in to what she was doing. It would be easy now to ask her to use her contacts, to bring Lou on board, to deploy her power and influence to advocate on behalf of the women. Even with the trouble Mirren was having with that exploitative arse who was trying to mine her name for clout, she was still a force to be reckoned with in this town. Having Mirren on board would give the women's words more credibility, which was a sad state of affairs, but true nonetheless.

But then... she was asking other women to stand up and tell the truth, so what kind of hypocrite would she be if she didn't show the same courage?

'There's something else – and I want you to hear it from me because it's going to be part of the story we're running. The reason I want to do this is a selfish one. I want revenge. No, maybe that's not the right word. It should be justice. Or maybe both. Because...'

The other two were silent as Sarah laid out what had happened to her that night in the hotel. Wes's violence. Blow by blow.

Mirren was forward in her chair, holding her hand by the time she'd finished.

'I should have killed him this morning,' Zander said, his face twisted with fury, his voice low and deadly.

'You might have to get in line. There are a few people in front of you.' She was being facetious, but she knew there was probably some truth in there.

'And Davie doesn't know?' Mirren asked.

Sarah shook her head.

'No. It was the reason I called off the wedding. I thought I was ready and then Wes arrived. Davie had invited him, and despite what Wes had done to me, he had the arrogance to show up. I freaked out. I told Davie that I had concerns and that I was investigating Wes, putting together a story and that there were victims out there. I just didn't tell him I was one of them, because I didn't want to be responsible for what he'd do. He would have gone after him. You know it.'

Mirren's expression darkened and Sarah knew that she was going back there, to when she was seventeen years old, and Jono Leith had brutalised her in the most horrific of ways. When Davie and Zander had found out, they'd both gone running to get him, and Davie had once said there was no doubt in his mind that they'd have killed him. Mirren's mother had got there first, murdered her lover with a knife through the heart.

The scars were with them still, in every demon they'd fought, every flaw in their personalities, and every relationship they struggled to maintain.

'Maybe that's the way it should be,' Zander murmured, and it scared Sarah that he seemed to mean that. She made a mental note to speak to Mirren when they were on their own because she was beginning to wonder if Zander should be left alone. He seemed... unstable. Like a tinderbox that was just a couple of degrees off combusting.

'You're right,' Mirren acknowledged. 'So let's get this done.' She stretched over to the countertop, retrieved her phone.

'What are you thinking?' Sarah asked, hoping Mirren wasn't about to call Davie. This wasn't the time. That was a problem for another day. Before Mirren could answer her question, her call connected.

'Hey, Lou, it's me. Listen, can you call me back when you get this message. Sarah and I have a situation that needs your input. Thanks, darling.'

For the first time all day, Sarah felt a real burning flame of confidence and hope as Mirren hung up.

'I'm thinking that if we're going to war,' Mirren said with icy determination, 'then it's best to bring the cavalry.'

'Did someone say cavalry?' The three of them spun around to see the new arrival. Davie Johnston was leaning against the frame of the open front door. Maybe it was the relief of having shared her story, perhaps it was the solace of knowing her friends had her back, but Sarah felt something happen inside her chest. A pang. A longing. Love. Affection. Regret. Had she made a mistake in shutting him out of her life?

Zander and Hollie had lost everything in a heartbeat, through a situation that was out of their control.

Mirren had lost Mike because of one mistake.

Davie Johnston was the person she had planned to spend the rest of her life with. Could she live really with herself if winning the battle against Wes came at the cost of a future with the man she loved?

21

DAVIE

'Someone Like You' – Adele

It was difficult not to stare at her.

It felt weird sitting at Zander's kitchen table with Mirren, Zander, Sarah – just like so many tables they'd congregated around over the years. All Davie wanted to do was to look at her face, her eyes, the way her lips pursed when she was thinking about something.

There was an air of sadness around her, and Davie knew that it was because, like all of them, they felt the emptiness of missing Hollie. Zander's suffering was right there for them all to see. Davie had known this guy almost his whole life, mates before they knew they were brothers, and he'd seen him wasted, stoned, after fights, in gutters, in jail and detoxing in rehab, but he'd never seen him look like he did now. Davie's heart broke for him. He almost felt like he had no right to be crushed and devastated about the news that the network had just delivered, when Zander was going through so much worse.

When he'd first come in, he'd sensed a weird atmosphere – that thing where you walk into a room, and everyone looks shifty because they were either discussing you or talking about something you weren't privy to. Now that they'd been there for a couple of hours, the tension had defused. They'd had some food, and the others had filled him in on what had happened with Wes earlier, including the part where Wes had insulted Mirren and Zander had smacked him.

'Holy shit. I wish I'd had a ticket for that. What did he say?'

Zander shrugged, staring straight ahead, in some kind of lethargic, defeated trance. 'Nothing.'

There was a few seconds' pause, before Zander blinked, moved his head as if shaking off dust.

'Hang on, that's not right. He said...' He stopped, thought about it. This was obviously news to Mirren and Sarah, because they both unconsciously leaned forward, interested, waiting to hear.

'He said something about me being the second son of a bitch that's hit him. And then he said...' Zander paused again, frowning as he tried to remember. *'Your pathetic little prick of a sidekick tried that too. He's still paying. Fucking cunts, all three of you.'*

'Your pathetic little prick of a sidekick?' Mirren repeated, clearly confused. 'But who—'

'I think that little prick would be me,' Davie admitted, with just a hint of sheepish amusement. 'Although I'd challenge him on the little part. I've been working out.' Anxiety. Joke. He couldn't help himself.

Mirren and Sarah weren't even trying to hide their surprise.

'Spill,' Mirren insisted, forcing Davie to oblige. Why not? His career had already been crushed today. His finances had been devastated. He had pretty much lost everything. May as well go for the full bingo card of humiliation.

'It was at the Callaghans' ranch. After my fiancée ruthlessly dumped me.' Again, he couldn't help himself. His cheeky gob had got him into trouble his whole life, but it was the only way he knew how to handle any form of emotional situation. It was one of those flaws he should probably admit upfront in all new relationships. My name is Davie Johnston and I use humour at inappropriate times to deflect emotional situations.

Sarah tilted her head to the side, rolled her eyes, but he caught the way her mouth lifted a little at the corners.

'Anyway, I went back out to where he was waiting at the helicopter, and told him to leave, and then he said a couple of dickhead things, so I punched him.'

Mirren's jaw dropped. 'What the hell is it with the two of you grown men going around decking people? Have you never heard of debate? Or insults? Or, you know, some kind of twisted revenge? Jesus. We're not in Crofthill anymore, boys. Sarah, I apologise for the behaviour of these savages. They didn't get hugged enough as children.'

Mirren was trying her best to lighten the mood too. Although, in all honesty, Davie knew she wasn't wrong about Crofthill. That was the area of Glasgow they'd grown up in, and it was just how things were done. She probably wasn't wrong about the hugs thing either. His mum had three jobs and his absent father turned out to be a psychopath that he'd buried when he was seventeen. Not exactly a recipe for a balanced individual.

He noticed that Zander had zoned out again, but Mirren and Sarah were still engaged.

'I need more details,' Mirren urged him. 'So what happened when you punched him? Did he go down?'

Davie was tempted to lie, but he tried really hard not to do that to the people he loved these days. Besides, one of these women was the first love of his life, and the other was the second and last love of his life – they were already very familiar with his shortcomings. Was it strange that he didn't count Jenny, the only woman he'd actually married, as someone he'd loved? Their marriage had been something else. Lust. Crazy attraction. Publicity. The combination of two stars to make a meteorite. One that crashed and burned.

Mirren was still waiting for an answer, so he went with honesty.

'Nope. I fell when I punched him and he got a couple of ferocious boots in. He walked away without a scratch and I broke two knuckles, a rib and my balls were the size of oranges for a week.'

The two women could barely hold it together and Davie gave a rueful shrug.

'Go on, mock me. I can take it.'

'It's so tempting, but as the "ruthless ex-fiancée", I feel that it's no longer my place.'

That one nearly squeezed the air out of his lungs. That, right there, was what he missed. The shorthand between them. The sarcasm. The cheek. The way he made her laugh and she kept him humble. He wondered, for a second, what she'd think if she knew about the decisions he'd made over the last few months, the ones that had dug his financial grave. The thought sent a burst of nausea from his stomach to his windpipe, and he almost gagged. He couldn't think about that now. There still had to be a way to save this situation. There had to be. He'd been down more times than he could count, and he had come back time after time. He hadn't made this life for himself by giving up when everything seemed impossible.

There had to be a way and he'd find it.

'Have you seen him since?' Mirren asked.

Davie shook his head. 'Only at Hollie's funeral, but I didn't go near him. Not the time. Nothing to say. We're done. I don't need him. Sorted the finances out on my own, and just need to pull in the ratings now.'

It wasn't bluster – he really believed it was possible. And, right now, that started with getting back to the studio to do tonight's show.

'Anyway, while I'm glad to have made you people smile at my pathetic prowess as a warrior, I need to go. Tonight's show isn't going to host itself.'

Sarah turned to him, and he wasn't sure, but he thought he saw a twinge of sadness that he was leaving. 'How is it going at the studio? Did you get all the problems sorted out?'

'Sure did,' he lied.

'Did you just go around punching people?' Mirren teased. She'd obviously enjoyed the banter too, and he understood that. Her life had gone to crap over the last couple of months as well. Before he could answer, Mirren's attention caught something over his shoulder.

'Shit, look at that,' she whistled, grabbing the remote control for the TV and turning the volume up. On the screen was a video, obviously shot from a helicopter circling above the helipad at Cedar Sinai, showing a team of medics surrounding a stretcher, one of them pumping air into the bag attached to the patient's mouth.

'I'm Myla Rivera for the Fame Channel in Beverly Hills and you're watching video of Wes Lomax, founder and recently retired CEO of Lomax Films, as he was brought by air ambulance to Cedar Sinai Hospital after what is being reported as a stroke.

'It's less than a year since Lomax suffered a heart attack, which came close to claiming his life. However, my sources tell me that he had been in good health in the last few months.

'As of yet, Lomax Films have not released any word on his condition, but we will keep you updated on events throughout this evening.

'The biggest box office success for Lomax films has been the Seb

Dunhill franchise, starring Zander Leith. Leith has also faced tragedy in recent months after the brutal murder of his wife...'

An image of Zander and Hollie, taken at the premiere of *Dunhill 10: The Last Second*, flashed on to the screen. Zander was almost unrecognisable as the stricken, broken man sitting at the table, and Hollie... Davie had to swallow the catch in his throat. Hollie was so beautiful, in her stunning, life-affirming, utterly gorgeous way. She was wearing a white toga-style dress, her waves of dark hair pulled up onto the top of her head, then flowing down her back, like a Greek goddess. Davie missed her fearlessness, her straight shooting and the laughter that came from any room she was in, especially when she and Sarah had what they called their Trash Telly nights – wine, chat, and as many inane reality shows as they could fit in. His gaze shot to Sarah now and he saw the heartbreak in every shadow of her face.

Fuck. He hadn't even been there for her, to support her through the death of her closest friend. Even though that wasn't through his choice, it still stung.

'Switch it off,' Zander said with a solemn finality that made Mirren stab at the remote control, eventually turning the screen to darkness. Without saying a word, he got up and left the table, heading in the direction of his bedroom.

Before any of them could say anything, a phone rang, and Mirren's attention immediately went to the cell phone on the table in front of her. 'It's Lou,' she told Sarah, and Davie was perceptive enough to pick up that there was some significance there. Probably something to do with news about Wes's condition.

Mirren slid open the doors to the pool terrace at the back of the house and stepped outside. He took advantage of the moment to continue making his own move. He still had three more weeks of shows to put on air, and he had to come up with a plan to salvage his entire life. Much as he wanted to sit here all night with his people, neither of those things were going to get done from Zander's kitchen.

He got up to leave, and was surprised when Sarah did the same. 'I'll walk with you,' she offered.

This was new. In the months since Hollie's death, they'd been in the same room many times. On every single occasion, she'd avoided being alone with him, made sure they were never in a position where she'd be forced to have a conversation.

Now, she was walking with him into the breeze of the early evening.

He stopped at his car, worried about not saying enough, and worried about saying too much. Fuck it.

'I miss you,' he said softly, waiting for some kind of pushback. It didn't come.

'I miss you too,' she said, but there was a sadness there, a finality that he didn't understand or like. He should leave it. Let it be. Not push it...

'Look, can we talk sometime? I still don't understand everything that happened, and I'd like to. And I...' Still no reaction, no objections. He'd gone this far, may as well plough on. 'I need to know if there's a chance...'

The sadness he'd seen earlier was back as she shrugged. 'Maybe.'

A long pause and for once Davie didn't rush to fill it.

After what felt like a lifetime, she went on, 'I just... this thing I'm doing, the story on Wes, I need to see it through and I can't think about anything else until it's done.'

The tone on the last word made it clear this wasn't up for argument, but she'd given him enough to spark a tiny flicker of optimism.

It was enough. For now.

'I'll wait,' he murmured, hoping she heard in his voice how much he meant that.

With a sad smile, he jumped in the Bugatti and left the property, heading up onto PCH and past Point Dume and Paradise Cove, where, just a few weeks before, whole swathes of the land, canyons and hillsides had been reduced to ashes by what was now simply known as the Woolsey Fire. It had taken almost three weeks for the fire to be categorised as contained, and in that time, it had burned through almost 100,000 acres of land, from the beaches, up through the Malibu Canyons, across the Santa Monica mountains, as far inland as the Agoura Hills, destroying almost everything in its path and forcing the evacuation of more than 250,000 people. Zander had stayed put, ignoring the evacuation order, and thankfully the flames hadn't spread as far as his home. Davie had a feeling Zander would rather have walked into the fire than leave the home he'd once shared with Hollie.

He was worried about his pal – saying 'his brother' still felt weird – and today hadn't alleviated that concern.

He was thinking back over the little that Zander had said today. The altercation with Wes. The words Zander had quoted Lomax as saying after the punch.

'Your pathetic little prick of a sidekick tried that too. He's still paying. Fucking cunts, all three of you.'

Something about that wasn't sitting right. Rewind.

'He's still paying.'

Davie had no idea what the old fucker meant by that.

But he was going to make it his mission to find out.

22

Mirren
'Don't You (Forget About Me)' – Simple Minds

Mirren drove through the protesters at the gates of the Pictor lot and the very sight of her turned their volume up to a level that no amount of Simple Minds on her car system could drown out. Jim Kerr, the lead singer of her favourite band as a teen, was belting out 'Don't You Forget About Me'. This crowd wasn't showing signs of forgetting about her any time soon.

Months after she'd last shared the same space as Jason Grimes, he was still waging a publicity war, in order to keep himself relevant and continue to exploit the situation for profit and profile. In the main, the public and the leading celebrity sites had lost interest, their attention span unable to sustain any lack of new information for more than a few days. Even the entertainment shows couldn't move the story forward. Grimes's insatiable appetite for publicity hadn't waned, but he must be running out of stuff to feed the media machine. Even he had to admit they only had sex once. Which meant that the persecution campaign had lasted about a thousand times longer than their physical intimacy.

That said, he now had a cult following online, and had set himself up as some kind of advocate for male empowerment. One who now had over 100,000 followers on Twitter and charged five thousand dollars for a tweet showing his naked pecs and endorsing protein powder, hair products, skin cream, taking money from any hand that would feed him. There was a rumour that he had a song in production. He was auditioning for acting roles. And he'd mentioned several times that he had a couple of reality TV shows in the pipeline, which made Mirren's teeth clench. Everyone in this town knew the only 'real' thing about reality shows was that the word was in the title. Mirren couldn't wait to find out whether he'd be discussing their relationship in a jungle, an isolated house, an exotic island or after doing a jive to 'Maneater' on *Dancing With The Stars*. She hoped it was the former and some wild creature damaged him for life.

What was worrying was that Lou hadn't been able to dig any dirt on him yet, so that meant there was probably none to be found. No criminal record. No past allegations. Not even a photo of him peeing in public.

She was pretty sure that the rent-a-crowd outside were from the Grimes school of self-publicity too. Every day, they showed up around 5 p.m. – notably avoiding having to rise from their slumbers early. Mirren had no idea whether they were genuine, but there were a lot of buff, aspiring actor/model-type gents out there, with groomed eyebrows and hints of Botox, who seemed to become particularly vocal, especially when it was a slow news day and a celebrity channel or online gossip website sent a camera along to find out if they were still going strong. Their placards also contained lots of natty soundbites. #SLAYTHEPUSSY was her favourite today. She wanted to get out of her car and take a blow-torch to the predictable, yet hackle-rising #JUSTICEFORJASON.

To her right, she saw Mike's car, parked in his own spot and sighed. He was here. And even though their divorce was well on the way to being final, that would probably be no consolation later, when he would have to drive through the protestors, ending his day on the inevitable high point. *Good night, Mr Feechan. Here's thirty placard-swinging blokes, providing a natty little reminder that your wife shagged a rabid, twenty-five-year-old asshole while she was still married to you.*

What pissed her off most was that she absolutely agreed with the principle of the argument. Not all predators were men. Women could be abusers. They could exploit, bully, coerce those weaker than them for sex, for money, for kicks. There were plenty of powerful women in Hollywood, from casting directors to studio heads, and she didn't blindly believe that they were all above reproach. That wasn't in question here.

Her defence, however, was to point out that wasn't what happened in this case. Yes, she was 100 per cent in the wrong to sleep with the devious prick. She was, although separated, still married. He meant nothing to her. He worked for her. All of which should have ruled out any kind of sexual encounter.

The point that they wouldn't hear, wouldn't accept, wouldn't consider, was that, much as it was wrong on many levels, there was no coercion. No power play on her part. Definitely no force or promise of reward. He'd come to her home, uninvited, and as far as she'd been concerned, they were just two consenting adults, in a slightly age-inappropriate sexual encounter. End of story.

If only.

The regret would never leave her, and she would never get back what that one act had taken away.

The Christmas holidays had been a bitter foreshadow of what

was to come for her. Mike's daughter, Jade, had been family to her for almost five years, so, after getting grudging agreement from Mike, Mirren had video-called her to wish her a Merry Christmas. The teenager had been as dismissive as Mirren deserved. No arguments there. Mirren respected that she was defending her dad, and again, the Gods of Self-Flagellation repeatedly reminded her that she deserved it. But still... what really stung was seeing Mike and his ex-wife, Jade's mother, in the background, cooking breakfast, drinking coffee, the picture of happy families. It was all Mirren could do not to smash up her own phone with a tinsel-wrapped mallet.

It didn't help that Logan and Lauren were in Rio, doing a Christmas Special live from the Maracana Stadium. Their first concert together had been a spectacle the fans had been in a frenzy for since they first got together. They'd sold 78,000 tickets in the stadium, and it was being streamed to over fifty countries, so they were set to make enough to buy a private jet or a home next door to her with the proceeds. Not that they would. Neither Logan nor Lauren were ostentatious and while there was nothing but love between them and Mirren, they all appreciated healthy boundaries.

They appreciated loyalty too. It must have been embarrassing for Logan to have his mother's sex life plastered across every tabloid, but he'd never shown that. Instead, both of them had been unfailingly supportive and made it clear they had her back. She liked to think that if Chloe was still with them, she'd feel the same. Although, with her girl's tempestuous nature, she'd probably have tracked Jason Grimes down and wreaked some kind of sinister revenge.

That thought brought her back to Zander. He had been her biggest worry over the holidays, refusing to join her, saying that he was heading up to Yellowstone to camp, alone, to forget what day it was. Mirren understood, but she still gave him endless options, even at one point offering to go with him, despite the fact that she'd managed to avoid camping her entire life. Beds had been invented for a reason. A part of her had been relieved when he'd declined, but she couldn't shake off the devastating thought that he'd be alone. He maintained that was the whole point. He wanted to escape the empty house, the memories, the continued press interest in his life and Hollie's death. The trial of the woman who had killed Hollie had been postponed indefinitely, her lawyers were arguing that she was unfit to stand, and the media was still reporting every detail. No wonder Zander wanted to block it all out and get away. In the end, they'd agreed that if he called her every day, she wouldn't send out a search party.

With Zander gone, her family absent, Davie spending the day with Jenny and the kids, Christmas 2018 had been her most solitary one yet. She'd woken on her own, then Lou had come over and they'd eaten turkey sandwiches, watched crap Christmas romcoms, and plotted the demise of Jason Grimes.

The last one wasn't particularly festive, but it was her favourite gift of the day. Lou still had some ideas up her Chanel sleeve, and whatever they were, Mirren knew that Grimes wouldn't come out well. That pleased her way more than a Hermès clutch.

Sarah had arrived later with wine, cake and the latest on Wes Lomax. Still in hospital. Surviving but critical. As a girl, Mirren had wished death on one other man in her life, but now Wes was on that list too. Even Grimes didn't come with a death wish. Almost, but not yet.

After Sarah's revelations, even thinking about that fucker, Lomax, made her teeth grind. Mirren would quite happily head for his hospital bed right now and smother the bastard with a pillow. She didn't say that lightly. She truly believed that men like him, like Jono, like all the others who thought they had some divine right to violate a woman's body, to take whatever they wanted, didn't deserve to inhabit this world. However, she also knew that Sarah had to do this herself, her way, for vindication, revenge, justice, and all the other resolutions that would bring to Sarah and his other victims.

As Mirren turned into Malibu Colony Road, she shook off the memories and dark thoughts. Time to look forward. To find a way to salvage this month. This year. This life.

Now that the holidays were behind her, she had another focus. In Hollywood, there were three seasons: Summer, Fall, and Awards. Right now, they were in the middle of the third of those periods and, so far, it wasn't going her way.

Before the scandal, last year's Clansman release had been expected to be nominated for best picture, and they'd hoped for either a best original screenplay or best director nod to Mirren. As with all the contenders, the studio's push to have it nominated had been relentless. It was almost like a presidential campaign. Pictor had brought in a specialist PR company, Seamus Andrews, to co-ordinate it all – adverts, interviews, trade-magazine articles, screenings... Studios all became like political parties, vying for their man, woman or movie to win the prize.

None of those had materialised at the BAFTAs. There had been nothing from the Golden Globes, despite those accolades generally being an indication of where the Oscars would find a home. Nothing. Nada. Zilch. But every year there were exceptions and maybe this year it was the Clansman. Or perhaps the scandal had been the death knell for them all. Mirren was only a few hours from finding out.

At home, she showered, her hair wrapped up to keep it dry, then she climbed, naked, into bed. A few hours' sleep. Alone.

At 4 a.m., her alarm went off, and she put on a bra and some cashmere lounge pants, threw a white T-shirt on top and pulled her red hair back into a ponytail. She'd have been happy to sleep through, but getting up for the crack-of-dawn Oscars nominations had been a tradition for over ten years and Lou and Logan had refused to let her change that now.

By the time Lou arrived, Mirren had the coffee ready and some bagels and pastries on the counter. Carbs. In this town, they were up there with crack on the vice list.

Lou hugged her tightly. 'There's only one person in the world I'd get out of bed at this time for,' she told her. 'But, sister, you better make it worth my while.' Her gaze went to an apple Danish the size of a side plate on the platter a few feet away. 'Oh, honey, you just did.'

Mirren was still laughing when Logan and Lauren came in, both of them wearing running pants and oversized sweatshirts.

'I've got a good feeling about this, mamma,' Lauren told her.

Mirren adored this young woman, had truly taken her to her heart as the daughter she didn't give birth to. However, she didn't place much stock in Lauren's 'feeling' because her son's wife had a good feeling about everything. It was a natural and pervasive optimism that only a few were born with. Mirren had missed that boat.

The last to arrive was Zander and Mirren exhaled with relief when he got there. She'd been worried he wouldn't come. He was almost entirely reclusive now, rarely left the house, and she'd had to apply serious emotional blackmail to get him to come.

She caught Lou's gaze and saw her friend was thinking the same thing she was – how he'd changed since this time last year. He was a shell of a man. He'd lost at least fifty pounds. His face was drawn and pale. His muscles, formed over twenty-odd years with the best personal trainers, had shrunk, leaving him looking more like the sinewy, slim guy she'd grown up with. His hair was long and he was unshaven and – maybe this was the point – his fans would walk past him in the street.

He was here. That was all that mattered for now.

She had a sudden thought that she should have invited Davie and Sarah, but in all honesty, she'd been blocking this out and wanted it to be as small and insignificant as possible. Less people to witness her rejection by the industry she'd devoted twenty years to.

'It's starting,' Logan said, turning up the volume on the TV. He'd already punched in the link to the livestream.

On the screen, Kumail Nanjiani and Tracee Ellis Ross, stunning in a pale pink trousers and top combo, introduced themselves, before Tracee got straight to it.

'We are so excited to announce this year's Oscar's nominees.'

It was 5.20 a.m. An ungodly hour for this to be happening, but this was how it rolled and Mirren wasn't going to question it. The next few minutes could change so much for her. They could tell her whether she had a chance of riding out this year and salvaging some kind of credibility, or maybe, at least, if she was about to go out in a blaze of glory.

They all stared, transfixed on the screen, for the next fifteen minutes, until the category that mattered. She'd lost out on this award twice now. Won once.

'The nominations for best director are...'

A list of names. In Mirren's head, it was all white noise until one line permeated the buzz.

'Mirren McLean, for *Clansman: Man Of War*.'

The room erupted. Lou punched the air, Logan rushed to hug her, swinging her around. When she was back on solid ground, Lauren's beautiful face was pure joy as she kissed her.

This nomination wasn't forgiveness, it didn't say the town had absolved her sins, but at least this meant she was in with a chance of scraping back up to the top.

Zander put his coffee on the side table, pushed himself off the sofa and hugged her.

'Congratulations, Mir. There are no words to tell you how proud I am.'

'Thank you, honey.'

A pause. She felt her words fight to escape from the tight, anxious depths of her throat. She'd promised herself she was going to do this. Not just for her sake, but for his too. Do it. Say it. Come on.

'But, Zander, if you really are proud of me, then I need to ask you to do something for me.'

23

ZANDER

'What Becomes of the Brokenhearted' – Jimmy Ruffin

A couple of early-morning surfers floated right by him, barely glancing in his direction. How ironic was it that being out in public wasn't a problem for him anymore? For thirty years, Zander had been swamped with unwanted attention, with overenthusiastic fans, with people wanting a piece of him, and now? These days, he bore so little resemblance to 'Zander Leith' that no one recognised him. And that was fine by him. He'd never wanted to be that guy anyway. That Zander Leith fucked everything up, didn't protect the person he loved and lost everything as a result. Who would want to be him?

A ripple in the water brought his attention back. He'd been out on the surfboard for so long, his fingers were shrivelled, and the sun had reddened his face. There were only a handful of other wave freaks out, and if any of them knew the loner who was out here every morning at 5 a.m., they didn't say.

Maybe they knew he was searching for peace, but even here, on the ocean he loved, he couldn't find it.

He no longer believed he ever would.

He swam back into shore, barely glancing at the architectural brilliance of the homes that lined this stretch of sand. The first time he'd walked here with Hollie, when they'd come to view their house before they bought it, she'd stopped on the beach, peered at the glistening frontages of some of the most expensive houses in the country and shrugged. 'Meh. Gutted there isn't a beach bar, but I can live with it.'

They'd put the offer in there and then and the deal was signed. Their home. For the rest of their lives. They'd barely got four years.

Back home, he showered, threw on jeans and a sweater, both of which were two sizes too big for him now. Only when he'd poured a coffee did he check his phone. His interest in anything it was going to tell him was zero. None of it mattered.

Still, it would pass the time, and that was his biggest enemy now. Time. It crawled by, the agony of it excruciating, because every hour was an hour without her, and an hour further away from when she was here.

He checked his emails first. One from his lawyer, updating him on Debbie Butler. After countless psychiatric evaluations and reports, she'd now been officially deemed unfit for trial by reason of insanity and was being held without limit of time at a forensic psychiatric hospital over in San Bernadino County. Zander wasn't fighting the decision. No sane person could have done what she did. The problem wasn't his stalker's insanity, it was his own inability to protect his wife. And yes, he could hear Hollie telling him she'd kick his ass for suggesting that she needed a man to protect her. In their relationship, the opposite had always been true – she was tougher and braver than anyone he'd ever known. A few years after she'd first come to work for him as his assistant, she'd summed up the dynamics of their relationship perfectly. 'I'm like a nun who devotes herself to God, except Mother Teresa never had to drag her main man out of a crack den,' she'd told him. He could hear her voice now, see that smart-ass smile, and fuck, he ached for her.

Every day, he wanted to drink to get through this, to block it out. Every single day. And every day so far, he'd managed not to. That would be breaking promises, to Chloe, to Mirren, to Hollie, to himself. But the problem was, he could only see one other answer. The only other way to make the pain stop was if he wasn't here.

Every day, he thought about just letting this life go. Sometimes every hour. When he'd been up in Yellowstone over Christmas, he'd seen a dozen ways he could end this. Just a nick to the wrist and he'd bleed out before anyone found him. A fall from a ridge that there was no chance of surviving. So far, he'd been too much of a damn coward to make that happen, and that made him hate himself even more, but it was coming. Every day, he was getting closer. Bolder. More at peace with his decision. Every day, he had a few more reasons to go, and a few less reasons to stay.

That's why he'd agreed to Mirren's request when she'd found out she was nominated for an Oscar.

'I need to ask you to do something for me. I know you were invited to present the award in my category. Win or lose, I need you there that night, so I'm asking you to say yes.'

He couldn't think of anything worse than putting himself up there in front of millions of people, but there was only one person he'd consider it for, and that was Mirren.

The ceremony was only weeks away, and he still wasn't certain he would show, but for her sake, he had to be seen to be going through the motions.

Months of emails, letters and calls had gone unanswered, so he wasn't even aware that he'd been invited to have a role in the ceremony. Hollie had taken care of his affairs, been his agent, his manager, his world, and he couldn't face going through her correspondence, so he'd made a call to the only other person who would have all the information he needed.

He'd been with Lomax Films his whole career, and Wes's people would have been all over this, ensuring that their stars maximised their share of the limelight.

The phone was answered on the second ring.

'Lomax Films, Monica speaking.' So she was still there, even though Wes was no longer involved in the day to day running of the company.

'Monica, it's Zander.'

A pause. He guessed she was trying to decide if it was really him. Their working relationship went back almost thirty years, and although they swapped pleasantries, they'd never been friends because Monica made it perfectly clear where her sole focus and her loyalties lay. She worshipped at the temple of Wes Lomax. Zander had heard the rumours that there might be something intimate between them, but he'd never seen any evidence of it, other than her blind loyalty and devotion.

'Hello, Zander.' She sounded brittle, and he wondered if it was because of the reason Wes had come to see him, his refusal to return to set for the final shoots. He dismissed that possibility. He'd heard from his stunt double that they'd managed to use him and a few touches of CGI to get it in the can, and he'd learned it now had a release date. Wes's threat of recasting him would now go ahead and Zander was cool with that. His days as Seb Dunhill were over. He'd said no. That was a word that stars and the big players in this business very, *very* rarely heard , but Zander had just discovered its power.

His second thought. Perhaps she knew he'd had an altercation with Wes on the day he took ill. But how could she? There had only been two people there. Zander and Wes. And Wes still wasn't talking. Sarah had reported back that he'd been moved from hospital to a long-term care facility. He wasn't sure how she got her information, but he didn't doubt it was true. According to Sarah's sources, the stroke had devastated Wes's cognitive capabilities and he was confused, had trouble recognising people and communicating. He'd been left paralysed down one side of his body, weak on the other and unable to take care of his own personal needs. His speech was gone, although they were hopeful that at some point it would return. Zander hadn't even given a second thought to the ire that would come his way if Wes recovered. Fuck him. After what Sarah had told him, Zander was more than happy to take anything Lomax threw at him, because it would only give him an excuse to retaliate. And right now, Zander was desperate to pick a fight.

'It's been a while since I heard from you...' Monica said, with a sneer that gave him his answer. Wes had been ill for two months and she was pissed that Zander hadn't come to pay homage.

Again, that same thought. Fuck him. And her.

'... so this is a surprise,' she went on, without pausing for pleasantries or small talk. Definitely copping an attitude with him.

However, he needed something from her, so he knew it was obligatory to play the game. 'I know. Just... well, things. How's Wes?'

She didn't hesitate. 'He's improving every day. Getting stronger. He'll be back to full strength soon.' The company line. Lies.

Jesus, how insidious and pervasive was the cancer that was Wes Lomax. Again, the question that crossed his mind every single day. How come someone so vile had lived, when someone as decent and loving as Hollie had died? How was that justice? Where was the karma there?

A seed of a thought began to bite somewhere in his subconscious. He flipped it forward to the front of his mind. 'Ah, that's good to hear.' Another lie. Followed by, 'Where is Wes recuperating now then?' If you could fake sincerity in this town, you had it made.

Monica hesitated, so Zander applied the softest of pressure.

'I'd just like to send him some gifts. Let him know I'm thinking about him.'

That worked. Of course it did.

'He's at the Hurston Centre. A wonderful location. They're taking great care of him.'

Zander knew it well, from back when he was a frequent flyer to a nearby rehab, Life Reborn. It wasn't far, located just up Latigo Canyon Road in the hills above Malibu.

'Great, thanks. Well, if you're speaking to him, please pass on my thoughts. Tell him I'm praying for his recovery.' Another lie. He'd never been religious. Too many times, he'd watched his dad beat his deeply religious mother to a pulp, and she'd respond by praying for his soul, then sticking around to let him do it again. His whole life, his mum would go to church every single day, and stay there for hours, on her knees, begging God to forgive the man who did that to her. Zander could never understand what God would tolerate that. Or what higher power would allow Hollie to be stabbed in the street. No. There was no God that Zander could believe in now.

Just being adjacent to this world again was making his skin crawl, so he moved on to the original reason for the call.

'While I've got you can I just ask a favour? I've been invited to present at the Academy Awards...'

'Yes. Although I declined on your behalf when I didn't hear from you.'

'Okay. Could you see if that offer is still there? I'm considering attending.'

Her tone was one of surprise. 'Oh. Erm, yes. Certainly. I'm sure Wes will be pleased to hear that.'

'I'm sure he will.' The lies were still coming thick and fast. 'Thanks, Monica,' he added, before hanging up.

It would be funny, if it wasn't so nauseating.

Monica's blind loyalty to Wes had undoubtedly contributed to his success and his ability to keep his secrets hidden. But then, hadn't Zander been culpable too? He'd stuck by him, even gone back after Wes had fired him, and over twenty years his Seb Dunhill movies had brought billions to the Lomax bank accounts and elevated Wes from being the head of a successful, mid-size studio, to the omnipotent mogul that he'd become. That strength and power were just two of the reasons that he'd been able to exert his sick, twisted deviance on unsuspecting women.

Zander should have seen it. Should have seen him for what he was.

But maybe it wasn't too late to make that right. The seed in his mind was growing now.

For weeks, months, Zander had been telling himself that he'd let Hollie down so he didn't deserve to live. Neither did Wes Lomax.

He hadn't been able to protect Hollie, but maybe he could do something for Sarah, for Mirren, for all the other women that prick had targeted.

Maybe he could kill two birds with one stone.

24

DAVIE

'That Don't Impress Me Much' – Shania Twain

Davie's housekeeper, Alina, tottered towards him, carrying his breakfast and a whole shitload of attitude. Her ire was, in her mind, completely justified, because he'd just told her that he wasn't paying for her to go to Vegas to see Shania Twain in concert.

It was his own fault. A year ago, he'd have thrown in a suite at the Wynn for her and her husband, Drego, to indulge in their wildest sexual fantasies. Now he was thinking he might have to trade her Audi Q7 for a bike. One that she could use to cycle to an employment agency to find a new job.

She slammed his three egg white omelette with a side of avocado on the breakfast bar and strutted off in her six-inch stilettos, singing 'That Don't Impress Me Much'. Davie made a mental note to get someone he didn't like to taste his dinner tonight. Alina and Drego had both been with him for over twenty years and she was snippy, quick-tempered, and prone to outbursts of straight-talking brutality, whether the recipient asked for her opinion or not. But as Davie had discovered countless times over the years, she was fiercely loyal and if anyone ever threatened him, or insulted him, she would probably have the skills to kill them with her thumbs.

Talking of which...

'That's the face of a man who just looked in a mirror and realised his life has gone to shit, he was never as great as he thought he was, and it's too late to do anything about it,' his ex-wife declared, as she strutted across the kitchen, picked a banana out of the fruit bowl and jumped up onto the counter while peeling it.

Davie put his fork down. 'I preferred you when you despised me so much, your brain exploded every time I came near you.'

Jenny shrugged. 'That still happens, but I just remind myself you've fucked up your whole life and that brings me sweet comfort.'

He didn't have the strength for her this morning. Verbal jousting with Jenny required laser focus and pinpoint accuracy. Today he was so wrapped up in his feelings, he wasn't sure which way he was facing. After careful contemplation and assessment of his current state, he decided his only way out was to fight the Patron Saint of Smart Mouths and Bitchiness with schoolboy insults. 'I hate you, you know that, right?'

'I do. But deep down I know you also still imagine me naked every time you see me.'

He didn't even justify that one with an answer. Mostly because he was only human, so it was pretty much true. Even at forty-six, Jenny Rico was regularly voted the sexiest woman in Hollywood, giving rise to numerous rumours about a lifelong rivalry with the other Jennifers.

Miss Aniston and Miss Lopez had refused to comment.

Jumping off the counter, she dropped the banana skin in the concealed trash, then joined him at the breakfast bar. Her long tawny hair, so natural it was applied with glue and cost over one thousand dollars a month in highlights, rolled down the perfect arc of her back. Her body, in ivory gym wear, could have been etched from marble. Jenny Rico was a goddess.

She just wasn't the goddess that he thought about every morning and night. Which was just as well, because since she'd left him for her female co-star and occasional threesome partner five years ago, she had absolutely zero interest in imagining him naked.

They'd gone through every permeation of relationship emotions. Love, obsession, passion, disdain, disgust, hatred, anger and now? Well, now neither of them had the energy for anything more than familial bickering.

'Okay, what's going on? I've been here five minutes and you haven't called me a bitch and I just walked past Alina, and she didn't look like she wanted to kill me. That hasn't happened since the day I walked out of here.'

Davie picked his fork back up and attempted a mouthful of omelette, ignoring the heartburn that was now making his chest ache. 'She's pissed off with me because I won't send her to Vegas for a Reba McEntire concert.'

'Shania Twain, you halfwit,' Alina spat in her thick Russian accent, as she came back in wearing rubber gloves and a plastic apron. Davie sent up a silent prayer of hope that she wasn't preparing a dump site for his body.

Jenny raised her eyebrows as much as her Botox would allow. 'You won't? But that totally comes under the banner of buying people's affections because you've got no one who loves you. I'd have thought you'd have thrown in a suite at the Wynn.'

Sometimes she knew him far too well.

Alina was now singing, 'Man! I Feel Like A Woman!'. If Jenny joined in, he was leaving the building.

'Okay, time for some brutal truths and, for the purposes of this exercise, try to forget I'm your ex-wife...'

'Been doing that for years.' He was down, but he wasn't dead yet.

That one made her smile.

'...and realise that I'm the only person who is here right now that might be able to help, or at least give you some moral support. So. How deep in the hole are you?'

Davie pushed his plate away, stomach going like a tumble dryer and refusing to accept incoming sustenance.

'How do you know I'm in a hole?' He could bluff it out, salvage some pride.

'Because your bank refused to honour the transfers for Bella's dog trainer, her voice coach and her monthly cleanse of her chakras by her shaman.'

'Her what? Do I pay for that?' he asked, astonished, thinking his chakras could do with a power-hose right now.

'You did. Until the payment didn't arrive this month. So, how deep?'

He was tired. Exhausted. So bone-weary he didn't even have the energy to fight any more.

'I think the banking term is "fucked".' Probably the most honest statement he'd uttered to her in years.

'Oh, shit, Davie.' To her credit, her expression was one of being absolutely crestfallen for him and he believed her. She wasn't that good an actress.

Rallying, she pulled her shoulders back and let out a long, slow breath. 'This is me trying not to gloat. Just so you can put a name to this reaction.'

He didn't mind. She was entitled to it. Ex-wife privilege.

'Thanks. I thought it was just you doing one of those cleansing breaths in an effort to clear your dark soul.' For once, there was a sadness in his words. The fight had gone out of him, and that was probably as upsetting to her as it was to him, given that it was the basis of their relationship.

'Tell me, from the start,' she went on, the empathy dial back up again.

'*War and Peace* or bullet points?'

'Somewhere in the middle. I've got a vaginal steaming booked at noon.'

He was tempted to suggest she just eat pineapple instead, but he wasn't that brave.

Instead, he gave it all to her. All the gory details.

When he finished, her first words were a familiar reproach. 'I will never until the day I die understand why you used your own cash. Actually, scratch that. I do understand. It's because it was bring-your-ego-to-work day, and you're so conceited you thought you'd pull off some big comeback.'

'What choice did I have?' he bit back.

She threw her hands up in despair. 'You could have kept what you already had and retired. Made investments in other shit. You could have played golf. You could have realised that you had enough money to never work another day in your damn life...'

He didn't even need to object to that, because he knew she'd get there herself any minute now.

'But you couldn't,' she answered slowly, realisation dawning, 'because you couldn't stand the thought of not being Mr Davie Big Shot Johnston, of not being on the nation's TV's every week, of not being a player. Give me marks out of ten,' she finished, her words loaded with resignation, rather than spite.

'Twelve.'

'Shit.'

'Nope, hang on – it gets worse.'

She got up, grabbed Alina's not-so-secret bottle of vodka from the wine fridge, poured two straight shots into glasses and slid one over to him. 'May as well be drunk for this.'

He didn't refuse.

'You know we had a million fuck-ups in the early months of the show.'

'Yeah. You said that when you roped me in to bail you out that night. You still owe Darcy and me a weekend in Newport Beach.'

The vodka stung as it went down his gullet. 'Talk to my creditors. There might be a line. Anyway, I couldn't catch a break. The cash was draining quicker than I could make it on the advertising. Halfway through the season, I was out of money...'

'I feel like I'm about to watch a nerf gun blow up the Star Ship Enterprise.'

'But I could feel that we were getting there. I knew it. I just needed a bit more capital to keep going...'

'So you mortgaged the house?' Her astonishment wasn't surprising. They'd bought this house when they'd first got married and he'd fought her to the bitter end to keep it in the divorce. She knew how much he adored it.

'Nope, didn't have time. I accepted a loan. High-interest payments.'

'Oh God.'

'And part of the deal was that I put the house up as security. Now, despite the fact that we got a huge ratings boost and finally made it work, the network is still cancelling us. Says it's been offered another show on more favourable terms. So I'm fucked. And in case you couldn't keep up, I've wiped out every cent I have and I'm twenty million in the hole, probably closer to thirty by the time you take interest and taxes, with no job, no show, no way of paying it back, except to try to get a mortgage on this place, which, even if I could somehow manage that, I couldn't afford the repayments, because... well, no job, no show. The only solution is to sell this place, but the market has just tanked, so that could take years, and with every month that passes, I'll go further down the tube until there's nothing left.'

Slowly, stunned, she put the glass down. 'I don't think day drinking is going to cover this,' she murmured, and he could see that she felt something worse than anger, worse than disgust, or rage, or any of the other emotions he'd happily evoked in her over the years. This time, she felt... sorry for him. And that was tougher to take than anything else.

'Just so you know, I'd cry, but I'm really trying to hang on to my very last shred of dignity,' he said, with raw honesty.

Jenny lifted the bottle, poured another two shots, they knocked them back, then she poured two more. 'So much for dry January,' she murmured, screwing the top back on the bottle.

'Okay. Let's think about this. There must be a way.'

'There isn't,' he answered. It was all he'd thought about since the last show aired in December. At the end of it, in a face-saving show of optimism and denial, he'd announced that they were taking a mid-season break and would be back in the spring. By some miracle, the press and the blogs hadn't picked up the lie yet, probably because the channel was filling in the gap before the new show premièred with reruns of *The Kardashians*. Or something about Housewives of somewhere. He didn't know or care. It was only a matter of time before people realised he wasn't coming back and a new show had permanently taken his place.

Jenny wasn't giving up yet. 'The guys you took the loan from. Are they cement-boots types or Russian Mafia dudes or are they reasonable businessmen who might be inclined to give you some time?'

The thought of that made Davie laugh. Or it might have been the vodka. 'Not cement boots.'

'Good.'

'Cowboy boots,' he blurted, finding his own joke hilarious. It was definitely the vodka. 'It was Lainey Anders. That's who loaned me the money. She's got investors, and she brokered the deal.'

Lainey. His friend. The woman he'd elevated to superstar status when he'd put her on the judging panel of *American Stars*. He missed her. And he really needed to stop drinking.

His mind was wandering so far down that winding street of melancholy that he didn't even notice the frown on the parts of Jenny's face that still moved.

'Give me your phone,' she said, giving off pensive now.

'Nope. Last time I did that you discovered I'd shagged a waitress in Vegas and you cut up my suits while I slept. The Versace one was vintage.'

'Davie, give me your phone. Come on. I've left mine in the car and I need it.'

Reluctantly, he opened it and handed it over.

Her long, white, silicon nails began tapping the screen. 'I've blocked caller ID so they don't see I'm calling from your phone. Don't think there's anyone in town who'll still take your calls.'

Davie now knew exactly what it was like to be the kid who didn't get invited to all his classmates' birthday parties. Jenny kept tapping, and then he heard a ringtone, followed by, 'Cal Wolfe's Office, Araminta speaking.'

'Fuck you,' he hissed, trying to grab it back, but she moved it out of his reach.

Great. She was calling his ex-agent, one of his sworn enemies in this town, to gloat. Life over. He poured another vodka.

'Araminta, this is Jenny Rico, can I speak to Cal, please?'

'Of course,' was the chirpy reply.

In the pause, Jenny covered the mic.

'Don't be an asshole. When you dropped him, I took him on. Better the devil you know, and all that bullshit.'

Okay, that made sense, but he was too hazy on vodka to fully understand why.

'Jenny!' his arch-nemesis crowed, as she flicked him onto speaker.

'Cal! Listen, just a quickie – and don't make some sexual innuendo about that comment or I'll have you in court. Anyway, last week, when I was in your office, you were floating a guest spot on a new chat show. A singer, you said. Can you tell me who?'

Davie's lungs began to shut down. It couldn't be.

'Baby, that's top secret. If I told you—'

'If you don't, I'm going back to CAA,' she retorted, citing her former agency.

'Okay, but you didn't hear this from me. It's mega hush-hush and not going public for at least another month. Lainey Anders.'

Davie almost fell off his bar stool, as Jenny gave him a knowing, furious grimace.

'And who's producing it?'

'Man, you're killing me...'

'I've still got CAA on speed dial.'

For the first time in many years, this woman might just be giving him a hard-on. In all the drama of the divorce and the eternal bickering, he'd forgotten what a kick-ass, formidable, class act of a woman she really was.

'Okay, but again, my balls will be removed and used for juggling if this gets out. I only know because the agent on the deal has a big mouth when I fill him with cognac in my cigar room...'

'Go on.'

'Lomax Films. Before his stroke, Wes fronted the funding for this. It's already gone through, so his illness is irrelevant. Strange move for him, but hey, it fucks our friend, Davie Johnston, out of that spot, so I'm all for it.'

Jenny hung up, and the two of them stared at each other, open-mouthed, every single puzzlement in the story falling into place. Wes. He'd had Lainey front the cash and take his house as collateral. He was also one of the few people in town with enough clout to make celebrities pull out, to have advertisers cancel deals, to offer great terms to a network, and the money it would take to make Lainey's show would be small change to him.

He'd destroyed Davie's career, his finances, taken his home and wrecked his life.

The comment he'd made to Zander now made total sense.

'Your pathetic little prick of a sidekick tried that too. He's still paying.'

Davie was still paying – with everything he had.

And Lainey. She'd been his friend. Or so he'd thought. Yet another Hollywood rule he'd forgotten. Rule number one: don't use your own cash. Rule number two: they're only friends when there's something in it for them.

'Fuck. Lainey sold me out. And that bastard, Lomax, has played me. He was behind it all.' Even saying it out loud couldn't make it seem real, yet it was.

Jenny drained her glass, put it back down on the counter. 'Sure looks like it, genius. Question is, what are you going to do about it?'

25

SARAH

'Not Ready To Make Nice' – The Chicks

'Wait a minute, he what?' There were very few times in life that Sarah had genuinely been caught off guard by the twisted acts of others. Jono Leith's depravity was one. Catching her ex-fiancé back in Scotland with his pants at his ankles having a mutual masturbation session with one of her friends on FaceTime was another. And, of course, a few years back, when a crazed madman almost killed them all as revenge for being dumped by Lauren, now Logan Gore's wife, was another. Hearing Davie recount how Wes Lomax had systematically destroyed his life was now up there on the list.

Davie carried on, until the very last twist of the story.

'I have so many questions,' she admitted when he'd finished, her suppressed fury turning the blood in her veins to cold, hard ice. She hadn't believed it was possible to hate Wes Lomax more, and yet now she did.

Davie's call had come out of the blue that morning, asking her to meet for lunch. Her first reaction had been to say no. The Lomax investigation was taking every single ounce of energy that she had. Some might have backed off after he had his stroke, but it had only fuelled Sarah more. She had to nail him while he was still alive.

They were getting close. After gentle approaches that consisted of long conversations and assurances of support, she now had three victims who were seriously considering going on the record, and with Lisa and Sarah, that gave weight that was beginning to afford some kind of comfort to the network's legal team. It was all about framing it now. All about finding the way to tell the story that was the least litigious, because Sarah was under no illusion – Wes might be retired and incapacitated, but the Lomax lawyers were like a pack of wolves in a doggy daycare. There was a very good reason that Wes had survived forty-five years of intimidation, shady deals, sexual deviance and all round fuckery and never been successfully sued even once.

That's why she'd almost declined Davie's offer of lunch. She needed to focus. Now, sitting across from him, she was glad she'd come. Even though it was devastating to hear what had happened to him, she knew it was all part of the same story – the Wes Lomax playbook.

Sarah leaned forward, both her elbows on the ornate wooden table in the corner of Pump, the West Hollywood restaurant owned by former Real Housewife of Beverly Hills, Lisa Vanderpump. Celebrity restaurants weren't usually her thing, but she made an exception for the stunning sister restaurant to Sur, which featured in *Vanderpump Rules*, the show that had been Sarah and Hollie's guilty pleasure.

Sarah pushed down the twinge of pain that each memory still brought. Perhaps one day, when she thought of Hollie, there would only be happiness for the friendship they'd shared, but that time was not yet.

'I guess my first question is why? Why would Wes come after you like that?'

Davie shrugged, and she noticed the women at the next table flicking glances in his direction. She could see why. Maybe they recognised him. Or maybe it was just because he was looking hot. Today, he was in a pale blue shirt, his brown wavy hair pushed back from his face, his skin bronzed by the sun, a thin gold chain she'd bought him round his neck and a Movado watch on his wrist. It cost a fraction of the price of the watches he usually wore, but again, she'd bought it for him, and it touched her that he'd worn it today.

'I don't know. I mean, I guess the obvious reason is the fight we had at the ranch. Even though he kicked my arse, that kind of shit would mess with Wes's ego. He always demanded blind loyalty and I guess that day I didn't show that.'

An alternative explanation began to form in Sarah's head and the pain of it almost made her wince. Was Wes doing this because of Davie's connection to Sarah? Was it payback? Did he know that she was trying to put a case together and this was some kind of fallback plan, the equivalent of putting his boot on Davie's neck, until he persuaded Sarah to drop the case? Or maybe he just couldn't stand the fact that he, Wes Lomax, had been rejected by them both. Maybe this was his version of a teachable moment on loyalty, executed by a demonic tosser of a psychopath.

'The thing I don't get is why Lainey would go along with it,' Davie went on. 'I mean, she's successful enough not to need Wes. She was my mate. And hell, she could have landed a talk show on any network. Why go into this fucked up partnership with Wes and do his bidding? I don't understand.'

The genuine confusion on his face made Sarah want to reach over and hug him. But what good would that do? What he really needed was answers to his questions about Wes, about Lainey, about the connection between them. Sarah didn't have them, but she knew one person who might.

'Davie, I need to go.'

His disappointment was so palpable that she almost stayed. Especially when, in true Davie style, he made a joke to cover his feelings. 'Is it because I'm poor now?'

'Yes,' she said, going along with it as she grabbed her jacket off the seat beside her. 'That's exactly it. I only have lunch with millionaires. It's my new rule. Listen, I just need to go see someone, but I'll call you later.'

'Promise?'

'I do. But in the meantime, the blonde at the next table is eyeing you up and you might be in with a chance.' She didn't mean that for a second, but she knew it would make him laugh, and he seemed to have been short on things that amused him lately. Hell, they all had.

Rushing out, she punched her destination into the maps app on her phone, then pressed start as soon as she reached her car. She knew the way, but she wasn't great at navigating any traffic issues, so she left that to technology. It didn't let her down.

After taking a circuitous but speedy route, she arrived at the café fifteen minutes later. At first, she wondered if she was too late. The park beside the café was busy with lunchtime strollers, joggers and chilled-out office workers sitting on the grass, but no sign of the person she was searching for. She was about to consider another approach when she spotted Monica's car pulling into a space at the other side of the lawn.

Perfect. Even if Monica fled, Sarah would have all the way between here and her car to try to get through to her. Slipping back behind the café wall, she bided her time, allowing Monica to come towards her, then side-track into the café for her usual lunch.

Ten minutes later, Wes's secretary emerged with a coffee and began her usual walk around the park. Sarah slipped into step beside her, making her jump.

It was obvious she was about to flee again, when Sarah stopped her with, 'Monica, please, this isn't about the accusations. I just want to ask you a couple of questions about Lainey Anders.'

The other woman flinched as soon as Sarah said Lainey's name, and that's when Sarah knew her hunch had been right.

Sarah had questions over why Wes would try to destroy Davie, but she was just as curious over why he would want to back Lainey. Television wasn't his thing. He was a movie mogul, and a retired one at that. Lainey wasn't some young pretty thing that he was lording power over and manipulating for sex. She was a woman in her late fifties. Maybe even sixties. Sarah hadn't had a chance to do her research on that yet, but she would. Also, Lainey was a strange choice for a talk show. She'd never so much as strayed from her wheelhouse of country music: no acting, no presenting, nothing but the judging panel on *American Stars*.

Nope, none of this made sense. To give a country music star of mature age her first TV show in the late-night slot was a massive risk, both financially and for his reputation as someone who always backed winners. There was only one obvious reason that he would do that.

Monica hadn't bolted yet, but she was definitely speeding up. Sarah had no problem keeping up with her. One of the consequences of a broken relationship and a workaholic personality was that she ran late at night to slow her mind down, or early in the morning to wake it up.

'Monica, please. This might actually help Wes.' It wouldn't, but she was throwing mud at the wall and hoping something would stick. 'I've learned that Wes and Lainey Anders were in a relationship and very much in love.' Not true. So far, that had only happened in Sarah's mind, but to her, it was the obvious conclusion. Some investigators used the mantra of follow the money. Sarah found that sometimes following the affairs had better success. It was how she'd solved the Jono Leith case and it might be her way in to solving this one.

Monica stopped so suddenly, Sarah almost kept going. 'No,' the older woman exclaimed. 'That's not true. He has no relationship with that woman. If he did, I would know.'

'Monica, are you sure? According to my sources, this wasn't just a fling or a casual thing. Apparently they were planning a future together.' Again, pure fishing. She just wanted to see how Monica would bite. And she did.

'I've already told you, there's nothing between them. Look, Wes has had... dalliances over the years, but since he divorced his last wife, there have been no other relationships. Certainly not with Lainey Anders.' She snorted as if that was preposterous. 'She's not his type at all.'

'What is his type, Monica?' Sarah challenged. It was probably pushing it too far, but she couldn't resist.

Monica reddened, and her face shut down like a garage door, as she realised she'd already said too much. Turning on her heel, she headed back in the direction of her car, and once again, Sarah had to rush to keep up with her.

As they approached the vehicle, Monica spat, 'I'm asking you to back off. I don't want to talk to you now or in the future and this is bordering on harassment.'

Sarah raised her hands, gesturing around her. 'I'm just a journalist taking a walk in a park, Monica. And I like to chat, that's all. So if you think you might want to talk some more, please call me.'

'The only person who'll be calling you is my lawyer, to tell you that I'm taking out a restraining order. Now, get away from my car, and don't bother me again.'

With that, for the second time, Wes Lomax's right-hand woman jumped into her Range Rover and fled the scene.

As soon as Sarah got back to her car, she hooked her phone up to the hands-free Carplay system and called Davie.

'Davie, do you think there's any chance Wes and Lainey Anders were in a romantic relationship?'

'Not a chance,' he blurted, then immediately back-pedalled. 'But then, we all know how great I am at sensing all that emotional stuff. Clueless. My ex-girlfriend was great at it, but she dumped me so I can't even ask her to help.'

Sarah struggled to suppress a grin. 'She sounds like a complete bitch. Anyway, more importantly... I don't care how you do it, but speak to Lainey Anders and get her to talk about Wes and their relationship. I need some kind of proof, evidence to show someone what was going on with them. Listen, I have to go. Stuff to do.' She hung up.

Davie was right. His ex-girlfriend was shit hot at detecting this kind of thing.

This was her jam. Her speciality. She was already on it. And what she was detecting now was that Monica's devotion to Wes wasn't just born of commitment and loyalty.

Monica was in love with him.

Maybe the way she was going to nail Wes was by turning that love against him.

26

23 FEBRUARY 2019 – THE DAY BEFORE THE OSCARS

Mirren
'Fake' – Alexander O'Neal

Mirren was behind her desk, working on the script for *Clansman ii: The Traitor In The Fold*. Of course, it was purely coincidental that in the first draft that she was currently writing, the aforementioned traitor in sixteenth-century Scotland was called Grimes, and he met a gruesome end when he was impaled by the women of the village on a manure-covered spear, and his penis was fed to a rabid wolf.

Sometimes, she just did whatever she had to do to get through the day.

The à la carte penis had been an afterthought, added after she'd received word from her lawyer that Jason Grimes had launched a lawsuit against her, seeking five million dollars in damages for loss of future earnings. His claim alleged that he'd been forced to leave his job for fear of intimidation by Mirren. The secondary claim was that he was now unable to find work in his chosen field, due to the notoriety incurred as a result of the publicity surrounding their relationship.

Obviously, there was no mention of the facts: that he had voluntarily left his job, or that he was the one who had gone public with the story, or that he had absolutely no intention of working in the therapy field again and that was why he was hawking himself around the entertainment industry, ready to sell his soul and every other part of his anatomy for some camera time and a pay cheque.

If Mirren wasn't 100 per cent sure that it would end with a one-way ticket to the nearest ER, she would have punched out the wall of her office.

Maybe she should just feed his balls to the wolves too.

It didn't help that her overriding feeling on the subject was that she only had herself to blame. No fool like a sad, lonely not-so-old fool looking for a distraction. Or something like that.

Picking up the phone, she made her fourth call of the last two days to the same number. As always, it went straight to voicemail. She didn't usually leave a message, but this time, she did. 'Hey, Mike, it's me. Can we talk? Just need to sort out what I'm doing tomorrow night.'

With a mumble of irritation, she tossed her phone on the desk, then almost immediately picked it up again and called Zander. No answer there either. She was about as popular as the fictional Grimes's penis around here today.

Leaning back on her old leather captain's chair, she stretched up, then rested her head on the top of the upholstery. To her right, her dress for the Academy Awards, taking place tomorrow evening, was hanging from the hook on the wall that she'd had put there for that very purpose. Before this whole debacle, she'd been required to show face at one or two formal events almost every week. Since the scandal broke, the invitations had stopped coming, with no one prepared to get snapped in the same shot as the woman who'd been accused of sexual misconduct. The pleas to dress her had dried up too. Every year, she was inundated with calls from the big fashion houses and cutting-edge new designers, begging her to wear their brand. The calls hadn't come, so she'd contacted the Fashion and Textile department at Glasgow School of Art back in Scotland and asked them to come up with a design that she could wear. The result was a spectacular gown of blush silk, embellished with thousands of hand-sewn crystals, and Mirren thought she'd never seen anything more beautiful. It might be the one wonderful thing to come out of all this, and if her star ever rose again, she knew exactly where she'd tell the feckless fashion houses to stick their haute couture.

Her assistant, Devlin, came into the room with the most exquisite arrangement of flowers and placed them on the coffee table across from her desk. Another weekly occurrence that had come to an abrupt stop when she'd been cancelled. Back then, the blooms would have been from Mike. Or from a director who wanted an audience. Or an actor who was pitching for a part. Or a journalist who wanted an interview.

Now?

'I'm scared to ask who they're from,' Mirren sighed, 'but I hope you've checked them for listening devices because I can't think of any other reason that anyone would want to send me flowers.'

'I can. They're from me.'

The surprise took her words away, so he filled in the blanks.

'My last day...' he reminded her, not that he needed to. She'd been dreading this moment for months, ever since the handsome big guy who'd come to work for her as a twenty-one-year-old intern straight out of college had landed the part of Brodie in the next Clansman movie, which was about to start shooting next week. 'I wanted to say thank you. You've changed my life and I love you.'

Tears didn't usually come easy to Mirren, but right now, one was trickling down her cheek. The kindness. The love. The goodness. There had been so little of that in her life lately and his gratitude overwhelmed her.

'You don't need to thank me, Devlin,' she sniffed, smiling. 'You earned this and you're going to be incredible. I can't wait to watch your star soar. I'd hug you, but I'm sure that contravenes some rule around here now.'

'I'll take the risk,' he told her, walking towards her with open arms.

She reciprocated, thinking the protesters that were still loitering outside would get another news cycle of outrage out of this. She couldn't care less.

'Right, I'll be at my desk for another...' he checked his watch, 'four hours. And then I'll be away practising to be an actor. I'm going to start with unreasonable tantrums, demanding good tables in restaurants and accepting tons of free stuff.' This sense of humour was what she'd miss the most around here.

'You do that. Add fake gratitude in the face of compliments and sycophantic adoration of talk-show hosts.'

Devlin gave a pensive nod, as if he was taking notes. 'Fake gratitude and sycophantic adoration. Got it. Big fan of your work.'

As he turned to leave, Mirren deadpanned, 'Oh, and Dev, for the benefit of the listening device in the flowers, can you confirm that I have not, in any way, demanded sexual favours in return for your role in this movie?'

As intended, that made Dev laugh. 'Sadly not, but I live in hope.'

A voice in the open doorway cut through the joke like a needle skidding across a vinyl record. 'This doesn't seem to be the kind of conversation I should be privy to.'

Mirren closed her eyes and wondered why the universe hated

her. Mike Feechan. Ex-husband. There, in the flesh, as clear as the divorce papers that were lying in her in-tray.

Devlin discreetly backed out of the room and left them to it.

'It was a joke. The kind that made you laugh once upon a time.' Mirren tried to make the point without sounding bitter. Antagonism wasn't going to get them anywhere today.

'Yeah, well I lost my sense of humour when the first lawsuit dropped. Anyway, I got your message and I was literally passing. What's up?'

He was so blunt and pissed off, it would have thrown her off balance if she wasn't getting used to this Mike. The disapproving one. The one who didn't trust her. The one she'd let down. The one who drove through protest lines at the gates twice a day, which probably reminded him how much he hated her. The one who, quite rightly, let her go.

There was no placating this Mike, and she didn't blame him one bit for that, so it was best to just get straight to the reason she'd called him.

'Tomorrow night. Obviously we're there representing the same movie.'

'Yes.'

That was all she got. He just stood, casually leaning against the wall, in black pants and a white Tom Ford shirt. Although, she did notice he was still wearing the Hermès belt she'd bought him. For the sake of her own self-esteem, she decided that it was a semi-positive sign. She then noticed the curves of his biceps under his sleeves, the tight set of his jaw, and it battered her self-esteem back down to a pulp for screwing up what she had with this man. *Regrets In Life* by Mirren McLean, Chapter 47 – Wrecking My Relationship with Mike Feechan.

'And, obviously, part of my job, as producer and director of the film is to promote it in interviews on the red carpet...'

He said nothing, and she felt herself squirming under his stare. *Buckle up, Mirren. Come on.*

She lifted her head, rising above the discomfort.

'So I'd like to request, that you, as the head of the studio that produces the Clansman franchise, accompany me to the event and support me while I do that.'

She knew him well enough to spot his raised eyebrow of surprise. Then she realised it was incredulity. And opposition.

'You have got to be kidding me.'

She added indignation to the list.

'Not kidding,' she shot back, her defensiveness showing.

'Mirren, we're divorcing. You destroyed our marriage...'

'But you ended it,' she countered.

'Because you slept with someone else!'

This was beginning to remind her of a dozen heated arguments they'd had in this office before, usually about business, and usually ferocious, animated and occasionally ending with them having passion-crazed sex on her desk. Clearly, that option wasn't going to be on the table – or the desk – today.

She held up her hands, took a breath and attempted to lower the temperature in the room by being measured and succinct. 'This is getting us nowhere. Mike, I'm sorry. I don't know how many times or how many ways I can say that. I loved you and I let you down. If you can't forgive me, I understand, because I don't forgive myself either. But I'm asking you, just for a moment, to put hostilities on hold, and support me tomorrow night. If I have to do it on my own, then I will, but please don't make me do that. This film is important to me, and it's important to the studio, so as CEO of Pictor, can you just treat this as a business decision and support the director of your movie? You can go back to hating me as soon as the ceremony is over.'

That took the air out of him, and he exhaled, as his gaze met hers. 'I don't hate you, Mir,' he said, the antagonism gone, leaving deflated sadness behind.

Mirren wasn't sure what was worse. Actually, scratch that. The sadness was so much worse. It made her ache for him.

He continued, but now his words were quiet bullets of despair and honesty. 'I just don't know if I can do that. I'm so fucking furious with you and I can't let it go. I feel like an asshole for saying it, but it's the truth.'

'I get that...' she answered truthfully, realising that there was a weird comfort in the thought that at least they were communicating now. Anything was better than the cold stand-off of the last few months. 'But, Mike, we work together and I can't carry on feeling like this here. Work is where I escape when I'm struggling.' He knew that was true. After Chloe died, she'd drowned herself in graft, staying at the office day and night to escape the memories at home. 'And it can't be my solace if you're still here, punishing me. If we can't come to some kind of amicable business relationship, then I can't continue to be here. And neither can the Clansman.'

It was intended to be an explanation, a plea to him to meet her halfway. It immediately became apparent that it had been received very differently.

'What, so you're threatening me now? You'll take Clansman away from Pictor because of our personal issues?' The heat was back up, and so was his fury.

'You know what, Mirren, I'll come with you tomorrow night. I'll do my job. I'll stand beside you and I'll smile and I'll tell the world that you're fucking fabulous. But after that you do what you have to do. And if that means taking Clansman to another studio, you go right ahead.'

With that, he turned and stormed back out, considerably more pissed off than he'd been when he'd arrived.

Groaning, Mirren let her head thud down onto the desk.

Fuck.

Maybe Davie and Zander's methods of conflict resolution were better after all, because she doubted that could have gone any worse if she'd punched Mike in the face. At least it would have been over quicker.

The thought took her back to the call that had gone unanswered earlier, and she raised herself back up and tried to rally. Okay, so it hadn't gone to plan, but at least Mike was coming tomorrow night and she wouldn't walk the red carpet alone.

Now she just had to make sure the other man that mattered would be there too.

For the fifth time, she rang Zander's number, praying he would answer. He'd been avoiding her all week, blanking her calls, and he hadn't been home the last twice she'd stopped by. She would be worried and rounding up a posse to go search for him, if he hadn't sent her the same text every night:

I'm fine. Don't worry about me. Just need some time to think. Love you.

Isolation, again. The Zander Leith way of dealing with pain. The one thing she'd asked him, the favour she'd requested was that he come to present the award for Best Director at the Oscars. Not for a single second did she think she would win it, but she'd hoped that for Zander it would be a gentle step back into the real world, that he'd feel the love people had for him and the support they were desperate to give.

Zander had promised her that he was going to be there.

She just wasn't sure if that was a promise that he could keep.

27

23RD FEBRUARY 2019 – THE DAY BEFORE THE
OSCARS

Zander
'Run' – Snow Patrol

She was with him.

Hollie.

She was there. They were sitting on the beach in front of their house, huddled together, her head on his shoulder. They were both barefoot, Zander in his favourite battered old jeans and a white T-shirt, Hollie in a pale yellow dress, with shoestring straps and layers that reached right down to the gold chains around her ankles. They'd bought those on holiday in the Maldives, where they'd spent two weeks in a bungalow on stilts over a turquoise ocean so clear they could watch the seaweed in the coral ebb and flow with the motion of the water.

There was no coral under them now. Just the sands of a Californian beach, and a view that they never tired of, especially, like now, at sunset.

Hollie nuzzled into his neck, her long chestnut hair tucked back off her face, her arm looped through his, both of their gazes fixed on the horizon. 'I feel like this is one of those moments in the movies where we should declare our undying love for each other and then the camera will pan back, and the titles will roll, and everyone who leaves the cinema will be so swept up in the romance of it all that they'll definitely get laid that night.'

The breeze took his laughter and carried it into the distance.

'I think you're right. And does the guy who declared his undying love get laid too?' Zander asked.

Hollie lifted her head from his shoulder, and he saw the glint in her eyes as she teased him. 'Depends how amazing the declaration of love is.'

Zander puffed out his cheeks, pulled his shoulders back, rolled his neck, like a boxer preparing for a challenge. 'Okay, I've got this. Brace yourself.'

Her laughter was infectious, but he tried to keep his words solemn and true, as he lifted her chin and moved his face closer to hers.

'Hollie Leith. I have adored you since the minute I met you...'

She shrieked, giggling. 'That's so not true. I was the biggest pain in your ass.'

'But I still loved you!' he objected. 'Right. Let me go with that again.'

Another shoulder stretch. Another neck roll. He gently lifted her beautiful face again...

'Hollie Leith, I have adored you since the moment I wised up and realised what was good for me...'

'Better,' she murmured.

'And I cherish every single moment I spend with you. You are my soul, my whole heart, my everything. You have showed me the kind of happiness I never knew existed and the kind of perfection that I never knew I could have. And if I never live another day, then I'll die a contented man, knowing that you were my love, and I was yours.'

There was a pause, then slowly, gently, she brought her mouth to his. 'Oh, you are so getting laid tonight,' she whispered, breaking the still perfection of the moment, but neither of them cared because she was laughing and he was punching the air.

Now it was his turn to throw down the challenge. 'Yeah, but this has to be a two-way thing and I've yet to hear a declaration of undying love coming my way.'

Clearing her throat, she got the giggles under control and gazed up at him.

'Zander Leith. I cherish every single moment I spend with you. You are my soul, my whole heart, my everything. You have showed me the kind of happiness I never knew existed and the kind of perfection that I never knew I could have. And... Hang on, what was the next bit? Never mind, I've got it. If I never live another day, then I'll die a contented woman, knowing that you were my love, and I was yours.'

'No, no, no,' he feigned objection and outrage. 'You just copied what I said! How can that be fair? Get your own script.'

'Damn. I was hoping you'd be too busy thinking about getting laid to notice.' Her squeals of hilarity didn't stop when he grabbed her, kissed her, or when they rolled back so they were lying on the sand, or when her legs wrapped around his, and they...

The beep of a dumper truck cut right through the moment and Zander jerked up, suddenly awake, confronted by a huge vehicle reversing towards him. He braced himself for impact, but it never came, the truck veering off to the right at the last second, then trundling away down the hill to the road that traversed the canyon.

It had probably not even seen him. He'd chosen to stop in a lay-by that was almost completely overgrown with trees and bushes, on the side of the hill, just outside the entrance to the Hurston Centre. If he got out of the car and crossed the narrow, winding road, he'd be able to see right down to the ocean in front of him. It was a spectacular view, but it didn't even come close to the one on the beach that he'd been dreaming about a few moments ago. He let the pain of that twist around his chest like a boa constrictor, squeezing the breath out of him until there was nothing left. If only that terminal prognosis were true, because then he wouldn't have to live with the agony of this life, every minute of every day. And if he was going to go, he was taking that bastard, Lomax, with him.

Dusk was beginning to change the colour of the sky from blue to grey, with streaks of red just visible in the distance. Now. This would be the best time. Before he'd dozed off, a succession of cars had come up the hill and through the open gates next to him, closely followed by another convoy of vehicles going in the opposite direction. Shift change. It was a familiar pattern to him. He'd lived in a rehab facility less than a mile up the canyon from here, and he knew the general pattern that these healthcare operations followed.

That's why he knew that there were far less staff on in the evenings. And he wanted as few people around as possible.

He started up the engine and drove the forty or so yards into the car park of the Hurston Centre. He'd dressed for the occasion in black jeans and a dark grey T-shirt, thrown a leather jacket into the passenger seat, next to the backpack that held the only possessions he truly loved or cared about. Hollie's wedding ring, her phone, which had every message they'd ever sent each other, Hollie's passport with all the stamps of their travels, his too, the small oak box containing her ashes, and a framed picture of them on the beach, snapped by a passer-by at Hollie's request, then printed off and placed on her dressing table. In it, he was wearing jeans and a white T-shirt and she was in a pale yellow dress, an exact replica of the scene that had just played out in his dream.

He climbed out of the car and walked towards the entrance, trying desperately to remember how to walk like Zander Leith, to talk like Zander Leith, to be Zander Leith.

At the door, he pressed the intercom buzzer and a voice responded immediately.

'Hi, how can I help you?'

'I'm here to visit one of your patients. Wes Lomax.'

'Oh. Right. Come on through to reception.'

The double doors buzzed open and he did as commanded, spotting a friendly face at the reception desk a few feet in front of him. A woman. Maybe in her fifties. Slightly ruddy cheeks and glasses. A blue jacket with a name badge on the side.

Walk like Zander Leith, talk like Zander Leith, be Zander Leith. He repeated the mantra in his head. He also, for the first time in months, resembled Zander Leith.

In preparation for tonight, he'd showered and shaved. His hair, now shoulder-length and inches longer than it had ever been, was pulled back with a black elastic band he'd found on Hollie's desk, even though he fucking hated that man-bun wankery. He was fifty pounds lighter, but he'd looked that way in the first couple of Dunhill movies, when he was in his twenties and fresh off the boat.

He hoped it was good enough, and as he saw the flicker of recognition cross the receptionist's face, he immediately knew it was.

He went first, aware that a lack of presumption always sparked an immediate connection.

'Hi, I'm Zander...'

'Mr Leith! I know who you are.' He immediately spotted the wide grin and sparkly eyes of someone who loved his movies.

Relief. This might just be okay. The staff in these facilities were trained to ignore status and fame, and just treat everyone with a cool, professional respect, but Zander knew it didn't always work that way. There had been a nurse in his last rehab who had brought him his favourite cappuccino from a coffee house in Calabasas every morning, then spent every break by his side, playing cards and singing Aretha Franklin songs to him. She still sent him a Christmas card every year. No one else in that centre had got that level of personal treatment.

'I was so sorry to hear about your wife, Mr Leith.'

A searing thrust of pain in his gut almost felled him. This, right here, was why he couldn't go back to a normal life. People knew. They felt they had to talk about it, and he was in no state to listen.

He managed a tight, 'Thank you,' then went straight on to his reason for being there.

'I've just stopped by to visit Wes Lomax. Could you let me know what room he's in?'

'Are you on the visitor list, Mr Leith?'

Shit. He should have pre-empted that one. The security in these places was always tight. Time to do the only thing he was actually good at – acting.

'Of course...' He leaned forward, peering at her name badge. 'Joy. That's a gorgeous name. And, yes, I'm on the visitor's list. Wes and I have been making movies together for thirty years. He's one of my closest friends.'

He held his breath and his best charming grin, hoping that this shit would work.

It did. She didn't check a thing, just took him at his word. The powers of fame.

'Mr Lomax is in room 18. Just round to the left. It was a pleasure to meet you.' Her cheeks were even ruddier now.

'You too, Joy.' Easy. Another example of never hearing the word 'no'.

Relief seeping from his pores, Zander followed the directions until he reached room 18. Various nurses, doctors and other staff passed him, but either ignored him or, with a glint of recognition, smiled his way.

When he reached the door, he put his fingers on the handle, exhaled, steadying himself to greet the devil.

His body moved slowly, the handle even slower, down, a barely audible click, then he began to push it open, but before he'd even cracked it an inch, he froze, peering through the space. He could see a bed, at the head of it, Wes Lomax, his head lolling to one side, sleeping. And right next to him, a problem. He could only see her back and her tendrils of blonde hair, but he didn't need anything more to identify her, because she was singing. Zander had been around this town long enough to recognise the hair, the voice and the song, a beautiful, heart-breaking country ballad that Hollie had sung for weeks when it came out.

Silently, he pulled the door closed again. She wouldn't even have known he was there. Retreat. For now.

On the way out, he passed Joy again. 'I'm going to come back. Mr Lomax already has a visitor.'

'Sorry, I should have said. Miss Anders came in a while ago. I hadn't realised she was still there.'

Another top-notch security measure from Joy.

'Well, I'll just come back later. I'll see you then, Joy.'

Her cheeks ruddied again as he gave her a wave.

He kept the amiable grin up until he got outside, then dropped it, swearing under his breath as he headed back to the car. Fuck.

He jumped in, left the car park, drove the few yards back down the canyon and into the same hidden spot he'd been in earlier.

That's when he saw the smoke in the distance.

He got out of the car, crossed the road and peered down to the coastline below, where the smoke was rising high above an area to his right.

He didn't need binoculars to know where that was. It was his neighbourhood. And the smoke was all the way to the water, so that meant it was his street. If the blaze was as ferocious as it looked from here, his home was in jeopardy. He should feel something, he knew that. There should be a reaction. A fear. A horror. Questions about why it was on fire. How it had started. Something. But there was nothing, except...

Zander made a calculation. If he drove as far as the flames allowed, then went the rest of the way on foot, he would be there within the hour.

That's when he decided he had two choices.

He could go back into the hospital, do what he had to do, then say goodbye to Zander Leith here and now.

Or he could just scrap his plans, go home, walk back into the flames and die with Hollie.

28

23RD FEBRUARY 2019 – THE DAY BEFORE THE
OSCARS

Davie
'Take A Bow' – Rihanna

Davie didn't even have to try hard to find her. He'd waited until just after seven o'clock before leaving the house, head bursting after four hours with his business manager, Cyril, who'd done a house call to go through his accounts – mainly because the accountant didn't want his whole office in the rarefied air of Beverly Hills to hear Davie screaming that Wes Lomax was a fucking cunt.

There was only one way out of the financial hole that he'd tunnelled in to. Sell the house, go for a knock-down price to get a quick sale, throw in the Bugatti, and he might just have enough left over to clear his debts and buy a one-bedroom shack in Oklahoma. Or maybe an RV that he could park in the street, so he could still stare at the house he loved. Fucker.

But one thing at a time. That was then, now he was pulling up to the striped awnings in front of the Beverly Hills hotel, and he was getting his game plan together. Go slow. Go easy. Don't charge in there threatening to stuff Lainey Anders up a buffalo's arse, or he'd be in jail before nightfall.

He tossed the car keys to the valet, with a word of thanks, then headed on inside, confident that she'd be exactly where she always was at this time of night.

Ten years ago, when he'd given Lainey Anders a seat on the judging panel on *American Stars*, she'd had it written into her contract that she'd have a bungalow at the Beverly Hills Hotel for the duration of the project.

When she'd appeared on his show a couple of months ago, she'd charged two nights at this hotel to his account.

And she'd also told him that she'd been staying there on and off for a few months already. The same place that Wes kept a crash pad. Where the old man ate every night. His home away from home. Of course they would have met. Would have known each other. Who knew how long they'd been planning all this? Why hadn't Davie connected it all before now? Fucking fool, he berated himself.

He should have suspected then that something was going on, should have drilled down on what it was, but he was just so grateful that she'd showed up to care.

And then... the ultimate twist of the knife... When he'd met her to sign the contracts for the loan, he'd done it right here, flanked by her lawyers, at a table in the Polo Lounge.

Her table.

And yep, there she was, right there, at the same spot in the corner, drinking Southern Comfort with a twist, no ice. Her usual drink.

She saw him coming, and smiled, wide-eyed with surprise. Davie caught the split-second hesitation while she got her own game plan together. Innocence and delight were clearly her starting points.

'Davie, my sweet sugar! Well, isn't this just a cherry on a cocktail. So great to see you. Come join this lonely mama right here.'

'Lainey,' he crooned, arms wide in greeting, before bending to kiss her on each cheek, before sliding into the booth beside her.

Stick to the strategy. Play it cool. Get the goods.

His mission was repeating on a loop in his mind.

The waiter was by his side in seconds, and he ordered a beer. No spirits. Nothing that could take the edge off his concentration.

All the while, his internal monologue was still going. *Game plan. Stick to the strategy. Play it cool. Get the goods.*

'So great to see you, sugar,' she crooned, sticking with small talk central. 'And I'm so glad I was able to take care of that little financial issue for you. Get you all sorted out and squared away.'

Game plan. Stick to the strategy. Play it cool. Get the goods.

'I just don't know how I'd have got through that without you. Saved my neck, Lainey, you really did.' As always when he was with her, he slipped into Southern lingo. He'd never been great at maintaining his accent. Mirren used to say he'd started speaking with an American twang the minute the plane left the runway at Glasgow airport. He put it down to an obsession with Starsky and Hutch when he was a boy. Ena had knitted him a Starsky cardigan and he'd worn that baby every day for years.

The waiter brought his beer and he immediately knocked back a slug as she replied, 'Well, we've known each other a long time and you've been good to me. Just payin' a little back.'

If Dolly Parton and Bernie Madoff had a love child, then gave it to a psychopathic serial killer to raise, this was her sitting right here.

'You sure did that,' he agreed. 'Is that really why you helped me, honey? As thanks for everything I did for you? For making you a legend by putting you on my show?'

A slight grit of the teeth there as she forced them into another big wide smile. Just as well she was a singer and a soon-to-be talk show presenter, because she was a shit actress.

'Sure was, sweetheart.'

Game plan. Stick to the strategy. Play it cool. Get the goods. But...

Fuck the game plan.

He leaned in towards her, still smiling, so that it looked like they were having an intimate conversation, and lowered his voice so that he wouldn't be overheard.

'Really? Because I thought it was because you were fucking that old bastard, Wes Lomax, and he gave you a shit-crazy deal to have your own talk show, if you just helped him bury me first.'

Her twelve-inch wide, country special wig barely trembled, but her fake smile froze, then morphed into a sneer. It was amazing how quickly someone so pretty could turn so ugly. 'Don't you dare talk about him like that, you little fucker,' she hissed, so close he could smell the garlic she'd had for dinner.

Ah, so she was on his game plan now too.

'That man made you and you had no fucking gratitude,' she spat.

'Really, Lainey? Is that where you're going with this? That man discovered me, I'll give him that, but I made myself. And I didn't have to fuck someone to do it. You on the other hand...'

'Don't you dare!' Now the wig was definitely vibrating. 'I did not fuck Wes Lomax for a job and where is your damn heart? That man is the love of my life and now he's lying in a hospital bed. Today should have been our wedding day and, instead, I sat by that man's side, singing my songs, begging him to come back to me. So cry me a fucking river. I couldn't give a snake's fart about you, your money or your life.'

Wow. That was news. For the first time, he noticed the huge ruby ring that she was wearing on her engagement finger. Shit. So this was way more than just business. She loved him. They were getting married. He supposed it made sense. Do you two evil fuckers take each other to be your lawfully wedded psycho?

'Well, congratulations,' he drawled, making it clear he meant the opposite. 'So what was I? Your wedding gift to each other? You screw me over so that you get a chat show and what? My house?'

A tiny twitch of a glance to her bottom right.

'Holy shit. You wanted my house!'

It was like a box had opened and all the answers were written right there. When she'd been on *American Stars*, Lainey had spent endless days at his home, and Alina, worshipper of all things country, had fussed over her, cooked her meals, treated her like a queen. Lainey wanted that for herself. She wanted the house, the staff, the life... And they knew that by writing it into the deal, he'd either have to surrender it to them or they'd be able to pick it up at a knock-down price in a forced sale.

Part of him almost admired the strategy and the execution. Well played.

And he'd done his job too. The camera on the buttonhole of his jacket had picked up what Sarah needed to know. Time to go. He just couldn't resist one last dig...

'You know, probably just as well he's on his way out. He'd have traded you in for a younger model before the month was out.'

That should have been it. It was a parting shot and a cheap dig, but it felt like enough to reclaim a shred of his pride.

He began to slide out of the booth when she came right back at him with a hollow laugh.

'You mean, like your little girlfriend? The one who begged him for it, offered herself up to him, and then started stirring up all sorts of trouble for him when he wouldn't screw her?'

For a second, Davie wasn't sure if it was her words or her hands that had slapped him.

'Sarah?' he blurted. It was out. Couldn't take it back.

She read his reaction immediately. 'Oh, Davie,' she laughed again. 'You didn't know. Well, there you go, sugar. I guess we're both having a bad day.'

An AR-15 was spraying bullets around the inside of his skull. Sarah? Memories dropped in. Sarah telling him she'd met Wes. Wes's smirk that day in the paddock up at the ranch. *'You got to learn that about women, son. They're just out for what they can get.'*

In the very back of his mind, something about that had always niggled at him. Wes turning up at his wedding. Sure, Davie had thrown out a casual invitation, but in hindsight, he'd come in with an agenda. An attitude. Now, like a sledgehammer bursting through a breeze block, the truth smashed through his understanding of events. Wes didn't pitch up on his wedding day for Davie. He came because there was something going on with Sarah.

Davie needed to see her. Needed to understand. But first he had to get away from here and this evil cow.

'You know, Lainey, the only reason I'm not dragging your flat arse out of here is because my mother brought me up better than that.'

With that, he knocked over the bottle of beer, so that it poured right into the crotch of her leather pant suit.

'She's paying,' he told the waiter as he passed him, moving out as quickly as he could without attracting attention. He had no idea who else was in the room, and he didn't want this splashed all over the internet within the hour.

With shaking hands on the steering wheel, he raced down to Marina Del Rey, breaking every speed limit on the way. Half an hour later, he was thumping her door until she opened it, startled at the ruckus.

He melted against the doorway, shaking, sweating, dread prickling his skin.

'What did he do to you?' he whispered, because this came from a place of love, of fear, of devastation. 'Wes Lomax. What did he do when you met him?' He desperately hoped he'd see confusion or bewilderment on Sarah's face, but no. As soon as she sighed, he knew it was true.

Her shoulders slumped, as she opened the door wider. 'You'd better come in.'

He followed her into the apartment, took the beer she pulled from the fridge, then watched her open another for herself. When she was ready, they sat at the tiny table for two in her kitchen.

'When I was researching my book on the #MeToo movement, I kept hearing his name. Nothing concrete. Rumours. Anecdotes. Horror stories. Way too many for there to be an innocent explanation or just some random speculation. I engineered a meeting. Went to his hotel when I knew he'd be there, bumped into him at the bar. I think I told you all that before...'

He nodded, gut twisting, feeling like he was watching a car speed towards a brick wall and he had no way to stop it. 'You did.'

'What I didn't tell you was that he invited me to see his bungalow, then gave me a drink with something in it. I realised pretty quickly, stopped drinking it, but not soon enough that he didn't take his chance. He held me down, he ripped my clothes, he tried to...'

'Don't.' He closed his eyes, thinking that maybe if he didn't see that pain on her face, then this could somehow not be real. Then he realised that what he was feeling had no relevance here. All that mattered was Sarah. He opened his eyes again, reached across the table, took her hand, his thumb automatically stroking the soft skin of her palm.

She began to speak again. 'I fought him off before he could rape me. I've no doubt that's what he was planning to do. It's what he does, what he's done to so many women over the years.'

'And you didn't tell me?'

Oh God, the pain on her face. It was almost unbearable.

'No. Because you'd want details that I wasn't ready to share. I needed to process it first. Sit with it. And when would have been the right time? Our wedding day? Davie, I love you, but I know you too well – if I'd told you, you'd have killed him and then I'd have lost you.'

'It would have been worth it.' He wasn't thinking about what he was saying. His heart was talking, his fury, his love, his rage, his sorrow. At the same time, his hopelessness in all situations that required emotional intelligence had already been well established, so he knew Sarah was right – he would have made a knee-jerk decision to go after Lomax that would have changed all their lives.

'And that's why I said nothing, Davie,' she replied, more animated now. 'When are you going to learn that I don't need you to fight my battles? This was my story. My body. My anger. My fight. I needed to do this my way. And I couldn't do that if I was constantly terrified that you'd torch him as he slept.'

'I get that.'

'I'm not done,' she chided him for interrupting. 'I was pissed off with you too. When I said I was doing a story on Wes, you wanted me to drop it, even though you'd heard all the rumours about him. So what does that mean, Davie? That you'll stand up and speak out against him when it's your girlfriend? What about all the others? What about the other men in this industry, the other Lomaxes, the other Weinsteins, who've been getting away with this for years? Don't they get your anger?'

His jaw was clamped shut. He understood his limitations, and one of them was trying to reason with Sarah McKenzie, especially when she was right.

'So leave this to me, Davie. Just tell me you've got the footage I need and then just leave me to it.'

'I got it,' he told her, taking his jacket off and removing the camera. 'Lainey and Wes were supposed to get married today. It's all there.'

She took it from him. 'Listen, I don't want to kick you out, but there's somewhere I need to be. You're welcome to stay here, and we can talk when I get back. I think that conversation is long overdue.'

He thought about it. 'You know, I love you, and I'm so sorry I wasn't there for you.'

'You weren't, but that was because I didn't let you,' she said. He took a tiny shred of comfort from that.

'No. You didn't.' He knew then that he wasn't going to stick around. He stood up, picked up his jacket.

'Davie, I'm warning you. Don't dare go near Wes Lomax. Promise me.'

He said nothing. Instead, he crossed the room, opened the door and left.

Because he didn't make promises he couldn't keep.

29

23RD FEBRUARY 2019 – THE NIGHT BEFORE THE
OSCARS

Sarah
'Toxic' – *Britney Spears*

The night was chilly, so Sarah pulled her long mauve cardigan
closed, covering her white sweatshirt and her blue skinny jeans,
glad she'd had the foresight to slip on ankle boots instead of the flat
pumps she wore most days.

She'd parked about fifty yards along from Monica's house, just
in case she wasn't home and Sarah had to go back and wait for her,
like some shady PI staking out a property. When she got to the front
of the building, she realised that wouldn't be necessary. Lights were
on and there was a shadow moving across the window in one of the
rooms.

This could have waited until tomorrow, but Sarah hadn't
wanted to put it off until then. Besides, getting Monica to talk to her
at the park had been a bust so far, and there was no way she was
getting onto the Lomax lot without a SWAT team being summoned

to take her out. Tomorrow evening was the Oscars, and she'd no idea where Monica would be for the biggest event of the year in Hollywood, so tonight it was.

Earlier, before she even knew if Davie had the footage she needed, she'd called Shandra and asked if she could find out Monica's address. The researcher had called back with it within twenty minutes. It was a small, two-bedroom cottage in Santa Monica, on a leafy street eight blocks back from the shore, and a couple of blocks east of Montana Avenue. In the town Sarah had grown up in back in Scotland, the same house would have cost about eighty grand. Not here. 'It was purchased for $2.2 million ten years ago, but get this...' Sarah could hear the intrigue in Shandra's voice, and she knew she was about to receive information of the jaw-dropping nature.

She'd decided to pre-empt the big reveal with a guess of her own. 'Wes Lomax owns it?'

'Ooooh, you're good,' Shandra had drawled, laughing. 'But not quite good enough.' Sarah loved this young woman. She had the perfect blend of resilience, intelligence, relentlessness and humour. Bringing her on to the team was the best move she'd made, and she'd proved that with her next nugget of information.

'It's owned by Lomax Films. It's a company property, but Monica has lived there since it was purchased. And there's something else...'

'I'm not even going to try to guess, oh wise one,' Sarah had replied, her mind whirring through a whole sequence of possibilities, questions and potential outcomes.

'It hit the MLS today.' Shandra had delivered that one with a touch of triumph.

'Can you repeat that in simple terms for the foreigner here, please?'

'The MLS,' Shandra had replied, slightly slower. 'Multiple

Listing Service. It's a property website that houses for sale are listed on.'

Sarah's brain had started spinning again, fitting that information into the equation. 'Wait a minute. Let me get this right. So Lomax Films owns the home Monica has lived in for the last ten years, and today it went up for sale.'

'Well done. You didn't keep up with my genius, but you were close.'

It was impossible to guess what the motivations and reasons behind the property sale were, but Sarah had filed the info away for later.

She was thinking about that now as she walked up towards Monica's house. She pulled out her phone and made another quick call. Mirren didn't answer, so she left a voicemail.

'Mirren, I told Davie about Wes Lomax and he's pissed. He left my flat half an hour ago and I don't know where he's gone. I'm worried that he'll do something stupid, but I'm just about to go into a work thing, so I can't track him down. Can you help please? Just see if you can find him and check if he's okay? Gotta go. Thanks.'

The uneven ground told her she'd reached the grey cobblestone path and she rang the doorbell. It was one of those ones that recorded the person at the door, so Sarah knew she could be seen. It was late to be calling on someone – almost 10 p.m., but what was the worst that could happen? Monica could ignore her, call the police or shoot her. Actually, maybe she should have thought this through a bit more carefully.

That was the thought that was going through her head when Monica did the most surprising thing of all – she opened the door.

Her first reaction was an agitated sigh. 'Jesus, lady, can you not give it a rest?'

Wow. The second surprise of the night. This wasn't the professional, sharp-suited, uber-efficient Monica that Sarah had met before. This woman was… a little dishevelled. Wearing yoga pants and a sweatshirt that was dropping off one shoulder. Hair tied back. Make-up somewhat smeared. Eyes bloodshot. And… going by the smell of alcohol that was almost knocking Sarah out… drunk.

Holy. Shit.

'Monica, I'm so sorry to bother you, I really am. I know you think I'm a pain in the ass, but I'd really like to speak with you and to show you some footage I've obtained.'

Monica rolled her eyes. 'I've warned you before that this is harassment. I could have the Lomax lawyers over here in a heartbeat.'

There was something in the way that she said it that told Sarah she was bluffing. Strange, because she'd have thought it would be true. As Wes Lomax's right arm, Monica wielded significant power, but this didn't seem like a woman who was in charge of her game.

Time to cut the bullshit, go with her gut, and see if that got her off the doorstep and into the house.

'You could,' Sarah admitted calmly. She didn't want it to be perceived as a challenge. 'But here's the thing, Monica. I think you're a good person. I think that you've been loyal to Wes Lomax and protected him for decades and he's probably rewarded you well. But things have changed now that he's no longer in charge. I don't think he's protecting you anymore, Monica. Your house is being sold and every single time I've seen you, you look unhappier than the last. So now, I think I might know why. I brought a video I'd like you to watch. It's on my tablet here…' She held up her iPad. 'And it's of Lainey Anders talking about her relationship with Wes. I think you're going to want to see it.'

'That bitch doesn't have a relationship with Wes.'

Sarah stood her ground, not easy when she was getting high on Monica's gin fumes. Her mum used to call gin 'mother's ruin' because she said it made women depressed. Sarah had always thought that was nonsense. Now she might have five foot four inches of evidence for the prosecution swaying right in front of her.

'She does, Monica. If Wes hadn't had his stroke, they were getting married today.'

The force of that statement made Monica stagger backwards, and Sarah only just managed to step forward in time to grab her. She carried on walking into the house, supporting Monica, kicking the door closed behind her with her foot.

It was an open-plan room, like most of these homes now, so Sarah half carried, half dragged her over to a round white ceramic dining table that separated a small but gorgeously appointed living area and a sleek white gloss modern kitchen with, Sarah could see, top-of-the-range Miele appliances and Calacatta marble worktops, under a beautiful bronze modern chandelier.

Guilty as charged, one bottle of Isle of Harris Gin sat in the middle of the table. Half empty. Definitely not half full. Next to it was an envelope, open, but Sarah couldn't see what was inside.

She made sure Monica was sitting steady, then poured some tap water into a glass that was by the sink and gave it to the other woman. Monica took a sip, then discarded it, picking up the gin bottle and partaking straight from that instead, throwing it back like a cowboy chugging whiskey.

'Okay, show me,' she demanded, rallying enough to focus.

Sarah almost felt sorry for her. Almost. She still hadn't forgotten the stories that several of Wes's victims had told her, about running out of his office, distressed, past his secretary sitting at her desk. Of the times Wes had said and done sexually inappropriate things to them and Monica had been close enough to see or hear. Monica had to know who he was, what he was, and she'd been prepared to protect him. She was the gatekeeper to the monster. But Sarah wasn't going to dwell on that or bring it up right now, because it wouldn't get her anywhere.

Instead, she played the part of the sympathetic friend, firing up her tablet and opening the file, warning Monica that this was going to hurt. Monica responded by drinking more gin straight from the bottle.

Sarah pressed play, and the crystal-clear image of Lainey Anders at a table in the instantly recognisable Polo Lounge filled the screen. Sarah turned the tablet so Monica had full view, as Lainey raged...

'I did not fuck Wes Lomax for a job and where is your damn heart? That man is the love of my life and now he's lying in a hospital bed. Today should have been our wedding day and, instead, I sat by that man's side, singing my songs, begging him to come back to me. So cry me a fucking river. I couldn't give a snake's fart about you, your money or your life.'

It was as if Lainey was talking directly to Monica and the response came in stages, all of them portrayed on her face. Confusion. Realisation. Fury. Contempt. Devastation. And then tears. Many of them. Sliding down her cheeks.

Sarah was about to stop the recording, when Monica, eyes still fixed on the screen, gasped, 'That is his mother's engagement ring.' A pause. A wail. 'He promised it would be mine.'

She slumped back in the chair, used her sleeve to wipe the fluid that was streaming from her nose. 'The bastard.' It was like a last whisper from a dying woman. 'He promised all that to me.'

Sarah wasn't sure whether to hug her, hold her while she cried, or just stay where she was and do nothing. She went with that one, worried that one false move would invoke a negative reaction. Her old editor at the *Daily Scot*, Ed McCallum, had drilled that into her when she was a rookie. *'Get them talking. Ask questions. Prompt them. But then shut up and let them fill the space, no matter how much it makes yer knickers curl.'*

Political correctness had never made its way to the offices of the *Daily Scot*.

Not for the first time, Ed McCallum was bang on.

'He promised all that to me,' Monica repeated, staring into the space in front of her. 'His mother's ring. The wedding. For twenty years, he's been promising that to me.'

Sarah's hunch was on the money, but she got no satisfaction out of being right.

'Do you know what that letter is?' Monica jerked her head to the envelope on the table.

'No.' But she was desperate to find out.

'That letter,' Monica spat, 'is my termination from Lomax Films. After forty years. Forty!' Her temper was rising now. 'Apparently, now that Wes has retired, I'm "surplus to requirements". Me! I ran that fucking place. They're taking my house, my career, my salary... And now that bitch has taken him too. He always said when he retired, we'd get married, we'd move to Montana, to a ranch. That was going to be our lives, our future.'

Sarah didn't have all the answers yet.

'But, Monica, the other women...?'

Monica gave a rueful snort. 'Getting that out of his system. He had an image to keep up, a persona to fulfil. He told me he thought of me every time. That it was a test of how strong we were. I watched him while he was with every single one of those whores and I knew he was telling the truth. It wasn't like that with me. With me, he made love.'

'Wait a minute... you watched him?'

Sarah tried not to gasp. Not for the first time tonight, the words holy shit seemed like the only adequate response. Monica knew. It was all part of some sick, twisted game, based on a forty-year-long promise. Just when she thought there were no more levels of crazy to discover, she'd just found another one.

'Don't you dare fucking judge me,' Monica warned.

'I'm not judging,' Sarah lied. Oh, she fucking was. Monica must have seen some of the violence, the attacks, the rapes. A thought made her shudder. Had she watched while Wes had climbed on top of her that night? While he ripped at her clothes? While he tried to…

'Now I see he lied. All of it. Everything I thought we had. It's all gone.'

Sarah leaned forward and, much as it disgusted her, put her hand on Monica's. Means to an end, she told herself.

'Monica, help me punish him. Help me make him pay for what he's done. I'll keep your name out of it and I'll make sure you're taken care of.' She was making promises she couldn't keep, but Monica was the only person who could hear her lie, and the other woman had already demonstrated that she wasn't great on truth or integrity either. 'Help me get justice for all the other women who've been used by him. And for you.'

Monica was still staring straight ahead, a sneer on her face.

Sarah stayed perfectly still and silent again for a moment… another moment… another… Until, in Ed McCallum's wise words, her knickers were well and truly curled. Just when she was about to surrender and plead with her again, Monica stood up, went through a door at the back of the room. Sarah debated whether to follow her when a bang made the decision for her. Shit. What had Monica done?

She ran over, went through the same door, stopped. Straight in front of her, Monica was standing next to an open closet, a biometric lock on the wall next to it. The door was open, flat against the wall. That must have been the noise she'd heard.

Monica turned to her.

'Take whatever you want. I'd stop you, but, apparently, I'm

surplus to requirements. I'll be next door.' With that, she staggered back into the lounge.

Sarah went to the open door, adrenaline making her whole body tremble. She could already see what was there, but when she got closer, it was even clearer.

Tapes. Hundreds of them. Rows and rows lined every wall of the cupboard. Some were old-fashioned VHS. Some were small cassettes from the video cameras of the nineties. There was a big, old, chunky hard-drive computer, with a monitor too. And then another box full of USB sticks sat on top of a laptop.

Sarah began to pull the tapes out one by one. Many had names on the spines that she recognised from the sixties, seventies, eighties. Lana Delasso. Sydney Carbery. Marisol Brookes. All movie icons in their day. A dozen more actresses that were familiar to her. Some names that weren't. And then the one that confirmed her hunch as to what this really was.

Lisa Arexo.

This was a catalogue of Wes Lomax's life, told through his victims. One. By. One.

Sarah felt a wave of vomit rise from her stomach as a question struck her. Was she on one of these? Did one of those little USB sticks contain a recording of the worst moment of her life?

There was only one person who could answer that.

After wedging the cupboard door open with a chair, just in case it had some kind of automatic closing mechanism, she went back into the lounge to ask the question.

It was empty.

The front door was open.

Monica Janson was gone.

30

FEBRUARY 24 2019 – THE ACADEMY AWARDS

Right Back Where We Started From – Maxine Nightingale

Myla Rivera reporting for the Fame Channel:

'Welcome to the 91st Academy Awards, live from the Dolby Theatre right in the heart of Hollywood. And what a night this promises to be! We'll be sharing every moment right here on the Fame Channel. Behind me, the stars are just beginning to arrive for Hollywood's biggest night and we'll be chatting with them soon and checking out all the fashion on the red carpet. Of course, we'll have some hot gossip for you too, plus we'll be sharing our predictions as to who will be heading home with the most wanted man in Hollywood... Oscar!'

We'll also be keeping you updated on the biggest story of the day so far, the tragic situation unfolding in Malibu right now, where an unseasonal wildfire has reportedly claimed the home of Zander Leith, a much-loved friend of many of the industry names who will be arriving this evening. Let's take a look at the moment Zander won his own Academy Award, back in 1993 for the original screen-play written by Leith, Davie Johnston and Mirren McLean.'

Cut to a VT package – The Academy Awards 1993. Actress Lana Delasso announces the winners in the category of Best Original Screen-play. Zander Leith, Mirren McLean and Davie Johnston, all barely in their twenties, take to the stage and pick up the gold statue for their movie The Brutal Circle. *Cut back to Myla Rivera...*

'At the moment, we've no information on Zander Leith's loca-tion, but prior to today's events, he was expected to attend tonight's ceremony to present the award for Best Director – a category in which one of the nominee's is his old friend, and no stranger to controversy this year, Mirren McLean.

'So, be one of the billion people worldwide tuning in tonight for all the latest news, fashion, and of course, the awards. Stay right here on the Fame Channel, and we'll be right back after these messages...'

Broadcast ends. Myla Rivera looks off camera, taps her earpiece, speaks to the producer in the gallery.

'Billion people, my ass. Why are we still peddling that bullshit? Lucky if it's even half of that. Okay, I need to know exactly what's happening with Leith. Let's run the package about his wife in the next segment, but you guys keep the cameras on the limos. Make sure you get Mirren McLean's face on a close-up when she arrives, and I want Davie Johnston's first words. Do your work, people. This is going to be a shitshow and we want the whole fucking world to be watching it here.'

31

THE ACADEMY AWARDS CEREMONY 2019

Mirren
'Tell Me Lies' – Fleetwood Mac

The Oscars.

A galaxy of stars.

Mirren and Mike had been seated near the end of a row, just a few feet from the stage, close enough that the camera could land on her if she won, but out of scope of the general audience shot, undoubtedly planned so that there was a possibility that the broadcast could go out in its entirety without a single frame of the woman who was embroiled in a sexual coercion scandal.

Bastards.

Clearly innocent until proven guilty didn't apply in Hollywood.

Mirren couldn't give a toss, because all she could think about right now was where was Zander? She hadn't been able to get him on the phone for a few days, he hadn't been at home when she'd stopped by to see him, and all she'd had were the texts...

I'm fine. I just need time to think.

Now, to make things so much worse, there was a wildfire raging in the area of his home. She was almost positive he wasn't there. After the Woolsey Fire, the authorities were vehement and meticulous with their evacuation plans, but who knew? He could be anywhere. He could be behind that curtain in front of her right now. He could be up a mountain somewhere, contemplating life without his love. Or he could be dead in a ditch or in the ashes of his home.

She'd found out about the fire earlier that day. She'd been in a bi-level bungalow at the Fairmont Miramar in Santa Monica since early morning preparing for the journey later that day to the Dolby Theatre, home of the Oscars ceremony. It was her new Santa Monica crash pad. She hadn't been back to the suite at the Casa Del Mar, because it was the last place she'd been with Hollie, and she wanted to preserve it in her memory, leave it unclouded by future occasions. It had been the perfect meal. The perfect view. The perfect friends. The perfect Hollie.

Mirren had been sitting back in the make up chair, her favourite Bio-Effect serum soothing her face, when she'd seen the reports of the Malibu fire on the news channel. Hair and make-up had been instantly suspended so that she could call Sarah straight away.

The hoarse voice that answered had surprised her.

'Hey, Mir. Thanks for tracking Davie down for me last night. The work thing lasted longer than I expected so I was pretty relieved to get your text.'

'No worries. Took me a couple of hours, though, and he was pretty distressed about what you'd told him.' Distressed had been an understatement. Davie had been drunk, upset, ranting, but she hadn't wanted to upset Sarah by telling her that. Instead, she'd gone on, 'He wouldn't say where he'd been. I'm not even sure he knew. I was just glad he was okay. Unlike you. You sound awful, honey. Are you ill?'

'No, it's just been a long night. And morning. The work thing – we found a whole stash of videos of... Actually, I'll tell you in person. Don't really want to discuss it on the phone. Why were you calling? Is everything okay?'

'No. Have you seen the news? There's a fire up in Malibu, and as far as I can see it's right by Zander's place. Pretty sure he's not there, but...'

Sarah must have heard the urgency in her voice. 'Bloody hell, if it's not one of these men, it's the other. Leave it with me and I'll see what I can find out. If any of our guys on the news channel are taking the chopper up, I'll hitch a lift.'

Mirren hadn't heard from her again, until Sarah had joined the FaceTime call with her and Davie out in the limos on the way here, and barked a desperate, 'Mirren! Mirren! He's... he's...' before getting cut off.

He's what? He's okay? He's hurt? He's dead?

Now, surrounded by the Hollywood glitterati, she wanted to throw up. She glanced over at Davie, at the other end of the same row, and even from here she could see the apprehension on his face. Not even his usual slather of Kiehl's Facial Fuel and Tom Ford bronzer could hide his grey pallor, or the fact that he was nervously chewing his bottom lip.

She sent him a subliminal message. Zander was going to be okay. He was fine. He was here. He had to be. She was starting to convince herself that was true when the producer came on to the stage and a hush descended as the audience realised that this wasn't part of the plan. This broadcast ran like clockwork. Was drilled and scheduled days, weeks and months in advance. They rarely veered off script. If there was a last-minute alteration to the plan, then it was something big, something unexpected, something way too cataclysmic to ignore.

Mirren felt her whole body begin to tremble as Paula Leno, head of publicity for Lomax Films, the studio that had launched Mirren's career, that had made all of Zander's movies, took to the stage. 'Ladies and gentlemen, the live broadcast will start in a few moments, but the Academy felt it only right that you should know that in the last few minutes we've learned of the death of a friend, of a legend, of a man that many of you know and love...'

No. No. No. Mirren was trembling now, shivering from head to toe, hands on her lap, making small rocking movements back and forwards. Zander. He was at home. The fire had reached him, claimed him, taken him to be with Hollie.

Her head was shaking from side to side as she grabbed Mike's hand and felt his gaze swing round to her.

'No. No. I'll do anything...' she murmured, under her breath, trying to bargain with the universe. 'Don't take Zander. Please. I beg you. Not after my girl. Then Hollie. Please, not Zander.'

On stage, Paula Leno paused, gathered herself. 'I am devastated to announce that Wes Lomax passed away last night. I know you'll all join me in sending thoughts and prayers to the family and friends of this incredible man.'

Mirren froze. Processing. Not Zander. Oh, thank God. The relief that flooded through her veins gave her such a rush she jolted to the side and Mike immediately squeezed her hand tighter to steady her.

He leaned in towards her, and there was a kindness that hadn't been there all day. Mirren got it. He was still pissed off and he was right to be. The tension in the car had been huge, the apprehension of what was ahead on the red carpet had escalated his irritation, but now that they were here, there was some relief. Now, he was closer to the old Mike. To her Mike. And her Mike was one of the most caring, decent men she'd ever known. He was showing that again now in every contour of concern on his face, because he knew what she'd just been through, knew what losing Zander would do to her. 'Are you okay? It wasn't Zander, Mir. Shame about Wes, though.'

That startled her until she realised that he didn't know. They'd split up before Sarah had shared what had happened to her, before they'd discovered that there were scores of victims of Wes's brutality.

'I hope he rots in hell,' she whispered, but her words got lost in the explosion of light and sound as Queen opened the show in a riot of smoke and attitude. Brian May's searing guitar, Adam Lambert's pitch-perfect vocals. Wes Lomax's death was already temporarily put on hold, parked to one side, as the stars got to their feet, clapping and dancing, aware that acting like they were having a great time would bring the camera focus to them for an extra second or two.

A video montage of some of the year's big movies followed the opening number, then Tina Fey, Maya Rudolph and Amy Poehler took to the stage to announce the first award.

Mirren wasn't listening, because all she could hear in her head were Sarah's words on her answering machine last night.

'Mirren, I told Davie about Wes Lomax and he's pissed. He left my flat half an hour ago and I don't know where he's gone. I'm worried that he'll do something stupid.'

Had he? Had Davie done something to Wes?

When Mirren had finally reached him hours later, he'd been wasted. Incoherent. Ranting. Raging.

The most frustrating thing of all was that, with the exception of a hostage situation, she was in one of the few environments that she couldn't just get up, go over to his seat and ask him. The production staff would have her taken out by a sniper for messing up the broadcast.

The next few hours were interminable. In the short advert breaks, she tried to attract Davie's attention, but he just sat there, staring straight ahead. That rang an alarm bell of its own. Why was he avoiding eye contact? That's what he did when he was ashamed, embarrassed or guilty.

Which one was it today?

The show had gone to yet another commercial break, and one of the producers was back on stage, issuing orders, checking mics, speaking to her colleagues up in the gallery.

'Okay, stand by, everyone, Award for Best Director up next. And we're back in five. Four. Three. Two. One... Applause please.'

She was off the stage and they were clapping as directed.

'Here we go,' Mike whispered, just at the point where Mirren's whole lower body had gone numb from sitting in the one spot for too long. It was a miracle none of the Oscar nominees had dropped from DVT over the years.

Moment of truth. All she wanted was for Zander Leith to walk out on that stage right now and present the award as promised. She didn't even care if she didn't win it. Didn't give a toss. All she wanted was him, safe, here.

'Ladies and Gentlemen, to present the award for directing, please welcome...'

Make it him.

'...winner of last year's award, Guillermo del Toro.'

Mirren's heart sank. He hadn't kept his promise. Or maybe he wasn't able to.

Under normal circumstances, she'd have been on her feet for Guillermo, thrilled that he still had the limelight after his win last year for his wonderful movie, *The Shape Of Water*.

Tonight, she just wanted to ask him if he'd seen Zander Leith.

He made a couple of comments and then read out the list of nominees.

Roma – Alfonso Cuarón

BlacKkKlansman – Spike Lee

Cold War – Paweł Pawlikowski

The Favourite – Yorgos Lanthimos

VICE – Adam McKay

Clansman: Man Of War – Mirren McLean

There was loud applause after each of the nominees were called out, until it reached her, and she managed to rustle up only a smattering of acclaim. Again, bastards. They were all her best friends last year when she was on top. Not that the audience watching at home would hear the reluctance to celebrate her. An applause track was played over the television broadcast so people at home would think she'd been just as popular as the other nominees.

'Okay, let's do this.' Mike whispered into the ether. He wanted to win, had no idea that she didn't care. That it didn't matter. That this nonsense was nothing compared to what was going on with Sarah, with Davie, with Zander. God, where was he? Panic started to rise again. Where. Was. He?

'And the winner is,' Guillermo began, then paused for suspense. '*Roma* – Alfonso Cuarón!'

The room went wild. Mirren wondered how soon she could get out of here.

'Sorry, Mir. I really thought you had it,' Mike said, and he actually sounded like he meant it.

'They'd never let me have it. Not after everything that's happened in the last few months.'

He put his hand over hers again, and there was an expression of such tenderness on his gorgeous face. She couldn't think about that now either.

Other things mattered so much more, and they were living in her mind right now.

Davie had gone missing for a couple of hours last night.

Zander Leith was also missing last night.

Wes Lomax died last night.

And both men had reasons to want him dead.

Question was, how badly?

And what would she do if one of them was responsible?

She already knew the answer to that.

They'd covered up a murder once before.

When it came to Wes Lomax, she was more than happy to do it again.

32

ZANDER

'Bohemian Rhapsody' – Queen

He'd tried. With everything he had, he'd tried to be there for Mirren, but the pain was just too strong. And the nightmares – the fucking awful nightmares – they wouldn't stop coming. He just had to close his eyes and there was Wes. In a bed. Lainey Anders singing to him. And Zander was on top of him, screaming, shouting, stabbing, stabbing, stabbing him until he was dead. Just like Hollie.

Justice. That's what it was. In his life, he'd known three monsters.

Jono Leith, the one who had spawned him.

Wes Lomax, the one who had discovered him.

And Zander Leith, the one who was inside him.

The one who'd always felt alone, despite the demons that took every step beside him.

The one who had more money than he could count, but who was empty.

The one that millions of people adored, yet who hated himself.
The one who could save the world, but couldn't save his wife.
In his nightmares, the other two monsters were dead.
Now it was time to kill the third one.
It was time for Zander Leith, the movie star, to die.

33

DAVIE

'Shallow' – Lady Gaga and Bradley Cooper

Rising from the end seat of an obscure row at The Dolby theatre, Davie now knew the answer to a question that had been tormenting him all week.

He'd lost his career. His fortune. The love of his life. His credibility in this town.

Could this shitshow get any worse?

Today he'd found out the answer to that question, and it had landed right at the same time as the hangover that was now seeping into his brain.

Zander hadn't shown up to present the award. Neither he nor Mirren could locate him. He was nowhere to be found.

So the answer was yes. It could get worse. He could lose his brother too. What the fuck was he doing in here when he should be out looking for Zander? What did any of this crap matter?

The show was over and all he wanted was to get out of here, but he was trapped by a celebrity crush – literally. Hundreds of them all leaving the theatre at the same time, moving in the same direction, and he had no choice but to go with the flow.

As he did, two other undeniable truths struck him. The first was that no one was making eye contact with him. Not the A-listers that he'd defended when they'd fucked up over the years. Or the agents who'd begged him to join them when he was at his peak. Or even the stars – male and female – who'd come on to him when he was the biggest producer in town. None of them. The news that his show had been cancelled was clearly out and he was now a pariah because he had touched the contagion that they feared more than any other. Failure.

The thing that twisted the knife that little bit more was that he now had enough self-awareness to admit that if he was in their two-thousand-dollar Louboutins, or in the case of a couple of diminutive action stars, two-thousand-dollar Prada brogues with custom lifts, he would be acting exactly the same way. He'd cut countless people dead over the years, ostracised them when they'd slumped, or flopped, or hit a scandal. So this? This was karma.

He kept on moving, up the stairs, this time tucking behind Bradley Cooper and Lady Gaga. They'd stunned the audience into jaw-dropping silence with their performance of 'Shallow', the song from their remake of *A Star Is Born*. Tonight, Gaga had the Oscar for Best Original Song to add to the other awards on her mantlepiece, and she'd earned it, for her talent, for her brilliance, for her iridescent star power – but all the gossip tomorrow would be about the sizzling heat between her and Cooper up on that stage and rumours of a romance. Davie didn't believe it for a second. He was way too long in the tooth to see it for any more than it was – a sensational performance by two actors. It didn't matter what he thought, though. It was all about the buzz and the drama and if they were talking about you in this town, then your value was rising, Oscar or no Oscar.

No one was talking about Davie anymore. Failures only attracted whispers and uncomfortable silences.

He reached the top of the stairs, still moving slowly, with the crowd.

The second undeniable truth? The other people who weren't discussed. The dead. All around him, stars were laughing, back-slapping, congratulating each other, when only a few hours ago they'd been told that someone who had been a legend in this industry had passed away.

Just thinking about Lomax made Davie's teeth grind and his fists clench. Other than Jono Leith, he'd never hated anyone more. Those two bastards were on the same level of evil. Forget Cooper and Gaga's epic performance. The official announcement of Wes's death was the best thing he'd listened to all day.

If Wes Lomax was here, they'd be circling him like the sun, desperate to bask in his limelight. Now he was gone, and he was already forgotten, irrelevant, out of sight, out of mind, at least until they were asked to give televised accolades or eulogies that would earn column inches or screen time. Unless, of course, they knew what an evil, malicious, depraved bastard he really was. Then there wouldn't be enough bargepoles in the western seaboard for this lot.

Yeah, this town, and all it stood for, was deplorable.

Yet, even in that moment of enlightenment, Davie knew he would sell his soul to get back on top again, because every single ion of his being belonged here. He was built for it. Worshipped it. Gaga's song could have been written just for him. Davie Johnston – shallow.

As they streamed out of the theatre, Davie felt a hand clutch the back of his arm, felt the breath on his neck, then the slow, familiar terror of Mirren McLean speaking through gritted teeth.

'Outside. Now.'

He was a forty-seven-year-old man, but suddenly he was sixteen again, in his spotlessly clean but run-down house on a dilapidated terrace in a Glasgow council estate, and the first love of his life was pissed off with him for putting salt and vinegar on her chips. Her wrath was as terrifying now as it had been back then, and he had a feeling her fury could be caused by something a whole lot more serious than a late night meal.

Was it anger or fear?

Mirren must have ditched Mike, because she was on her own as she steered him out into the dusk of the early evening, then waited until his car was summoned. There were too many people to talk without being overheard, so nothing was said until they were in the limo. Normally they'd be heading to one of the after-parties now. The iconic Governor's Ball. The glittering Vanity Fair party. The annual Elton John fundraiser for his Aids Foundation.

Not tonight. As soon as they got into the limo, they both pulled out their phones and switched them back on.

Mirren's started beeping like a reversing dumper truck. Davie's was silent. There it was again. The aftermath of failure.

Before Mirren opened her phone, she eyed him with a stare that made him squirm. 'I'll come back to you in a minute. I want to know exactly where you were last night and what you were doing, Davie, because I need to know if you did something that can't be undone.'

He knew exactly what she was alluding to, and he'd expected it. He opened his mouth, but she cut him off.

'Not yet. We need to know if they've found Zander before we talk about anything else.'

Her first call was to Sarah, who answered almost immediately and Mirren flicked straight to loud speaker so Davie could hear.

'Sarah! Any news? Have you found him?'

'No, but I know a bit more. Shit, Mirren, this isn't good. We've had surveillance on the clinic since Wes was moved there. Drones. Stationary cameras. We've got the whole lot set up, trying to find out who's coming or going.'

Davie felt his stomach begin to twist, and desperately wanted a fast-forward button, to hear what they'd seen.

'We've got footage of Zander, parked in a concealed spot outside the Hurston Centre last night. Then more of him entering the building. They found his car, burnt out in his driveway. His house has been destroyed too. But there's no sign of him.'

Mirren groaned. 'Where is he, Sarah? We need to find him.'

'Mirren, there's more. Looking at the time stamp of when he drove away from the Hurston Centre, the fire was already well underway. He drove right into it. They can't get in to search his house yet because the fire marshalls haven't deemed it safe, but I think you need to prepare yourself because none of this is making sense. What was he doing at the Hurston? And why did he drive home afterwards, straight into the carnage?'

Davie knew what she was implying, but he didn't want to hear it. No. Zander was depressed, he was struggling and lost, but... no. Fuck right off. He wasn't losing his brother.

'I don't know the answers,' Mirren croaked, and Davie could hear the raw pain there. Zander was like a brother to her too, one who had held her together when Chloe died. He saw her trying to open her mouth to speak, but the words wouldn't come out, so he reached over and gently took the phone from her, keeping it on loudspeaker so they could both hear.

'Sarah, it's Davie. Where are you now?'

'I'm back at the office. I'm just going through some tapes – horrific stuff – that we found at Monica Janson's place. That's where I went last night after you left. And that's another conversation, Davie, because you scared the crap out of me. Where did you go?'

He saw Mirren's anguished gaze come back round to him and he cleared his throat.

'Nowhere. Got drunk. Passed out.'

He wasn't sure that either of them believed him, so he just brushed right on past it.

'Look, we'll talk later. What's on the tapes? Does it help you?'

'Davie, I... I can't even tell you. It's bad. The most depraved thing I've ever seen. He taped everything. So many women and they had no idea. And, Mirren, can you hear me?'

That snapped Mirren out of her pain, focused her on the present again. She leaned towards him, so she could hear better.

'Mirren, I don't know how to say this... but there's something I need you to see.'

Even under the expertly applied make-up, Davie could see the colour drain from her face.

'Sarah, what is it? Oh God, Sarah. Tell me. Is it Chloe? Is she on a tape?'

Chloe had been eighteen when she'd died, but she'd lived on the wild side of addiction and vice for years before. At one point, she was dating some messed-up, junkie, trust-fund kid and he'd tried to blackmail her with a sex tape. Mirren had gone to the guy's hotel room with a gun and threatened to put a bullet in him if he didn't give her his phone. He made the right decision that time, but it was the last one he made. A couple of months after Chloe died, he'd been found in a canyon off Laurel with his fingers missing. Maybe the mother of the next young woman that he'd fucked with hadn't been quite as restrained as Mirren.

Sarah hadn't answered yet, so Mirren jumped back in. 'Sarah! Did that bastard do something to her? Did he film her?'

The two of them were staring at the phone, waiting for Sarah's reply.

'Mirren, it's not Chloe that's on one of the tapes... It's you.'

34

SARAH

'Nightmare' – Halsey

Sarah left the meeting room and crossed the open-plan office, passing her own desk on the way.

She'd moved her laptop, phone and all the playback equipment she needed into the secure, lockable, empty boardroom at the *Out Of The Shadow's* offices when she'd got back from searching for Zander up in Malibu. At that time, the office was still busy, and she didn't want anyone else looking at the tapes, or overhearing her conversations.

Now, it was 8 p.m. and the floor was deserted, except for two other people: Shandra and Meilin. Both of them were out at their desks, typing furiously on their keyboards, both on the hunt for knowledge and details that were supposed to stay hidden.

Sarah hoped they wouldn't be hidden for much longer.

'Anything yet, Shandra? Bank details. Background. Connections?'

'I'm brilliant but I'm not Jesus. I'll need a bit longer for miracles,' Shandra quipped, without even glancing up from her computer.

Sarah's phone buzzed in her hand and she answered it immediately. 'Okay, I'll come let them in.'

'They're here?' Meilin asked, as Sarah headed for the doors.

She nodded, dread robbing her of her words. She wasn't looking forward to this. Of all the things she expected to see on those tapes today, this wasn't one of them.

That said, the whole experience had been traumatic. It didn't matter that she'd stayed up all last night watching them, and now hadn't been to sleep for thirty-seven hours, because after what she'd seen, she doubted she would ever sleep again. Chip Chasner, her boss and executive producer, had sat with her for hours today, going through the videos, and they'd called in Legal to clarify their position and ensure this was handled to the letter of the law. The answer was a grey area. Monica had given them to Sarah, so she had every right to have them. Without the testimonies of the women involved, it couldn't be confirmed that crimes had taken place, so they couldn't be categorised as evidence yet. However, there was no way that any of this stuff should be anywhere near the public domain, so they'd made the decision to catalogue everything and turn it all over to the authorities.

However, there had been exceptions. Sarah had contacted all the women in their existing investigation and notified them of the existence of the tapes. If the women had requested that the recordings of their assaults be excluded from the handover, and given directly to them instead, Sarah had agreed. These ladies had been through enough. Sarah wasn't going to do a single thing against their will.

The authorities wouldn't be made aware of those particular tapes.

Or one other.

At the security doors for the floor, Sarah punched in a code and opened them, allowing Mirren McLean and Davie Johnston to enter. 'Thanks, Leon,' she said to the security guard who'd escorted them up there.

She hugged Mirren, feeling the tremble that was running through her body, then cast a subdued glance at Davie. She wasn't hugging him yet. Not until she found out exactly what he'd done last night.

She'd told herself over and over today that he wouldn't have killed Wes. Couldn't have. Didn't have it in him. But… at the same time, she knew exactly what Zander, Davie and Mirren had gone through as youngsters, and she knew what they'd had to do to survive. Deep down, Sarah had a feeling that when it came to protecting the people they loved, all three of them were capable of anything.

'Have you heard anything more about Zander?' The question from Mirren surprised Sarah a little. Despite the reason they were here, Mirren's first thought was Zander. Not herself.

'No, nothing. We've got contacts with every sheriff's office, fire service and hospital – if someone finds him, we'll be the first to know,' she reported, squeezing Mirren's hand.

'I've got everyone I know on it too,' Mirren told her. 'Lou is going through the city like a tornado.'

'We'll find him,' Sarah vowed, not sure that was the case, but going with positivity because, right now, she was about to download something so awful, she couldn't bear to add to Mirren's suffering. 'Okay, let's go.'

They followed her across the office and when Meilin and Shandra reacted with raised eyebrows, she realised why. The duo were an incongruous sight. Davie, in his custom, midnight blue Andrew Brookes tuxedo, looking every inch the most dashing celebrity, and Mirren in a full-length, utterly stunning, red-carpet dress.

'I feel underdressed,' Meilin quipped when Sarah introduced them.

Sarah took them into the boardroom, locked the door, took a USB stick from her handbag and plugged it into her laptop. 'Are you sure about this?' she asked Mirren.

The reply was a firm nod.

'Even with Davie here?'

Mirren shrugged, threw a glance at Davie. 'Nothing he hasn't seen before.' It was a nervous joke in terrible taste, but Sarah fully understood.

'I need you to know I didn't watch it all. I switched it off as soon as I realised...' She didn't finish. 'So just tell me as soon as you want me to stop it.'

Sarah pressed play, then kept her finger by the keyboard, ready to shut it down as soon as Mirren said the word. The very existence of this tape was enough of a violation of Mirren's privacy. Sarah wasn't going to exacerbate that by showing a second more than was needed to identify it.

The scene opened and Mirren gasped straight away. 'That's my bedroom. No. No. No. Who was...?'

She didn't get any further, because the answer to her question walked across the shot.

'Jason. That's Jason Grimes. How did he do that? How did he film without me knowing?' Mirren was wide-eyed with astonishment.

'The fucker,' Davie spat.

Sarah pressed stop, took the USB out of the port and handed it over to Mirren. 'Here you go. As far as I know, there are no copies. This is the only one.'

Mirren was still trying to get to grips with what she'd seen.

'But... you said you found this in Monica's home? It belonged to Wes?'

'Yes,' Sarah confirmed. 'He set this all up. This is the only tape with Jason in it though – Wes is in all the others. He made tapes of everything, and Monica stored them in her home. Apparently, she liked to watch them, convinced herself of some mad theory that the way he was with other women proved his love for her.'

Mirren's eyes flared. 'What the hell? That's so fucking sick.'

Sarah didn't have time to agree before Mirren went on, 'But why would Wes do this in the first place? What did any of this have to do with me? With Jason?'

Sarah had given this a lot of thought over the last few hours. 'I think Wes had some kind of shit list. A collection of people he felt had wronged him. Maybe his heart attack gave him a taste of mortality and he wanted to settle scores. Or maybe he just wanted a game to play in retirement. I've no idea.'

'What score did he have with me?'

Sarah leaned forward in her chair. 'Like Davie, and Zander, he discovered you. And therefore he thinks you owe him everything. Lifelong loyalty. You took the Clansman movies back from Lomax to Pictor, lost him millions. I think that was the score he was settling.'

Even as she said it, she knew how despicable it sounded.

Mirren was still shaking her head, stunned. 'Oh God. It terrifies me now that it makes so much sense. I mean this with every bit of me – I want to raise the evil bastard from the dead so I can kill him myself. I still don't understand how he got my tape though? What's the connection with Jason?'

Sarah didn't have all the pieces yet. 'I don't know. We're still working on that.'

Mirren was quiet for a moment, processing, before exhaling. 'It's unbelievable.'

Sarah sat back. 'Is it though? Weinstein. Cosby. Larry Nassar. There would be no #MeToo movement if there wasn't an under-belly of horror and deviance out there.'

'You're right. I guess it's just unfathomable that he got away with it for so long.'

'He had Monica on his side. She protected him at all costs. And who was going to investigate Wes without proof? He'd been around for decades so he had everyone in his pocket. Cops. Politicians. I think he had the power to make just about anything go away. Until a few brave women tried to fight back.'

That was the biggest takeaway from all this.

None of it would have come to light if Lisa Arexo, and the other women who had talked to her, hadn't told their stories.

'What about Monica? Where is she now? Because there's a special place in hell for a woman who would do that.'

'We don't know. She left the house last night after showing me where the tapes were. I—'

A knock at the door interrupted her, and she waved at Shandra to come in.

The young woman burst forward like she was storming the building. 'Okay, Jesus can move over, because I have that miracle you were looking for,' she announced.

Sarah waited patiently, appreciating that the preamble would undoubtedly be worth it.

'I found the link. Jason Grimes...' Sarah saw Mirren's posture stiffen. 'Son of Wendy and Dirk Grimes. Both deceased. Killed in a car accident. Dirk Grimes was found to have high quantities of methamphetamine in his bloodstream. Jason was fourteen years old. He was then placed in foster care until he was seventeen. However, at that point, his education, expenses and care were fully supported and funded by his late mother's estranged brother, one Wesley Lomax.'

'Christ,' Davie exhaled. 'He groomed him.'

'Maybe.' Sarah conceded. 'Or maybe it was just a family disposition to weird, shady shit.'

'But why wouldn't Wes just give him a job and a great start in life? Why do this?' That came from Mirren.

'But then, who would he have to do that shady shit for him, with blind loyalty and no risk of comeback? The boy that he picked up from nothing ends up with a pretty cool life – that buys a shitload of blind loyalty and a lifetime of working off the debt,' Sarah suggested.

Meilin came in behind Shandra. 'Wes's will. A million dollars for Jason Grimes. Five million dollars to Monica. Everything else to Lainey Anders.'

The two other women left a silence behind them when they went back to their desks to carry on with their investigations.

'So now we know her pay-off,' Sarah said. 'Five million dollars. Not the lifetime with Wes that she expected, but enough to keep her quiet. Do you think she knew?'

'I don't know anything anymore,' Davie admitted, opening the top couple of buttons of his shirt. Sarah had always loved him in a suit. It was his sexiest look. But she couldn't even think of anything personal until she had answers.

'Okay, before we go any further, I need to know. Davie. Where did you go when you left my flat last night? You dropped out of contact. Please, please tell me you weren't away doing some kind of vigilante shit on my behalf? Please tell me you didn't go near Wes Lomax?'

Sarah noticed Mirren lean in, interested in the answer.

'No. I didn't go near Wes. I don't know if that makes me smart or a coward,' he told her, his brown eyes going straight through her soul as the relief came in one huge wave.

'So where were you?' Mirren probed. 'It took me hours to track you down.'

'I told you in the limo. I was nowhere. Passed out.'

Both women zeroed in like Exocets.

'Davie, don't...' Sarah warned him, suddenly worried again. 'If you're lying to me...'

He grunted, exasperated. 'Urgh. It's like the fucking CIA in here.' He threw his arms up. 'Right, full confession. And pay attention, because I'm never telling this story again. I got wrecked in a bar, got caught peeing on Lainey Anders' star on the Hollywood Walk Of Fame, Jenny had to come bail me out. So next time someone says I couldn't get arrested in this town, well... there you fucking are. The only shining light is that I'm now so fucking irrelevant that the cops didn't tip off TMZ.'

Sarah's hand flew to her mouth. This wasn't a time for laughter, but this one would definitely be stored for later.

'Zander will love that,' Mirren said softly.

The mention of his name refocused Sarah's mind. 'We still haven't found him, Mir. Last sighting was still of him driving away from the Hurston Centre last night.'

None of them vocalised the obvious assumption.

'So what's the plan?' Mirren asked, then answered her own question.

'How about we go home, change, then head up to Broad Beach. If we can get access to his house, then...'

She didn't get any further because her phone rang. Lou.

Mirren answered immediately. 'Hey, you're on loudspeaker. Davie and Sarah are here too.'

'Just as well I wasn't calling to talk about my pap smear. Okay, gang, I have news. My contact at LAX came through. Zander flew out of there last night.'

Mirren gasped. 'To where?'

'London.'

Davie reacted with a blurted, 'What?'

Sarah was pretty sure he had heard the first time, but was just expressing confusion.

'London,' Lou repeated. 'Left late last night.'

'Lou, you're incredible and I love you. I'll buzz you back.' Mirren ended the call.

Sarah sat back. 'Why is he going to London? I don't get it.'

'Me either,' Mirren said. 'Aaargh, I'm just so relieved he's alive. But... listen, whatever he's doing, he doesn't want us to know. And with Zander that usually means it's something that won't end well for him. He only goes secretive when he's in a dark place. Change of plan,' she said, getting up. 'I'm going to London.'

'Not without me,' Davie argued. 'I need to come because... He's my brother.'

It was the first time Sarah had ever heard him say that. She flipped her laptop open. 'There are three free seats on the BA flight tonight. Leaves in an hour and a half though. Can you get them to keep the gate open if we're a few minutes late?' she asked Mirren, fully aware that she probably could. Either way, Sarah was going with them. The urgency was off the Lomax investigation now that they had all the evidence and Wes was dead. The lawyers would want a few weeks with all the details before they cleared it. In the meantime, Zander's disappearance was, right now, far more time critical.

Mirren shook her head. 'No. If we fly commercial, it'll be all over Twitter by the time we land.'

Sarah knew she was right. It was the thing she'd hated about life with Davie. They'd be having a romantic dinner somewhere, and by the time they got home, there would be photographs of them eating their carbonara all over social media.

Mirren picked her phone up again, made a call, rhyming off her requests.

When she disconnected, everything was arranged. 'Jet will be ready at Burbank in an hour.'

Sarah closed her laptop. 'This is why I hang out with rich people.'

'Passports?' Mirren asked.

'I'll get Drego to meet me at the airport with mine,' Davie said.

'Logan and Lauren are at my place tonight. They wanted to keep me company whether I won or lost. I'll get them to bike mine over to the airport, with some clothes too.'

Sarah had almost forgot that Mirren had been up for an Oscar just a few hours ago. How could it be that that wasn't the most significant thing that happened in her day?

'Mine is in my purse. Don't go anywhere without it,' Sarah added.

Mirren stood up, looked from Davie to Sarah. 'Okay. We're doing this? Just the three of us? No one else gets to know until we're sure of what we're dealing with. Until we find him.'

Sarah began packing up her things, getting ready to go. 'Agreed.'

'Shit, I can't go like this. Sarah, do you have anything here I can wear for now?'

'Sure. I keep sweats in my drawer. Hang on.'

She was back in two minutes, and yes, there was a tiny pang of irrational and unwarranted jealousy when she saw Mirren was holding up her hair, and Davie was pulling down the zipper on her dress.

Mirren let it fall to the floor, revealing a nude body suit, then threw on the gym leggings, sweatshirt and sliders that Sarah handed over. 'Okay, let's go.'

Out in the main office, Sarah gave the other two a vague explanation. 'There are a couple of things I need to check out, so I might not be in tomorrow. You can get me on my cell though.'

If Shandra and Meilin were surprised, they were too professional to show it.

Sarah opened the door and held it as the others trooped through.

Davie pressed the elevator button for the ground floor, then held open the door that took them out into the cold night air.

As they went, Sarah wondered if the others were thinking the same thing as her.

Where was Zander going? What was he going to do? Was he running because he'd already done it? Was Zander leaving the country because he killed Wes Lomax?

Given that the last place he'd been seen was the Hurston, there was a definite possibility of a link between Zander bolting and Wes's sudden death. Sarah had ignored one murder for this group. Was she going to have to do it again?

She didn't know for sure, but she did know that the most dangerous kind of man was one who was in a situation like Zander Leith.

He had nothing left that mattered to him. So what did he have to lose?

35

MIRREN

'Hold On, I'm Coming' – Sam and Dave

As soon as they were airborne, Mirren made her first call, to Jonah, her new assistant, hired to replace Devlin, who had ridden off into the Scottish sunset in his new role as Brodie McLure in Clansman. Jonah was an old friend of Logan and Chloe, a sweet guy who used to hang out at the house with her kids when they were young teens. They'd been so close, Mirren remembered thinking that they were the next generation of Mirren, Zander and Davie. If only they'd stayed that way. Logan and Jonah were still good mates, but Chloe had left them behind, chosen another route. One that Zander had tried to save her from several times. Chloe hadn't made it, but at least with Zander's help, she'd had a chance. And now it was Mirren's time to try to save him, from whatever he was running from, or running to.

Devlin had left a brilliantly detailed, comprehensive handover manual for his successor, so Jonah had got up to speed with impressive efficiency. He also knew that he was renumerated exceptionally well because the job required him to be on call twenty-four hours a day, although this was the first time that Mirren had called him out of normal office hours.

'Jonah, I'm on a flight on the way to London right now, but that's 100 per cent confidential and if anyone asks, I'm taking some well-earned personal time. Everyone will just think that I'm sulking about the Oscar, so they'll buy it.'

'No problem. And I'm sorry about that.'

'About what?'

'The Oscar.'

It was so far down her list of concerns that she almost laughed. 'Ah, thank you. But you'll learn there'll be many more crushing disappointments, so it's best not to get fussed about any of those things.' Even as she was saying it, she knew it was true.

'Anyway, what I need is for you to book my usual suite at the Goring, please – if that's not available, two adjacent suites will do.' She wasn't being presumptuous about Davie and Sarah's relationship. Her usual suite had two bedrooms and a sofa bed in the lounge, so they'd be fine, even if they wanted separate sleeping spaces.

'If you check Devlin's notes, you'll see the pseudonym he uses for me when I'm staying there. When you call, ask for Jeremy Goring. He owns the hotel and he's the soul of discretion and a really good guy. If you give him that name, he'll know it's me.'

It was a common tactic when any celebrity wanted privacy and anonymity in a hotel. Hotels like the Goring were wonderfully discreet, but a false name guaranteed that extra level of privacy. God knows, she didn't want to arrive to a picket line organised by some radical incel group claiming she was a sex pest.

Fucking Wes. And fucking Jason Grimes.

That snide little shit would get what was coming, but for now, she had far more important things on her mind.

When she hung up, she realised she had a voicemail. She assumed it would be from Logan, checking that she'd got her passport, delivered just in time to the VIP rep at the airport. She clicked to listen.

Not Logan. Mike.

'Mir, it's me. Listen, I came to the house – I'm here with Logan and Lauren. I just wanted… I guess I just wanted to talk. Logan isn't sure when you'll be back, and he's turning pink when I ask him about it, so I'm guessing there's probably something you don't want me to know.'

That made her smile. They both knew that her son was the worst liar on earth. The slightest hint of an untruth and he went into some internal panic that flushed his cheeks. Sometimes they put him on the spot just to mess with him.

'I totally respect that. You don't owe me anything. But I just wanted to say that I'm sorry. And tonight, you were beautiful, and I'm an asshole. Call me back if you can talk. I lo…'

Her chest fluttered. He was going to say he loved her, like he had ended every single call until the day he'd found out about Jason. Even when they were apart, he still said it. This time, he caught himself, stuttered.

'I… I hope I can talk to you soon.'

She glanced across the plane. Sarah and Davie were in deep conversation on the sofas in front of her, both of them holding bottles of beer, their body language open to each other. She really hoped they would work it out. Especially now that the secrets were out.

Keen to avoid playing gooseberry, and inspired by their communication with each other, she picked up her phone and her glass of wine and headed through to the bedroom behind her. It was a compact, but stunning room, almost like a cabin on a luxury cruise ship. The walls were cream, but there was a glossy wood veneer behind the pale gold velvet headboard and co-ordinating side tables below brass art deco wall lights. The sheets she recognised as Frette, 800 thread count. Like sleeping on clouds. None of this was on her initial request – it just so happened that this jet had been the only one available when she'd called. She'd have been happy with just a standard private plane, with two rows of chairs across an aisle. Hell, right now she'd sleep in a cramped seat next to the toilets on Slum Air if it got her to Zander quicker.

Using the jet's Wi-Fi, she FaceTimed Mike. He answered on the second ring, and she could see he was in his car. 'Hang on, I'll pull over,' he told her, and she watched as he manoeuvred, then stopped the engine and got out of the vehicle. When he sat down on the small, sandstone wall and she heard the ocean, she knew exactly where he was.

'I just left your house,' he said, telling her what she already knew.

He was at one of their favourite spots, the little cove at the end of her road. He was sitting on a wall they'd sat on a hundred times at night, watching the ocean slip on to the sand in front of them, then retreat, then come back for more. Sometimes when they were there, they'd sort out the world, or they'd laugh, and sip beer from the bottles they'd brought in the pockets of their hoodies. Other times, they'd just say nothing. Mirren would lie on the wall, with her head on his lap, and they'd just savour the silence, and the love that was in every stroke of his thumb against her cheek.

'I see that,' she said softly.

There was a pause, as it became clear that neither of them knew where to start. Too much pain. Too much distance. Too much love. Too much of everything was getting in the way.

When he spoke, he caught her off guard, with a tender, 'I love you.'

Another pause before he went on, 'And I just want to say that to you first in case this turns into one of those conversations that starts off calm and well-intended, then all goes to shit, usually because I'm an asshole.'

Hearing him say he loved her made her smile, melted away one of the many layers of stress that was crushing her. 'You mentioned that already. The asshole bit. On your message.'

'I did,' he agreed. 'Just repeating for emphasis, I guess.'

A couple of seconds passed with just the ocean waves making conversation.

'Is it okay if I just talk?' he asked. 'Just tell you everything that's on my mind? Get it all out there. And that way, you'll know, with no doubts or cross purposes, what I'm thinking?'

She'd always loved that about him. He said what he felt. No games. No demands. It's why he was one of the very few studio heads in this town that didn't have a queue of people lining up to say what a dick he was. In business, he was fair and he was reasonable and people respected his intelligence and his ability to negotiate a tough deal and make hard decisions, without taking a blowtorch to the room.

As a husband, though, he had an emotional intelligence that she adored, and sure, sometimes it got swept away by passion or pain, but for the most part, Mike Feechan was a good and decent man who didn't deserve what she'd done to him.

He was still waiting for her answer.

'I think I'd like that.' She hoped he could see that she was smiling when she spoke.

'Okay. Here goes...' His eyebrows frowned as he prepared his words, and Mirren thought he'd never been more handsome.

'The first time we separated, I didn't leave because I didn't love you. I left because I loved you too much to be an afterthought in your life. It felt like everything – your work, your foundation, Chloe's Care, your grief, your pain – all of it came before me. And I know that sounds selfish, but you just wouldn't let me in. I wanted to be your husband. I wanted to love you.'

There was nothing he'd said so far that wasn't true.

'When I left, it was to let you breathe, in the hope that you'd see we should be important. So when you came back and told me that you wanted us to work... Man, that was everything. I was so happy, but it was more than that. It was right. It felt like it was forever. And I was all in, Mir. That's why... when it happened...'

She appreciated that he wasn't spelling out the truth of it. *When she'd had sex with another man.*

'It wasn't just my marriage that changed, it was every single day of my life after that. It felt like I couldn't ever imagine a day that I wouldn't be angry about what happened, that I wouldn't be embarrassed, or devastated, or worried, or fucked right off...'

The waves again. Crashing now, in time with the beats of her heart.

'But the thing is... I don't want to do it. The last time, you realised we could make it, that we had to be together. This time, I've realised it too. I want us to sort this, Mir. It's taken me a while to get here, but the alternative is never having you again, and that's too much to lose. I want to be your husband and forget everything that's happened. Clean slate. Just me and you. Do you think you can do that? Start over? I really hope you say yes, because I love you, Mir.'

He was staring straight at her now, and she wanted to lean into him, to kiss him, to fall into his chest and let him hold her. She didn't even pause to think through her answer.

'Yes. I love you too, Mike. No matter what, I'll never stop being sorry for breaking what we had.'

'I don't know that I like the sound of "no matter what". I think I was hoping for more, for something like, "Thank God, I'll be round in twenty minutes with my toothbrush."'

She loved that about him too. He made her laugh. Made her lighten up. Even when she was feeling way too dark inside.

'That one would be a bit tough right now,' she said, pulling the phone back so he could see her surroundings.

He recognised them immediately.

'You're on a jet?'

She nodded. 'Yes. I've got so much to tell you, Mike, but this isn't the time to go into it all.'

'At least tell me where you're going.'

She could see it was from genuine concern, not intrusion.

'London. I think Zander has gone there. He's in a really bad way and I need to find him, to make sure he's okay.'

'Is there anything I can do?'

He was a powerful guy, and she knew he could pull strings, move mountains. But the thing was, in their world, she was his equal. If she needed anything, she'd get it herself. And that was the crux of their problems. Mirren McLean had had to fend for herself since she was a child and she'd been too scared, or too selfish, or too damn stupid, to change that when she'd married Mike.

'No, we're good. Davie and Sarah are with me. But thank you.'

She contemplated telling him about Jason, and Wes, and everything else that had happened, but no. That was a conversation for another time, when she could concentrate on them and nothing else.

A beep on her phone, then a notification on the screen took her attention. Lou was trying to reach her.

Now she just had to work out how to tell the guy who'd just shared his whole heart with her that she had to go.

He read it on her face. 'You have to go? Something's happened?'

'Lou is trying to get me. She's tracking Zander, so I'm guessing she's found something.'

'Listen, I know you've got that going on just now, and I get it. I've kinda ambushed you with all this tonight. Just... think about it. About us. And when you're ready, come back to me, Mir. I love you.'

'I love you too.'

All she wanted to do was stay on the phone, talk to him, fix this. But not yet.

'Lou!' she said, as she answered the incoming call.

'Change of plan,' Lou blurted. 'He took a second flight.'

Mirren's heart sank. Where the hell was he?

'To where?'

There was a crackle on the line.

'Glasgow.'

Mirren felt like she'd been shot in the chest. She hadn't been back to Glasgow since she'd left almost thirty years ago. Neither had Zander. Nor Davie. They all loved their home city, their roots, but too much had happened there and all of them had vowed they would never return. Until now.

'Lou Cole, I love you. I'm going to ply you with cocktails when I get back.'

'Throw in a spa day and I'm there. Love you.'

Mirren hung up and immediately picked up the internal phone that went directly to the cockpit.

'I'm sorry to do this, but change of plan. Can we reroute to Glasgow?'

'Of course. I'll arrange it straight away,' the captain assured her. The jet company didn't charge sixty thousand dollars for this flight, and then say no to anything she wanted.

Mirren rested her head back against the headboard.

So she was going home.

Glasgow.

To Zander.

If he was going there, it was because he wanted to feel pain, to remember the unthinkable. That made her determination to be there for him even stronger.

If he was guilty. She would keep his secret.

If he was innocent. She'd defend him.

Either way, she was going to find him.

And she wasn't going to let him go.

36

ZANDER

'Caledonia' – Dougie MacLean

He still wasn't sure what had brought him here. A compulsion. Maybe a need to say goodbye. Or maybe a need to belong to something. Anything.

There had just been a moment, two nights ago, when he knew he couldn't leave this earth without coming back here.

It hadn't even been a conscious decision.

When he'd left the Hurston Centre that night, he'd had a plan in his mind. A solid one. Go home. Walk into the flames. Feel Hollie's presence in every room, in every single thing he touched. And then wait until she came for him.

But it hadn't worked out that way. When he'd got there, the flames were already dying, his house had been consumed by them and now they were lying down to sleep. He'd abandoned his car and walked down to the beach, sat there, watched the ocean, then raised his eyes to the sky to speak to her.

The plane had been the first thing he'd seen. It was in the distance, taking off from LAX, soaring heavenwards.

And he had no idea why, but it felt like a sign.

He'd thrown his backpack over his shoulder and jogged a couple of miles along the beach, to a spot where he knew he could cut up on to the road. That's when he'd summoned an Uber to LAX.

'Which terminal?'

He didn't speak. But someone else took charge, maybe divine intervention, maybe the universe, maybe his wife, directing him...

'Terminal B.'

That's when he knew exactly where he was going. Home. Glasgow.

On the day Hollie Callan strolled into his office looking for a job, she'd told him she'd always wanted to go to Scotland. For years, he'd been promising he'd bring her, but they'd just never got round to it. Now they were here. She was beside him. In a small oak box with her name etched on the top.

For the first time in thirty years of being out in public, not one person had recognised him. He took that back. Maybe the guy at the check-in desk in LAX, who'd looked at him quizzically when he spotted his name in his passport. But even then, it had his given name: Alexander Leith. Not Zander. And Zander could see the agent deciding that the dishevelled man in front of him was no movie star. Baseball cap. Sunken face. Glasses. And flying economy. Perfectly understandable that the agent had shaken his head, decided it couldn't possibly be the A-list actor Zander Leith and waved him through.

When he'd landed, he'd left the terminal building at Glasgow and his body had immediately reacted. Shivering. Cold. He'd forgotten how fucking freezing it was in this place in February.

'All right, pal?' That was the driver in the white taxi at the front of a line of identical vehicles.

'Aye,' he'd said, his Glasgow brogue thick and low, with the guarded disdain of someone who doesn't want to chat about the weather all the way into the city.

The driver could read the room.

Zander had given him the street name, and he'd seen that the driver immediately understood. Maybe he was from a nearby area, a nicer one, where the people took care of each other, where there were problems, addictions, antisocial elements, but they were overshadowed by a community spirit that strived to make life better for them all.

It wasn't like that in the street that the driver had punched into his satnav. The men who came from there didn't do small talk. They did aggression. Irritation. Violence.

In the back seat, the bloke who'd sat in hostile silence all the way there knew that he fitted in. He was built for that place. He'd proved it time and time again, from the first day that he'd taken a baseball bat to the back of his father's head, until the last time, only a few years ago, that he'd fallen out of a nightclub in Los Angeles, fists flying, pummelling some prick who had it coming.

When they'd reached the destination, Zander had given the driver fifty quid, from the two hundred he'd taken out of a cash machine while he'd waited in London for his connecting flight. If the driver was surprised about the tenner tip, he hadn't shown it, probably too focused on getting out of there before it all went horribly wrong. Because in that street, it always did.

The rest had been easy. Until he was sixteen years old, he and Davie had spent every free hour in the shed at the end of Ena Johnston's garden. Muscle memory had the whole thing covered. Zander had cut down the alley at the side of Davie's house, jumped the fence, slipped in at the back of the shed. They'd been gone for thirty years, but he could see Ena Johnston hadn't replaced or changed a thing. Zander knew why. He knew that she would probably come out here every year and add a coat of some kind of varnish to preserve the wood of the shed. Always herself. Never a tradesman. No. Mrs Johnston was way too savvy to let anyone near this place.

He also knew that if the back four panels on the right-hand side were twisted to an exact angle, they would then slip to the side, creating a space that sixteen-year-old Zander could slide through without a problem. Forty-eight-year-old Zander, body decimated by heartbreak, had managed it too.

He'd crawled in. Replaced the panels. He'd used his backpack as a pillow and he'd pulled a couple of old rugs over the top of him so he didn't freeze to death before the day was out.

Now he was where he was supposed to be.

Zander Leith, the movie star, was finally dead.

He'd let him go. Killed him off.

This was all he was now. Homeless. Cold. Alone. Nothing left. And this was the Zander Leith he deserved to be.

For the first time in months, he closed his eyes, and he slept without hearing Hollie's screams...

'Zander.' A whisper. A woman's voice.

Hollie. She was back.

'Zander.' The voice again. Now it was closer, and someone was rubbing his arm, gently shaking his shoulder. 'Zander, it's me.'

Not Hollie. Mirren. She must have got out of the house tonight. Maybe her mother was in there as usual, screwing his old man, and Mirren had done what she did every night – come to escape the sound of the headboard banging on the wall upstairs, of her mother's whispers and screams of pleasure. Mirren had come to find him and Davie, to be with people she didn't hate.

'Zander.' More insistent now.

He opened one eye, squinted as the daylight contracted his pupils. It took a moment for them to focus, but when they did, he saw he was right.

Almost.

It wasn't that Mirren; it was this one. The grown one, who'd lived a whole lifetime since they were here last.

He pushed himself up so that he was sitting with his back against the wooden wall panels, then reached out to accept the steaming mug she was handing to him.

As soon as he took it, she lifted the old rugs, slipped in underneath them, so that she was sitting next to him. Their positions and postures identical.

'How did you know I was here?' he asked, hearing his voice come out in a husky croak. He had no clue how long he'd been sleeping, but he felt the clench of his gut as hunger made its presence known.

'Davie's mum saw you come in last night, but it didn't matter. We knew this was where you'd come to.'

Some people might think it strange that Ena had seen him enter here but not come to check, to speak to him, but that was her way. Thirty years ago, she'd watched from the kitchen window as a blood-spattered Mirren had run past, had stormed in here screaming, and seconds later, Zander and Davie had burst out, racing towards Mirren's house.

Later, Ena had watched as they'd carried Jono Leith's body in here.

And over the next two days, she'd ignored the sounds of them digging until they had a hole big enough to bury him.

Ena Johnston had watched it all, and she'd stayed here ever since, protecting their secret.

'Old times,' Mirren said, her sad smile telling him that she was right back there with him.

'Shit times,' he countered, correcting her.

'Not all of them.'

She was right. Not all of them. Not the times they were together, just the three of them, her, him, Davie, lying on this floor, smoking cigarettes they'd stolen from her mum, drinking vodka Zander had stolen from his dad, laughing, listening to the radio, Davie singing along because he thought Simple Minds were going to discover him in a shit shed, in a shit street, in a shit part of town.

Davie had always been the optimist, the hustler, the one who'd get them out of here. Wes had discovered them, true. But it was Davie who had got in front of Wes and made it happen.

Mirren took a sip from the mug in her hands. 'I need to ask you something.'

A pause. He waited. It came.

'Did you kill Wes?'

A sigh. 'He's dead?'

'He's dead,' she confirmed. He could see her shoulders sag with relief, and he wondered if she'd doubted him. He wouldn't blame her. He'd doubted himself.

'No, but I really wish I had. I have nightmares every night. And every single time I stab the bastard again and again until he's not breathing. Until he's gone. Just like Hollie.'

He let that lie for a second. 'I went to his hospital to do it. I really thought I would, but when I got to his room, Lainey Anders was there, so I left. I parked up, thought about waiting, but then I changed my mind. Went home, then came here.'

He thought about telling her the rest, that he'd gone back to his house planning a different ending, but he didn't. Not now. Another time, maybe.

He could feel her body heat permeating the fabric of his jacket, forcing his blood to circulate, his heart to beat, and he was grateful for it.

'I'm sorry I didn't show for you at the Awards.'

'You don't need to say that. You never need to apologise to me.'

'I couldn't stay there, Mirren.'

'I know.'

This was what she did. She let him breathe. Let him tell her his thoughts in his own time.

'Hollie is everywhere, but she's nowhere at the same time. I can't do it.'

'I know that too.'

The way she said it had such weight, he knew immediately where her words came from.

'When Chloe died, I was in that place too.'

'And how did you get out of it?'

'You,' she said, making Zander's throat close. 'And Logan. And my work. And Chloe's Care. And Mike. The hole was still there. I just learned to fill little bits of it, piece by piece, until I wasn't lost in it every moment of the day.'

He took her hand, wrapped his fingers around hers.

'I don't think I can do that, Mir.'

'Then we'll do it for you until you can. If you let us.'

He didn't believe her, didn't see how it was possible, but for now he kept quiet. The sleep had helped. Her presence even more. Maybe that was enough for the time being.

Before he could get a chance to say that, the door opened, and Davie barged in.

'Can you not just come into a room without making a dramatic entrance?' Mirren asked and he watched her find a smile, then lose it almost immediately. Zander was way ahead of her. He could see the panic on Davie's face, and the anxiety in his movements.

'You need to come inside. We have a problem. And it's a fucking huge one that is going to end us all.'

37

DAVIE

'Let Me Go' – Gary Barlow

There had almost been a feeling of comfort being home, in the same kitchen he'd grown up in. His mum frying up a Lorne sausage and thumping it on to a bread roll. His aversion to carbs and his need for avocados had apparently been lost at some point over the Atlantic. As had his natural slide back into speaking to his mum exactly as he had as a teenager. Not his mum. His maw. He was the Scottish version of Davie Johnston again.

'Thanks, Mrs Johnston,' Sarah had said, as his mum gave her a mug of tea, to accompany her roll. Ladies first. He'd have been astonished if his mum had done it any other way. She'd drilled manners into him since he was old enough to hold a door open for anyone younger, older or female. Last week, he'd held the door open for a woman exiting a Starbucks in West Hollywood and was told he was a sexist tool of the patriarchy. He couldn't keep up anymore.

Maybe best just to stay in his mum's kitchen, drinking tea from the mug that had sat for thirty years in the same spot in the cupboard, waiting for him to come back for it.

It was the strangest feeling. For three decades, the very thought of this place, this street, of the ghosts that lived here, had filled him with dread and horror, yet now, there was a strange comfort, a familiarity that he could barely comprehend. It felt like home. Even more so because Sarah was in it too.

He'd been idly staring at her as she'd scrolled on her phone, when she'd gasped so loudly he'd almost dropped his roll.

'Holy shit!' she'd exclaimed. Then followed immediately with a rushed, 'Sorry, Mrs Johnston.'

His mum didn't tolerate profanity, which made it even more of a mystery that she'd stuck around Jono Leith for the half-hour or so it took to get her pregnant.

'Davie, look.' Sarah had passed her phone over, and he saw she'd been watching a video clip. LA News. Myla Rivera. She'd once offered him a blow job in the toilets at the Golden Globes. He'd refused, because his wife at the time, Jenny Rico, had been sitting right outside, chatting to her new friend and co-star, Darcy Jay. If only he'd had a crystal ball, he might have made a different decision.

He'd turned up the volume, just as the shot cut to a different video, with Myla's commentary over it.

'This footage obtained by the Fame Channel was captured outside the Hurston Centre in Malibu, on the evening of the twenty-third of February. The woman you see in handcuffs, being removed from the clinic by police, is Monica Jansen, who was, sources claim, a personal assistant to Wes Lomax for over forty years until her employment was very recently terminated. Mr Lomax died at some point that evening. However, a spokesperson for the clinic refused to comment on whether Ms

Jansen is implicated in Mr Lomax's death. We will keep you updated on this breaking story as events unfold.'

Davie had rewound, watched as a staggering, sullen-faced Monica was manhandled out of the clinic doors, almost dragged across the driveway at the entrance to the building and then, with an officer's hand on her head, pushed into the waiting police car.

Davie had lifted his head, chin dropped, as he'd handed the phone back to Sarah.

'Monica killed Wes?'

He'd seen that Sarah was struggling to digest that. 'It's my fault. I shouldn't have let her out of my sight that night. I thought she was just going to another room in the house. I had no idea... Shit.' Then another hasty, 'Sorry, Mrs Johnston.'

Davie had realised his mother wasn't listening, a red flag in any world. Nothing got past Ena. He'd turned to see what was up, fearing it must be something life-threatening for her to have missed a swear word, but no. She was hastily shoving something into the front pocket of her apron. His spidey senses had gone straight to high alert.

'Maw, what's that?'

'What?'

'The thing you just shoved in yer pocket.'

'Nothing.'

'Maw, really...'

'What?'

'What are you hiding?'

'Nothing.'

'Jesus Christ, Maw, this is like the reverse of every conversation you and I had for my whole teenage years. It's how you found my porn collection.'

That had set her off. 'Don't you dare utter blasphemous words in this house, Davie Johnston. And I will not hear talk of those filthy magazines either. I didn't sleep for a week.'

He'd leant against the worktop, arms folded, aware that he was reduced to acting like the sixteen-year-old kid who'd done double shifts for a week in the chippy to get the money to buy more porn. 'Well, I tell you what, Maw. Two choices here. Either you tell me what you're hiding, or Sarah and I will go grab the other two and we'll be off.'

It was a risk, but he'd known it was his best move. Ena Johnston wasn't an easy woman, but the truth was that she loved her son, her grandkids, the poor souls she fed on the soup bus at night... She was a woman of fierce loyalty, and the last thing on earth she would do was make her only child walk away from her.

Reluctantly, staring daggers at him, she'd pulled a brown envelope out of her apron pouch. Davie realised that he'd seen it on her worktop when he'd astonished her by walking in the door earlier. His only assumption had been that she'd realised he might read it and she was removing that possibility. Clumsily. Busted.

He'd opened the letter, praying that it wasn't from a hospital or a doctor, that he wasn't about to discover she was sick or worse. If his mother was dying and she hadn't told him, he'd never forgive her.

'Maw, this better not be...' He'd stopped when he spotted the header. Glasgow City Council.

Shit, she must be late with her council tax. Or her wheelie bin payment.

'*Dear Mrs Johnston,*' he'd begun reading. '*Further to our recent communication regarding the repurposing of the land comprising...*'

Davie had carried on, even though panic was making the words blur and meld into one big fat block of fucking carnage.

'Davie, what is it?' Sarah had asked, concern making the pitch of her voice slide up a notch.

'I'll be back in a minute.' That's when he'd stormed out, down the garden, burst into the shed.

Now he was back, with Mirren and Zander following behind.

Zander automatically leant down and hugged Ena.

'Sorry I didn't come in to say hello when I got here, Mrs Johnston. I was a bit... wrapped up in my head.'

'Don't worry, son, but, my God, you're way too thin. I'll put some sausage in the pan and make you a roll.'

Davie couldn't take it anymore. 'For Christ's sake, Mother!' he blurted, making everyone in the room freeze in anticipation of the reaction.

Ena raised her spatula. 'I warned you, Davie Johnston. If. You. Ever...' The gritted teeth were on. They used to scare the crap out of him when he was a kid. Actually, still did. But anyway...

'Maw, just show them the letter. In fact, never mind.' He turned to the others, took a deep breath, tried to quell the panic. 'There's a letter there from the council. They've condemned this street. Repossessing all the houses, compulsory purchases on any that have been bought, decanting the residents to other homes and selling the land.'

There was a stunned silence, before, in synchronised, almost robotic fashion, all three of them turned to face the kitchen window and focused their eyes on the shed at the end of the garden. The one that sat on top of Jono Leith's thirty-year-dead remains.

Davie had no idea how long the silence lasted, but it was right up until his mother handed over Zander's breakfast, with, 'Here's your roll and sausage, son.'

It broke the silence, snapped them all back to the room.

'Why didn't you tell me, Maw?'

'I didn't want to worry you, son. You've got enough on your plate with the wedding disaster and that job of yours falling through.'

Davie didn't check to see if Sarah was looking sheepish about her part in that.

'But you couldn't put it off forever.'

'I'd have told you when I was good and ready,' she said, obstinately, washing down the worktop now with the cloth that was never far from her hand.

'When, Maw? When they're coming down the streets with wrecking balls and diggers?'

She stopped, hand on hip, a stark reminder that she was no pushover. She had survived on this street for nearly fifty years. She worked in the city centre, helping the homeless and the street workers during cold dark nights – not a safe or secure place for an almost seventy-year-old woman to be. Yet, when Sarah was a reporter, covering the work of the bus, she once saw his mother drag a rabid pimp off the bus by the hair, and she'd battered him all the way down Sauchiehall Street for attacking one of her regular girls. Ena was not to be challenged. Especially by her son. 'What did I tell you about taking that tone with me?'

He sighed, defeated. 'Sorry, Maw. I am. I just don't get what the game plan was here.'

His mum shook her head. 'Son, I wasn't out of ideas yet. Agnes Caldwell over on Barclaven Street has stalled out her compulsory purchase for nearly a decade. I still had time.'

That crushed him. She still had time to save him. To protect him. Christ, what kind of son was he that his mother was going through this for him?

'I'm sorry, Maw. I should never have left you with this.' He went to her, wrapped his arms around her, making her turn puce. Public displays of affection were up there with swear words in her book.

'Mrs Johnston, has the land been sold yet?' Mirren spoke for the first time.

'That's the thing – they don't even have a buyer for it! I mean, who's going to buy land around here? No one wants to live here. They can't build shops because the junkies will steal from them or the wee gits that run wild will burn them down for fun. It's a nonsense. It's probably some upstart at the council, that thinks he's smart, when he's not got a clue. Not. A. Clue.'

Mirren nodded, then Davie saw her purse her lips, her jaw setting into that ruthless determination that he knew no one could break. Sometimes he forgot that this classy, awe-inspiring Hollywood writer, producer, director, was from around here too.

'Can you give me that letter, please, Mrs Johnston? I'll take care of it.'

38

THREE MONTHS LATER – SARAH

'Unstoppable' – Sia

Sarah sat in the editing suit on the production floor of *Out Of The Shadows*, working on laying down her narration over the footage of a special extended edition of the show: The Wes Lomax Story – Exposed: Downfall Of A Hollywood Legend

The whole programme had been storyboarded and scripted, debated and run past Legal time after time. They had to get it right. This was going to be the most shocking, most explosive, most controversial show of the year and the anticipation across Hollywood was building to a frenzy.

And no wonder. This was the story that had everything. Sex. Drugs. Money. Power. Crime. It was a documentary that would chart the life and crimes of Wes Lomax and expose the shocking dark side of an industry legend.

Nothing was going to be left out. Sarah, Chip Chasner, Meilin

Chong and Shandra Walker had made this their obsession and it showed.

It would begin with Wes's rise to success, his triumphs as he built Lomax Films up to be the titan it had become, with his unfailingly loyal assistant, Monica, by his side every step of the way.

They would then use interviews with victims, in chronological order, to prove that his abuse of power and sexual assaults went back over forty years. Some of his victims had relinquished their anonymity, some of them had even agreed to allow the footage of their assaults to be shown. The scenes would be carefully edited, of course, to protect them from any further trauma.

Lisa Arexo was one of the women who'd agreed to that, determined that the world would see what an evil bastard Wes Lomax really was.

Monica didn't escape scrutiny either. She remained in LA County jail, oscillating between protesting her innocence and raging against Wes, against Lomax Films, against the world. And, of course, against Sarah too. In the cold, sober light of day, she'd regretted handing the tapes over to Sarah and had brought in the lawyers to block her using them. It hadn't worked, which had enraged her to the point of derangement. Every day, another handwritten death threat from Monica appeared in Sarah's mail. She could have reported them to the prison authorities, requested that they be stopped, but that defeated the purpose. They were evidence. Part of the story of how two sick, perverted individuals with deviant predispositions collided in this world, formed an alliance built on some twisted triffid of love, obsession and dysfunction. And all the while, they did it in plain sight, camouflaged only by power, money and success in a town that was forever afraid to scratch beneath the glitter on the streets in case they were confronted with the horrors in the gutter.

Not even the biggest stars were safe or protected from Lomax's evil, as shown in one story involving an Oscar-winning writer and director.

In the documentary, Sarah would expose the real truth behind the recent scandal involving Mirren McLean, reveal the links between Wes and his nephew, and the chilling footage, secretly shot by Jason Grimes, proving that he was the instigator of the encounter. Mirren had done a piece to camera, explaining the full story of what had really happened. Some of that footage had been deliberately leaked, and the wave of support for her had been phenomenal.

Jason Grimes's culpability had yet to be decided by the authorities, but in the meantime, all lawsuits against Mirren had been dropped and his legal team, his PR team, his agent and his manager had all publicly withdrawn their representation. Jason Grimes was now officially cancelled.

Sarah knew Mirren was pleased with the outcome, but she wouldn't be in Los Angeles when the programme went to air, because she was currently living in her hometown of Glasgow, where she had recently procured land in a run-down, deprived area of the city, for the construction of the first international branch of Chloe's Care, the non-profit facilities that cared for young people with addictions. The new centre was to feature a two-storey, four-sided quadrant structure, with a large lawned courtyard in the middle, formed primarily from the gardens of the houses that used to sit on the land.

There was another interesting aspect to that story. The land she'd bought used to house a terrace row that included the childhood homes of Mirren, Davie Johnston and Zander McLean, who, as a former addict, was also currently in Scotland, working with Mirren to bring the centre to fruition. Sarah was planning another story on that in the future.

Sarah felt the door open behind her and Chip Chasner popped his head through the gap. 'How are you getting on in here?'

'Yeah, great. I won't be much longer. Just one more clip to finish and then we're done. Eric here is making it plain sailing.' She gestured to the affable gentleman beside her. Eric Kaufman, an editor in his sixties, had been with the show for two decades, and he'd been a guiding light in teaching Sarah everything she needed to know to put these episodes together.

'Okay, come up to the boardroom when you're done and we'll run the rough edits on the big screen. Let everyone know where we are with it.'

'Will do.'

She turned back to Eric. 'Okay. Let's see how my audio and this clip synch and make sure we're good to go.'

'Let's do it.'

They ran through the thirty-second clip, one that Sarah had watched countless times already. This time, her voice was dubbed over the top of it, explaining exactly what was happening.

Monica Jansen, being taken out of the Hurston Centre in handcuffs on the night Wes Lomax died. It was the last shocking story of the episode and the one unanswered question.

A post-mortem had proven inconclusive as to whether Wes had been murdered or had died of natural causes due to the after-effects of his stroke.

Monica was currently in prison awaiting trial on twenty-seven different charges, including coercion, conspiracy and assault on three medical professionals in the Hurston Centre. That's why she'd been removed in handcuffs that evening. She'd arrived to be told that Wes had passed away, and she had flown into a rage, wrecking the reception area and assaulting members of staff, including Joy, a receptionist who had since resigned from the clinic, citing trauma.

'Okay, one more time. Sorry. I know I'm a pain in the ass, Eric.'

'Not at all. Let's just do it until you're happy.'

He ran it again, and this time Sarah leaned forward, her face only a couple of feet from the monitor, focusing intently on the clip, her voice, the blend of the two and…

It was right at the end. Something jarred but she couldn't even say what it was.

'Can you roll it again, please? Slow it down this time.'

Eric did as he was asked, half-speed this time, cutting the volume so they didn't need to listen to Sarah's distorted vocals.

She stared at the screen. There was something. Something. Something.

'Pause!'

There it was. The very last frame of the clip.

If Eric noticed her sharp intake of breath, he didn't question it. Why would he? There was nothing in there that seemed odd. Just a car park outside a clinic. A police car in the foreground. The outline of Monica Janson's head in the back seat.

But Sarah's focus wasn't there.

It was on the slightly blurred outline of a nurse, in scrubs, over at the doors of the building. A woman. Clearly exiting, coming out of the doors, at an angle that would suggest she was about to turn left.

Only if someone was to look this closely, and stare at it, would they perhaps, by a million to one chance, recognise that face.

Sarah knew it because she'd looked at it for countless days over the last few months. She'd met this woman for lunch. She'd interviewed her both on and off the camera. She'd become a friend, found her a therapist, and was helping her reclaim the career and the status that she'd had before Wes Lomax took everything from her.

She was looking at Lisa Arexo.

Exiting the building where Wes Lomax was a patient.

Dressed in nursing scrubs.

Barely an hour after he'd passed away.

The truth of Wes Lomax's death was right in front of her.

Sarah closed her eyes, weighed up her options. This would send Lisa to prison for the rest of her life, something that would never have happened if Wes Lomax hadn't destroyed her.

Right from the start, Sarah had said she wanted justice.

Now that was in her own hands and she had to do the right thing.

'Eric, can you do me a favour please? I think the video runs just a touch too long. Can you delete that last frame and then, my friend, we are done.'

EPILOGUE

SEPTEMBER 2019

'Thinking Out Loud' – Ed Sheeran

There were clear blue skies over the Callaghan ranch, as Mirren stood at the end of the aisle, book in hand, marrying two of her best friends.

'Do you, Sarah McKenzie, take Davie Johnston to be your lawfully wedded husband?'

'I do.'

Davie cut in with, 'Wrap it up, Mirren, before she changes her mind again.'

'Do you, Davie Johnston...'

'I do.'

'Then by the powers invested in me by a dodgy internet website, I hereby pronounce you man and wife.'

Davie picked his wife up, swung her around and waltzed her back off down the aisle.

Cara had set it up beautifully, and everyone pretended that they had no idea all the wedding decorations had been in storage for over a year, since the last time they'd all made their way here to watch Davie and Sarah promise the whole richer and poorer thing.

Now, that line of the vows was particularly apt, given the sorry state of Davie Johnston's finances. His fortune was gone. There was no miracle that would bring it back. At least not yet. However, he was very fortunate to have a personal connection to the investigative journalist behind the sensational Wes Lomax documentary, *Exposed: Downfall Of A Hollywood Legend*, which had run a few months ago on network TV, to the highest ratings of any true crime show in the last five years. It had been such a sensation, the production company behind it had taken the unprecedented step of repackaging it and selling it to dozens of streaming services. At one point it was in the Top 10 on Netflix, Amazon Prime, Paramount+, Hulu and several others, all at the same time.

As a result, that same investigative journalist had been offered high six-figure TV deals for all three books she'd already penned – one on the dark side of Hollywood, one on the scandals in the music industry, and the third, a perceptive look at the phenomena of the #MeToo movement and its success in bringing about social change.

Sarah McKenzie had become someone to watch in this town and Davie had stepped behind the scenes to produce and direct her new projects. Now that she was the one signing megabucks deals, and he was working for her, Sarah regularly threatened that her next project would be a romcom about a couple whose fortunes had switched. Davie wasn't sure she was kidding.

Still, at least the whole saga was giving his ex-wife a laugh. That situation was a sitcom all of its own. Much as it pained him to admit it, Jenny and Darcy had saved his ass. They'd bought his house from him for market value, all cash, quick close, giving him enough to pay off his debts, hold on to his car and put enough money in the bank to keep him in gas and Tom Ford bronzer. Sarah had given up her flat in Marina Del Rey, because it was too small for both of them, and Jenny and Darcy were letting them live in the guest house. It wasn't big enough for his daughter's shoe collection, but it did him and Sarah just fine. Drego and Alina worked for Jenny now, but Alina still cooked his meals and added an extra ingredient of disdain before she put them in front of him. Jenny had arranged the suite at the Wynn and the Shania Twain tickets, so his ex-wife was Alina's favourite employer now.

Hopefully, it wouldn't be long before Davie could get her back onside by stumping up for Tim McGraw tickets, because the Fame Network had offered him his talk show back, fully commissioned by them, after Lainey Anders bombed. He'd told them he'd think it over, but, of course, they all knew he would accept. It was the ultimate 'fuck you' to Lainey. Apparently, her link to Wes Lomax had been a turn-off for the viewers. And sadly for her, after all the lawsuits filed by Lomax victims were settled and paid by his estate, there was nothing left there for her either. She was going to have to go back to singing for a living. She might even meet Jason Grimes on the circuit. Now that the duplicitous prick had realised Uncle Wes's money wasn't coming to him either, he'd bought a guitar and last they'd heard, he was busking on Hollywood and Vine.

Monica Jansen wasn't up on her luck either. She'd been sentenced to fifteen years for conspiring with Wes to commit a shit-load of sex crimes and she'd be spending the crumbs of her severance cheque on snacks in prison.

His maw couldn't even hear Monica's name without pursing her lips in disgust. She didn't come over to LA much now that she knew Davie and Sarah were happy, and because she was busy with her new job as the live-in facility manager of the Glasgow branch of Chloe's Care. They'd only had to move her stuff twenty yards to the new building, on the site of their old terraced row of homes. She'd made sure no one ever dug into the newly-lawned meditation area, formed from the gardens of the old properties. Even now she was protecting them.

* * *

The happy couple were dancing to Logan and Lauren's live duet of Marvin Gaye and Kim Weston's 'It Takes Two', when Mirren, her duties over for the day, kicked off her heels and wandered barefoot over to the fence surrounding the nearby paddock.

Of course that was where he'd be. It was a special place for Zander. It was where he'd first tried to kiss Hollie, and although, on that occasion, she'd told him to piss off, he'd got her in the end.

Sometimes Mirren had thought he would never come back. It helped that they'd finished the few outstanding scenes of his last Dunhill movie using a double and CGI, and that it had created a huge buzz in the industry already. The word was that it was the best one yet and Zander was incredible in it. Lomax Films were betting on it. Their share price had plummeted and the board that was now running it were panicking. There was talk of them changing the company name, removing all connection with the man who had built the studio to be a titan in the industry, then tainted it with his evil.

It was progress that he could be here and not fall apart. Six months in Scotland, overseeing the construction and preparations for Glasgow's first Chloe's Care Centre, had put a few pieces of him back together again. Not all. He still had a long way to go. Working on the soup bus helped too. If he had a pound for every time someone told him he looked a bit like like that movie star, Zander Leith, he could feed half the city.

Standing next to him, Mirren leaned on the fence too, subconsciously mirroring his body language. They'd done that since they were kids and they didn't even notice it any more.

'No Mike?' he asked her, glancing around.

'No Mike,' she confirmed, wondering why she hadn't told him that last night, when he arrived at the ranch, after coming straight from the airport. Or why she hadn't told him during one of their daily FaceTime calls. After she checked on the progress of the build and ironed out any issues, they always chatted for a while, but somehow it had never come up.

Mirren and Mike had tried. For a couple of months after she'd come back from Scotland, they'd tried to make it work again, and for a moment they'd both thought it would.

Zander squinted his eyes against the sun as he turned to her. 'How come?'

She shrugged. 'Lots of reasons. We parted as friends though. I'm keeping Clansman at Pictor and it's all very professional.' That was true. Probably because this time, neither of them had hurt the other one. They'd both just come to the same conclusion that something was missing. Mike thought it was the security of knowing nothing could tear them apart.

He didn't know that, once again, something already had.

No, not something.

Someone.

Mirren wasn't sure when she'd realised it. When she thought she'd lost him. When she was on the jet. When they were back in Glasgow. When she'd left him there and a part of her had ached for him every moment since then. It was complicated. But then, with him, it always was. She'd known Zander Leith all her life and it had taken her until now to realise she was in love with him.

And as her head dropped on to his shoulder, as it always did, and Zander's hand brushed against hers, she knew she could wait until he saw it too.

MORE FROM SHARI LOW AND ROSS KING

We hope you enjoyed reading *The Fall*. If you did, please leave a review.

If you'd like to gift a copy, this book is also available as an ebook, large print, hardback, digital audio download and audiobook CD.

Sign up to Shari Low and Ross King's mailing list for news, competitions and updates on future books.

https://bit.ly/ShariLowRossKing

Explore the complete Hollywood Thriller Trilogy...

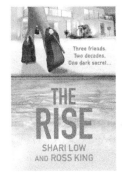

Three friends.
Two decades.
One dark secret...

THE
RISE

SHARI LOW
AND ROSS KING

Someone, somewhere
always knows
the truth...

THE
CATCH

SHARI LOW
AND ROSS KING

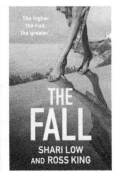

The higher
the rise,
the greater...

THE
FALL

SHARI LOW
AND ROSS KING

Boldw∞d

Boldwood Books is an award-winning fiction publishing company seeking out the best stories from around the world.

Find out more at www.boldwoodbooks.com

Join our reader community for brilliant books, competitions and offers!

Follow us

@BoldwoodBooks

@BookandTonic

Sign up to our weekly deals newsletter

https://bit.ly/BoldwoodBNewsletter

Made in the USA
Monee, IL
11 August 2023

40841051R00193